Ken McClellan

The Last Byzantine

Confessions of a Would-Be Messiah

Outskirts Press, Inc.
Denver, Colorado

This is a work of fiction. The events and characters described herein are imaginary or are used fictitiously and are not intended to refer to specific places or living persons. The opinions expressed in this manuscript are solely the opinions of the author and do not represent the opinions or thoughts of the publisher. The author has represented and warranted full ownership and/or legal right to publish all the materials in this book.

The Last Byzantine
Confessions of a Would-Be Messiah
All Rights Reserved.
Copyright © 2009 Ken McClellan
V3.0

Cover Photo: All rights reserved - used with permission.

The Palaeologus emblem of the double eagle used on the cover is a composite image derived from:

    Russian Emblem: ©iStockphoto.com/Oleksii Boiko
    Presidential Seal: ©iStockphoto.com/niknikon
    Golden State Emblem Of Russia On Marble: ©iStockphoto.com/Alex Kotlov

The back cover image was composed from:

    Fireball: ©iStockphoto.com/Rosica Daskalova
    and Emperor Constantine's Standard modeled from the book
    Tesoro Militar de Cavalleria by Ioseph Micheli Marquez, 1642

This book may not be reproduced, transmitted, or stored in whole or in part by any means, including graphic, electronic, or mechanical without the express written consent of the publisher except in the case of brief quotations embodied in critical articles and reviews.

Outskirts Press, Inc.
http://www.outskirtspress.com

ISBN: 978-1-4327-3981-2 (Hardback)
           978-1-4327-2385-9 (Paperback)

Library of Congress Control Number: 2009927226

Outskirts Press and the "OP" logo are trademarks belonging to Outskirts Press, Inc.

PRINTED IN THE UNITED STATES OF AMERICA

To Kenny, Tony, Melody & Ashley
May you live to see a better world!

To Archbishop Ximenes de Cisneros

*I have chosen the way of Truth: thy judgments have I laid before me.
I have stuck unto thy testimonies:* O LORD, *put me not to shame.*
Psalm 119:30-31

Most Illustrious Sir,

I confess I am the one you seek. By a dozen condemnable names you have known me and my brethren. However, before you toss yet another soul onto your pyre, I will offer you the secret to the seeds that bore us, the ground that nourished us, and the circumstances that multiplied our ranks. I will tell you the Truth and trust to God's Mercy after that.

As you ask of all your guests, I freely give my confession and I thank you for the opportunity in which to repent. I thank you as well for the 40 days and the paper on which to write it. Thank you too for allowing me the constant companion of my youth, my commonplace book.

I will do my best to describe the circumstances in which I found myself, and perhaps God will forgive me the path I took. It was full of stones and I was not well shod before being forced to take it ... but let me start at the beginning.

I was born in a cold year of a cold age – the sort that breeds depression, rats and lice. It was the Year of Our Lord 1444. The priest that baptized me sang Mass, swung censers of frankincense and myrrh and forgave us our sins. He taught us to try to live the Commandments, to be Holy, and told us we might one day aspire to *apotheosis* in our own resurrection. This divinization or deification of the departed may not be considered a proper idea here for any but a few saints, but with us, it was our call to eternal Communion.

At home with the people who raised me, I remember thinking the Scriptures they read aloud applied personally to me. That it was my responsibility to build God's Kingdom on Earth. In that sense, I failed.

A lifetime does not build a great deal. We are lucky if we heal our souls' self-inflicted wounds by the time we are ready for the worm.

Wounded or not, healed or not, I recognize that my chastised life was also blessed. I would have lived happily forever in the hills of Sparta, but the old Sultan Murad left his domain in the hands of a young tyrant with grand ambitions.

His son Mehmed's grand strategy to choke Christendom continues to unfold. You can set back his plan by centuries if you will continue your drive south. Fail to strike soon and your new nation will return to slavery and share the fate of Byzantium.

For nearly three centuries, your kings of Castile sought the Imperial Throne of Rome. If Spain would now bear the Sword of Caesar, let me tell you of what it was made.

John IX Palaeologus

Chapter One

Speak to me now Alitheia – my Muse, my Sun, my Home.
Grant me one cup of your Wisdom before I leave this Tomb.
On the road to Lethe you'll find me, at the path to Our Mother's lake.
I pray Our Father accepts me or grants us a New Life to make.
One Phoenix is left 'ere we find it, our Temple of Heaven on Earth.
Alpha Omega is coming; once again let us witness his Birth.

Mystras, 1444

My birth was that of any child of Adam. I cleaved the Rock, emerging Mother's peaceful waters. Landing in the dust, I awoke with my first breath. The first voice I uttered was a cry of pain. I was nursed in swaddling clothes and care. No king has any other beginning. For all have one entrance into this life, and the like going out. [Wisdom of Solomon 7]

I was born at Mystras in the Peloponnese, a land called the Morea. In this life, my troubles arrived early. I did not know my father; and my mother left me for Constantinople soon after I learned to walk. Death was dancing across the land, bringing a return of the Plague. When the sides of my neck swelled big and black, my natural mother Caterina Notaras panicked and left me for dead. In the early days of Sparta or Rome, she might have thrown me from the cliff behind the palace – the *Apothetai*. There would be days when I wished she had.

Instead, at my point of death, the woman who cared for me, Diana, wrapped my neck with warm ashes from the fire in a strip of fur. Next morning, she peeled off the poultice and tossed it in the flames. The sides of my neck bled, but most of the infection was gone.

The Hellenes fear children returned from the dead, considering them unlucky. Old people called me the ancient words for "second born."

3

It was like a curse of the Evil Eye, only with scars to prove my misfortune.

To be accepted back into our superstitious village, I had to be passed through my new mother's lap and gown as if leaving the birth canal and seeing light for the first time. I was baptized again, and that is when I acquired the surname Emanuelis – son of Emanuel. It was the only way he and Diana were ever going to have a child.

My adoptive parents were secretly Bogomils, he a young warrior for the Despot of Morea Constantine and she an attendant at the court. Neither of them believed in contributing yet more souls to this Devil's playground. Their barren "marriage" was to fool the world into believing they were Orthodox. We would go to St. George's chapel for services, and at home they would read me stories from a *Bible* written in Greek – a rare thing before the new printing presses. The courage of my new parents to lead double lives in a world condemning their beliefs would later give me strength. For one day, I too would live in an enemy camp.

One of my earliest memories – I must have been four years old – was a conversation with my adopted mother before going out to play. "Tell me about when I was little, Mother. I can't remember," I said. She was gazing out the window to the northwest, toward a spot she sometimes looked in the evening, shedding a tear.

She turned and smiled: "You were born here one morning in late June, as the morning breeze brought the smell of the sea up the plain of Sparta. Jupiter and Saturn were together in Gemini communing as they sometimes do, plotting how to try a new generation of souls."

It amazed me she knew such things. Christianity frowns on anyone but priests taking notice of the stars and planets. She said it was always good to look for signs, that there are prophets who can read the intent of God in the sky, as the ancients once read a sheep's liver.

She continued: "You were unusual. From the first day, you would reach out to be held; you would smile; and if I laid you on your belly, you would push yourself up to look outside your basket!

"At the time, Sparta felt as victorious as if we had again defeated the Persians. Your father and the king had taken back most of Greece from the Franks and Florentines, and wrested Serbia from the Turks. The old Sultan was busy marching on Hungary; and for one fleeting moment, we were safe in our homeland. It was a time of great hope."

She laughed: "You wanted to be a warrior like your father. By the time you were two, you were winning more battles than one might have expected with your little carved sword against his Mandoble. You would stand there with a foot on his chest, your sword raised high, exclaiming 'By the Sword of St. George!' Then he would scoop you up in his arms and march you off to a story, the two of you laughing infectiously.

"You would sit there listening to him read, recounting the greatness of Rome or you would tell him stories you had heard, the two of you dreaming of better worlds. You could speak gravely of goings-on in Iberia or Gaul as if you had been there ... as if you could see the places beyond his words. You spoke of ancient things too, though I have no idea where you heard those stories – perhaps the old men.

"He taught you quite a lot in your little time together, but you were only two and a half when he died protecting the Emperor at the Hexamilion Wall. One night, about two weeks before the winter solstice and the birth of our Lord, you pointed to a comet flying past the mouth of Draco, near the North Star, and said, 'Look, Mama, my father's soul flies to Heaven!' You didn't cry. You knew, as surely as if he had kissed you goodnight.

"At Christmas, Grandpa Lucas returned from the battle at Corinth. You had been right about when Papa died. The wall and our soldiers had been no match for great cannon. Had your father lived, the king might have made him a governor. That is what the king did for George Sphrantzes after the battle at Patras, where your uncle 'saved' the king by stopping his horse. Since Papa did not live, he was given a hero's burial.

"I am thankful the king kept us in his household, but I suspect we will have to move – perhaps to Trebizond, perhaps to my father's people in Mallorca or Catalonia. Soon, Constantinople will fall, and with it Byzantium. We must not be here when that happens. Enough of this ... go out and play. It's still light out!"

Soon the old Emperor John VIII died and the winds of our fortune were shifting. John had too many brothers and no sons. The emperor had been sick for years. His elder brothers Andronicus and Theodore had died. Next in line would be Constantine, though his younger brothers seemed anxious for power. Demetrius was playing demagogue, promising to keep the Great Church from joining "the

Whore of Rome." Under ultimogeniture, he might have been regent with the crown passing to his daughter Helena – the youngest marriageable daughter of a junior line. Thomas' only chance would be to take the throne by force, sometimes a successful strategy. Byzantium had not followed these alternate Roman rules of succession for ages. The concern was that we would lack a clear heir and the old sultan or his son would be at our throats.

The Emperor's mother Helena saw to it that her younger sons behaved while our King Constantine assumed the imperial throne. Emperor John died late in October when I was four. Constantine, the named successor, was with us at Mystras as our Despot of the Morea. Thomas made it to Constantinople in two weeks. Demetrius rushed there from Selymbria.

To prevent problems, Helena, widow of the earlier Emperor Manuel II, took power as regent in the name of Constantine. Constantine had been regent when John was in Florence trying to reunite Christianity and to bring Western support against the Turks. Empress Helena's act, and the acquiescence of the old sultan, would keep Byzantium together for a time.

It took three months to move our little court to Constantinople. In the meantime, I observed some curious things – ancient things that had kept our empire alive for more than a thousand years.

Before I go on, I should confess that if a soul's compass has four cardinal directions – of Love, Faith, Power and Truth – I always erred in the direction of curiosity and Truth. If that might lead one day to simple Faith, I was ever happy to be taking the longer road. I do believe what separates the forces of good and evil in this world is whether our intent is primarily to serve others or serve ourselves. Truth and Faith were harder for me to sort out.

At almost sunset one evening, about the time of the winter solstice, I noticed some of the older men dressing in cloaks and heading out as a group. It was not a night for Mass and there was no battle calling, so I decided to follow. I snuck out the servant entrance of the palace and hung back along the stone wall. They followed the old defenses of the city down the hill, through the arched Monemvassias Gate of the second wall, then north a few hundred yards down the hill from the new Pantanassa Church. At the town's third wall of defenses, just before the last gate, was the Mitropolis Church with its three-sided grand patio open to the northeast. They gathered on the patio, facing a much smaller group on the balcony. I went in through the church to a window in the back adjoining the courtyard.

The first thing the nobles did was some sort of group ritual prayer involving kneeling, then prostrating oneself as one might have done before a Persian monarch – hardly something proper for Greeks or Spartans. It sounded and looked as if they were directing a prayer to the Sun. I cannot say whether it was directed to the Sun setting on the opposite side of the church, to the Emperor as grand master of the Holy Order of St. George, or to Plethon as head of a Pythagorean brotherhood called the "Phatria." The men lit a large fire in the center of the patio and began to trace concentric circles around it in a dance, some spinning from time to time.

In the center of the balcony was the king. The performance was obviously for his benefit. At his side was Gemistos Plethon, the oldest man in the village – in his 90s. The man was a mystagogue and philosopher. Even Latin churchmen found him irresistible. Cardinal Bessarion, a former disciple, once called him the reincarnation of Plato.

Plethon had been at the Academy in Constantinople. Later, Emperor John banished him to Mystras for ideas on how we are all brothers and sisters – and how the Old Religion, Orphism, Judaism, Christianity, Zoroastrianism, Islam and Platonism are merely derivations of one true religion. He said we should search for the similarities, identify the shared mysteries, and act on the best ideas of each. Byzantine authorities had little interest in such eclecticism.

The Mitropolis event appeared to be an initiation or an invocation of ancient magic to support the throne. Plethon explained that in times of old, the emperor was master of all the mysteries. So Plethon began explaining the orbits of the planets about the Sun and how what to us appear as stops and reverses by a planet are illusions due to our relative movements. He said the Seal of Solomon belongs to Mercury, the Pentagon to Venus, the 20-year generations to Jupiter-Saturn conjunctions, and corrections of the calendar to Venus and the Moon.

The dancers took up torches as the sky darkened. Now they formed constellations of the zodiac and slowly made their way across the bonfire "Sun's" path. Plethon explained that at the birth of Sparta, when we were still the tribe of the Serpent and Phrygia the land of the Lions, it was the age of the *Dioscouri* – Twins of the Goddess Leda.

We held them as a symbol for Sparta's consuls – our ancient system of governorship adopted by Rome.

In the Age of Gemini, about 8,000 years ago, we were still a small tribe of Asia Minor. The twin lights of day and night were our gods. Among people from Sumer to Judea, the brothers were Ea and El, the Deep and the Moon – sons of Father Sky and Mother Earth. In several places, the Old Testament retells their tragic story of competition over the right ways for men to worship and a "stolen birthright." In Egypt, they were Osiris and Seth. The Sun crossed the twins in the sky when our people still worshipped the Queen and we sacrificed the King at winter solstice so the tribe might prosper.

Dawn flew to Taurus about 6,000 years ago. Mithras Sun crossed the heart of the Bull to renew the Earth. At noon, January 1, 4317 BC (Julian), a Phoenix set Rome's calendar. In this age, Cretan Zeus stole Queen Europa from Phoenicia to establish our race in a new land. Gods and heroes fought between this date that God spelled his name in the Heavens and when Zeus brought the Flood of 3113 BC.

Then came the time almost 4,000 years ago of Aries, God of War. Alexander the Great, "The Two-Horned," wore the horns of the Ram. This is the Age when the Golden Fleece was found; People of the Sea attacked Egypt; and Greeks won the Battle of Troy.

In the current era, we live in the Age of Pisces. Jesus was born when the age was new. Sun, piercing the heart of the Lamb, was aimed to strike the first Fish when, in Judaea, the Spirit returned to Earth.

Plethon said Constantine the Great had watched a similar ceremony at a forest in Gaul on a vernal equinox. The tetrarch had asked where Apollo's Sun rose that day perpendicular to the V formed by the two fish. The Druids (or rather their successors in Wisdom) told him "Byzantium" was the center of Pisces and that he was fated to be the next Phoenix of the Age. From that day forth, Constantine the Great strove to be the prophesied *military* savior of the world just as the Christ was now its spiritual head. Not for the first or last time, Power would supplant the rule of Love.

From the "star" formed by the zenith parting the vernal equinox and the ecliptic (as well as the two fish), Constantine conceived his sign of the Labarum and decided where to move the power of Rome.

To show the world he had moved the Prime Meridian and the center of the Earth, home of the Sol Invictus, Constantine brought the tripod from the Temple of Apollo at Delphi to the city that would take his name.

Now the Sun overshoots the second fish and the ages begin their return to the Water Bearer, who will accept us back into the Assembly of the Gods and bring Earth a new life. Winds of the Old World are shifting. Creation is about to be renewed. ...

Behind me, I heard a muffled footstep. A hand grabbed my shoulder and spun me around. I nearly cried out, but decided I was more afraid of the group than just one man. The stern familiar voice of my grandfather asked, "What brings a young spy to our midst and what should be his punishment?" In reality, he asked no one. The old man leaned his head close to mine, put two fingers to his lips, and tipped his hand toward me to stop me, saying in his deep voice, "No harm done. One day you would be asked to join. For now, this must remain our secret. Go. Tell no one where you have been nor what you have seen. Can you do this?" I nodded ... and arrived at the palace long before the men returned. Thankfully, the Moon was not too old in the sky. I could see the stone path and nobody had noticed me.

That night, there was a small but festive get-together in the palace. I saw table service for twelve. Six noblewomen – among them my natural mother Caterina – and six noblemen would gather later for a private revelry.

The men invited included my grandfather, the king, and some knights I did not know. I would learn this was another ritual that had kept Rome alive – the *dodecatheos* – a gathering of 12 gods of the zodiac whose issue would replenish the ranks of Rome's nobility. I remember wondering that day who my real father might be, and for the moment was happy not to know.

Two weeks later, on Epiphany, there was another evening ceremony, again at the Mitropolis Church. The Metropolitan presided over a low-key coronation. Few dignitaries attended the king's anointing as Emperor. My grandfather said it took place over the great seal of Byzantium, the family shield of the House Palaeologus.

The coronation stone, my grandfather once showed me in the church, is a mystical rock with two carved images, one obvious and the other hidden. The obvious one is a double-eagle in the shape of the Labarum, Constantine the Great's conquering symbol for Christianity. Nestled darkly in the center of that Phoenix is a crowned owl, symbol for Athena and Egypt's Word of Truth – Ma'at. If he attended, and I imagine he did, Plethon would have remarked the symbol as a key to the Trinity and Plato's Logos. My grandfather said they used the double eagle (or double peacock) to signify both the rays of the Sun and the Emperor's immortality, recalling the words of Job, *I shall die in my nest, and I shall multiply my days as the sand.*[Job 29:18]

On that day, Constantine took his holy vows as our Emperor and as a Servant of God. Grandpa said the priest intoned the Ascension Day hymn based on Psalm 72: *Christ, having called upon all nations to Serve the Truth, has accomplished the Divine Economy in our regard.* Later, God would call on my king to lay down his life as well.

Constantinople, 1449

In January, we arrived in Constantinople with great fanfare. There were banquets, tournaments, and merrymaking of all sorts – all out of proportion to our real situation, or perhaps because of it. Danger can be exciting. Gifts for the new Emperor arrived from afar, but no offers of soldiers or ships or arms for what everyone knew to be the coming war. As for a boy, not yet five years of age, life was mostly a matter of playing at being grown up. Mother was busy around Blachernae Palace and I was making new friends.

Of the next three years, I remember little beyond games with my friends and studying in a vault below Justinian's much older palace with my uncles. It was part of the old city. My grandfather the Megadux (or Prime Minister) was the end of the line of presidents at the Academy of Constantinople. Besides prime minister, he was our Sun of Science, our "Sol Invictus" as it were, our latest incarnation of Apollo and the one in whom resided Truth. He had been "Aquarius" under George Gemistos Plethon before the old master was banished to Mystras.

In addition to the president, there were 12 "professors" – each chair a sign of the zodiac. We no longer really had that large an academic aristocracy. Just a few brilliant minds and good translators were left. Mostly, "chairs" were older students assuming a mantle of leadership. Like the old pantheons of gods in their council, the institution was hierarchical.

For centuries, there had been few students picked from the royal houses or gifted children from the schools and monasteries to receive this training. I did not know what role we might eventually play, or whether the students were supposed to graduate to some other group such as the Order, or the Phatria, which may be just as old. I could see education had been key to our well-ordered, now-dying society; but for too long Orthodoxy had been pruning back the tree of knowledge. If eating the tree's first fruit was humankind's great sin, then by now we surely had regained our innocence!

Many of the library's 40,000 tomes had been destroyed or lost in the time since Constantine the Great. Many had been burned by Leo the Isaurian. Many had been shipped to Baghdad by treaty of Michael III. Many had gone with refugees to Venice or to Florence. Ours was a remnant of what had been one of the grand libraries of its day:

> *The Emperor has recalled and raised from the dead the souls of wise men and heroes for the welfare of the city; for the souls of wise men are in their wisdom, mind, and intelligence, while their monuments are the books and writings in which their remains are to be found.* Themistius

Manuscripts had been shared with monasteries and the palace, but here were some works found in neither. The Church and many of our previous emperors failed to see how pagan writers might contribute to knowledge. Besides occasional purges of the collection for orthodoxy, there were losses to mold, fire, worms, and a few thieving scholars.

Grandpa used to say, "Knowledge is like a jewel. To be truly precious, it must be kept and it must be passed along." He never seemed upset by our dwindling collection. Perhaps he was having some of it moved to Mt. Athos or Venice for safety. Perhaps he was selling it off to pay mercenaries. I know he used some of the older students to make copies.

Between lessons of rhetoric and mathematics, there were two thousand manuscripts and codices we were encouraged to rediscover, some written and illustrated in precious inks like lapis lazuli and powdered gold. Each of us kept our own book of wisdom – notes we found significant. To graduate, all we had to do was commit our book to memory! It may seem strange to say that I spent my childhood with Homer, Plato, Herodotus and Zoroaster but they were as real to me as my grandfather or my best friend Constantine.

When I was not studying and my mother found me sitting at home or wandering where I did not belong, she would push me out the door saying: "Jason and his friends will want you to capture a Golden Fleece or give you a Herculean task to perform. Perhaps Grandpa Lucas will show you an old soldier trick. Now go, enjoy your youth!"

One afternoon in the spring of 1453, she must have spoken to my grandfather or "Uncle George" about leaving. She said that the next day we would begin to lay aside things for a trip. Soldiers had been arriving from Genoa and there would be ships returning that way. A little farther upstream, the young Sultan had built a fortress at the neck of the Dardanelles and was sinking ships not paying his new toll. The strategic waterway for European commerce now had a bandit with a knife to its jugular. Mother was saying we were going to abandon many of the things we had brought from Mystras. This time we would not be traveling with the permission of the Sultan or in the train of an Emperor. She said we would be lucky to get away from our home of four years. Then she gave her little speech and shoved me out the door.

That afternoon I cared nothing for news. I grabbed my wooden sword and started to go. Thinking better of it, I ran to another part of the palace to find something. Mother was right, of course. Out on the courtyard, several children of the palace had gathered. Jason, the oldest of our friends, was ordering Constantine to achieve the 11th task of Hercules – to steal "golden apples" from the "Hesperides" (an Armenian's garden down the street).

One might as well steal gold from an Arab! Constantine ran off to the Petrion district, to a garden we all knew, hoping to avoid the beating our friend George had suffered the week before for just such a feat. While we were waiting for a piece of orange or colorful stories of bravery from our friends, Jason ordered Stavros to capture the girdle of the visiting "Queen of the Amazons."

Lady Anna was the more worthy daughter of my grandfather. For a time she was betrothed to Emperor Constantine. It was rumored that "Uncle" Sphrantzes, and I have no idea why Mother called him that beyond everyone's familiarity with the Emperor's best friend, had advised against the marriage. Perhaps he detested my grandfather and wanted to seek new allies. Perhaps Lady Anna tired of competing with her little sister for the Emperor's affections. Unkind souls suggested Grandfather had promised Anna to the new Sultan. She would soon leave us again for Venice, but for now the visiting lady left a sash on her bed, probably in the knowledge it was valuable to certain intrepid young heroes.

For coming late, I received the most feared task (because in our tame version of the game we didn't slay lions or nine-headed hydras). Jason instructed me to bring "Cerburus, the Hound of Hell" – an old greyhound that had tired of our games. Cerburus would often bark, bite or run to avoid playing the game. I found him near the Gate of Phanar, not far from where I could see Constantine running from the Armenian fruit seller – a magnificent sight!

Today, I bribed the hound with a bone I had saved for just such an occasion. When he leaned down to chew on it, I collared him with a braided rope of goat's hair. When he tried to get away, he realized there would be no escaping my trap. Such a rope is tough as rock and lasts twice as long! My prize trotting with his mouth full, I headed back to the courtyard of St. Mary, running to catch up with Constantine.

Constantine was a friendly youth. He was the smartest, tallest and best looking of any of us. He would have been popular with any group. He slowed as I caught up, and he began juggling four oranges.

The orchard owner having given up, we could walk today rather than race to see who would be first or last back to "base." He would have won easily, of course, but I had reason to believe at least Stavros would not be waiting there with his prize. I pulled Lady Anna's sash from my shirt. Constantine laughed loudly, and nearly dropped the fruit.

CHAPTER TWO

*For in much wisdom is much grief;
and he that increaseth knowledge increaseth sorrow.* Ecclesiastes 1:18

The Hippodrome, 1453

When the World gives up her brightest jewels and darkest secrets, her lessons are rarely favors. Blessings and curses run hand-in-hand. Turn a truth this way and that. View a person from all angles and you will see. Everything below the one perfect Truth is flawed.

Throughout my life, I chased Truth like a boy tracking clues to a treasure. I was sure each manuscript, each situation, each new person was about to provide "The Answer." What I eventually found is that on this side of the Styx, there can be joy in a mystery and grief in perfect understanding.

One day I abandoned my friends near Blachernae Palace and made off for my grandfather's house down in the old city. It was good to walk along the ancient columns that marked the road toward St. Sophia, Our Lady of Holy Wisdom, the Great Church. One could still feel the grandeur of our city and empire. Long ago, this road had once been the world's greatest display of statuary. Now, it was merely surprising how many ruined columns can stand stripped of their marbles and bronze.

I would sometimes follow the road to the harbors and market area to see what the sailors and vendors were saying. I figured they would be first to know if help was on the way. If, after visiting Grandpa or our hall of study I still had time, I might take another road back up the hill.

Sometimes I would stop to watch knights at the Hippodrome while they practiced their archery and horsemanship. The old race circuit had been the center of an Empire that had straddled the world. Entertainment, trade and armed might had been the core of Constantine the Great's capital. A thousand years ago, this was where the Blues, Reds, Greens, and Whites raced their colors. Once, two of those parties revolted against the Emperor. When General Belisarius put down their revolt, 30,000 people were massacred right there in the stands. Roman politics had not been democratic for quite some time.

On this day, sunny and quiet as an empty field except for the call of an occasional seagull, I stopped just short of the Great Church. From a stairwell within Constantine's Column, I could hear a young girl weeping. I stuck my head inside to see if I might help.

I called to her and asked her name. She answered that her name was Alítheia (a name meaning Truth). I asked her what was wrong and she cried all the more. "Just leave me be," she sobbed. But I had never heard anyone crying who did not wish to be found, so I went in.

I found her about 10 feet up the stairs. She was sitting with her face in her sleeves, her arms resting on her knees. She looked up, and her eyes widened when she saw me, as if surprised to see someone again after a long absence. She haltingly caught her breath as if to stop crying and asked me who I was. "Nobody special," I said, "just someone who would like to help, or at least to listen." She protested that I could not help, that she should not say anything. Then, of course, she began.

Tearfully, she told me how, when she was seven, her father had begun to visit her at night, to hurt her, or in his sick version, "to teach her how to please a man" and that he was a selfish drunk merchant who hid his abuse from her mother. She said now he was teaching her things she did not want to know and hurting her in ways that were "bad for her soul." I had no idea what she meant. To me, she did not appear someone who could violate the Ten Commandments and, therefore, had no reason to worry.

Looking back, I realize she probably meant one of the sins of Jeroboam, one of Julian's complaints against the Christians, a Roman slave's practice beneath the banquet table.

I said what I imagined my adopted parents would have said, "The sins of selfishness do not belong to the victim." That no matter what her father did or said, there was no way it could taint her soul in the eyes of Merciful God. I sat down next to her, took her hand and suggested she not think about what a foolish man might do to please himself. She could repent of his evil before God and never question her salvation. "The sinner is the one with reason to worry!" Hearing the force of my argument, she stopped crying.

Then I pulled her to her feet and suggested we "climb to the clouds" and see what we might see. Some said the column we were in had once been a great monument to Constantine the Great. The tower had been sheathed top to bottom in burnished brass plaques arranged in a spiral portraying his glorious deeds. If there had been a statue above, it had long ago been pillaged and the plaques on its sides melted down by the Latins in their "Fourth Crusade" that never quite made it to Jerusalem. Now it was just a tall pillar, and a rather unsightly one.

We emerged at the top, a hundred feet from the ground, and she sat at the stair. I stood raising my arms to the heavens and said: "Father, show mercy upon your daughter Truth. Teach any man who would harm her to repent of his ways; and if a man cannot learn and if a man will not repent, then slay him and never let him return as a man!" Then I folded my hands together and bowed my head, "Father, Son and Holy Spirit have mercy on us. Amen." It must have looked funny, because she smiled past her tears to laugh at the little Stylite monk invoking the power of Heaven on Earth.

Alítheia's smile was wide, bright and tilted up slightly on one side. Her eyes were the large ovals of a deer, only blue, the left always shining brighter than the right. When she stopped crying and smiled, her wavy golden locks and strong chin looked so familiar. I felt we might have spent eternity together and that this should ever be the plan. She stood to thank me, hugged me and we sat down together on the edge to watch boats sail out the Golden Horn into the Sea of Marmara. For hours, we talked about where they were going and of things we might see if we could follow the setting sun. I did not get to visit much with Grandpa that day, but I had something to eat and he let me ride a warhorse back to the palace.

Church of the Apostles, 1453

One day, Alítheia and I were admiring frescoes in the Church of the Apostles, which was up the hill, closer to my end of town. The priest was droning on and on, then took a detour at Matthew 10 – the one about Christians being "sheep in the midst of wolves." I suppose it was sort of on everyone's minds because of the ravenous Turks we all knew would soon be pounding our gates with all the tender mercy of a Caligula.

When the priest finished, I said to that most precious soul next to me, "More than anything, one day I want to know the Truth. I want to be

'Wise as the Serpent.' If you want to be 'harmless as the Dove,' then you can pity the Wolves while you are at it. The Beasts will die before you and I – I swear it!"

I had spent too much time in the Morea threatened by Turks. They killed my stepfather. The Latins betrayed my king and Turks now surrounded him. I had spent too much time hearing what happened to those who fight the Moslems rather than surrender to their will. I was sure that when it came to battle, I would be up to the challenge, whatever my age. What I would soon learn is that the will to live is terribly strong. It can be strong enough to betray one's heroic self-image, strong enough even to betray one's beliefs.

When the fighting came, I remember thinking only Christs or those with nothing to live for would fight on in the face of unstoppable opposition. Yet soon we would see thousands of such people, and those martyrs would shame the rest of us.

> *As gold in the furnace hath He tried them, and received them as a burnt offering. And in the time of their visitation they shall shine. ... They shall judge the nations, and have dominion over the people, and their Lord shall reign for ever.* Wisdom of Solomon 3:6-8

The Old City, 1453

Often I would see Alítheia near St. Sophia and we would walk through the old city to see what we might discover. We puzzled over the Delphic Tripod and the obelisks in the Hippodrome. We explored ruins. We visited silk weavers in the underground cisterns. We watched equestrians play polo. We went to churches to stare at icons, breathe the incense and light candles. Sometimes she would come to the Blachernae, but she would not join the games.

We never spoke again about her father, though I noted she sometimes looked bruised. The man slow-to-learn would be among the first to die when Turks took the city a few months later. If, as Pythagoras, Origen and Clement believed, we have levels of existence below that of reason when we die, then Alítheia's father is spending the rest of this age as a stone, a plant or an animal. Better for my soul that I never knew which one!

Despite our misfortunes and living too far apart for so long, Alítheia was my greatest love. I hope sharing her secret ended her fear that day. I know it did not end her suffering, for soon all of us would suffer.

Those not killed in the fighting were brutalized with woes over which we had no control. All would learn the evil men do – even the ones who thought to ingratiate themselves with the new leaders and ransom their way back to freedom.

The year 1453 would define my life in all its shades of tragedy and comedy. The legend on the compass of my life had been set. My true north would ever point to Truth, with a girl named Alítheia the beacon of my soul. I could see even then that my greatest happiness, my eternal hope, Heaven itself, would be in knowing she lives. Hell would be a life apart, seeing her only in my dreams.

My life here in Purgatory has been as blessed as it was cursed. The Wheel of Life often stretched me until my bones cracked. Yet there was joy.

CHAPTER THREE

The Most High has power over human kingdoms. He gives them to whom he will. He places the basest of men in charge of them. ^{Daniel 4:17}

Little children, these are the End Times, and as you heard, the Antichrist is coming. Even now, many antichrists have arisen. By this we know it is the final hour. ^{1 John 2:18}

Adrianople (Edirne), 1453

Antichrist – the archetype of power, lust and greed – sometimes walks among us. He thinks himself the One and will humble the entire Earth to establish his dominion. You have heard of Nero, of Diocletian, and of Caligula. In this lifetime, Al-Masih Ad-Dajjal was named Muhammad II, son of Sultan Murad II.

Those who adored him would call him El Fatih, The Conqueror. Mehmed-i sānī we called him or "Mehmed." I understand he had been an impossible child. His father, Murad, had been an honorable man dedicated to military victories and contemplation. However, instilling values and discipline in his son of a slave was left to servants hardly qualified for the task.

Murad decided he was ready for peace and quiet by the time Mehmed was twelve. Sultan Murad retired with his manuscripts to join the Dervish in Magnesia ... and the West saw an opportunity. The Vatican preached "Crusade" and gathered forces near the Black Sea to push the Turks from Europe. This, I suspect, is the moment Constantinople became the sacrificial lamb who would pay for all Christianity's sins. Up to that point, we had been an empty threat to the Sultan.

Still, the young Mehmed was not ready for such a confrontation. For example, there was a mutiny of the janissaries when the new Sultan went hunting and forgot to pay them for six months. There was uneasiness among the irregulars about following a child into what looked to be the biggest battle of a generation. Realizing his weakness, the boy king panicked and sent his father a note: "If you are Sultan, come lead your armies. If I am Sultan, then I order you to come lead my armies." Murad donned his armor and crushed the Europeans at Varna, then went back to retirement with the Sufi mystics. So now, the boy with a terrible temper could add personal humiliation to his list of demons to overcome.

When he was younger, this Prophet's namesake heard a hadith saying, *Verily you shall conquer Constantinople. What a wonderful leader will that leader be, and what a wonderful army will that army be!* Mehmed felt the need to be this leader foretold by the Prophet, though for centuries the Ottomans had periodically tried to reduce our city by siege and each time found it impossible. Just as the Western nations had seen a need to stop Mehmed before he gained strength, he saw a need to stop them before they united the Churches. He had carefully observed battles his father had won using cannon. His plan would be to forge the largest cannons ever seen – and both East and West would be his!

Mehmed's vanity was extraordinary. In his mind, he was the measure for all Scriptures, legends or famous sayings. For example, Aristophanes once said of Zeus, *Open your mouth, shut your eyes, and see what Zeus will send you.* The young man's appetite was every bit as omnivorous as Bacchus and certainly as hard to please. For a time, he contented himself playing Zeus with a beautiful girl named Irene, a Greek of some nobility.

Mehmed's caprice became Irene's humiliation. He called her his "Sin Eater" since to stay alive she was willing to worship him in his manner. Cathars had believed that what they ate they purified. Mehmed had no care that calling Irene a Cathar was calling her a witch.

Like Caesars before him, Mehmed had little use for discretion. He was *zill Allah*, the very "Shadow of God" who could do no wrong. His troops so seldom saw him in the field that there were rumors among the janissaries he might marry this girl if she accepted the Law of the Prophet. The Sultan's former tutor and now-vizier Zaganos Pasha recommended Mehmed end the affair before rumors could lead to disorder in the ranks.

Therefore, one day, Mehmed brought Irene in front of his officers. Some say he was humiliating her one last time and caught her as she finished. Others say merely that, disrobing her to show her off, he then caught her by the hair with one hand and by the neck with his *kılıç* (scimitar), and raising her bloody head with its sad eyes to the crowd, he shouted, "By this, judge whether your emperor is able to bridle his affections!" Zaganos' joy must have been complete, but for Mehmed, this had to be a wretched moment – that is, if he still possessed a soul.

I heard from several of the janissaries who had been present that they and some of the irregulars had secretly loved the girl. That "her beauty had shone with the light of God." That she had been "a kind and gentle soul." That many "would have defended her" had they guessed what the Sultan was going to do.

Later, trying to contain the damage of the Sultan's violent act against a submissive woman, the mullahs let out that Mehmed had married the girl and that he was counting on her to give him eternal bliss in the hereafter. They said, "Just as Muhammad knew his favorite wife Aisha would join him in Paradise, Irene will be there for Mehmed's pleasure."

The truth, of course, was that the *enfant terrible* lived in a world where only his desires counted. We were all intimidated – and perhaps this was his calculated aim – some by his violent temper, many by his twisted will. He was loved or hated, but Mehmed was always feared. One of my more spiritual friends asked if killing the woman he loved had slain the soul of Mehmed. Another, less appreciative of the great man, said that moment had come years earlier when he had ordered his better-born half-brothers murdered – Aladdin by strangling and Ahmed by drowning.

The only person with any kind of sway over Mehmed was his intimate friend Zaganos, and Zaganos defended nobody but the Sultan. All of us knew that as slaves we were disposable and defenseless. We were sure that any freedom we exercised would have to be secret – or it would be fatal.

Our greatest shame was that we never cherished freedom so much as Spartans, Athenians, Romans or Byzantines as we would as Ottoman slaves. Why do people value most what they have lost? When the Ottomans begin to fail, it will be because freedom is a lesson they teach with their oppression. Perhaps the Turks learned their arrogance from us. After all, we had conquered half the world for Christianity. In the end, Christianity divided and we handed over to Antichrist the great walled city at the crossroads of world trade.

Old-timers among the janissary said that before the young Sultan set out to accomplish the sayings of the Prophet or to become a man of legend, he had been a better and freer soul. Before he became the student of Zaganos, he had received the teachings of a janissary. This is to say, that in his heart, he might still be a Bektashi – an eclectic sort of Sufi mystic. I can see where he might have become confused.

Hajji Bektash, the cult's patron saint, taught a doctrine of the Heart wherein the kingdom and will of God are contained in us and we are contained in it. Like the Bogomils of the Balkans (and one of the founders of the Bektashi had a Bulgarian mother), the Bektashi also highly regarded those who took vows of celibacy. A Baba who took the vow at one of the sacred tombs would wear an earring in the shape of a horseshoe, an ancient symbol of the Mother Goddess. Perhaps this influence was the one by which Mehmed became enamored of himself as godlike and acquired his ambivalence toward women.

The Bektashi were extremely open-minded, and this was advantageous to the janissaries. For one thing, it made Islam appear a more tolerant and reasonable theology than either Judaism or Christianity. Plethon had spent time in Adrianople associating with these ideas prior to bringing his eclecticism to Constantinople and carrying it in a royal entourage to the Vatican council of Ferrara and Florence. Looking back, I wonder if perhaps the neoplatonic Phatria was Plethon's own little Bektashi lodge! One could argue that the mystical dance of his Pythagorean followers derived from the sema of the *Mevlevi* (Swirling Dervishes).

The janissaries also made a good bond with Ottoman subjects. About a thousand Christian children were rounded up for training each year as a tax from the Empire's captive populations called the *devshirma*. Those who excelled would, in four or five years, graduate to become personal slaves to the Sultan.

As an honored aristocracy of sorts, the Janissary Corps was kind of an embassy between the Ottomans and their subject populations. Through them, everyone knew someone who worked for the empire, who in turn knew whom to bribe or whom to please to get ahead. This was much easier, of course, than trying to please the man at the top.

Once he finally began his studies, Mehmed was in an intense search for wisdom and power. Some say he could read and write in six languages (others that he had plenty of interpreters to read for him).

Either way, he surrounded himself with Sufi mystics, Hurufis (cabbalists of the *Koran*) and old warriors who could bring him theories of the soul, the universe and military strategy. The young sultan reportedly saw himself as the very Right Hand of God.

The Grand Vizier Halil Pasha, a half-Serb, half-Greek janissary who had risen through the ranks, encouraged Mehmed's interest in the *Mevlana* (Jalal al-Din al-Rumi), a pantheist given to love poetry and spiritual perfection. I found this civilized hobby ironic in a young man who could murder both his first love and two brothers without shame!

When Mehmed finally entered the Great Palace of the Caesars, he would quote a line from Rumi: "The spider weaves the curtains in the Palace of the Caesars; the owl calls the watches in the towers of Afrasiyab." Afrasiyab had been an ancient king of the Turks and a fierce enemy of Iran. So it would eventually become clear to us: Mehmed saw himself as the new Alexander. Where once cavalry and infantry had ruled mountain passes and valleys, now artillery might bring a reign of terror to cities from the Atlantic to the Euphrates.

In the ongoing Holy War, another such target will one day be Rome. In this, the Prophet agreed with the Apostle John. Again, a hadith points the way: The Prophet Muhammad was asked, "What city will be conquered first, Constantinople or Rome?" He answered, "The city of Heraclius will be conquered first." Rome should know it is still in danger.

Spain too must prepare, looking south from her ancient Phoenician port Cartagena. Across the water, in the Gulf of Oman, at the *Portus Magnus* of Mers el Kébir, you will find Turkish pirates working alongside the Arabs who have been raiding your coasts for slaves. They are expanding the port. If you do not act soon, one day when you little expect it, you will find an enemy controlling your straits and your commerce subject to the Sultan's tariff.

Let me tell you how he caught us at Constantinople, while we counted on the Western Powers to come save their brethren of the "United Catholic and Apostolic Church."

Chapter Four

I will briefly tell you why He willed Satan to be what he is. I put the question: Is virtue a good thing or a bad? Good undeniably. If virtue is a good, vice is an evil. If vice is evil because it wars against virtue, and virtue good because it casts down vice, virtue as a consequence cannot exist without vice; and if you take vice away, the merits of virtue will also be taken; for there can be no victory without an enemy. Hence good cannot exist without evil. ... It was with supreme reason, then, that God placed the 'stuff' of virtue in evil, His aim being to prepare for us a contest, and to crown the victor therein with immortality as his reward. Lactantius, the Epitome of the Divine Institutes, Chap. 29

The Dardanelles, 1452

The wages of sin is death; and the seeds of our destruction were planted nearly as soon as Constantine's capital was inaugurated. In imperial arrogance, they bore their fruit.

The proximate cause of Byzantium's destruction was "Union." George Sphrantzes, the chamberlain who aspired to be prime minister, used to say our fall began with John and Constantine implementing edicts from the Council of Florence – a decision of men that the Holy Spirit should henceforth proceed "from the Father *and the Son*."

Against the advice of their father Emperor Manuel II, John VIII and Constantine XI had pursued a policy of uniting the Great Church with the Catholic. They did it hoping to ignite another Crusade. They did it to threaten the Sultan. Instead, it availed their subjects murder, rape and slavery. The brothers' crime was simple – forgetting the meaning of Christianity's original and unadulterated creed.

I do not wish to reengage the old debate over the Filioque clause, because it was just one more example of Christianity's leadership deciding the best way to have a divine mystery is to defy common sense and the laws of Nature. Where humanity for thousands of years had remembered a family divine with a Father, a Mother and a Son – Church Fathers beginning with Augustine chose to postulate an all-male Trinity where Father and Son somehow generated a third male! Such is the thinking of men trying too hard to avoid women.

I refuse to imagine how a process of "in-Spiration" for ordination or succession might now be necessary if, originally, a bishop breathing on the candidate and the congregation laying hands on him were sufficient for early believers to become professing Christians!

There were three basic parts to the original Nicene Creed that had lasted a thousand years:

- *We believe in one God, the Father Almighty, Maker of all things visible and invisible.*
- *And in one Lord Jesus Christ, the Son of God ... (with added explanations of his relationship to the Father and to us)*
- *And in the Holy Ghost.*

There was no need for a genealogy of the Spirit. In the beginning, the Spirit had moved upon the face of the waters. She was the voice of Holy Wisdom. The Θεοτόκος (Theotokos) "Mother of God" required no sex change. In the earliest stories, the Dove at the River Jordan did not alight on Jesus – it symbolically flew inside Him! Wisdom came to reside in Him at the moment of His spiritual adoption!

So there was no need for Schism. Texts of the original Creed were sent to the three churches – in Latin, Greek and Armenian. Only exceeding arrogance could cause a break in Christianity's line of defense stretching from Armenia to England. But where "unity of Faith" is key, arrogance and contests for Power soon overthrow Love and Truth.

Perhaps the error was Constantine the Great's need for a "unified creed" – a simple doctrine or slogan to unite all men in the one pure and true religion. Only the Gnostics (the first condemned) resisted, asking, "Did Jesus issue a doctrine before John would baptize him? No, like us, He only needed to repent and accept the Spirit!" We had forgotten so much in the three centuries and 700 miles separating the Jordan River and the Bosporus.

Lord knows there had been ample room for misunderstanding as the fourth century began. Two years before Nicaea, Constantine the Great was still "Sol Invictus" – our Emperor the Invincible Sun. As if to underscore the idea, he erected a statue of Phrygian "Apollo" (or

Mithran "Cautes") wearing a seven-rayed crown and holding a torch aloft a column brought from Rome. The royal mint stamped out coins making the Sol Invictus a "companion" of the Emperor. Later, theologians would make the Emperor a "companion" to Him, likening Christ to the sun god Helios and convincing Constantine that Christ was the "Sun of Righteousness." [Malachi 4:2] However, all of this was really just a colossal reversal and a new telling of the ancient story of the Sun Deity's incarnation. Ironically, Constantine's former master Diocletian had ordered the sacrifice of Christians, Jews and anyone refusing the Sun God His ancient rites. Then it turned out they had always been privy to the same mysteries!

So "Union" can be a problem. Human belief long separated from its author or the circumstances that gave it rise cannot be confined to a single Hymn to the Sun, holy rite, Holy Book or one-sentence dogma.

This idea of "Union" divided us from the beginning! For example, it cleaved Armenia from Byzantium with Gregory's intolerance – ceding Armenians, Nestorians and Paulicians to the Turks. Now, by my king pretending his dream of Union was real, he would alienate himself from his own people; he would still fail to engage the West; and he would invite Mehmed to our gates with a pretext for war! A principled stand can prove terribly expensive.

Rumeli Hisar, 1452

A year before the siege, at the narrowest bend of the Bosporus and about six miles northeast of the city, Mehmed had made known his plans that another old church would be torn apart. Across from the Turkish fortress at Anatolia Rock (*Anadolu Hisar*) built by his grandfather, he dismantled Saint Michael the Archangel's Church and an old Roman fort to erect in one summer a magnificent fortress on the European side of the straits.

Christians had once blocked his path at this strait by ship, and now the fort would achieve several of Mehmed's objectives at once. It could bottle up help coming from the Black Sea in an end run. It could effectively cut off sea trade and ensure tariffs for the Sultan. Most importantly, it would prevent Byzantium from using its small fleet to slow supplies or troop movements across the Bosporus. The half-mile stretch would be perfect for funneling troops into Europe.

The new fortress, with 14 towers (five covered in lead to protect against artillery) was armed with a battalion of janissaries and cannon capable of reaching the main channel. When Emperor Constantine XI sent diplomats to protest the Sultan's annexation of this area behind Pera, Mehmed sent back two of their heads and began deploying his first 50,000 troops.

Mehmed saw that Christianity could be pulled down church-by-church and city-state by city-state. He only needed to help along a process begun long ago by the West itself. Byzantium's patriarchs earned their institutional blindness by putting out the eyes and destroying the lives of Paulicians and Armenians. After the Battle of Tephrike, which decimated the Paulicians in the 9th century, it was better for a heterodox Christian (anyone not reporting to the Patriarch or the Pope) to accept Moslem rule than court the friendship of the Great Church. After the "Fourth Crusade" that sacked Constantinople, perhaps Byzantium too should have broken away rather than put any trust in Rome. Now a lonelier Catholicism will face the future staring into the glowering eyes of ambitious Islam.

Mehmed would one day walk into Saint Sophia's (the Great Church of Holy Wisdom) exclaiming he was there "to dedicate the Church to the One True God." He climbed onto God's altar and knelt to Mecca.

This barbarian was God's perfect punishment for Christian arrogance. By the law of divide-and-rule, he would be the strong and crushing hand for a people who had forgotten what they believed. His creed was simple – so simple even Constantine the Great might have marvelled:

There is no God but God, and Muhammad is His Prophet.

CHAPTER FIVE

Do not look awry at the Saint; the Universe is in his hand. He is the one who governs the world; the authority of the Sovereign is in his hand. The Divine Reality sent him to give right guidance to his servants here; He guides aright whom he will; the curse and the blessing are in his hand. You think he is a man like yourself. The Saint has a mystery. The mystery of God is in his hand. Kaygusuz Sultan

Adrianople (Edirne), 1445

Wisdom and Power Mehmed asked of the Serpent. Wisdom and Power the Serpent would teach. How did the Athenians rule the Aegean? By triremes swift with rams of brass! How did Carthage rule the Mediterranean? By capturing the gate from the Southern Shore! How does a fortress rise? By strong foundation, rock and sweat! How does a city come to fall? By hunger, disease, thirst and fire! Dreams of glory he gathered from legend. Power and riches he promised to make them come true.

Some of the answers Mehmed needed he could gather from military men and old manuscripts. They did not always give him answers relevant to our time, but answers on military strategy could generally be had from the great battles of mankind's past. For example, triremes did not work out very well against tall galleys. However, his drive to conquer ... this came from elsewhere.

"For 800 years," his flattering teachers said, "we have waited for a Mahdi to conquer Constantinople." The Prophet said it would happen, and the *Koran* predicts: *The Romans are vanquished in a near land, and they, after being vanquished, shall overcome.* Koran 30:2-3 It will fall to whomever picks up the mantle of Rome to make good the rest of that prophecy.

Mehmed el Fatih, Conqueror of Byzantium

The Hurufi were among the most excited by the Turks' sacred mission of conquest. They were Persian followers of Fazlallah Astarabadi. They were anxious to see Anatolia's new sultan pick up the mantle of Mahdi. Their hope was that he would free their shrine in Khorasan from the Timurids, ally with Mecca, and conquer Constantinople. They came to visit the young sultan during Mehmed's first reign as a boy of 12 to 14. The Hurufi had influenced the Bektashi with their literature; and now a Hurufi had an audience with Mehmed. I learned of this conversation from one of my Bektashi instructors.

Mehmed asked, "Will I be the one?" The Hurufi told him, "Yes, you are the reincarnation of a Great One. Mighty will be the sword you wield for Allah and great will be the reward of His blessings. You will surpass all sultans before you in your glory and wealth." Mehmed replied, "Will I destroy House Palaeologus?" The Hurufi said, "You will smite the heart of the old Phoenix, but a son will hunt you down." Mehmed asked, "Can you give me a sign to watch for, that I might avoid this fate?" The Hurufi said: "An archer will play the part of Mithras to strike the heart of the Bull of Heaven. Then beware the sign of Athena, for she will bring you wisdom at great cost."

Mehmed wondered, "You say I am the reincarnation of a Great One? Who?" The Hurufi hesitated. "We have waited three generations for the return of Fazlallah to begin the End Times. The Prophet would instruct me to say the Spirit comes by the command of our Lord and only a little knowledge is allowed to us men." The boy insisted, "And if I am the one to be inspired by Allah's command?" The old man had been backed into a corner. He said, "From time to time, a Mahdi is given us. Whether he is inhabited by something Divine himself or whether he is merely inspired, this is not for us to know."

With this, one of Halil Pasha's men, a scholar named Fahreddin Efendi, jumped out from behind a curtain shouting "Heresy!" The poor accursed Hurufi and several of his compatriots and manuscripts were rounded up by the grand vizier's men and sent to the new Mosque of the Three Galleries. There, the muezzin gave out a call for prayer.

When the people gathered, the scholar delivered an angry sermon on the heresy of *hulul* – the idea of a human being inhabited by the divine. A fire was lit around the leader of the group while his compatriots were beheaded. Fahreddin, the fanatic, was so absorbed fanning the flames of his enemy that he singed off half his beard!

It was too late to save the soul of Mehmed from such heresies if that was the Grand Vizier's intent. The young man was already an initiate of the Bektashi and Hurufi orders. Grand Vizier Halil Pasha Çandarlı would henceforth do his best to distance the boy from these groups and to encourage him to study the works of Rumi and the *Koran*.

For awhile, the Sultan would be more circumspect when it came to talking to heretics while holding court. In ultraconservative circles, we janissaries and our Bektashi instructors began to be regarded as "tainted with Persian beliefs" similar to the way Manichaeans had been regarded as Persian traitors to be burned at the stake by my Byzantine ancestors.

We might well have picked up some unorthodox ideas, but we came by them honestly. We had a mystical bent from the Bektashi and the Hurufi. Our Christianity had been derived from the Nestorians with whom the Prophet had studied. Then there was the ancient root of Abraham and Ishmael's heritage. If we had a tendency to favor the idea that we were ever in a battle between the forces of Light and Darkness, it was one the Hebrews had received in the land of Mithras, Zoroaster and Mani. It is a shame that this dividing the world into believers and heathens goes on, even between sister religions of the same family tree. Alas, Jesus said he came *not to send peace, but a sword.* [Matthew 10:34] The same has been the eternal legacy of Persia.

For me, it was all very confusing. I was born into the West, but the East absorbed me. I was born in freedom, yet I would live as a slave. I was brought up in two Christian traditions but would now live in a world of the *Koran*, the poetry of Rumi, the dance of dervishes and secrets of the Bektashi. In the end, I concluded Light must reside on my side and Darkness surely resides with the man about to strike me. Perhaps it is ever this way in the affairs of men.

Chapter Six

Every Kingdom divided against itself is brought to desolation; and every city or house divided against itself shall not stand. Matthew 12:25

Now is another age worn away by civil wars, and Rome herself falls by her own strength, whom neither the neighboring Marsi could destroy, nor the Etrurian band ... [nor Capua nor Spartacus nor Germany nor Hannibal]; but we of an impious race, whose blood is devoted to perdition, shall destroy her. Horace, Ode XVI

Constantinople, 1453

Our Lord is generally merciful to children. He cleanses our memories of the worst of times, leaving little more than the lessons that saved us.

Thankfully, I do not remember much from when the city fell. The most frightening lesson was learning the Most High will use the darkest powers to chastise us when we sin against Him. What does Scripture say? *All have sinned and fallen short of the glory of God.* Romans 3:23 We had, and the price we paid was terrible.

By the time Byzantium's army was low on manpower and our sole defense from the Turks became an old stone wall, we had wasted centuries at battle with other Christians, trading lives and land with the Franks and Venetians. We could have been forging cannon and raising armies to protect us from the forces of the Crescent Moon, but we were busy offering Christianity's generations of first-born to the Son in unholy sacrifice.

After destroying Nestorians and Paulicians, it somehow still made more sense to Orthodoxy and Catholicism to inflict the Bogomils with inquisitors rather than use them to fend off Turanian apostates! We played right into the Turks' hands. Each time Christians were intolerant, Moslems would say, "Show us your holy book, pay the tax and you too will be safe." By peace, Mehmed destroyed many. ^{Daniel 8:25}

In this way, villages of good Christians went from being defenders of the Faith to raising sons for the Sultan's army. It was just easier than fighting and being condemned by one's own brethren.

From God's standpoint, I suppose empires rise and fall as often as the Sun and Moon. Even to us with our limited sight, it seems whole nations are replaced by the very next barbarians to arrive. One dynasty gives way to another family even more greedy and ruthless. Since the end of the Age of Gemini and Most High's quarreling grandsons, human royalty and governments have been corrupt, overreaching, and generally short-lived. Byzantium and its longevity of more than a thousand years was something of a miracle among nations. Nonetheless, our fate had been sealed long ago in the heavens.

In the ninth century, Abu Masar claimed the fortune of Byzantium and her *basileos* (emperor) could be read in the stars. By this astrologer's methods, known to Mehmed, two months after we arrived in Constantinople a conjunction of Venus over Mars in Aries announced that our new Emperor Constantine XI would be "of no importance." The astrologer had also said when Jupiter passed over Mars it would foretell the death of Byzantium's Emperor, the death of most of his nobles, and conflagrations in the city. In May 1452, such a conjunction occurred.

At the time, we were just beginning to hear rumors of a fortress taking shape across the Golden Horn behind Pera. Had we known of the signs, perhaps we would have looked to the stars and loaded into our wagons and ships instead of praying to icons of Jesus, Mary and the Saints. Unfortunately, the prophecies we heeded were much more confusing.

Methodius of Patra, Emperor Leo the Wise and St. Daniel the Stylite had all predicted our fall – the latter noting that the last Emperor would be named Constantine as the first. Others saw us in a battle between the Eagle and the Snake, Christianity and Islam, but that the Eagle would eventually triumph over the Snake, like the one remembered when Constantine the Great decided to make the seven hills his capital city. The Emperor saw an eagle struggling with a snake then and thought it an evil omen, but his sages convinced him Christianity would triumph over the apostates "after a setback." The prophecy was ascribed to Apollonius of Tyana.

In truth, I was not a good eyewitness to the dramatic events of the next few months. While I could, I lived in youthful oblivion, happy to spend an afternoon wandering with Alítheia or sword fighting with the boys. I knew my mother worried about the Turks, but she was always worried about something. She did not trust the "Moors," as she called them, any farther than she could throw one. I suppose it had to do with her origins.

"How many centuries has it taken to reconquer Spain from the Arabs?" she would demand. "Eight centuries! Constantinople will be a hard lesson for Europe, because the West treats Byzantium with less care than a Briton regards a Persian. They will leave it to intermediaries – Genoese, Jews and Venetians – to one day reopen the East. We are lost!" In her way, mother was brilliant. Unfortunately, women rarely sit on the councils of kings. In ancient times, even Yahweh had a consort who spoke Wisdom. Our Emperor received no such counsel, or if he did, he had ignored it long ago and now it was too late.

My first real memory of the gathering storm was the winter of 1452 to 1453. The Sultan started sinking ships, I think, in December. Since we could not initially get aid beyond some archers from the Pope, my grandfather took ships up along the Marmara coast to raid Turkish villages for supplies.

He and his sailors came back celebrating victory, but I know there were some on the Council who, up until that very moment, had hoped war might be avoided – the difference between denial and cowardice being exceedingly small. While the Megadux was sure life under the Turks would be more tolerant of Orthodoxy than under the Latins, he said he was "glad to strike one last blow for freedom." The action probably shortened his life, as it would one day depend on Mehmed's forgiving nature.

In January, 700 Genoese arrived under the leadership of Giustiniani. How odd that Byzantium's last hero would be the namesake of our greatest emperor, Justinian, just as the man he served would be namesake of Byzantium's first Caesar, Constantine the Great.

How could a nation so very rich in history have become so terribly low in resources? The recurring Plague was part of it, having decimated our population, but neither had we ever recovered from the Fourth

Crusade in 1204. Our poverty was made worse when merchants and nobles alike moved their wealth to Italy or buried it rather than give it to the Council to prepare for war. So beyond these armored sailors of Giustiniani and the 200 archers brought by Cardinal Isidore, there would not be much armed help on the way. We had a few Frankish and Armenian volunteers, but nothing sizable.

At the end of February, Lady Anna returned to Venice with about 700 of the city's aristocracy. I do not fault them for abandoning our lost cause. However, I am sure their desire to safeguard their families and wealth was the death knell for our little empire. For example, the inability of the Emperor to pay for large cannon in the summer of 1452 led the Hungarian engineer Urban to join the ranks of the Ottomans in September. He added a dozen supercannon to Mehmed's 50 ordinaries to shatter walls that had stood a millennium.

I am not sure why my mother and I did not leave on one of the boats in February. Perhaps she could not afford the passage; perhaps she thought the Emperor might join us; or perhaps she was waiting for the Megadux to do something. Whatever the case, it looked as though we might have lost our chance.

Only two cities on the Turks' way to Constantinople chose to defend their freedom: Selymbria and Epibatos. The Turks simply went around them, focusing on Constantinople. Sever a hand and the warrior fights on. Slice off his head and you win the day.

In March, the Turkish armada arrived in the Marmara. Troops crossing the Bosporus came ashore at the new fortress. Now there was no way to block their path.

In April, Mehmed and his thousands showed up at the walls in force and Emperor Constantine ordered the chain boom strung across the Golden Horn. There was a minor skirmish there when the Turks attempted to reopen the Horn (estuary of the ancient Dathynio and Athyra Rivers), but you could say the war really began with a shot from Urban's huge cannon "Basilike" on April 11th.

As our bad luck (or our past transgressions and God's will) would have it, Mehmed had an ambassador from Hungary with artillery experience. The ambassador showed him that by bombarding in a triangle and then hitting the triangulated area with one of the giant cannon, he could level an entire section of wall!

The Ottoman troops had drawn to within a mile of the city and had begun erecting their engines of war. Our sole victory that month was a Byzantine galley and three Genoese fighting off the Turkish armada of 145 boats to bring in a shipment of wheat. Looking back, it was not such a beacon of hope. At the time, it felt as if Heaven had taken up our cause.

When that minor miracle happened, it was wonderful to watch Mehmed going insane, whipping his horse into the surf, shouting at the top of his lungs, livid that his little triremes could not sink tall galleys firing down on his sailors with cannon and Greek fire! I later saw impressive scars on Admiral Baltaoglu's back where Mehmed had pounded him with his scepter, breaking ribs. Mehmed in such a moment must have viewed himself as Orion with his great mace. Lucky for the admiral, the madman had not been dreaming of Achilles and his spear! The old man was also whipped for his defeat, leaving him blind in one eye when the lash went astray.

The victory in April for the Turks was skirting the boom with about 70 of their small warships. An Italian renegade showed them how to do it. They greased a timber slipway assembled over a creek behind Pera to drop some of the smaller boats right next to our northeastern wall to threaten our ships. Mehmed also stationed cannon on a hill behind Pera for the same purpose. One morning we woke up to find a small armada had sailed over land into our harbor! It was definitely a bad omen. For years, people had said: "Constantinople will fall when ships sail on dry land!" Mehmed had apparently taken us at our word.

Then the atrocities began. The Sultan impaled a number of prisoners outside our walls, a horrible cry to hear. Our Emperor responded by beheading 260 Ottoman prisoners. The Angel of Death was now taking people so quickly that both sides took to burning bodies rather than digging graves. Those with shovels were employed digging mines to weaken Constantinople's walls – or countermines to burn out Turkish miners. By the end of April, my grandfather said we had lost about 6,000 men and the sultan "about five times as many." I imagine Mehmed received similarly optimistic reports.

Both sides were cautious, experiencing failures to take advantage. A tower collapsed at the St. Romanos Gate and the Turks gave us time to repair it rather than rush into the breach. We failed to quickly burn the little armada they infiltrated into the Golden Horn. The Turks were warned before we could move against them and thwarted our attack as soon as it began.

Uncle George, used to playing the beggar in the courts of Europe, suggested the Emperor make a run for safety and bring back an army from the West to save us. The Emperor said his place would be to die with his beloved people if that was God's will. Grandpa suggested we destroy the city and kill ourselves rather than accept the slave's yolk from a greedy lunatic. The Emperor repeated, "Let God's will be done!" In the end, each man would get what he wanted. George would beg for his life and pay a ransom to live. The Emperor would die trying to defend his people. My grandfather? He would play all angles until it killed him.

Our position was increasingly desperate. Within the walls, we really did not have sufficient food for a siege. In 718, we had withstood a siege by 180,000 Arabs and a great fleet. Mehmed was now doing his best to recreate the event, only he would hold out for victory.

I remember the great cannon sounded as though they might split the seven hills as well as the walls. Smoke covered the enemy camp and the city in a fog so dark the two opposing forces could barely see each other. Round stones from the supercannon wider than the biggest man and weighing more than five men crashed into our walls. There were smaller explosions and smoke from muskets (or *Arkibuza*), which were a new invention used by both sides. Arrows rained in with more accuracy and stones slung from mangonels spread destruction along the city's edge. In reprisal, we flung hot pitch and Greek Fire at the Turks and they were unable to approach with their towers.

Sometimes early on, my friends and I would throw rocks from the walls at the Turks – a futile effort since they were generally too far away, but it felt good. After a few weeks of fighting, all able-bodied people were pressed into moving rock and dirt toward the walls so we could rebuild them almost as quickly as the Turks could tear them down with cannon.

I have heard unkind souls say Byzantium "had to fall" because we had not united the churches, but we had! The one thing Emperor Manuel had told his sons NOT to do we had done. I went to St. Sophia and heard Mass said with the Filioque. Women wept and men quietly raged that we had finally committed the unforgivable sin against the Holy Spirit.

> *He who blasphemes against the Holy Spirit never has forgiveness, but is subject to eternal condemnation.* ^{Mark 3:29}

Some people think we did not pray fervently enough, but I was there many an evening when icons were paraded through the streets, women cried prayers to the *Theotokos* and men prayed the Jesus Prayer unceasingly. In the spirit of the hesychasts, I had my own one-breath version that I had adapted for myself. Instead of *Lord Jesus Christ, Son of God, have mercy on me, a sinner* – I would say, *Father, Son, Holy Spirit, have mercy on us*. During the war I remember saying it in my mind so many times that it became my very breath. In the end I lived, so perhaps all the praying worked. At the time, it didn't feel like it.

People did not lose faith in God before the city fell, though some surely did once they lost everything. More often, they would lose faith in themselves, in their neighbors, in the nobles, in the mercenaries, in the city ... and in our collective ability to face down the Sultan's army of 200,000 with 5,000 proper soldiers and 40,000 people theoretically under arms. I think most of us realized that if the walls fell, all would be hopeless, and on this Mehmed focused his efforts. In the end, the unwillingness of the populace to fund our defense and the mercenary treachery of one engineer determined the fate of an empire.

In early May, my grandfather called for me. The messenger said the matter was urgent. The servant said the old man was pacing back and forth like an animal in a cage and that his only desire was to speak to me. I mounted a charger and we quickly rode past the Aqueduct, the Venetian Quarter, the Hippodrome, and the Forum of Constantine and stopped at the manor in front of St. Andrew's.

House Notaras, 1453

Grandfather dismissed the servant, and then proceeded loud and fast: "You must sail to Venice and take up with your mother or your Aunt Anna. The end is near and things are not going to work out as planned. Old Halil is being pushed aside for the Sultan's boyfriend, so I expect no quarter to be given. Constantine will not surrender or accept terms, so condemns the city to rape and plunder. Our brave Genoans are quietly readying their boats for the moment there is a major breach in the walls. The Turks know what we're doing before we do it! They've mined under the walls. My cannon cannot stop theirs. That greedy Godforsaken little Hungarian repairs and reinforces them too quickly! With spies and arrows, the Turks are issuing notices here in the city that the neighborhood first to surrender a gate will keep its property and lives. I'm down to one ace in my hand and I'm not about to give it up to that son of a slave!"

I just stood there wide-eyed. At the time, I had precious little idea as to what was going on beyond what people said in the streets. Now he pointed at me, drew close and said quietly, "YOU are my last hope." And with that, he gave me a hug and we both sat down.

"All is sometimes not as it seems," he said, collecting himself and continuing quietly. "Ruling a nation is dirty business. There are secrets to keep from the enemy, and that causes you to have secrets from your own people. Sometimes, if the Emperor is truly a good man, there are secrets to keep from him. What I'm about to tell you is so secret, I would kill anyone but family or its keepers for knowing it. It is more important than the recipe to Greek Fire – and the old men knowing that little secret will be killing themselves one day soon to keep it from Mehmed! Do you understand what I am saying?" I nodded that I did. "Then I'll tell you a story and we must be quick. Hold your questions until I finish."

The old man stood up to go back to pacing. No matter how tiring the councils or patrolling his wall and speaking to archers and cannon crews along the Golden Horn, he was not one for relaxing in a time of war. "You are almost nine years old now, old enough for Holy Communion. In the days of the sacred mysteries, old enough for initiation."

He continued, "Do you remember what you saw back in Mystras?" I replied that I did. "That was a ceremony of the Phatria. Most of the men you saw that night were followers of Gemistos Plethon. Some you knew from your classes. Others you will meet in Rome or Venice, men such as Bessarion. To them, you can entrust your life. If you do not know them, but you think you have met a member of the Brotherhood, tell him you are a child of Athens and ask him if he knows the way home. Only a member will know the password and the answer.

"Home is not Greece; it is the extreme north of Heaven above the Logos following the Milky Way from where Zeus was weaned, past the Cupbearer of the Gods, the Phoenix and the Seven Spheres. The secret of the Phatria is the secret of the Grand Cross, the 'Phoenix' that occurs every 500 years or so. But you are not here to be initiated into the Phatria. The Brotherhood will work with you. They will shelter you if you are in danger; but you are not theirs and they are not yours to control. They are the inner circle who will one day restore the Republics of Plato, Athens and Rome to this evil world.

"No, today you are here for another kind of initiation. You should have been older. You should have remained awake all night keeping watch. You should be attended by the Emperor and your brethren, but now there is no time. You will spend your life searching for truths we would have taught you." He walked back to his chair and strapped on his sword as I had seen him do many times before.

"Kneel here, in front of the icons and the sacred Labarum." I obediently moved to the little prayer rail at the front of his miniature chapel. Now bow your head and answer me.

"Do you swear to Serve the Lord your God all your life?" I do.
"Do you swear to Seek Justice and Overthrow Tyranny?" I do.
"Do you promise to Relieve Suffering of the Oppressed?" I do.
"Do you promise to Seek Wisdom and to Serve the Truth?" I do.

With his sword, he dubbed me a Knight Captain of St. George, and stepped back to touch the stone Labarum behind him. "Your mission is to do all in your power to build the Kingdom of God on Earth and to bring down His enemies. Pick your men well. They will be the lifeblood of Rome. Choose your words and your actions carefully, for the path you follow will be steep to climb. The way is narrow that leads to life, and few are those who find it. EN TOUTO NIKA. In Hoc Signo Vinces!" (By this sign conquer!) And my induction was over.

I had joined an order dating back to 313 *Anno Domini*. Constantine the Great founded it as a band of warriors whose duty was to ensure Christianity's battle standard never fell. He deployed the standard wherever he needed to concentrate forces to procure victory.

> *Out of the warriors that were with him, he selected such men as excelled in bodily strength, in courage of mind, and in exemplary piety; and on these he imposed a single duty: that they should uphold the standard. These persons were in number no less than fifty, on whom nothing else was incumbent, but to surround, defend and guard the standard.* [Eusebius, Vita Constantini]

Grandpa explained the symbol of St. George and the Dragon as a mystery of ancient astronomy, its connection to a mystery of the

Genesis, one from Isaiah, and a tie to the End Times. He explained the meaning of the Labarum. Finally, he gave me the Prayer to the Celestial King that also dates back to the time of Constantine the Great:

Thee we acknowledge our only God. Thee we declare our Eternal King. Thee we acknowledge our Comrade-in-arms. Victory is Thy gift. By Thee we vanquish our enemies. To Thee we give our thanks. We are Thy humble servants. Keep our Emperor and his family safe among us. And let us die with honor or live victorious and free! Amen.

Then he turned to a subject I had always wanted, but always dreaded, to hear. "I'm sorry, my boy," he said, "but it is high time that you learn what brought you here to this place and this time. I am not proud of the role I played. I regret that God entrusted you to Caterina instead of Anna, but so far, I think you've done exceedingly well considering. But now I'm speaking in riddles! Let me tell you what happened."

He went on but now lowered his voice again, "Try not to be angry with me or with your mother or with the Emperor, but your life will always hang by a slender thread of secrecy. No one may know of your identity but those in whom you would entrust your very life, because the day you are betrayed, Rome and Greece may die with you. We must keep you alive and for that you must listen carefully."

My grandfather, the biggest, most powerful, most confident and loud man I knew now glanced about to make sure we were alone and nearly whispered: "The day Byzantium falls – and it falls almost as we speak – the Sultan will want to eliminate any and all competition. And you," he said, quietly poking my chest, "will be the only person standing in the way of that slave's son's legitimacy as Caesar. You are the rightful heir to the Byzantine throne, and though you were not born in the purple room, you carry the blood of a dynasty." I opened my mouth to ask a question.

"No questions, hear me out. That self-serving chambermaid the Emperor chose as his chamberlain … forgive me … I mean your 'Uncle George,' recommended against your father and your Aunt Anna from marrying. He wanted to use a marriage to enlist better allies than a millennium of history might provide. So while that dandy was running around Europe at our expense for 10 years, I did something necessary but questionable. I reinstituted the *dodecatheos*.

"The family of the Emperor was always supposed to survive, no matter what. It was the Phoenix itself, according to Eusebius. Just as a seed brings forth an ear of corn with the Lord's blessing, from Constantine would spring dynasties."

The old man handed me a chalice and told me to look inside. It contained 18 naked figures, half of them men and half women. The chalice must have been gnostic. He explained that the winged dragon in the center was Draco and each of the gods surrounding it held a seat on the Divine Council. Apparently, the number of members varied over the years, but the idea was the same. As long as we held the capital, the aristocracy would ensure there was an heir to the throne.

Now I understood what had happened at Mystras. While I was a little angry at being regarded all my life as a "twice-born" *deuteropotmoi*, I could see the beauty in what the Megadux had done. To legitimize the pregnancy, there was a secret ceremony at Mystras with only Constantine (then-Despot of Morea), Caterina, Anna, the priest and himself — all sworn to secrecy. What might they have done if Sphrantzes had returned with a bride for Constantine?

This all came as a bit of a shock, of course. One moment I was the happiest and best-connected bastard in the Kingdom and the next I was royalty kneeling there with my neck out, waiting for a *kılıç* to fall. I did not know where to begin with my questions or objections — and of course, they would not matter. The King was calling for a meeting of the Council and Grandpa had to go. The old man gave me a hug and promised we would have a bit more time to talk before the end and that he would devise a means for my escape.

I returned home that night terribly agitated and with a deep sense of foreboding. How would I escape? What would I do if I did? The mantle of empire weighs heavy on the shoulders of a nine-year-old.

Blachernae Palace, 1453

By the second week of May, much had changed. The churches were taking special offerings to provide food for men on the walls. The Emperor had dispatched a small ship beyond the Dardanelles to find out where our relief was, since the Vatican and the Venetians had supposedly promised aid.

By using a high trajectory and a smaller charge over Galata, the Turks meanwhile worked out how to hit galleys inside the Golden Horn. They blasted a neutral Genoese ship to the bottom. One night assault by the Turks made it all the way to Blachernae Palace, but they were turned back. No doubt a spy had left open one of the minor gates. My mother, as many of the others, was almost hysterical with concern.

Mehmed must have been quite the student of history. I guess he heard that Xerxes had built a pontoon bridge over the Hellespont and now the Sultan would do the same here. The Turks were in the process of lashing boats together in the Golden Horn when Grandpa again called for me. The servant found me with my friends along the top of Grandpa's wall just southeast of the Blachernae Palace, behind St. Mary's. It was not the safest place to be with Zaganos firing cannon from behind Pera, but we had never seen a bridge in progress before.

In no time, the servant and I had crossed the city by horse. It was a beautiful day, the kind you might lose a cloak by leaving it most anywhere. Instead of going to the house, we pulled up in front of the old Great Palace. The mornings were sunny but cool and the rains had just about stopped for the season. Grandpa was looking worn. His cape was soiled, his big blue eyes had bags under them and his beard needed a trim. Nonetheless, he gave me a bright smile and a hug.

"It's all set," he said. He handed me a fist-sized leather bag. Inside were 50 gold coins and two signet rings, one of the House Palaeologus and one of the House Notaras. "That is your passport," he said. "Give Captain Doria half the coins and show him the Notaras ring. He will take you to Caterina and Anna. Never part with the rings unless you are captured – and then lose them as quickly as you can. Doria's ship will be among the first to depart in the event of a major breach in the walls."

The walls were already frequently breached and repaired, but I knew what he meant. The final push would be a madhouse of Turks flowing in through a break in the walls, and the Venetians and Genoans and much of the populace would be running for the harbors. I am not sure how he thought a nine-year-old would fare in all of that, but that was our plan. I asked if my stepmother could go with me. He said she could, that he had spoken to her already, as well as the captain.

I asked him what he expected me to do in Italy that would contribute to reviving a fallen empire. "God will show you the path," he said, "You must believe that, or we have lost already." I had expected more in the way of a grand strategy, but I think the old man was having doubts in man-made plans at the moment. His plan for the war definitely was not working. His agents were being caught and tortured. He was a Megadux without a navy at his disposal. His old friend Halil was losing influence with the Sultan. The Emperor, always a good man and a kind leader, appeared on the verge or in the midst of a major depression. The *basileos* usually said and did the right thing, but now he resigned himself to dying at the Romanos Gate in defense of his people, and Mehmed was sure to oblige him.

"Come with me," said my grandfather, lighting a torch and then leading me through a long dark corridor. We stopped about 100 feet from the scriptorium where our manuscripts were stored in a secret vault. He went to a niche in the wall and moved a statue of a saint. On the other side of the gallery, there was a small stack of porphyry balls. He took one and set the ball at the base of where the statue had been, then reset the statue. A plunger of some sort unlatched a lock below the floor. Then he pulled aside a large tapestry and gave the wall a shove.

Behind the tapestry, a narrow stairway descended to a little room directly below the ground-floor gallery. The room held some old decorative items and the occasional sword, mace or piece of armor. It looked like an old storage room of some sort. In the back on the right, below the bottom shelf was a small chest about two palms width and a forearm in length. He pulled it out.

"This," he said, "you take with you when you leave. I will assign you a brother of the Order, but this must not stay behind when the city falls. Take it to a defensible site built by the Old Empire. Use it when you must, but otherwise hide it well. It belonged to Julius Caesar and Constantine the Great. Now it belongs to you."

I opened the aged box. Inside was an oiled leather scabbard, obviously newer than the hilt, which appeared to be of ebony with a gilt bronze pommel and half-ball guard. It was not much to look at until one pulled out the blade. The steel had been worked like a Damascus blade – black lines showed where carbon had been worked into the billet in very unusual patterns of color. Grandpa said the blade was forged from a shooting star blue-silver in color. The edge looked as if it had been in more than one fight, but it was still deadly. On one side of the guard it had an inset medallion of Apollo, the Sol Invictus. On the other, it had one of St. George slaying the Dragon.

"Legend had it that the Gauls kept it in a wounded oak tree from the time Caesar left it with them in honor of one of their chiefs – Vercingetorix, I believe. He told them to keep it for him until a rightful heir came to claim it. Centuries later, Constantine the Great found himself in the same forest near a Temple of Apollo where he met the Druids or one of their successors in star wisdom who taught him astronomy as they had Caesar (though I imagine he had recourse to the writings of Hipparchus as well). Constantine went looking for the sword, and the story is that the tree split open from a lightning strike on a clear day – as if Theos Himself wanted him to have it! Of course, the magicians might have used gunpowder or Greek Fire – like the priest of Apollo bringing down the cliffs of Delphi on the Persians! The point is, it is a very special blade never defeated in battle. Perhaps it will one day defend you." I promised to value it as nothing from this world. He said it was called *Agheu Glas*, "The Gray Death."

We left the gallery as we had found it and went on to the vault. My education was far from complete. Grandpa had given me good tutors and Diana and Emanuel had always read to me, but there is so much to know in this world and so little time to relearn even the basics. I vaguely remember Apollonius, Plato, Philo, Tacitus, Thucydides, Diodorus, Virgil, Homer, Herodotus, Lactantius, Clement, Dionysius the Areopagite, Plotinus, Ovid, Julian, Strabo, Eusebius and the plays. Sometimes their words still come unbidden to illuminate a situation.

The way we accelerated our studies was everyone would read a work, then return to the group and report on important lessons we had learned. We would discuss them, share the best quotes for our commonplace books and figure out what we wanted to read next. It was a much faster way to get through the classics than in a regular academy. We burned many candles at night. It seemed like the manuscripts were letters from old friends with important things to say.

I felt by now that I would never graduate, that there just would not be time. I would have to find a school in Italy, and who knew if they would have such materials at their disposal? Later, I would be pleased to find such a school in Florence for my children. For now, life was good, but my education would soon take a detour through Hell.

For the moment, I had my friends, my notes, and my sword. I had a way to escape and a future. At the age of nine, what more could a boy want? I think Grandpa sensed it and resolved to see what he could do.

Chapter Seven

Hope is ever the curse of man; it drives state against state for ambition and greed. When men vote on the question of war, no man takes his own death into account, but thinks another will meet his fate. If we had seen death when we cast our votes, Hellas would never have rushed to her doom in mad desire for battle. Any man can choose between good and evil, and how much better is peace than war? Peace, the Muses' chiefest friend, the foe of sorrow, whose joy is in healthy children and prosperity. These are the blessings we cast away when we wickedly start wars to make the losers slaves. Euripides, Suppliant Maidens

The victorious barbarian, alas! shall trample upon the ashes of the city, and the horseman shall smite it with the sounding hoofs. Horace, Ode XVI

Blachernae Palace, 1453

By May 21st, we were near our last reserves of food and will and hope. Months of blockade and a month of shelling were having their effect. I believe the West's sole attempt to keep us alive was the one shipment of wheat. Everyone was exhausted.

When the Turks lit their bonfires that evening, the light reflected on the dome of *Agia Sophia*, and the guards and the people were by turns excited and concerned. Some saw the reflection on the dome as a cross. Some thought the tower at the top had ignited and the city was burning. Others saw a supernatural flame in which the light flashed and then floated up to the sky. Some cried out that Our Lady of Wisdom had abandoned us, that Her Light had returned to the heavens! In the end, it was no more than the reflection of campfires and smoke.

Constantine XI, last emperor of the Romans

One night later that week, the moon turned blood red in an eclipse. Our doomsayers took it as a sign of the End Times; [Revelation 6:12] and I am sure Mehmed had both known the prophecy and anticipated the sign.

There was parading of icons and fervent prayers. We hoped God and Allah would come to blows over Constantinople as Homer's gods had squared off over the fall of Troy.

It was an eventful couple of days. Johannes Grant's countermining team captured an Ottoman officer and a soldier. When Grant's team burned out the mine, most of the Turks suffocated. Under torture, the two survivors revealed locations of remaining mines. Then it was a matter of locating barrels of water along the walls to see exactly where they were burrowing in – and laying more traps. The next day was crazy. The Turks had not enjoyed seeing burnt and decapitated comrades tumbling over the walls. They blasted us and darkened the skies with arrows throughout the day. The north wall from the Romanos Gate to the Blachernae Palace suffered great damage.

One evening I came in from our neighborhood games and a couple of hours loading wagons of stone for the walls and found Grandpa at the Blachernae Palace talking to Mother. Most of the time, he avoided the palace, probably out of his dislike for Uncle George. These days, it was also not the usual place to find the Emperor. Constantine spent most of his time at the Romanos Gate with Giustiniani when the two were not out trying to maintain troop morale along the walls.

Grandpa took me aside, and said, "There is someone I would like you to meet." He walked me down the hall to an area I had been taught to avoid – the throne room. It was much plainer than I had imagined. There had been a time when the Byzantine throne had been magical, mechanically rising up to tower over anything else and surrounded by courtiers and pomp. Today, in this smaller palace, it was just a nice room with a bit of gilt and some large tapestries. However, on this day, the Emperor was home!

I think our Emperor had always been vaguely aware that I existed as a person. After all, we had lived in the same palace in Mystras and come to Constantinople together. However, until that moment, I had not imagined he might have noticed me; and now he wanted to meet me!

Looking back, I do not envy his position. Here he was on the brink of losing to heathens the Empire that brought Christianity to the world.

Here he was concerned about which gate would be first to open to save a few lives and houses, about the spies in our midst, about the bloodshed and rapine to come – and he was just now meeting a son raised right under his nose!

I fell to one knee. The Emperor tossed off his black cloak with the dynasty's insignia and closed the distance. He asked my grandfather, "Does he know?" My grandfather nodded. My Emperor had tears in his eyes. He looked as though he had not rested in weeks. However, he raised me up, gave me a giant hug, and invited me to have a seat. He asked about my lessons. He asked after my mother. He said he regretted all the secrecy. Indeed, he said he had thought me dead when Caterina returned to Constantinople alone while he was out fighting Turks and Franks. He said I was my grandfather's biggest secret. I could never be his son publicly – not if I was to live. He said the only Palaeologus or Notaras that might survive this war would be the Sultan's agent, an escapee to Italy, or disguised.

On the other hand, there is nothing as invisible as what is in plain sight everyday. That definitely applied to me. I had been a nobody for so long, my own mother would scarcely believe I met the Emperor!

He looked exhausted. Yet there was something in him so tough there could be no compromise before death. He said as almost the last true Roman: "Constantinople as a city may change rulers before this battle is out. Even now, her great stone walls cry out for mercy. But know this: The greatness that was Rome will not be lost if we remember what she stood for. Our Greek ancestors gave us a philosophy of freedom and democracy. Christianity gave us virtue and faith in the Supreme Being. We expanded His Kingdom across the world with armed might and by bringing education to the barbarians. Each of us gave our best years to the service of the Empire. And wherever our banner flew across the world, we knew honor. Each of us was a Knight of St. George, for none would willingly let the standard fall."

My grandfather told him that he had initiated me into the Order. My Emperor father smiled, congratulated me and told me to *Serve Truth* all my life. He said his greatest shame was in knowing that the Empire would end on his watch, but that his greatest hope was in knowing that the tradition and line of the Phoenix, that of Constantine the Great, would not die with him.

He cupped my face in his hands, kissed my forehead and thanked my grandfather. Then my grandfather took me out a side door and back to the section of the castle where my mother and I lived. The old man quietly reminded me never to forget who I was – just a boy of the household. Anything else could be fatal.

Grandpa said I could tell my mother I met the Emperor – it was just something special he wanted to do for his grandson, but that telling her my secret could only place her in danger. I told her the King and the Megadux had shown me the throne room. Mama was thrilled.

The Enemy Camp, 1453

There are conflicting stories about what was going on during the 26th and 27th of May in the Ottoman camp. Wishful thinking in Constantinople had it that the pause in action was because our reinforcements were on the way from Genoa and the Turks were concerned. The rumor circulated due to the return of a scout ship on the 23rd to Langa Harbor on the western shore of the city. My grandfather wined and dined the ship's crew and debriefed them so they would not give away the bad news. The tragic truth was that nobody was coming, not even the Emperor's brothers Thomas and Demetrius, nor the 15,000 troops from the Morea we had hoped would come. I guess Grandpa's hope was that Mehmed might get the wrong idea from his spies observing our reception of the scout ship's crew or perhaps there was strategic advantage in our people retaining hope.

Mehmed may well have been having doubts, but he had scouts to debunk disinformation. Within our walls, some said the Hungarians were on the move and that more Venetians were on the way. We entertained such daydreams while the Sultan's forces spread out surrounding the city, preparing their scaling ladders and filling in ditches for a rapid assault.

The Faithless One might have been concerned he could be caught at the end of a narrowing peninsula without defensible supply lines ... backed up against a hornets' nest of pent-up rage. I imagine his Grand Vizier Halil was counseling time to pull out, that if five months of blockade had not forced us to surrender, what made anyone think five more would do the trick ... but the more likely possibility was that the Sultan just wanted his men rested up before the final push. His leaders wandered through the encampment promising high rank to the first man to scale the walls of Constantinople. He set his order of battle and went out to visit his fleet in the Horn.

The new admiral, Hamza Bey, would attack sea walls with scaling ladders wherever possible (ensuring few of Grandpa's troops could redeploy to the Romanos Gate). Zaganos Pasha would divide his forces between the Horn and attacking the single wall of the city near Blachernae Palace. Karaja Pasha would be to the right. Ishak Pasha and Mahmud Pasha would take from the Romanos Gate to the Marmara shore. Meanwhile, the Sultan and his Grand Vizier Halil Pasha would direct the main attack up the Lycus Valley to the Romanos Gate, where the giant cannon had been tearing at the walls for weeks. Mehmed's old admiral, a rehabilitated Baltaoglu, would command the janissaries and palace guard as a strategic reserve.

Constantinople, 1453

Defense did not look good. Big chunks of all three walls of the Lycus Valley were missing. There had been plenty of hand-to-hand combat in areas between the walls. Brave warriors on both sides had met their maker there chopping each other to bits. Manuel of Genoa had about 200 archers and crossbowmen defending the main land wall. Giustiniani and the Emperor led the defense of our most threatened sector, the Romanos – the gate nearest the river. At the center, they still had 400 armored Italians and a couple of thousand Byzantines. Girolamo Minotto and the Venetians defended us at Blachernae Palace. Grandpa had 500 archers and men on cannon and musket to defend the Golden Horn's wall. Some of our fiercest defenders, the Catalanes, held harbors in the south.

On the 28th, I took advantage of the situation to visit the Emperor in the morning before Mass. One of my tutors, Michael, was on guard duty and let me through when I said I had a message from the Megadux for the Emperor. I guess Michael figured extraordinary times call for extraordinary measures. He did not question the idea of a nine-year-old as a messenger. When I made it to the Emperor's tent, my father walked with me up to the tower as if to show me something he wanted the Megadux to know.

Looking across the battlefield, he said: "Tomorrow will be the day I return home and you find your future. Tomorrow, take your stepmother and go with Girolamo Minotto, governor of the Venetian Quarter and the man to whom I have entrusted Blachernae Palace.

In the confusion when the Turks breach the walls, he will get you out. If you can, convince your grandfather to go with you. Italy is where his daughters are and where you will be, and that is where he should be – watching over his grandson. Of course, it would offend him were I to say that, so let the request come from you."

He went on: "Tomorrow will be the death of the Roman Empire. I hope the barbarians appreciate what a millennium of history has built and do not destroy it out of hand. We have fought a good fight, but the walls cannot take more bombardment. Our soldiers have neither the strength nor the munitions to hold back the enemy once the walls give out. Our brave allies will run to their ships once the situation becomes desperate. This was never really their fight.

"My biggest regret is that I listened to the promises of Europe when I should have been listening to my father. They said they could mobilize more than 100,000 troops for this war. With just a few more from our brethren in the Morea and a few rebels in the conquered territories, we might have made a glorious stand – but it is better to spare those lives that some may live to remember the glory of Greece and Rome. One day our people will free themselves, God willing.

"I regret not having had a family. If I had been less eager to gain back our land, perhaps we might have saved the city by paying tribute. You might have had the life of a prince. Your grandfather could have taught you to lead a fleet. Now, I fear for what may become of you.

"Whatever you do, wherever you go, try to remember what we stood for, not how we failed. Remember we did not sacrifice our religion when the Latins conquered us in the 13th century, and we did not bow to superior force when the Moslems conquered us in the 15th. That was as our history demanded. God and Freedom were what mattered to a Byzantine. If the trespasses we committed in our freedom were more than He could countenance, then we bravely accepted His judgment."

He placed his hands on my shoulders, saying: "Go get ready for Church. Today is a day for speeches and prayers, for tomorrow we fight!" I bowed and left.

I rode back to Blachernae to get my friend Constantine. It was time to make my own plans.

Chapter Eight

Did we for these Barbarians plant and sow,
On these, on these, our happy Fields bestow?
Good Heaven what dire Effects from civil Discord flow!
Virgil, the First Pastoral

Constantinople, 1453

I rushed to find my friend Constantine Comnenus. Listening to my grandfather and father, I now had two ways to escape whereas he had none. He was a royal from one of the great dynastic families. He would make a great ally wherever we landed. With a bit of luck, he could take the first boat out and I might have time to talk my grandfather into coming, see if Alítheia could get out, and see about the sword. I had to try.

This morning, though, would be no time to be trying to get to the Great Palace. The streets would be packed around the Forum and the *Agia Sophia*. Everyone was keyed up, scared, perhaps angry, but all wanting to see what the Emperor had to say. If ever he had a need for courage, patience and the right words, it would be this morning. When my friend was not home, I followed the throng to Our Lady of Holy Wisdom.

The Emperor arrived on a white charger, my grandfather and some of their senior warriors in tow. The people hushed, realizing the gravity of the moment. Everyone filed in to the sound of chanted Psalms, first the Patriarch, then the presbyters by rank, and then the Council. The people followed, some singing chants, some weeping, and some beating their chests with their fists.

The Patriarch made a prayer to the Trinity. Then he made another to the Virgin:

Oh, Theotokos, most Holy Mother of God, stay with us in this hour of our greatest need. Intercede for us to the Father that He might forgive our transgressions and His wrath be pacified. Mother of the Christian race, have mercy on us. We repent of our sins. Please save us from the hellfire that surrounds us. Lift from us this darkness and give us hope. We pray to you and your Son to keep us alert, to fortify our strength, and to help us defend our families and our city. As one who loves the Greeks and Romans, as a merciful Mother, protect the great city, your inheritance. May your magnificent Name be praised forever.

And all the multitude said, "Amen."

Ironically, my mother was in the audience and was in the last days of her *endura* – a total fast to starvation after having received *consolamentum*, which is sort of a gnostic baptism and last rites. A gnostic "Perfect" in that state is a *Theotokos*, or God-bearer. I wondered what blessings she was procuring for us as the Empire crumbled to nothing and death appeared the sane alternative to waiting for Mehmed and his hordes.

Our Emperor was deep in prayer that morning. He left his imperial chair and approached the screen separating the nave and the altar. There, he prostrated himself before the great icons of the Christ and the Mother. After praying, he approached each prelate and each member of the Council. He asked the pardon of each in case he had ever offended any; he embraced each one and then went to the altar to receive Holy Communion. It had ever been the object of his predecessors to end up in holy orders before meeting their Maker. Now, as a Christian soldier he prepared to meet his God. Those in the West have their rules of saints and perhaps a cloister in which to end their days. Our Emperor had long ago taken his Oath of St. George and received his Lord's anointing as our temporal and spiritual leader. He would take his stand at the Romanos Gate with his brethren.

When he emerged from the Great Church, he faced the crowd:

Gentlemen, great captains of the army, most-Christian comrades in arms – the hour of battle again approaches. You have fought with glory against the enemies of Christ, as bravely as any of your predecessors of Rome, Genoa and Venice. The defense of our Faith and our Fatherland is committed to your brave spirits.

Our impious enemy again breaks the peace without cause. The infidel violated the oath and treaty he made with us; he massacred our farmers during the harvest; he erected a fortress on the straits to slay Christians as they pass to the Holy Lands and to hold at ransom the world's commerce. Under pretense of peace he has surrounded our neighbors of Galata and held them hostage to his plans.

Now he threatens to capture the great city of Constantine the Great, refuge of Christianity and guardian of Freedom. His desire is to destroy what is dear and to profane what is holy.

Men of Rome, Venice and Genoa – valiant heroes – lift high your spirits. You have slain thousands of the infidels. The Sultan dashes them against our defenses, hoping to tumble walls that have stood a thousand years! Continue to crush them with your valor!

Men of Constantinople and Armenia, strike deep your weapons into the heart of this enemy. Shedding your blood with us in this battle of the Sons of Light and the Sons of Darkness, you will win for yourselves crowns of martyrdom and eternal fame! Either way, Glory is yours!

Let us make our stand here for Roman Law and Christian Liberty. Into your hands, I commit my Empire, my scepter and my life! Crowns await you in Heaven; and on Earth your names will never die. Let us commend our spirits to God, and may His will prevail!

The words had their intended effect. Men forgot their differences; they embraced each other and resolved loudly to win or die, "For God and Constantine!" For each other, they withstood the tides of Hell.

If ever the various Christianities stood united in one body, in one "Holy Catholic and Apostolic Church," this was the day. Like other days, it lasted only 24 hours – but still, it was marvelous to see!

That afternoon, I caught up with my friend, gave him the Notaras ring and 25 gold ducats and told him to look up Captain Doria. They would not know Constantine from me. I suggested he take the Notaras ring to Bessarion with a request to join the Phatria as soon as they would take him. Grandpa was sending a couple of chests of manuscripts to the Cardinal, so I asked him to write a note recommending my friend.

Grandpa had also told me that a knight can create other knights as easily as a Christian can baptize new believers. I gave Constantine the oath of the Order, presented him a sword and told him the history.

I embraced him and said, "See you on the other side." "Of the Styx?" he asked with a grin. "Of the Adriatic … now go with God!"

Alítheia was going to stay put. Her father was convinced he could sell to Turks as easily as he could sell to Greeks. I swear, drunks must not think very well. How could a father and husband think such a thing with the pack of wolves gathering at our gates?

Grandpa said he would remain with the Emperor and greet the Sultan if the time came for that. He said he was ready to die if that was what God willed. He told me to get as far away as the waves would carry me. Pleading was of no use. He told me to be in touch with Michael, that he would protect me. Michael was with my father and Giustiniani at the Romanos Gate. He would not stand a chance.

Of the people I knew, some were blind optimists to the very end. The wise and truly faint of heart had left long ago. Now, at the moment of truth, there were mostly various grades of fools and heroes: warriors ready to meet death, a few innocents ready to accept whatever the Lord brought them, and opportunists thinking to profit in the city's change of hands. I found relatively few ignoble rats like me, ready to jump from the burning ship. Until the very end, people are happy to think they can survive most anything without taking action.

Mother and I went to see the Bailo. He promised us safe passage if such could be had.

The Enemy Camp, 1453

The morning began with trumpets blaring throughout the camps. Under the pain of death, pashas and their men were at their posts in preparation for the general attack of the next day. Some 2,000 ladders were carried to the walls. The moat was filled in. The ships pulled as close to the walls as they dared, using their cannon to ward off opposing fire. Javelins and lances were stacked for the irregulars. Arrows were distributed to the janissaries. Each man sharpened his blades and prepared distinctive flags to plant his claims on the morrow. After killing any who resisted him, he would mark a house with his flag to signify that all inside was his – and he could resume battle without losing time in the pillage. When preparations were finished, the young sultan addressed his troops at each of the camps. That afternoon, he rode with thousands of cavalrymen to his fleets in the Horn and beyond neutral Galata (Pera) to issue his final orders and deliver a short message:

Children of Muhammad! Victory is ours! As the Prophet predicted, the city of Heraclius falls to the force of Allah, praise be His Name!

In this fight, he who dies in the Prophet's service enters directly into the pleasures of Paradise! You who survive will receive double pay on Earth until you too join the houris.

Tomorrow, you will be rich men! When we take the city, it is yours for three days! Save the buildings for me, but the rest is yours!

From the beards of Greeks we shall make leashes to tie up our dogs! Their wives and their children are your slaves. The gold, silver, silk and jewels are yours!

Praise Allah, children of Muhammad! Whether you die tomorrow as a martyr or live to be old, each of you is a hero!!

All the men cried *La illah il-Allah, Muhammad ressoul-Allah!* (There is only one God, and Muhammad is His Prophet.)

In the afternoon, the Sultan ordered the shelling to resume. The bombardment of stones and ball this day may have been the last, but it was more terrible than any previous. Until evening, the blasts continued. I heard one old man ask under his breath, "Does he want to conquer a city or just a pile of rocks?" In this way, the Turks inflicted much more damage than we could possibly repair in one night; and the following morning Mehmed's artillerymen could join the infantry in breaching our walls and harvesting the spoils. Slowly that night, the bonfires were lit. At midnight, they were smothered and all was still as death.

Constantinople, 1453

The next morning, a few brave men gathered inside our gates. About 4,000 combatants remained to defend us against the horde. Archers gathered behind palisades or took their places along the wall and remaining towers. A few cannon were aimed at choke points along the main roads into the city. The populace would be able to do little but try to blockade their neighborhoods.

The battle began not long before noon. The Romans and their allies fought valiantly, repulsing waves of irregulars from the walls and gates. As comrades dropped around them, defenders fought on despite their hunger, sleeplessness and wounds.

After rotating division upon Ottoman division in fighting at the gates, and ensuring fresh troops were at the fore, the Sultan soon tired of the now-familiar lack of progress. He called up to the line Baltaoglu Suleyman Bey and the janissaries.

The Sultan called them, urging them forward as the heroes who would turn the tide. He led them to the moat, calling hundreds of bowmen, slingers and musketeers to fire against defenders along the just-erected palisade of logs and earthworks defending what remained of the walls. With opposing archers and musketeers pinned down, he called forward his armored infantry and shield bearers to demolish the palisade.

With a terrifying shout, the janissaries rushed across the moat and overwhelmed all opposition. I know the janissaries. They were young. They were fresh to the battle that had wearied our defenders nonstop for a month. There were 12,000 of those brave young men full of strength and hardened to pain. Each was as ready to lay down his life as to deal death. My father and his men did not stand a chance for all their prayers and skill. The janissaries knocked down all in their path and the defenders began their retreat, leaving behind supplies.

Giustiniani and his force of Genoans came forward with battle-axes, lances, pikes, and javelins. Hand-to-hand combat was fierce until a crossbowman put a shaft through Giustiniani's armor. He had been a great captain for Constantinople, but as the Genoans carried him away, all lost spirit, wanting only to retreat and live.

That left my father in a terrible position. Four hundred of his best-armored and bravest troops now beat a path to the harbor and he had no reserves with which to fill gaps in the line. He did the only thing he could. He led a regiment into the breach, hoping to find Mehmed. Instead, he found a great press of janissaries and Turkish irregulars rushing forward. This was a black day for the Order of St. George. By its end, all but the oldest and youngest standard-bearers (my grandfather and I) were ground down by *kılıç* and battle-axe.

The great slaughter began. Troops were frenzied from being long held back by Greek Fire and arrows and cannon and walls. Now nothing could keep them from their blood lust. Mehmed's men cut people in half, and gutted or maimed others who resisted. Some of us ran to churches, hoping for safety but there was none to be had.

Terrible deeds can happen in a house of God as quickly as a battlefield. Soldiers fell on us everywhere with a wrath inspired in Hell. They killed until they were tired of killing and then they began to terrorize and enslave the survivors.

Each man has his own idea of wealth. They went in bands to the mansions to plunder the rich. Others went to the churches. Others spread out to the homes of the peasants and merchants, raping, robbing, and enslaving. Age counted for nothing that day. All were taken – virgins, nuns, priests, young and old. The truth is that there were no virgins that day – male or female. To be old was to stand only that much closer to brutality and death.

Turks carried nuns and noblewomen to the ships and central places to be abused again and again. Young boys were carried off as quickly as a pretty girl, to no better purpose. Men and women of every race and age were hauled out of their homes to endure nightmares. Old men were beat mercilessly and dragged around by their long hair and beards. Babies were snatched from their mothers. Young brides were separated from their husbands. Each victim suffered many crimes, for there were five times more Turks than we had people.

Those who would deny happiness to the demons threw themselves from walls or down wells to die. Others rushed in a panic toward the ships, often to find retreating soldiers had locked the gate and tossed the key. It was an evil day for everyone but one gloating young man who felt like one of his heroes – Achilles, Xerxes, Julius Caesar, Alexander the Great or the Prophet! He was indeed a "great one" returned to life ... Nero, the scourge of Christians! [Augustine, City of God 20:19]

The loot piled high for the Sultan's share. Churches and tombs were stripped of gold. Our malefactors shared us and beat or killed those who resisted. If Roman arrogance merited punishment, then Mehmed and his hordes were the rough rod of justice to our backs.

Another 4,000 Romans died that day and 36,000 were enslaved. My mother and I were captured well before we made it to Minotto's ship. Looking to help me, she kicked a Turkish irregular so hard she bent his sword – so he killed her with his metal one. I guess she had not spent a life of purity for the privilege of being passed around the barracks of heathens. I do not remember much past that. As I rushed to help her, I was caught in the head by a very large fist. Later I awoke bleeding, bruised and hurting everywhere.

Alítheia was captured at one of the locked gates trying to get to a ship. Of my friends, the only ones who escaped were Constantine and his little brother Isaac. The rest of us were slaves in an inferno none could have imagined. For the longest time I had nightmares.

That afternoon, Mehmed surveyed his city and began to rein in his soldiers' three days of pillage – it was ruining his buildings. He had everyone gather at the *Agia Sophia*, where he told us not to be afraid, that there would be "no inimical act" committed! By that time, we the bloody and the bruised were wondering what inimical acts were left to be committed! Those of us unclaimed by a soldier were handed over to the Master of the Horse for sorting into whom would be kept or sold.

Mehmed took his share of the loot and rewarded men who had distinguished themselves. He took his pick of the women and boys. He and Zaganos had voracious appetites. Alítheia was picked for the harem. Some slaves he took for political marriages. Some he took for ransoms. Others he took for pleasure. Some were merchandise for profit taking later. Mehmed did not have much of a soul, but he had a good eye for pleasure and business.

That evening, Mehmed met and interrogated some of the city's surviving elders, including my grandfather. By several reports, the Sultan contemplated making my grandfather commandant of the city. By another, my grandfather refused to hand over one of his sons to the *Saray* (palace) – so the Sultan called for his head. Perhaps Zaganos suggested it out of meanness. Maybe Halil Pasha wanted to cover up his long life of profitable treachery as a double agent. Perhaps jealous Uncle George suggested my grandfather was too dangerous a man to keep around.

Whatever the case, Grandpa begged the executioner to slay his two sons before his eyes to ensure in their terror they did not abjure their faith. He told them, "God's will be done. I will embrace you in Heaven." Then they went to the block with dignity ... and the rest of my family was gone. I survived because nobody knew who I was and because God was not through challenging me. Now the boy "twice-born" was also twice-orphaned.

Later that day, the Bailo died, the Venetian governor who had almost been my savior. I suppose he was another gentleman of too high a caliber for the new administration. No greater crime was needed to earn a death sentence than to sport gray hair, speak well, and possess a sense of dignity. Many old men would be hanged the next day for no better reason. Tyrants cannot stand loose dogs, I guess. There were many beards for leashes!

Never was a nation so quickly and utterly deprived of all wealth, wisdom, honor, and leadership. Buildings were spared for the Sultan, and to us all was lost. May 29th, 1453, I learned the name of the Antichrist announcing the start of the End Times: *Mehmed Al-Masih Ad-Dajjal.* Now we had antichrists both East and West!

In the year 800, Pope Leo III, a money-grubbing apostate liar and adulterer, wrongfully crowned Charlemagne Emperor of the Romans. Pope Innocent III sponsored a Crusade that sent Franks to conquer my city! Pope Nicholas V, a great librarian but a poor commander, sent 200 archers to fend off 200,000 Turks as his grand strategy to defend Christendom! As far as I was concerned, the Vatican had betrayed Byzantium at least three times. In my lifetime, it would betray Christianity as well.

In my eyes, then, I had two enemies – the Sultan and the Pope. There are few things a nine-year-old boy is genuinely good at, but nurturing a smoldering hatred is certainly one of them. My path to enlightenment would have to wait. In this life, there are beasts to slay!

My priorities were to survive and to learn the nature of my enemies. If the death of my city and its elders could serve the purposes of Almighty God, then how much better would be the death of two incarnations of his Shadow?

Chapter Nine

The tyrant should lop off those who are too high and put to death men of spirit. He must be on his guard against anything that might inspire courage or confidence among his subjects. ... He must compel people to appear in public and at his gates so he knows what they are doing. In short, he must practice these and the like Persian and barbaric actions all designed for the same object. ... The tyrant is also fond of waging war so his subjects will have something to do, always in need of a leader. ^{Aristotle, On Politics}

Constantinople ("Istanbul"), 1453

Everything was about to change. Mehmed was the new occupant of Blachernae when he wasn't at Adrianople or on campaign. The wise but corrupt Grand Vizier Halil Pasha was killed to make way for the Sultan's teacher as Grand Vizier Zaganos Pasha. A crescent replaced the cross atop the Great Church, and construction began to raise the southwest turret as a minaret. Constantinople would be Stamboul or Istanbul – the way the Turks had always mispronounced it. The worst was that we, the former masters, would now be slaves in our own imperial city! God's justice can be severe: *But many that are first shall be last; and the last shall be first.* [Matthew 19:30] I had always thought that verse was about reincarnation and divine justice. I had never dreamed I would start paying right away for the sins of my forefathers.

During his grand tour of the vanquished city, the Sultan came across an ancient building marked by the moon and a five-pointed star. Since Rome had worshipped the Sun, first as Apollo and later as Christ the Celestial King, Mehmed could see nothing more appropriate than resurrecting a symbol of competing deities long ago suppressed.

Ironically, it had been Constantine the Great, our Emperor of the Unconquerable Sun, later turned Christian, who had added Venus as a symbol of the Virgin Mary and Holy Spirit to the early Byzantine flag of the Moon. Since the days of the ancient Goddess and the later Book of Genesis, the solar calendar has been corrected by observing cycles of the Moon and Venus.

> *God said, Let there be lights in the firmament of the heaven to divide the day from the night; and let them be for signs, and for seasons, and for days, and years: And let them be for lights in the firmament of the heaven to give light upon the earth: and it was so.* Genesis 1: 14-15

Like our first Emperor, Mehmed became a student of history, science and the mysteries. According to local legend, our city of Byzantium centuries before Christ had won a decisive battle under a bright waxing moon. The Byzantines took this as a sign of their goddess Artemis (Diana, sister of Apollo). Since a lunar eclipse had figured in Mehmed's victory, and since the moon was also the ancient Arabian symbol for their god Hubal/Sin – the Crescent and Star symbol of the vanquished Old City seemed doubly appropriate as the new standard.

The next big change for me was being sorted by the Master of the Horse. I suppose the humane thing about the system of the janissaries was taking in the orphans generated by wars against Christians. The horrific aspect of it for us was the potential of becoming a Christian in training to kill Christians, a sex object or manservant for shameless barbarians, a scribe, or a slave in some faraway land. The scribe thing did not sound like a bad deal, that is, until an older student explained to me that any palace job put one in line for becoming a eunuch. We, of course, would have no say in which of these futures would be ours.

The taller, stronger and good-looking were potential janissaries. The very best looking and smartest would go to the palace and the "best jobs." I was fortunate enough to be in the first group and not the second. (When they were testing us for skills in writing, I misspelled many words, flunked the reading test and professed to know nothing beyond Greek myths and Christian scripture.)

We were issued baggy blue pantaloons, red smocks and long, limp conical hats of the same material. We were told we could retain whatever possessions might fit in the small leather sack they gave us. While this would have been big enough for the imperial signet ring, I had tossed the royal seal into the Horn just before we were captured.

The Sword of the Caesars could keep in the old imperial palace until they tore the place down. It would be quite some time before I would have the right to wander my city again. My only possession would be my *florilegium*, my little book of quotes. My 25 gold coins were gone.

We were housed in tents as barracks were being erected for us near the old market district. I had tent mates from Albania, Armenia, Bulgaria, Morea and Serbia. Not one from the City. Perhaps it was all part of a plan to force us to learn Turkish quickly – giving us a common language with each other and our masters. I found it terribly depressing. I felt as though I had been adopted by a very dysfunctional family of foreigners who now wanted to punish *me* for speaking the "wrong language" in *their* new hometown! It was as if our instructors had deliberately separated us from all friends to further divide and conquer us.

Kreshnik was the first fellow student I met. The Albanian name means "knight." He was a studious fellow who did not talk much. Like most of us, he was pretty much scared witless the first week, not knowing what to expect. He was almost as tall as me, so ended up next to me as one of the leads in formation.

We received a mat and bedroll. Then we met our *hodja* (instructor), our *ortabaşı* (captain) and our *imam* (chaplain). We would spend our time learning Turkish, studying the *Koran*, saying five prayers a day, and exercising. If we did nothing else in our first year, we had to learn the basics of wrestling, sword fighting, and shooting the bow. We also spent a good deal of time running and jumping and riding. Most would be destined for infantry, so we never did enough riding for my liking.

When we lost an event against a fellow student, we received a lash from the hodja. If we won, we would get a treat. We were in sort of a race to see who would be the quickest, the toughest, the meanest, and the biggest the soonest. At no point in that process was one allowed to demonstrate pride, because pride leads to sedition and corruption. Some came to live for the challenge. Some grew meeker until they were given another fate by the Master of the Horse, which might lead to a sale ... or an operation at the hands of the barber.

The Master of the Horse was not the only one doing the sorting. On occasion, we would receive a visit from someone like Zaganos Pasha, an Albanian janissary who had risen through the ranks. Even with his five-horsetail rank (only Mehmed had more), he really enjoyed showing off for an audience.

He would pick out a target of the day – someone overly meek, brash, popular or attractive. He would toss them a stave or a wooden sword, tell us to forget his rank and order us to attack him. It was invariably an unfair fight in which his object was to, as quickly as possible, defeat and emasculate the victim with a kick declaring "Another scribe for the *Saray*!" For him, I am sure it was a hilarious game. We dreaded to see him coming because it meant someone was about to be terribly victimized and was destined to be a prize of possibly the worst pervert in the realm.

Hippodrome (Ok Meydanı), 1454

One day, when I had just turned 10, we saw something grand. We were going to meet the Sultan. We had eaten some rice and mutton and been inspected by our *Ortabaşı* and his *Çorbacı* (like a colonel, but literally "The Maker of the Soup"). We had all been duly humble, never raising our eyes to meet theirs and standing at attention until called upon. On this day, it was announced that we would go to the *Ok Meydani*, which was really the Hippodrome now renamed "Archers Field." Instead of chariot races around the monuments of old, these days the arena had become a training field and archery range. Today promised to be special.

We had recently received our second bows, moving in strength from a 40-pound draw to more respectable 70-pounders. Some of the aristocracy, like Zaganos, boasted 160-pound bows. With such a bow (or *yay*) and seated on the ground using both feet and both arms, one could overshoot the entire Hippodrome end-to-end. While this kind of flight shooting demonstrates a great deal of strength, I did not find very practical the idea of shooting up to 1,000 yards and hitting nothing!

That day, there would be contests for shooting distance *(menzeel atishi)* and horseback archery *(kabak atishi)*, penetrating armor with an arrow *(darp voorma)*, and shooting targets *(puta atishi)* at distances up to half the arena away! The latter is what impressed me. The Turkmen were people of the horse and were naturally fans of *kabak atishi*. Most of us would end up infantry troops, so target practice was all we knew so far. Target shooters were on our side of the arena. Riders were opposite us across the median where the obelisks and columns stood. There was some netting strung across the median so animals would not cross the field. "Flight" shooters like Zaganos, meanwhile, were at the curve of the Hippodrome aiming out between a break in the opposite walls.

The contests were sort of the Turkish version of the ancient Olympics. Some of my new friends were impressed by the flight shoots, in which the winner would place a stone with his name on the new record distance. Everybody wants to be immortal, I suppose.

Archers were aristocracy, and janissaries were well represented among the best archers. As one's marks improved, so did one's chances for advancement. While it might now look on the field of stones as if the Ottomans were exaggerating flight records of their sultans and viziers with marks at 700 and 800 yards, the truth is, the regime was designed to raise warriors, and such marks are not at all surprising.

Our new bows were war bows. If we could consistently hit targets with them, we could bring down a man at a fair distance. Turkish bows were reputed to be more accurate than those used by the Europeans, and this is probably why knights whom I had met in Byzantium much preferred the recurved war bow to the longbow.

Earning the title of Archer was quite the ordeal. Aside from our usual lessons on Turkish and the *Koran*, we spent what seemed an eternity just pulling bows. Mind you, we were not shooting them at all for the first months. We received light bows and we simply pointed them and pulled back on the string – until we could do 500 pulls a day without tiring. Around the 12,000[th] pull, we were given a real bow and a sack of shavings to fire into – hung where it would receive our arrows at a 44-degree angle. After about 6,000 of these sack arrows, we were ready for the range – and about 3,000 practice arrows. To join the Guild, the test was firing a flight arrow accurately into the stands from the opposite end of the arena. That is not something most of us were prepared to do at 10 years old. By now we had developed the right muscles and some proficiency with a bow, but we were hardly ready for combat or competition.

So there we were, sitting on the field of the Hippodrome, about 200 yards from the Serpentine Column that Byzantium's first Emperor had brought from Delphi. Immediately behind us was the grandstand with the Sultan and his court, or rather his high-ranking officers who were not competing at the moment. All the junior officers were out on the field participating or officiating. About 100 yards down the field to my right and seated in another group was Jason and his class. I had not seen him in a year and had not previously known he survived. I waved, but he did not see me. He was looking up in the sky. Beyond my group to the left, a falconer was demonstrating his craft.

On the opposite side of the arena, I was observing some of the most amazing feats of horsemanship imaginable. Early on, there was a game of 20-man teams stealing a wet-sand-filled calfskin from each other, rounding a pole and dropping it back in the starting circle. There were riders throwing javelins at each other (points off for hitting a horse). There were riders shooting targets while standing on the saddle. Some could unsaddle and saddle their horses while riding. Some could stand while riding two horses. The Romans had their gladiators and chariot races. The Portuguese have bullfights on horseback. Well, this was entertainment Turkish style. It had been a long time since the Hippodrome had seen anything so colorful.

Despite the thrills and distractions, there have been times in my life when I have acted like an old soul who has seen things go wrong too many times. This was one of those moments. Next to the rider coming up was a cage holding a lion. I remember thinking this was a fool's idea since lions see horses as food. For good reason, hunting lions by horse bow has long been considered impractical! We were about to witness one of Mehmed's history dramatizations. Ashurbanipal or Nimrod might have been proud, but shocked to see a horse running *behind* the lion. I looked to the median and noticed the netting about 10 feet high. I asked myself, "So how high can a lion jump?" The net sagged a bit lower in front of Jason's group.

I used a *kemend* to string my bow – sort of a lasso we used to bend the bow back on itself far enough to place the waxed bowstring. One way to use it is sitting, bracing against one's feet, forcing the bow back by hand at first and then using the rope around one's back to pull the bow tight as one twists and places the second loop of the bowstring on its nock. The *kemend* was handy because I wore it as a belt with the ends tucked into my sash.

On the other side of the arena, someone opened the cage while another prodded the animal from behind and an assistant fired his gun. The lion sprinted down the old chariot raceway. The horseman took off after him and placed an arrow in his bow. As soon as the lion saw the low spot on the net, he suddenly veered left, away from the arena track. Still aiming straight down the raceway, the rider's first shot missed the animal entirely. Mounted archers fire their bows from the right side, not the left as infantry, so the shot had been a little more difficult for the rider to correct. He would not miss twice.

The lion was clearly making for the median. The second shot hit him on the rump, but did not even slow him down. He pounded the ground quick as a racehorse, but without noise. Now the rider would have to leave off shooting. From his vantage point, everything around the lion was people – and a hunting arrow can go right through its prey.

I rose up with my bow, popped an arrow onto the string and waited. The lion leapt about 12 feet into the air, even in a sprint. I raised my bow and fired just as the beast cleared the net. I caught him in the torso. He kept running from the rider toward Jason. On the second shot, I caught him through the right eye and now he made his wound worse, rearing up to swipe at it with his front paws. As he reared up, I stuck him again in the chest. Finally, he went down. Muskets might have stopped him quicker, but they could not match our bows in accuracy, distance or speed in reloading!

Everyone that had seen what had happened was shocked. While they were glad the lion had not mauled its way through the students, I had broken some rules. We were not supposed to be stringing and firing our new bows that day. We were there for show (and our bows just never left our sides). Worse for me, I had stood out – and the first rule of tyrants and gardeners is to clip anything rising above the rest.

Some of my fellows cheered, but across the arena, I had just made an adult enemy. I prayed it was not Zaganos. It wasn't! That day I would earn the nickname *Yay Burcu* – the Turkish phrase for Sagittarius ("Sign of the Bowman"). Fortunately, I was neither to be punished nor commended. The leaders determined I had done the right thing despite bending the rules. Later, on the way out, Jason would thank me and congratulate me for finally completing the first task of Hercules! We both laughed. It had been so long.

Fortunately, the next contest was less dramatic but much more important. The Sultan was the next rider up and Mehmed rode at a full gallop firing arrows into a pumpkin on top a post. He got off three shots in one pass, all striking the mark. The crowd went wild. A bit later, a real show-off placed an orange on his young slave's head and shot it off – also at a full gallop. Everyone but the slave thought this mighty impressive. I wondered how many slaves the hero went through while perfecting such a technique!

Zaganos set a flight record that day sitting on his butt, and that afternoon erected a "mother stone" to his perpetual honor (or at least until they moved Archers Field). His would be a mark archers would have to beat in the future. We went back to our barracks after target practice and evening prayers. Some of the students now thought I was great, and some, no doubt, in their competitive souls hated me.

Plane Tree of the Janissaries, 1454

In the *Ok Meydani*, there was a centuries-old plane tree where we gathered. It became our standard meeting place since it was convenient to our barracks and to the old palace and *Agia Sophia* (now called the "Great Mosque"). Sometimes we met there for a class on the *Koran* taught by one of our Arab or Persian instructors. Sometimes it was for wrestling. Sometimes we went just to socialize in the evening between exercise, dinner and prayers.

Today, we were there for some wrestling. Kreshnik had just been switched for losing to a Serbian kid named Stefan. An Armenian youth named Vahan prevailed over a Bulgarian named Mihail. It was my turn. I wondered who they would pair me up with.

Into the circle walked Zaganos. He said to our *Ortabaşi*, "My good friend Hassan tells me one of your students embarrassed him the other day at the games. He said I should meet the boy people are calling *Yay Burcu*. Let's see what he's made of." With that, he took off his turban and green velvet smock and picked up two staves.

I stood up and bowed low to the vizier crossing my hands in front of my chest in submission, saying "Excellency." I took off my smock and waited. He threw me a stave saying, "You know the rules. I'm just a janissary here to instruct you. Defend yourself as best you can." With that, he took a swipe at my head and I blocked. He went for my side. I blocked. He went for my legs. I leaped over it. He reversed direction and caught me square in the back. I fell forward winded, rolled and came up. Again, he went for my head and I blocked. Side and block. Legs and block. Side and he broke one of my ribs. Then a powerful rush and he shoved me so I would fall on my back. At that moment, I had a choice. I could defend myself or take what comes next – a kick to the nuts and a trip to the barber to have them cut off.

I decided to remain a janissary and a man. As he pulled back his right foot, I spun over and kicked his left knee hard enough to where it touched the ground. He caught his balance and spun around with the stick. Instead of giving my head a good bashing as I started to rise to my feet facing away from him, he stopped short, laughed and then roared. "It's about time someone did that! It is good to know your opponent and use his own strategy against him! Do not cut this one. He is ready for the country! Lesson over." We bowed to each other and that was my last day of regular school that year. I had always sort of hoped the faded scars on my neck from when I was little would save me from the palace. Perhaps they had!

For the next three years, I would be a servant to the former Admiral Baltaoglu. If he needed rocks removed from his field, I would be the one to do it. If he needed a galley slave, I would be the one. If he needed a chamberlain, a cook hand, a boy to clean his stables, it would be me. He had lost his properties near Adrianople when he disgraced the realm trying to conquer galleys with little triremes. When Mehmed theatrically ordered his life taken, Zaganos and old Halil had played their roles and begged the Admiral's life be spared. The trireme idea had not been the Admiral's idea to begin with, but then that hardly mattered. Now he had a nice villa in the old Venetian Quarter. My further studies and exercises would be to his specifications.

On occasion, maybe once a month, my *hodja* would come check up on me to make sure I was being utilized, was physically okay and had not lost my talent with the war bow. Other than that, I was an *Acemi Oğlan,* one of the foreign boys divorced from the school and destined for the *Kapikulu* (Slaves of the Gate).

It was soon obvious the admiral did not have much need of a bow-shooting apprentice, but the old man was kind. He set me up on pretty much the same schedule I had always kept. He had a son by his third wife (or "Middle Lady") about my age. For convenience, he kept us together when it was time for wrestling or sword fighting or archery. We also shared tutors for Arabic and *Koran.*

The best part of living there was that we had a real cook and nobody played favorites (switching the loser or giving treats to the winner). Ahmed and I could have been brothers. He would be destined for *Sipahi* cavalry or the navy. He was not sure yet.

They called me the ancient name for John – Ohannes. According to Berosus the Babylonian, Oannes was the ancient god who taught mankind Wisdom. It was another name for the Sumerians' Ea, the Fish of Heaven. I was glad to keep my name for now and happy not to have to live up to my nickname just yet! Students for the Janissary Corps were not supposed to receive new names until we were blooded in combat. That would be awhile.

Sometimes, the old man had no work for me so he would leave me with one of his old friends, a bowyer by the name of Yasin. The bowyer had lots of work and appreciated the help. While a janissary is not really supposed to learn a trade beyond freeing souls from their bodies, the post of armorer (or *djebedji*) is an honored profession, and the admiral appreciated not having to watch me all the time. I was with his family to learn the ways of the country and to learn to empathize with our Sultan's people. "Country" assignments were also to teach hard work and humility.

Yasin was the holy man of bowyers. He knew all the sayings of Muhammad related to archery, of which there are at least forty. I remember only a few of his favorites, but they were the sort of thing I am sure were being taught at the school, if I ever returned there. The *hadiths* made the profession of archers *(Okçus)* an essential element of *jihad* – a man's struggle to perfect himself and the world:

> *Use archery, for the casting of arrows is useful in war …*
>
> *Whoever shoots an arrow in the way of Allah receives the reward of freeing a slave; and this is his ransom from the Fire.*
>
> *He whose arrow reaches the enemy, Allah raises a level in Paradise.*

So on top of anything I had going on with my archery, my studies and helping the admiral, I was cutting and curing wood, cooking fish glue and sinew, laminating wood and horn, tillering bows to make their draw even, finishing and then heat-treating bows. It takes at least five years from cutting the wood to finish a war bow. So, of the many bows I worked on at every stage, there really was not one I had taken all the way through the process. Final assembly took about a year, beginning in the fall with the fitting of the parts.

In the meantime, there was always much to do, and the people were great. I was always enthusiastic and busy enough at whatever I was doing to where the admiral was flexible as to when he would see me;

and Yasin was flexible as to when I could spare the time for him. So once in awhile, Ahmed and I would use this to advantage and wander the town or ride horses. Two years flew by and in the third, a miracle happened.

Venetian Quarter, 1456

I was walking down the street alone one day in the direction of Yasin's shop and I saw the most familiar pair of eyes. Big deep-blue eyes ... left one a bit brighter than the other ... a wisp of wavy golden hair visible beneath the veil. I was sure I had died and gone to Heaven! I followed her for a bit to see whom she was with and could not find any obvious connection. I casually walked by and said something like, "I have never known anyone to get out of that place on holiday." She turned and gasped, then murmured, "I can't talk now, but I'm free of there. Tomorrow meet me at the Column before *Dhuhr*."

That afternoon I boiled and braced two Hercules-type bows for a couple of three-horsetail beys looking to leave mother stones on the *Ok Meydani*. Yasin pegged them for me as I drew them into shape. Then I tilled two others. The work was tough but rewarding. I could not believe Alítheia was free of Mehmed. I wondered what it had cost someone to rescue her.

The next day, before noon prayer, I went to the Column of Constantine and waited inside. About 20 minutes later, she came in and removed her veil. "I can't stay long," she said, grasping my hands. "I am just a servant and I have given my eunuch the slip. He is out buying food so he'll be a little while. I still have to buy ink and wax and some trifles for the ladies. But I'm so glad you're okay and look, a janissary too!" "Well, not a janissary yet," I said, "but soon to be if I can learn to avoid trouble. So how did you escape the Harem? I have never heard of anyone doing that." We sat on the steps rather than standing awkwardly.

"It's a long story," she said, "but the truth is, it wasn't too difficult. Once the Chief Eunuch and the Great Lady (first wife of the Sultan and daughter of Zaganos Pasha) decided their newest pleasure girl would never satisfy a man ... that I was somehow too plain, too sensitive, too boring, or too prudish, I was given back to the Master of Horse to sell to the first old man with four wives. I'm servant to a retired *Çorbacı*. He's a very civilized man who mostly uses me as a scribe. He lost his right arm at Varna and he has family in Adrianople with whom he likes to stay in touch. If you like, I will put in a good word for you. I'm sure he still has connections."

I laughed and said: "I already have plenty of connections. I should have been back to the school or a camp a year ago, but there is a *bey* and a *pasha* angry with me. I may never graduate! I never saw such a place where you get in trouble just for trying to do the right thing!"

She looked at me questioningly. She is one of those few souls that always knows the right thing to do and why, the right thing to say (or not say), and I was not quite sure if it was her intelligence that made her that way or her virtue. It was as if she had been given a heart, mind and soul four times larger than any sense of self, if she even had one. I wondered how she would have handled Zaganos and somehow I knew he would never have picked her as a target. I am pretty sure demons generally steer clear of the angels – breaking the prideful being much more interesting.

Alítheia was living proof that every good person is free. Philo said it, but Alítheia knew it in her soul. I envied her. I think a person with the patience of Job can live quite a happy life. Me? Well, I never had the patience. I wanted to fix things or slay the devils. Even back then, I could tell she held the key to Heaven. Even then, I hoped she would pass up her heavenly crown to spend another lifetime with me. Love like that is pure bliss. Missing a love like that? It can change a person.

After about 20 minutes of catching up, she went back to her eunuch. I waited another 10 minutes to leave so people would not see us together. We hardly knew when we might see each other, but discussed what parts of the city we both frequented. Happily, we did not live too far apart so it would be theoretically possible to see each other if we could arrange a go-between or a signal.

Inside the column was a loose stone 20 steps up. We agreed to leave notes with a symbol for the place, a moon phase for the week, a planetary symbol for the day and two numbers indicating between which prayer times. Since nobody did business near the ruined column, we hoped to avoid suspicion. That was the plan, but as Grandpa Notaras discovered, good plans do not always play out as one intends.

I was sure I had died and gone to Heaven!

Neorion Harbor, 1456

In early July, Ahmed and I were looking for something to do. We got the old man talking about his days with the navy. Baltaoglu was raised like me, a janissary, but when Mehmed decided he was going to need a navy to gain control of the Bosporus and Black Sea, he drafted the old cavalry officer to establish sea supremacy.

So after retelling the victory of Lesbos (every old man has a dozen favorite stories he will tell you again no matter how many times you have heard them), the admiral walked us down to Neorion Harbor. It was the harbor closest to our area and he knew some people.

As it turned out, there would be a mission headed up into the Black Sea enforcing a trade blockade of the Danube. We had troops marching on Belgrade and archers were welcome. A captain agreed we could go up with some of the irregulars. Unless someone mounted a naval battle, the trip would take a week or two. Before the ship was ready to sail, the admiral presented us with our own swords – beautiful damascene steel in leather scabbards. I guess he had been looking forward to this day. He gave us each a hug and wished us well. Then he left us in the hands of an *Ortabaşı* and we were off on our adventure.

On the evening of the second day, I heard the oddest sound. It was like the singing of little girls. I asked one of the old sailors what it was. He said, "Sirens! Pay them no mind." Well, having been a student of myths and folklore, "Pay them no mind" was hardly an option. I asked the *Ortabaşı* if Ahmed and I could go see where this sound was coming from. "No problem," said the captain-bashi, "take a boat and spend the evening. More of our boats are coming. We'll see you when you get to the fight." Ahmed and I took some hard biscuits and dried meat in a sack, grabbed our bows, quivers and water bags, and we were about to be off when the *Ortabaşı* handed me a lamp. "You'll need this," he said, "You won't find much driftwood or trees for a fire. The island was logged for ship lumber and now is barren."

It was five days before the full moon, so he need not have worried. The island was called Λευκός, or White Island, by the Greeks. To the Romans, it was *Alba*. It was the scene of one of the most mournful moments in history – the burial of Achilles near Apollo's temple.

> *'Till seventeen nights and seventeen days return'd*
> *All that was mortal or immortal mourn'd,*

To flames we gave thee, the succeeding day,
And fatted sheep and sable oxen slay;
With oils and honey blazed the augmented fires,
And like a god adorn'd, thy earthly part expires.
Homer, Odyssey, Bk XXIV

    Today, it is called Snake Island (perhaps because of its profile when viewed from the sea). I would have seen snakes had there been any. There was little to look at – just a pile of white marble in the Black Sea, but for two young men who had never traveled, it held great mystery.

    We beached the little boat on the low-lying eastern shore of the tiny island and scrambled up the limestone rocks. There was not much to see, so we went looking for those sirens, for here was the home of Thetis, the sea nymph. We found a narrow cave on the western shoreline and wriggled our way in. We could see very little, even with the lamp. Finding nothing, Ahmed was soon bored and went exploring along the tiny sea cliffs. I told him to take the lamp with him.

    I remained behind, backed into the crevice as far as I could go, just beyond a patch of water. I stopped moving and waited. The sound of the surf outside the cave was soothing. In a little while, a couple of small creatures resembling tiny dragons crawled out of the water, looked up at the moon and began to sing in harmony. Apparently, these little creatures – some kind of newt or salamander – have lungs!

    I relaxed in the cave and began to sense something new to the smell of the air, though I do not know if it was a mold or a gas seeping up from far below. I think I dozed off, listening to the music of the dragons and I saw a great battle unfolding. Some of the janissaries I knew were there and there was great bloodshed. They were opposed by a mob armed with Magyar bows, axes, two-handed swords, scythes and pitchforks! Several galleys (including the one we had originally shipped on) exploded and sank to the bottom of a great river. There was a huge fire cutting off the janissary from the irregulars; and then Mehmed was carried from the fight wounded and unconscious. Unbelievably, our great cannon tumbled into the river! Finally, a peasant rushed at me with an axe. I awoke with a yell! Yards away from the tomb of Achilles and a temple of Apollo, I silently thanked Apollo the Sol Invictus for this vision.

    Apologizing to the little creatures for interrupting their song, I crawled past them as they slipped back into the water. I emerged from the cliff on the opposite side of the island from where Ahmed and the boat were. At its widest, the island is less than half a mile from side to side. In the moonlight, it was easy to find my way back. Ahmed said he thought he had seen a small ship in the distance across the water.

Snake Island, 1456

We hopped in the boat and made for the coming twin-masted xebec. It was not going to swing around the island before going into the Danube delta. We called for the captain, but he could not hear us. So I did something pretty stupid. I picked up my bow, nocked a feather and shot his main mast. Thankfully, one of the sailors on board recognized a Turkish arrow when he saw one. They slowed down to let us catch up. They had no room for rowboats and told us to hurry up and climb the ladder. We did, but I did not relish the thought of having to pay back the friendly *Ortabaşı* for a rowboat when we returned to Stamboul.

Actually, that prospect would have been more fun than trying to explain why a young janissary and an irregular on the way to a blockade were floating around the Black Sea by themselves. Our worthy craft was not big enough to go to war so the sailors found the situation quite amusing. Fortunately, someone knew Ahmed's father and then everything was fine. We found ourselves up in the bow watching the land go by as we wound our way toward the blockade.

Standing there, Ahmed asked me, "So what did you do back on the island? I didn't see you for quite awhile." I said, "I think I fell asleep in the cave. You?" "I shot a seagull," he said, "but then I didn't find enough wood or dry grass to cook it with." I told him about the dream. He laughed, saying my imagination was too good, and that I was wasting it if I was not thinking about girls! We laughed and joined a couple of sailors playing dice. Nothing was wagered, so I suppose it was lawful. Among janissary, the best entertainments have to do with war: wrestling, horseracing and archery. We were told the only other activity overseen by angels has to do with the pleasantries between a man and his wife! I soon bored, ducked into a forward hatch and fell asleep on a sail.

Next morning, Ahmed did something wonderful. As we were sailing up the Danube he saw a giant sturgeon. Alongside the cabin, he spotted a spear, which I suppose was just for such occasions. He somehow knew how to correct for the distortion of the water. Personally, at that time I would have had no idea. The spear had an arrowhead design, so it would not come loose. He speared the fish through its spine just behind the head. In no time at all, we were able to net it. The fish weighed more than 100 pounds. About 200 of us had fresh meat and caviar for supper.

It took another day to negotiate the Danube. We helped with the rowing when there was no wind. By the time we arrived at Belgrade, disaster had struck. The Hungarian general, János Hunyadi, had initially set fire to three of our galleys. He was now in the process of capturing or sinking a few dozen more.

Our captain joined the fray, going in with cannon and muskets blasting. The scene is hard to describe, but what had started out as a couple dozen galleys and a multitude of smaller boats in a blockade was now a churning, burning, shouting, thundering destructive free-for-all with lots of casualties to one's brethren in arms. Cannonball, musket ball, arrows, stones, and burning projectiles were flying in every direction. Ahmed and I got off our 40 arrows each before our ship had passed through the melee and began to turn about for another pass.

We took that as our signal to bail out. A wet bow is weak, but a bow with no arrows is worthless. We jumped ship, making for the horsetails of the *sipahis*. It was not long before we each had a drawn sword in our hand and a horse beneath us. The battle had turned bloodbath and the dead were piling up. I figured the janissary did not want me back in their ranks just yet, so I joined the fight without my smock.

Basically, Belgrade was the Battle of Constantinople played out again, but with a popular uprising and an effective navy working against Mehmed! He had found the limit of his capacities. It is one thing to pick off an isolated animal (or a lone city) and quite another to take on the pack! He had marched into Europe expecting to play his divide-and-conquer games when everyone had seen his ideas of fair play at Byzantium. Belgrade was the war my father had dreamt of and the diplomats had promised. I was secretly happy for the Hungarians and Serbs, even while they were shooting at me with everything they had.

That night, Ahmed and I hooked up with the Anatolian Corps. They were past the city on the other side of the battlefield. I donned the jacket of a dead man and appropriated his light armor and small round wooden shield. One of the *sipahi* lords was glad to have two replacement fighters and I was glad to be on a horse. It was more complicated for archery, but provided one a good perspective of the battle. We restocked our quivers.

At the camp, I approached a captain-bashi and asked if I might have a word later. He said he could talk to me later when we doused the fire since he had a council to attend. I sat next to the fire drying out my bow until he returned around midnight.

I told him I was concerned about the course of the battle. I laid out the vision I'd had and related how, so far, it seemed to be coming true. He said the mind sometimes plays tricks on one before a battle and not to worry about it.

Next day, we saw plenty of action. We were facing the sorts of weapons and peasantry I had seen in my dream. Our leaders had expected minor nobility and a few mercenaries. This popular uprising was unusual, especially in these numbers. Hunyadi and a Franciscan cardinal had amassed an army of 50,000 to augment the defending Serbs and Hungarians.

The next few days were more of the same mayhem. Cannon were breaching the walls. Our miners were undermining towers. Engines of war were tossing stones and flame in both directions. Each evening, the smell of burning bodies assaulted our senses.

On our fourth day of battle, (the siege having begun two weeks earlier), the captain-bashi introduced me to his *Çorbacı*, instructing me to tell him my vision. I explained that I am no prophet, but I had seen the ships destroyed, I had seen the peasant uprising, and I had seen the Sultan carried from the field. He made me swear that what I was telling him was true and I so swore. He told me from now on to keep my visions to myself.

Now soldiers can be a superstitious lot. Commanders will take intelligence from wherever they can get it; and there are precious few secrets that can really be kept. They are the currency of trust, and a battlefield is one place signs of trust are necessary. This is why lies, propaganda and other deceptions work. They lead us to believe what we are prepared to believe and prepare us to believe the unbelievable. In war, rumors fly up and down the chain of command – with rapid verification all but impossible.

Well, this was precisely the sort of thing leadership should hear about. So at the risk of telling our Grand Vizier he was not wearing any clothes (the Sultan being absent for this meeting), the *Çorbacı* attended the war council and said one of his troops had foreseen our troubles up to now and anticipated more in the future. Someone in the council asked who the "prophet" was – no doubt hostile to the idea that we had a naysayer in our ranks. The *Çorbacı* said "just a kid who showed up with the fleet on the 14th." Depending on who heard the rumor, an almost-12-year-old had just lit a powder keg beneath Ottoman morale.

Chapter Ten

Even if you are pressed hard and beset with fierce violence, yet it is a disgrace to retreat; maintain the post that Nature assigned you. Do you ask what this may be? The post of a hero. ^{Seneca, On Firmness}

Men directing their weapons against each other – under doom of death yet neatly lined up to fight as in the pyrrhic sword-dances of their sport – this is enough to tell us that all human intentions are but play, that death is nothing terrible, that to die in a war or in a fight is but to taste a little beforehand what old age has in store, to go away earlier and come back the sooner. ^{Plotinus, Third Ennead}

Belgrade, 1456

We each have a greater impact than we can foresee. Seeking glory, however, can greatly diminish it. Mehmed taught me this at Belgrade. The examples we set are not always the ones we intend.

"The Conqueror" rode into Europe as the new Alexander, intent on smashing anything in his path as he had at Constantinople. He had giant cannon. He had miners. He had engineers. He had truce agreements to break. He had troops and boats and machines of war. What he lacked was a good assessment of what he inspired in his enemies. There seems to be an axiom of the universe that a great force will generally be opposed by as many small forces as it takes to restore balance. If the fear of Athens could provoke Sparta to war, perhaps Mehmed could inspire Christianity to save itself. Fear is a wonderful spur to action.

So while Belgrade was designed similar to Constantinople, the result was much different. This was not Varna and Mehmed was not his father. This time, the besieged city was not surrounded by Ottoman territory, as had been our case looking out the Romanos Gate. There was plenty of room here and motive for armies, peasants, and interested crusaders from Germany, Poland, Bohemia and Austria to gather and harass the invader.

This, of course, made no impression on the 24-year-old who had forever silenced the single voice of caution in his council. Had old Halil been available, he might have mentioned that Hunyadi had been severely punishing Ottoman forces since Mehmed was five years old!

The next day, it was becoming obvious, to me at least, that this fight was not a replay of Constantinople. Hunyadi knew how Mehmed fought. He knew where the main force would be, where the janissary would be, how they would finally blitz the city after it had been softened. Anticipating all this, he picked away at the flanks, continued to recruit reinforcements outside, and waited for the big attack. At no point in time did it occur to Mehmed that he might have met his match.

Sometime about the 20th, my vision started to make the rounds. Fortunately, for me, my name was detached from it. Some called it an oracle; some said it came from a sailor who overheard it; some said it came from an officer; and some said it came from a holy man. The rumor cited fact after fact that had come true and mentioned some of the signs still to come ... cannon going into the river and the Sultan carried off the field with injuries. Fortunately, the officers I had related the story to were by now dead and Ahmed and I were keeping quiet except for when we were firing arrows or slashing our way across the field. For now, "The Prophet of Belgrade" could remain nameless.

On the 21st, exploitable breaks in the walls came. True to plan, Mehmed ordered the janissary into the city, exhorting them to carry the day. Hunyadi ordered them cut off, telling his defenders to throw down as much flammables as they could at every break in the walls and every gate. We had been filling the moat for the attack, unfortunately with lots of dead trees, so it too went up in flames like the gates! While the crusaders inside the walls ground away at the janissaries working to conquer the city or extricate themselves, reinforcements for Hunyadi began pouring across the river. Mehmed found himself in the two-front war my father had wanted for Constantinople.

Next morning, as we were piling up our dead, crusaders in the city decided to earn their wings to Paradise, pouring out of the walls and again hitting us in a pincer movement against their reinforcements. Not surprisingly, the Shadow of God let his temper get the best of him and he rushed into the fight with his sword. In the course of events that afternoon, he earned a few cuts and an arrow deep in his thigh. He passed out and guards had to carry him off the field.

As with Giustiniani, the sight of one's commander being carried off the field can be a potent reminder of one's own mortality. It was 10 times as powerful, however, because of the "oracle." Not even the janissary could contain the fear produced by this event. Zaganos ordered the cannon destroyed or pushed into the river. Since this too had been part of the prophecy, that evening we started *en masse* and without orders to beat a retreat. We did not burn or bury bodies that day. We left them to rot. Many in the city would die of Plague in the coming weeks.

Ahmed helped me kill the axe man when he came for me. We were glad to be alive, but a bit concerned. Our leadership might be as happy to kill us as the Hungarians or Serbs would be.

At Belgrade, we had lost about a quarter of a force of 150,000 men. The retreat cost us another 15,000. When Mehmed came to and learned he had lost so many troops and leaders like Karaja (his Governor of Europe), his dreams of being the next Augustus Caesar dashed on the headstones of reality. His depression was long and deep. Some said he had to be talked out of poisoning himself.

When he learned later of the prophecy, he reportedly did not know whether to chop heads for nobody telling him or chop heads until he found the person who had spooked his troops. Ahmed kept my secret and I lived to fight another day.

Chapter Eleven

Does not everyone know that I based the world solely on love?
I have said, "The world is built by love."
It is love that sustains the world. [The Zohar]

Love is from the infinite, and remains for all eternity.
The seeker of love escapes the chains of birth and death.
Tomorrow, when resurrection comes,
The heart that is not in love will fail the test. [Jalal al-Din al-Rumi]

Istanbul, 1456

Heaven and Hell are contained in Love. Were there no God, no Spirit, no Son and no Satan, I wonder if the world could be any different. For where there is Life, there is Love. Where there is Love, there is every joy and misery caused by our oft-misguided affections. Give Love sufficient time to act and your greatest source of bliss will become your greatest loss. We live to hope, love, despair and remember. For me, happiness was mostly in the remembering.

My greatest year was the summer of 1456 to the following spring. Mehmed was rebuilding his army instead of playing lover of glory and seeker of Power. I had survived my first battle and now trained for cavalry. My *hodja* had learned of my Belgrade experience with the *Sipahi* and recommended me for *Kapikulu* cavalry. The best, of course, was that Alítheia and I found some out-of-the-way spots where we could enjoy each other's company.

Leaving each other coded notes at the column worked well. Her master was as lenient as mine, and so long as we were not gone too long, an hour or two away from our labors was hardly to be missed. We came to live for those moments.

I guess in every relationship, there is the one who knows and the one about to find out – whether there is the basis for a relationship, whether there is genuine attraction, when it will move to the next level, and whether the relationship is doomed. In ours, the one who always knew was Alítheia. I was just happy and amazed that this beautiful older girl had time for me.

We talked about it once. I asked her what it all meant and how she thought it would all work out. "Eventually," she said, "our masters will discover us. I will be locked away somewhere you are not allowed and you will go off to war. It won't matter what we would have done had we been free because we aren't. I love you here and now because one day I won't be able. When that happens, I will only regret the days I could have been with you and wasn't." To which I replied, "Then, if there is holy justice, I shall see you in Heaven and God will see us back together for our new life!"

That day, it must have been September because the weather was delicious, she decided to initiate me into the greater mysteries. We had been talking, daydreaming, playing, a bit of kissing, and as young developing bodies are wont to do, we began exploring some of our differences. Now 14 or 15, she had grown breasts. I had finally passed her in height, where I had been barely keeping up for two years, and had started sprouting hair everywhere. Parts of us that had previously never gotten excited now did so almost constantly.

So I am happy to report the Great Lady of the Sultan and her Chief Eunuch had no idea what they were talking about when they sold off the Sultan's youngest *odalisque*. I suspect they were doing the little girl a favor in allowing her to escape Mehmed.

She was wonderful at all she tried and there was little we did not attempt. For that matter, my body had no selfishness in it, so after two-and-a-half hours, I had not known how to finish while she had been happy many times. The lesson had to be cut short and my first torment of loss was intense, but what a thrill to finally understand one of the mysteries of life!

The next day we could see each other worked out much better. We borrowed a rowboat from a silk weaver we knew and spent the afternoon floating among the more than 300 pillars of the *Yèrè Batan Serai Sarniçi*, an underground cistern with the size and architecture of a palace, designed to protect the city from drought during sieges. There is no stranger place in all Istanbul. Ancient pagan imagery is visible in this place where time stands still. We tried not to make noise in the echoing shadows, but our old friend grinned as we returned her boat.

The Yèrè Batan Serai Sarniçi was a place one could escape prying eyes.

We went on like this for almost a year, when one day my *hodja* came looking for me and I was not at the admiral's and I was not at the bowyer's. They found me with Alítheia down by the Market. This led to questions about her. That led to the old *Çorbacı* being informed he might have a slave involved in an improper relationship with a janissary. Since janissaries are supposedly celibate (though never held to such a ridiculous standard that can only lead to vice), the colonel put her up for sale with the Master of the Horse the day of a visit from the Sultan of Oran, who took an instant liking to her.

I cannot blame the man for suffering love at the first sight of her naked flesh, but I would forever resent Abu Abdallah Muhammad VI at-Thabiti. There had been no goodbyes for Alítheia and I. There would be little possibility for correspondence and I was certain I could never visit or hear from her again. I would rather have lost my bow arm! For a time, I was greatly depressed. Eventually, I learned to treasure her memory. She had known what would happen and had loved me anyway! I could think of no greater gift.

The *hodja* took me back to the school. We would have a large graduating class to begin replacing troops lost at Belgrade. One of the casualties there, though indirectly, had been Zaganos! His love of cruelty had encouraged men to desert and enemies to toughen rather than sue for peace. He had recommended against a longer battering of the walls by cannon, which had led to the fiasco of the fiery gate. The premature blitz of the city cost us many lives and Zaganos had been in charge when the Sultan was wounded. By the time Mehmed came to in Sarona, the battle and its aftermath had turned to total disgrace. Zaganos had performed so much worse than my admiral, yet instead of a beating he received a fiefdom in Asia! Going back to school without his visits would be pleasant indeed. I was ready to earn my white turban.

Chapter Twelve

Enmity is anger waiting for a chance for revenge. Cicero, Disputations

Istanbul, 1457

The same people who had destroyed my family had stolen and then sold my beloved! For a primitive like me, there is only one thing to do with anger. Since you cannot dam it up and you cannot dissolve it, one must give it a focus – a way to use it without being too destructive. I chose archery. In my mind, targets became sultans' turbans and my ability to hit bull's eyes improved.

We were moving up the draw weights on our bows again, this time to about 100 pounds. Once again, it was time to suffer in the tendons of the left elbow, the muscles and joint of the left shoulder, and the right thumb. Europe need not marvel over the Turkish bow. The bow does not shoot faster or farther or more accurately or pierce armor better than any other bow. The man conditioned to use it does these things. There was nothing we did on the battlefield with our arrows we had not done many thousand times at the *ok meydani*.

I eventually realized that though I had reason to hate them, my target was not so much one sultan or one pope. The problem was this evil world maintained by Power, in which the caprice of a few corrupt men is only the worst symptom. What they do, they do with the help of greedy nobles and *beylerbegs* (commanders), landholders, priests and tax collectors – all standing on the heads of a population of slaves and peasants. A man should be free to farm his land, love his wife and raise his children, and not have to worry about who is marching up the road to deprive him of everything. That was what the farmers of Belgrade had said by taking to arms.

I realized what needed destroying were these systems of parasitism and superstition whereby the people are cheated of half their wealth and a fifth of their children. It was not just Greeks who needed to be freed of their chains, it was all humanity. I had gained a new respect for the Phatria. When they questioned everything, they eroded the foundations of all nobility's pillars. While I had been focused on a Christian order to free the Greeks, they were busy establishing a brotherhood of man – a more important enterprise. I wanted to do my part, but it took awhile to figure out what that might be.

I also realized that my love for Alítheia had taught me nearly everything worth knowing. For years, I had prided myself in learning how to be a good student or a good soldier and now all I wanted was to learn to be a good man. I was pretty sure Istanbul was not the place for me to do this – that regardless of your cause there is something fundamentally wrong with spending 10 hours a day training to kill people who have done you no harm, and another hour groveling to someone (or bribing him) to get him to do his job.

It had not taken long for this old city to tame the nomads who had come to stay. Their court was soon as slothful and decadent, and as self-interested and regulated as ours had ever aspired to be. Indeed, the great Moslem historian Ibn Khaldun would have been ashamed:

> *When a tribe has achieved a certain measure of superiority with the help of its group feeling, it gains control over a corresponding amount of wealth and comes to share prosperity and abundance with those who have been in possession of these things. ... As a result, the toughness of desert life is lost. Group feeling and courage weaken. Members of the tribe revel in the well-being that God has given them. Their children and offspring grow up too proud to look after themselves or to attend to their own needs. ... This finally becomes a character trait and natural characteristic of theirs. ... Eventually, group feeling is altogether destroyed. They thus invite their own destruction. The greater their luxury and the easier the life they enjoy, the closer they are to extinction.* ^{Ibn Khaldun, Muqaddimah}

With us slaves, just the opposite was happening. We, upon losing everything, realized that Greece and Rome had stood for something these newcomers may never understand. I could see the possibility of reviving the Order if I could find the right kind of people. It would have to be a secret within a secret if we were going to plant the desires for liberty and truth and expect them to grow. But I began to see a bright lining to our oppression. The Sun's rays are never more visible than when the Moon stands in the way!

In the meantime, I also began looking for spiritual people from whom I might learn. On occasion, I would visit with the Admiral, Ahmed or Yasin. However, more and more I looked for people who might provide me an idea of what my life was missing (aside from the love of a girl 2,000 miles away). I spoke to Jews, Bektashi, Dervishes and Bogomils – anyone that seemed to have a religious education beyond the *Bible* and the *Koran*. I spoke to Yezidis, Mandaeans and Cabbalists. Savages from lands beyond Islam or Christianity. I listened always for wisdom whencever it might come.

I met a Kurdish holy man through his son. When he prayed and opened his hands, there would be a flame dancing there. I met a Jew who, with enough time, could recite the entire Torah and Mishnah. I met a Dervish who knew the rotation of the planets and the stars as well as you might know what time the sun will rise tomorrow. I met a Christian who could cure people with his touch. What I was finding is that while each religion has its particular rules and beliefs that sound like foolishness to anyone else, they all share the big ideas, the signs in the stars, the milestones of the soul, and the ceremonies of life. We just use different words to describe them.

Even my fatalistic *hodja* had a certain holiness about him. One day, after calmly beating the soles of a student's feet for a major infraction, he said: "Look at the world around you neither as good nor evil. Rather, see it as a reality that contents you or that you might change for the better. The key is to apply the right thought, right words and right deeds. Never despair. Be brave and of good cheer. And as often as you can, BE the Hand of God!" Up to that moment, I had thought his temperament resembled that of a piece of driftwood – but now I could see his wisdom. The happiest people do all this without much introspection. The unhappiest? Well, they spend too much time thinking of their wants and not of their needs.

As part of my self-education, I also looked for people who knew the properties of plants. I found a gypsy woman who had gathered flowers, leaves and roots from Valencia to Istanbul. She taught me their uses as well as how to recognize them by their shapes and tastes. I do not think it is true that these women can make you fall in love or curse you, but I know their mixtures can make you feel incredibly good, staunch a wound or make you feel unbelievably bad. Extending life or cutting it short was surely in her power.

Because I was going to be *Kapikulu* cavalry, I was able to get out riding, and much of my archery practice was now from horseback. We practiced over on the new *ok meydani*. The Hippodrome had become too small for all the students coming through the schools, so Mehmed gave us a large field just north of Galata (Pera) and new camps were being set up.

Most of my old classmates went infantry. A few, such as Kreshnik, had gone off to the lesser chamber of the Sultan's palace to be a scribe. I ran into him one day near the old Great Palace. He said he was translating old scrolls of pagan works – that he had found a cache of them downstairs. I congratulated him and asked him if I could see. He took me there. I asked him how he had found it. He said, "We've been going through the old churches and palaces to see what niches were missed conquering the city and what old texts might be found. You never know what might be useful. We found manuscripts on medicine, astronomy and navigation and some maps ages old. Of course, we also found tons of useless theology not even worth scraping for the parchment. Some of this will be sold. Much will just be destroyed. Here, take some if you're interested."

I went over to one of my favorite old shelves and grabbed a scroll of the first book of Diodorus Siculus, the first three books of Strabo, a codex of Eusebius' *Vita Constantini*, a *Golden Verses* of Pythagoras, a scroll of the *Iliad*, the works of Dionysius the Areopagite, a *Timaeus* of Plato with a Proclus *Commentary* and the *Aeneid* of Virgil. I tossed them in a box and asked if he would help me stash them away for safekeeping until I could get to them. He agreed, so I showed him the secret closet below the gallery and asked him to keep it a secret. Again, he agreed. I guess some people lead terribly boring lives and a little conspiracy is an invitation to live.

I tossed the manuscript collection next to the sword box in the corner and told him he was welcome to anything else in the room – that these two boxes would leave with me if ever I could one day have my own place. I told him back in the vault he was sitting on a gold mine. The Patriarch George Scholarios would love to get his hands on the old theology and Catholic Cardinal Bessarion (who could be contacted through the Venetians) was a philosopher and a heresiologist who would love copies of the rest if the new scriptorium was looking to make some money. I warned him not to alert Scholarios to the pagan works. Best not to excite the old man's torch hand! He thanked me and went back to exploring old papers. I envied him. He really did have a good job for a scholar.

The most fun of my final year of training was practicing for "The Games." We grew proficient in racing horses and throwing javelins at each other or tagging each other with sticks on horseback. We played polo too, but our favorite was Kökbörü – the game of steal-the-calf (or steal-the-goat) that goes back to when the Turks were the Kök Böri (Blue Wolf Tribe) of the Altai Mountains. It is a combination of horse riding, teamwork and wrestling. You have not lived until you have wrestled 39 horsemen! We occasionally lost a man or a horse in these contests, but they were great fun and kept us in condition during winter.

Graduating from the school, I now rode with the 64th Orta of the *Cemaat* Division. When we were not at war, we were the "Greyhound Keepers," a unit of the Sultan's hunting establishment. While many of my fellows were lancers, the brothers in my *boluk* (company) carried bow, *kılıç*, dagger and an 8-inch *sipar* (small shield) on our bow hand that doubled as an arrow guide. My infantry brethren were beginning to use firearms, but for light cavalry reloading is much faster with a bow. I lost track of Ahmed for a time. Meanwhile, Jason would ride with me in the 64th. Finally, I would be back with an old friend!

Chapter Thirteen

So to thee Light by Darkness is made known:
Since God hath none, He, seeing all, denies
Himself eternally to mortal eyes. ^{Jalal al-Din al-Rumi}

Maslak, 1458

One night after we had been out hunting in the hills with the Sultan a few miles north of Istanbul, I was granted another vision. In this one, I was high above the Earth looking down on the Imperial City. Darkness had settled over Istanbul like an ink stain on a map, but from the edges of that pool of black, blue fires raced out in the rays of a star, just in front of a conflagration of the world. I heard Christ the Unconquered Sun saying: *Enlighten them that sit in darkness and the shadow of Death, and guide them in the way of peace.*

What I understood Him to be saying is that we need a way to link and communicate the Truth possessed by the brotherhoods of East and West. Their mysteries are related and tremendously important – just as the ancient Greeks and Jews shared the same God at their root. ^{Plutarch, Moralia, Table Talk}

We need a way to teach the dignity of every human soul. We need to convert the time, energy and treasure we sacrifice to the God of War into an internal battle to face the evil of our own systems, cities and hearts. I believe this is what Epictetus touched on when he said:

> *If these statements of the philosophers are true, that God and men are akin, there is but one course open to men, to do as Socrates did: never to reply to one who asks his country, 'I am an Athenian,' or, 'I am a Corinthian,' but 'I am a citizen of the universe.'* ^{Epictetus, Discourses}

What I thought we needed first was a symbol, one that could be explained in such a way as to be acceptable to our Ottoman masters.

We needed one that could also carry secret meanings for the initiated.

There are many messages and symbols that transcend Judaism, Christianity and Islam and reach back to the noble and sublime beliefs from which those religions emerged. Before I go too far, I should note that Muhammad would hardly agree with such a notion, claiming Islam was its own true original. ^{Koran 109:1-6} Basically, we needed a symbol that could be used to begin to construct the Kingdom of God on Earth and one we could begin to use to teach the eternal verities of this world.

The image came to me just after we had our left inner forearms tattooed with the Black Moon insignia of the 64th Orta. I did not have to search very far to hit on a symbol for the cadre of friends I hoped to dedicate to Truth and an empire of the Spirit.

A friend of mine in the armorers was an ironworker. I had him make me a brand of eight spokes radiating out of an empty circle (to fit the standard-sized janissary tattoo). If questioned, I would explain it as Rumi's Light from the Darkness. To soldiers with a bit of pride and historical knowledge, we could see ourselves as Rome's *Praetoriani*.

To a Roman Christian, it could be the Labarum, the Chi Rho of the Christus, the Cross of St. George or St. Andrew, or the Christ Sol Invictus. To an Armenian or Greek nationalist, it could be a sign of the Phoenix. The idea was to scar initiates with a symbol not too obvious, but one where if the right people were brought in early, it would signify an elite order within an order, just as the Phatria and the Order of St. George had been hidden to most Romans.

We would be janissaries within the Guild of Archers, but we would be *Gazi* gathering the ancient secrets. We would unite with like-minded souls wherever we met them and share their stories and sacred symbols. Together, we would begin to forge a New Age for mankind! Such are the idealistic fantasies of youth.

I would never use such a group to confront our commander, the *Zağarcıbaşı*. However, we could carry a doctrine of the universalist Bektashi to a new level and plant the seeds of Truth, Freedom and Justice in the very heart of our oppressive regime. We would be the *Lux ex Tenebris* (light from the darkness), Plato's Light of Truth proceeding from the Good. To us, secrets would gravitate. From us, wisdom would come. Swear a man to Truth and he will begin to weigh his philosophy, religion or science for what is real and reasonable.

We could meet in the middle. The more East and West understood each other, the closer to peace we would be. I thought, if we could grasp our commonalities, maybe we would not need to engage in Crusades to take each other as slaves, and that the first step should be taken here and now. It should only require a few good souls, and the seed of such an idea would begin to grow back the Tree of Knowledge.

It would be a matter of initiates specializing in what they were most interested in learning, and allowing them to suggest changes in policy or doctrine or stories that would make our group more valuable to the regime and more relevant to other soldiers and other nations.

I realized that in its janissary-centered military, the Ottomans had committed the error of my Byzantine forebears. The Sultans had placed their destinies in the hands of a mercenary arm, and one bound to Islam only as tightly as Islam could be explained as a reform of Christianity. Otherwise, my Greek, Roman and Armenian brethren were apt to seek a middle way that condemned neither themselves nor the Christian families they had left behind. I saw the bloodshed of *Jihad* as the usual arrogant, self-aggrandizing worldly imperialism, but the *internal* struggle it implied as the one essential element of all religion.

The one reality we had lost touch with in Christianity, by focusing on one man's story, and in Islam by relying on one or two men's stories, is that all humankind is born with the same earthy clay of an animal inheritance and the same holy breath of the Divine. Our true object in this life should be to engage our descended spirits in the ongoing Creation and to reawaken our Divinity.

With the right ideology and the right "group feeling" there eventually could be moments in which the interests of such an order might even override those of the tyrant *du jour*. Such a network could reach into the palace, the conquered lands and Europe's courts. It was a matter of identifying brethren in a position to make those connections and providing them a means for trading valuable information. I had no doubt it is the same sort of friendly relationship that had kept my grandfather and Halil in power for so long – two wise old spiders whose webs of intrigue connected along a single thread of mutual trust.

For the janissaries, as in the Roman legions of old, the most logical basic military unit was the tent of 10 men who fight as brothers and who mess, camp and hang out together. For the nomadic Turks, this reality was viewed in terms of people eating together – the Sultan being "the Father who feeds us." The *Yoldaş*, or travelling companions, were people who gathered around one kettle with one cook (*Aşçi*), who worked for a master cook *Aşçi Usta*, who worked for the *Ortabaşi*, who worked for the *Çorbacı*.

In truth, I cared nothing for formal chains of command. Around each campfire of men eating mutton stew, drying their bows, honing their blades, drinking *boza* (a beer made of fermented grain) and munching on hot bread is a popular storyteller, the informal leader in whom the men confide, an *Amelimanda* (combat veteran) of proven valor. Through these storytellers, we could unite an army in ways far beyond the edicts of the Sultan's proclamations and the orders of the *Ağasi* (janissary commander).

All that was required was a little organization, a structure for gathering information, and a wealth of story material. Each battlefield has its brotherhood of veterans assisting the officers and imams. Over time, the collective memory of these troubadours has much to do with who rises in the ranks and what can be accomplished. All the ingredients were there. What we needed was a cause for action.

I administered the first branding to myself, surrounding the Black Moon with what would become the white scar of a sunburst. It burned like Hell; and well it should have. The Prophet frowned on such a practice. I bandaged it with salve and covered it with my sleeve. Later I knew questions would come, and I began my search for answers.

Chapter Fourteen

Jewish: *If you will not have faith, your kingdom will be broken.* [Isaiah 7:9]

Christian: *Pray that we may be rescued from worthless and evil people, since not everyone shares our faith.* [2 Thessalonians 3:2]

Moslem: *Ask not questions about things which, if made plain to you, may cause you trouble. ... Some people before you did ask such questions, and on that account lost their faith.* [Muhammad, Koran 5:101-102]

Istanbul, 1458

A religious creed is only as sharp as the executioner's axe. A cleric claiming to be tolerant of questions or other opinion dissembles, only to delay his opening gambit in his game of ideological chess. In the end, he stands prepared to enforce the commandment against heresy: *Thou shalt not suffer a witch to live.* [Exodus 22:18]

Unfortunately, "Faith" – this phenomenon demanding such fierce and uncompromising loyalty – begins with alarming simplicity, and, for an intelligent person, a suspension of logic. I probably had a tough time comprehending Scriptures for the sole reason that Emanuel and Diana always insisted I explore the *Bible* for myself whenever I had a question. They used to say "A religion or a heresy is founded on a dozen verses of God's Word taken out of context. The true believer must study the works and consult the Spirit."

In this way, my wrestling with God began. Jacob strove one night with the Angel of God and remained upright, earning himself the name Israel, [Genesis 32:24-28] as well as a second chance at life. [Jeremiah 30:10] I was not so successful. For the years 1453 to 1463, had it not been for my brief time with Alítheia, I felt my name would have been "Forsaken." For throughout my search for Truth in those years, she was my one Epiphany – the one reality that made sense. Otherwise, I had felt lost.

For example, the *Bible* says Yahweh is God and Yahweh is One [Deuteronomy 6:4] and all the kings shall fall down for Him and all nations will serve Him. [Psalm 72:11] If that is true, which version of the One are we talking about? El? Yahweh? Apollo? Jesus? Allah? Anyone who thinks them identical was not paying attention. It speaks of Him as "among the gods." [Psalm 86:8] So does that refer to the *Elohim* or to us? The same *Bible* that says "God sent his *only* begotten Son into the world" [1 John 4:9] also implies He has more than one and that Satan figures among them. [Job 1:6] It says our souls descend from above, [Psalm 18:16 & Revelation 2:5] that we too are gods and children of the Most High, [Psalm 82:6] and that we all shall rise on the third day! [Hosea 6:2]

I suspect it is for readings like this that we are encouraged to *train up a child in the way he should go and, when he is old, he will not depart from it.* [Proverbs 22:6] Perhaps this is why sultans take children from Christian captives to raise as janissaries, enforcing the edicts of Muhammad. With simple answers to all life's mysteries, a child's mind can be locked shut forever. On the other hand, a disciple of God (in whom God walks and in whom the Kingdom ultimately resides) [Colossians 1:27] will spend a lifetime searching out the mysteries with guidance from the Spirit whom God ordained before the Creation [1 Corinthians 2:7] to show us the path to eternal life. A disciple seeks to understand rather than merely submit. Conversely, clerics demand submission before understanding!

The *Bible* that calls the Hebrews His chosen people [Genesis 17:8] also says He will sow the house of Israel *with the seed of man and with the seed of the beast* [Jeremiah 31:27] and that He will one day be beheld among people *not called by my name.* [Isaiah 65:1] That a seed will come forth out of Jacob [Isaiah 65:9] who will be a curse unto the chosen people and whose servants will have another name [Isaiah 65:15] – but that the chosen people and the new servants will one day be reconciled. [Isaiah 65:19-25]

While there is a commandment in the *Torah* and the Gospels to *Love thy neighbor as thyself* [Leviticus 19:18; Galatians 5:14] ... there are others, just as in the *Koran*, calling for People of the Book to be spectacularly intolerant. The Jews, who have a God for all nations, were invited to destroy the people of Zobah, Jebus, Moab, Edom and Ammon. Christians are reportedly told the Jews descend from the Devil. [John 8:44] Yet Jesus and his apostles were Jews who said *We know what we worship; for salvation is of the Jews* [John 4:22] and *all Israel shall be saved.* [Romans 11:26]

The *Koran*, though written by one man's inspiration, has similar problems. Muhammad said People of the Book should be held to their own scriptures – the *Torah* and *Injil* (Gospels) – and *Those who believe and those who are Jews and Christians, and Sabaeans, whoever believe in God and the Last Day and do righteous deeds shall have their reward with their Lord, and on them shall be no fear, nor shall they grieve.* ^{Koran 2:62}

Yet awhile later he reportedly said: *They are surely infidels, who say, 'Verily God is Christ the son of Mary'* ^{Koran 5:17} and *take not the Jews or Christians for your friends* ^{Koran 5:51} and *kill the idolaters wheresoever ye find them* ^{Koran 9:5} and *strike off their heads until ye have made a great slaughter of them.* ^{Koran 47:4} So much for my brotherhood of man!

So it was, in this vague and harsh ecumenism, that people who survived the rapine and slaughter were allowed a Patriarch and some small churches, but they would live as slaves. As Christians and "People of the Book" we janissaries should have been free of the strictures of the *Koran*, there being *no compulsion in religion,* ^{Koran 2:256} but my brothers-in-arms and I were raised Moslem. Nor did this confer freedom from slavery. We too were property of the Sultan.

Predictably, given the bent of my difficult soul, I would sometimes receive extra attention from my company's imam, a Sunni from Arabia. Mostly I succeeded in avoiding the man, preferring to speak to the Bektashi who lived in a lodge adjacent to our barracks. I found them much more open-minded about nearly everything, including women and *boza* beer or *raki* (a liquor made from anise we called "Bull's Milk" when mixed with water).

One day, I met the Bektashi Sheikh, the *Baba*. I figured I would one day be in need of some sort of religious sanction if I was to achieve my vision. The meeting would be fortuitous. I was visiting the *tekke* (or lodge) nearest the Hippodrome, being invited by one of the brethren, a fellow janissary. We were returning from the Great Mosque to the barracks when we became involved in a conversation on the relationship of Truth to Faith. My friend did not feel qualified to wax philosophic on such a theme, which can easily end in a beating by the nearest *mullah*. He took me to meet the *Baba* (or Father).

At the door, we took off our boots, exchanged our red cloaks and white turbans for white jackets, and donned white caps of the brethren. We advanced to a shaded area adjacent to an octagonal gardened courtyard and waited to be served some *chai*, a sweet tea enjoyed at all hours of business throughout the city. After awhile, we were joined by the master of the place, the Sheikh.

My friend said I was an "interested associate" of the place, that I was searching for all of God's Truth, far beyond the words or actions that might lead one to Paradise. The Sheikh smiled and said, "One seeking to understand already is on the path, for God's Name is Truth. Our observations of Reality reveal Him. He is revealed through Love. He is revealed through the Law. He is revealed through the Perfection of our hearts. He is revealed through Meditation. He is revealed in the words of His Messengers and Prophets. He is revealed in every thought of the *qutb-i aqtab* (Supreme Axis), who is an incarnation of the Ancient One, head of the Perfect Masters, Axis of this world and Sustainer of the Creation. Such a Messenger was our master, Hajji Bektash Veli of Khorassan, a man in whom lived the thoughts of God, which is not the same as calling him an intercessor or a Godman. No, such things would be an abomination." [Koran 21:28-29]

What one might learn from such a man! Yet in the end, the Sheikh had a role to play, and his dogma, his place and his uniform circumscribed that role. Even so, he was the sort of man to study and to emulate. I told him I had chosen a difficult path, *Al Haqq* (The Truth). That I would not be content until Scripture, science, philosophy and my life made sense in each other's light. He laughed and said, "You have indeed set for yourself a tortuous path. Live righteously and perhaps Allah may one day grant you wisdom!"

I told him of my vision. I explained that of all the orders of Islam, his was the one with a chance of opening a conversation with the West. He asked me why such a thing would be of value now, after centuries of Crusade. I said the West was again searching for Truth and that Sufi, such as the Bektashi, could offer insights seemingly unavailable to Orthodox, Catholics or even primitive Christians such as the Waldensians. In my estimation, only a handful of mystics really understood what Jesus and Paul were talking about. The rest of the Church was going through rituals hoping to win Heaven. I said there is much more to Christianity than can be found in the *Injil* and more to Truth than can be found in Scripture. I said I saw Truth as the path to the Kingdom of Heaven. He smiled one of those smiles the old sometimes grant a child in whom they are well pleased.

Now beneath the exterior of every inquisitor is a committed believer looking for a chance to affirm or propagate his own belief. Even Jews who do not believe in evangelism will allow intermarriage and admit converts. He said he would speak to the other sheikhs and perhaps the idea of a bridge for understanding other cultures might be of interest to the *Ağasi*, the Vizier or the Sultan.

Then he made an interesting observation: "The Messengers of God have always formed an intellectual bridge for people to reach out to each other and to the future. Adam gave us language. Abraham and Muhammad observed the polytheistic confusion of Sumeria and Arabia and preached the One. Abraham observed the barbarity of the Phoenicians and brought a halt to sacrificing children. Zoroaster reformed the polytheistic confusion of the Brahmans. Moses reformed, syncretized and transmitted the wisdom of Sumerians, Persians, Babylonians, Egyptians and Hebrews and brought his people to the Promised Land. Jesus brought the truths of Judaism to the rest of the world. Muhammad sought to reform Christianity by removing its idolatry of the Son and focusing back on God."

I said, "Then what is needed, or will be needed, is a message that shows the common beliefs and the continuity between the various religions. The day we preach these things is the day each janissary becomes an emissary for Allah, praised be His Name. Thus far, we have only confusion as to what to tell our former family and friends. There is no way to teach them how we became who we are, what it means or how they might join us."

The Sheikh promised to get back to me, though there was no reason to suspect a 14-year-old boy's opinion would carry much weight in the *Saray* or with the Sufi. No, a typical answer would be no answer. I did not see the Sheikh again for a month, but I would be pleasantly surprised.

Chapter Fifteen

Wisdom is the principal thing; therefore get wisdom; and with all thy getting, get understanding. Proverbs 4:7

A prudent man sees evil coming and will take steps to avoid it. Simple men rush ahead and suffer their punishment. Proverbs 27:12

Ayazaga, 1458

One of the things well taught by the hunting grounds is the mind of a beast. Over time, one learns where they like to hunt, where they prefer to raise their young, where and how one will fight, where and how it will attempt to escape if it senses danger.

Some said Mehmed spent far too much time in the hunting grounds, but I understood his affection for the sport. In his mind, he was the predator at the top of the food chain. No bear, no lynx, no boar, no mountain goat should be able to match his strength, his agility, his speed or his lack of fear. Indeed, none did. He was a great hunter, happy to face a bear with lance or bow, telling us not to interfere. He was content shooting birds or deploying his falcons. He was happy to kill whatever ran from his dogs.

I think the only beast he never wholly understood is the one sometimes lurking in the human breast. In that case, an appeal to his vanity could leave him with a huge blind spot – and earn him an evil companion or temporary father-in-law like Zaganos. I think he admired people like himself and so would sometimes reel them in close and later banish them to where they might still serve his interests while doing him no harm.

Between wars, Mehmed could be humorous, generous and, sometimes, even charming. However, his word meant very little. The second an earlier treaty or friendship became inconvenient, he would change his mind until he accomplished whatever he now sought to achieve.

One of the old pashas on this trip had a huge gray wolf for a pet, perhaps remembering the tribe's history. I suppose he had picked it up and raised it when he had killed the mother long ago. Now it was getting old and cantankerous like its master. I noticed it had one gray eye and one blue. The gray eye looked as if it had cataracts; and I noticed that the animal seemed content with what went on to its left or straight ahead, but what suddenly appeared to its right field of vision would make it bristle. The old man kept the wolf on a heavy iron chain, but given the animal's size and strength, I would not want to test its ability to hold.

This night, we were enjoying some fortified *boza* and some slaves brought in by a khan of the Crimean Tartars who sometimes supplied us with berserker cavalry. In addition to carrying an extra helping of alcohol, the drink apparently also contained some poppy seed or opium. Mehmed was at his roaring best, showering a favorite group of dancing boys *(sodomitai)* with gold for a performance of the dance of veils. Then he was walking about teasing his old warriors, regaling them with tales of each other's heroic misbehavior.

At one point, he wandered over toward the old pasha's tent. The wolf lunged at the Sultan and the iron chain snapped. Standing nearby, I shoved the wolf with both arms as it began to close its mouth around his left bicep and tore instead his coat. The wolf turned on me now, catching my left forearm in its mouth just after I had hit its head with my left fist and *sipar*. Finding its purchase on my armguard ineffective (though I felt a bone snap underneath), it let the arm go and lunged for my throat.

This time, the Sultan stopped the wolf. He leaned into the animal, traversing its chest and ripping with his *kılıç*. The fight quickly left the animal when Mehmed withdrew the sword and chopped off its head, saying, "That is twice you've seen the future."

I nearly died, thinking he was referring to Belgrade! He smiled and said, "Many thanks, *Sinan Yay Burcu*." (Sinan is the usual name given to us converts.) I replied, "Many thanks to you, Excellency. You should not have risked your life for a poor bowman. But, if ever I write a book of prophecies, I will send it to you." He laughed. I was sore, but immensely relieved. He remembered me from the Hippodrome – not the Battle of Belgrade.

That night, perhaps under influence of the *boza*, God granted me a vision of Alítheia. She was breast-feeding a baby about 18 months old. She was dressed richly, not like a slave, but like a fourth and favorite wife. She looked so happy sitting next to her husband. As I awoke, I felt crushed. I wondered about the Sultan of Oran's youngest son. I rejoiced to know she was happy, but my heart ached much worse than the arm that would take three months to heal.

One afternoon, now on light duty (unable to carry, much less draw, my bow), I returned to the *tekke* with my Sufi warrior friend. Again we sat down for *chai* and again, the Sheikh joined us. The old man smiled and stroked his beard. "I see no good deed goes unpunished with you," he said, "but I hear good things about your proposal." I replied, "I do not think much of the Devil's beasts. Sometimes they must be put out of their misery." He laughed, "The old pasha would have had you beaten if you had been the one who killed his pet. As it is, he thanked the Sultan for doing all of us a service and ridding him of that dangerous animal!"

We sipped on our *chai*, waiting to see what he had to say. "I spoke to the Sultan, the Vizier and the *Ağasi*. There will be an intelligence officer position established in the 99th Orta for you to report to and who can provide you guidance and supplies or finances you might need. He is not one of mine. You will remain assigned to the 64th until we figure this thing out, since you are no chaplain. The *ulema* insisted on their involvement to keep things on the side of orthodoxy. After all, *Shariah* (the Law) precedes *Tariqah* (the Way); and *Marifa* (Knowledge) precedes *Haqiqah* (the ultimate Truth)."

I opened my mouth to say something and he held up his hand. "You know as well as I that this may limit your success. Therefore, do what you can in the spirit of your proposal and report what you can in the spirit of their support. In this way, all of God's intent can be fulfilled."

I thanked him and stayed to watch some of the dervishes as they meditated, spinning to the sound of the chanting, and the play of the *oud*, flute and drum. In their ecstasy, they looked happier than a janissary holding an emptied bottle of *raki*. I would have enjoyed learning how to meditate like that, but frankly, spinning has never been kind to me. For that matter, neither has a bottle of *raki*. I drank my *chai* and left as my friend donned a weighted white skirt, a black cloak, and a tall camel hair hat to join in the *sema* dancing the soul's progress up Jacob's Ladder to Paradise.

They say a war plan does not survive contact with the enemy – that nearly every detail beyond the overall strategy must be adapted before success on the battlefield. I dare say, religious plans fare no better in the hands of man. I wonder if the boat Noah built was exactly to the specifications of God. I wonder if Hippodamus of Miletus designed good plumbing into his plans for Piraeus and Rhodes or whether these were a trivial matter left to others as he drew up his architectural grand schemes and wrote out the Constitutions for government. Planning is easy compared to execution.

The officer they gave me to work with, a chaplain named Davut, was an upright human being, but he was also withdrawn, suspicious and analytical. He could occasionally be good-humored and even brilliant. The best thing about him was that he was an indefatigable systematizer. If I came up with the contacts and the content, he would come up with a methodology for reporting and archiving.

I think he realized from the first day that we could not simply be generating propaganda for the furtherance of the Ottoman regime or Islam – that we would have to be relevant to our targets and offer them something they valued. He said he found the idea distasteful – the idea that an enemy might have something to offer us, that we would have something to offer them, or that dirty means might be required to accomplish pure ends.

In the end, though, there is not much a zealot cannot stomach. For example, how many of the faithful in the sects have gone through an initiation *ad suppositorum* or through the "Middle Way" of the "Mount of Perfection" to analogously "experience" God? In the days of Kempis, I guess it was much more typical than today. Mystics sometimes lose their bearings.

I suspect many of the practices and problems of today's religions descend from hoary traditions going back to the days of El's temple virgins and the Goddess with her *castrati* priests. How else to understand so many eunuchs, men in feminine dress, and writers of love poetry vaunted as discipline, enlightenment and the most sublime spirituality?

I could see the Phatria, who would eventually have to work out such challenges for themselves, was going to be an obvious ally in reaching across cultures. However, I was a bit disappointed with myself for believing such groups may eventually be key to guiding mankind back to Truth and the way of peace. Is the rest of humanity so mired in patriarchy that the sexes cannot work together for the greater good?

Beyond Plato and Plotinus, the great believers in Truth as identical to Beauty and the Good were Dante, Petrach and Boccaccio. Truth for them, for me, was – is – embodied in a specific woman, not just some philosophical abstract. I believe the Spirit returns to us. Call her Beatrice; call her Laura; call her Fiammetta. I call her Alítheia. Like God, she is with us always, the holy twin to our earthly Love. Without a Beloved, we are lost in delusions and the frustrations of selfishness.

Married and with a child on the other end of the sea, Alítheia continued to be my compass rose, as well as my now-impossible dream. Still, in my sorrow for our separation lived a constant joy in her existence. By her Light, I had glimpsed God's love.

Did I sin in loving this wife of another? I suppose I did covet her at the time. Do I now repent of that sin? I know I should, but I hope God has forgiven me. How could I deny the desire of my soul to be whole? Were I blind, I would have wished for eyes. Were I deaf, I would pray for my ears to work. Were I corrupt, I would seek baptism.

We all seek to be whole. In this, we do not sin. Were she the flame and I the moth, I would die happily to draw close to her. How often can one think of a person before it borders on obsession? Even knowing I had to live without her, I easily surpassed the mark.

Chapter Sixteen

If anyone introduces an innovation in religion or gives shelter to a man who introduces such an innovation, he is cursed by Allah, by His angels, and by all the people. ^{Hadith, 'Ali ibn AbuTalib}

Istanbul, 1459

Islam is not a peaceful religion at its heart. Within it, there are some peaceful and wonderful people, but they are not really supposed to feel at ease with the world until they have fully conquered the rest of us. "Peace" is someone else's delusion.

There is the House of Islam (the Faithful) and the House of War (the Infidels). Anyone from the House of War seeking to avoid force of arms had best be paying *jizya* (the poll tax for religious minorities). When you think about it, Christianity is similar in its self-righteous outlook – demanding everyone wise up before Judgment Day or there will be Hell to pay. Both religions exist as empires of the mind, neither content to cede people to the other.

Once, briefly, in the 13th Century, it appeared the two could come together with an *Introduction of the Eternal Gospel* by the Joachimites, on the supposition that the Spiritual Franciscans had found the keys to Truth. One of the keys involved an understanding of Islam as a continuation of Christianity – the eternal Christianity, not the one begun by Jesus, James and Paul. Alas, not even to inaugurate the Age of the Spirit was Catholicism willing to end its secular hold on Europe.

One day, soon enough, certainly by the end of this Age of Pisces, the Catholic Church will look to the stars and embrace the permanent religion of mankind it veiled in stories. Otherwise, I am not sure how it can possibly remain relevant. Whatever the case, I do not believe anyone in the Vatican has tried to reconcile with Islam in centuries.

The Phatria, when reestablished, was willing to meet with Moslems; and Moslems were willing to associate with such a fellowship. While the Phatria has had various names during its long history, it has also varied its character as it widened its sphere of influence. My friend Constantine Comnenus told me some of their members are students of alchemy, kabala and other esoteric subjects. Their little conspiracy of freedom has been quite successful in gathering people to its banner – but I get ahead of myself. I had very little to do with it.

My first request for my new *Çorbacı* (my part-time boss in the 99th) was for a small group of men who could read and write in their native languages and represent the thinking of a nationality of Europe. The idea was for each of them to become an expert on the activities of their former nation's respective army, court and populace. Obviously, they would each need money, a scribe for generating correspondence, and the ability to travel. That request was easy. The second was trickier.

I then requested for some men – preferably not military – who, in exchange for their freedom, would provide us information through correspondence and contacts from throughout Europe, Asia and Africa. I encouraged the colonel to have as many of these contacts as possible come from friends of the first group, making the maintenance of those relationships easy, and more liable to last. We would use these freemen to cultivate additional contacts and to act as our listeners and messengers.

For my part, I began to send out letters to Constantine at Venice, my Aunt Anna (also at Venice), and to the old Metropolitan at Mystras, whom I hoped might put me in contact with remaining elements of the Order. I had no such entrée with the extended Palaeologus family, for whom I was, and remain, a nobody.

The price of all this activity was having to render analyses to the *Çorbacı*. We attempted to discern: who was friendly to whom, what group had a gripe with the nobles, what group of heretics was militating for its own freedom, who had cornered what market of goods, who owned what land, which fortress was strong, whence came its water, how big was their army and with whom were they allied. ... There were many questions and not everything was discernible in a timely manner from a distance, but we tried.

My first lessons in all this were pretty negative: Mankind has a real problem with commitment. We are fickle in our friendships.

Our leaders are selfish, our governments full of disguised corruption. Nations are unreliable in their treaties.

To take over, one needs only ask *Cui bono* ... who benefits from the status quo and who will benefit from the New Order. If you tell each group what it most wants to hear, people will line up to pummel each other despite any hypocritical protestations about how they would "unite" against a common enemy. Wolves masquerade as sheep, and devils as honest men.

The only place we had not seen divide-and-conquer politics work was Belgrade – so Belgrade was off the target list. To use Ibn Khaldun's phrase, their "group feeling" was too strong. However, the rest of Serbia was clearly up for grabs.

With each exploit and each little victory, we would feed the network of our storytellers. The number of janissaries with a brand surrounding their tattoo grew. Everyone wanted to know what was really going on at home and abroad. With recommendations from three members, we would let you in. You just had to be able to sort out what "everyone" knew from what the experts knew ... and remember to whom you were speaking.

Men are hierarchical, so the higher one's rank, the more "accurate" and "comprehensive" was the information we would provide. Truth is, one's intelligence service can play divide-and-conquer games with one's own country as easily as diplomats play with another!

I was not a great man in the Turkish camp, but I was growing a web of trusted agents and feeding them ideas I hoped might one day blossom into a desire for something more than Mehmed's ideal: tyranny in a perpetual state of war. In doing so, I nearly forgot the first rule of tyrants – clip the tall ones first.

The Spirit was quietly reminding me, "I shall meet thee on the path of sin; and on the path of pride I shall humble thee." However, by now I was hard of hearing. I suppose success early in life can be deafening.

Serbia, 1459

After Belgrade, one might have expected Mehmed to give up on his dream of conquest, but giving up was not in the character of the young man who had grown up wanting to be Alexander the Great and who now had soldiers to match his ambitions. He was Caesar, the Sultan of Rome! Serbia would provide the proof of concept for our Special Organization *(Teshkilat-i Mahsusa)*.

Three years after the Prophet of Belgrade's whispered warnings of disaster came true, we returned to Serbia to find a world where much had changed. General Hunyadi and Capistrano, for instance, had died of Plague within weeks of our hasty retreat.

Europe had returned to its divisive ways and Lazar Branković, chief of the Triballi, had brokered a deal with Mehmed to pay tribute in exchange for a nonaggression pact, thereby freeing Lazar to cause trouble for his former Hungarian masters across the river. Such an agreement between the Sultan and Lazar's father had previously failed ... but how often do we learn from the mistakes of our elders? For that matter, how often do we learn the lessons of our own lives?

Earlier, Mehmed had coaxed Lazar's mother away from her tyrannical son, encouraging her to bring her children and jewels to our territory and he would treat her according to her rank! Two of her children made it to our protection, though the old woman was overtaken by her son and died soon thereafter. Mehmed understood that divide-and-conquer applies even (or perhaps especially) to royal families. I do not recall the reports from Semendria that led to covert action, but intelligence was crucial to many a conquest.

The Sultan had promised to leave Serbia alone as long as Branković lived, but then that despot mysteriously and conveniently died of illness in 1458. The regency set up to succeed him then fell apart just as quickly. (We bought off Lazar's wife and daughter with towns in Dalmatia and Bosnia to make up for their loss of estates.) The Hungarians, meanwhile, were having domestic disagreements, so now there was nothing but distance to slow us down. Ignoring Belgrade, the Sultan settled for taking Smederovo and the Serbian countryside. Making occupation palatable to the people was simple. We promised and provided them religious freedom to retain their Orthodox faith.

Lemnos, 1458

In Lemnos, we tried a new strategy. We secretly sent our agent, Kritovoulos the Imbriote, into an area held by the Italians and had him explain advantages for the local Greek aristocracy if we took over. They sent a letter to the Sultan requesting the island be "liberated." Kritovoulos sent another letter to Demetrius, advising my uncle to remind the Sultan that he had sufficient forces to expel the Italians from the islands. My uncle promised the Sultan 3,000 ducats a year if he could have this estate. The Sultan so promised, and now

Kritovoulos undertook to have the locals help us expel the Italians in a bloodless revolution. Holdouts caved in when we sent a small force to begin a siege. Most everyone by now understood that one's fate in surrendering a town was infinitely better than making us bleed to capture it.

Albania, 1459

The Illyrians stopped paying the tribute to which they had agreed with the Sultan's father Murad. Mehmed sent Mahmud Pasha to secure the mountain passes. Then, sending in the main force, the Sultan had the wheat harvest destroyed; and our army carried off a great number of people and cattle. Left with no other wealth, the Illyrians would henceforth pay their tribute in children and sheep.

Peloponnesus, 1460

Many kingdoms would rather pay gold than suffer invasion. This was the solution of my uncles in the Morea, who never did learn to get along. For a time, they bought their freedom as vassals for 20,000 ducats a year. When they failed to pay, the Sultan sent his men to burn fields and decapitate or break the legs of anyone not paying the poll tax.

Mehmed subjected Corinth to siege, then set off to pillage and burn other towns in the Morea. Tegea fell. Patras began to desert to Venice, leaving the castle above to defend itself. The men inside saw our cannon and surrendered. We then promised the townspeople immunity from taxes and the return of their possessions if they returned. Most did. Elis and Messenia resisted and were pillaged. Vostitsa surrendered. Gardikion gave up after a day's siege, but her men were killed and the women and children enslaved for not surrendering the day before.

After four months of sweeping the Peloponnese before us, Corinth still held out. So my uncle Demetrius, in a move designed to ingratiate himself with the Sultan and to alienate his brother Thomas, sent in Matthew Asanes with food on a daring rescue mission. Asanes and his men scaled steep cliffs to avoid us. Seeing the people starving inside, Asanes sent a messenger to the Sultan to discuss surrender.

Ultimately, my uncle and his wife were instructed to report to Adrianople as members of the court. My Uncle Demetrius thus became a foreign deputy to the Sultan and a well-paid servant. A Turk named Balabanaga became the *Voivode* of Mystras. Uncle Thomas and his chiefs gathered in Mantinea. Seeing all was lost, they hopped in their triremes and sailed for Corfu. "Uncle" George Sphrantzes had tied his fate to that branch of the family and now would finish his days as a monk in Corfu writing his self-congratulatory memoirs, puffing himself up from chamberlain to "Great Chancellor."

We resupplied and manned the better fortresses and stationed a force of 400 janissaries at Corinth. Most of the other fortifications of the Morea we destroyed.

On our way back to Adrianople, we stopped at Athens. The Sultan, long a student of ancient Greece, was excited to walk through the old market area, to stand in the theater where Sophocles' tragedies were staged, and to hike up the Acropolis to see where Paul had preached and Socrates debated. Thankfully, while in Greece I never had to fight anyone I had known growing up. I would rather have died.

People from towns whose fortresses we dismantled were sent to repopulate Constantinople. People with wealth or talent settled into the city proper, while others were invited to move into the countryside. Mehmed's idea was to begin reconstruction of the city and to restore some of Byzantium's earlier power and glory.

At the same time, the Sultan was expanding the navy with an eye to the Mediterranean. More triremes, galleys and xebecs. More mahonnes, galiots and brigantines. More cannon and mortars. Like his sudden move to construct Rumeli Hisar to throttle Black Sea trade, Mehmed was looking to control the seas from the Bosporus to the Pillars of Hercules. We expanded our activities in far-flung islands and harbors, and we put some foreign sailors on our payrolls.

Priests and sailors often seemed the guardians of mankind's most ancient wisdom. They were easy with their knowledge, given a bit of drink or a little money and a sympathetic ear.

Black Sea Coast, 1461

To put the Greeks wholly under his thumb, Mehmed now undertook to snuff out their last enclaves of freedom. He expanded the army's rolls and had more ships built for a Black Sea expedition. It was time to ensure the southern coast of that sea was his.

Until the Sultan choked off Black Sea commerce, Trebizond and Sinope were important cities along the old caravan routes to the Orient. Trebizond was the little empire of my friend Constantine's royal family, the Comneni. Sinope had been important for its mines, but now the area was much poorer and fractured by domestic unrest. When it began to ally itself with neighboring nations through marriage and had trouble paying the annual tribute, it came time for action. If we delayed, the Sultan felt rebellion was going to be right around the corner. There were also indications that Hasan, king of the adjacent Tigranocerta (an ancient capital of Armenia), had designs on the area.

We headed out with 300 ships, 60,000 cavalry, 80,000 infantry and a huge train of cargo and camp followers to Sinope. When Ismail, ruler of the city, saw us, he loaded up wagons with treasure and came out to meet the Sultan. Mehmed offered him a province of Macedonia in exchange for his city and Ismail took it, making Sinope's harbor a base from which to attack Trebizond.

Now the Sultan ordered the fleet and army to press ahead along the coast, to take the harbors at Trebizond and invade the city by land and sea. The citizens of Trebizond defeated our irregulars outside the city's gates. Driven back into the city's walls, they were then weakened by six weeks of siege. The Sultan sent in Thomas Katabolenus, one of our agents. Thomas offered the leaders a choice: "Own lands and live unmolested with your families ... or die and leave your families as our slaves. " The key, he said, was whether they surrendered to the Sultan when he arrived the next day.

The ruler and his city sent out their captains the next day with gifts to pay obeisance to the Sultan. The Sultan sent our navy back to Constantinople with 1,500 children destined for the Janissary Corps or the Harem. Again, the wealthy received notice that they should move their families and goods to Constantinople rather than reinforce their ancestral lands. Mehmed appointed an admiral as the new governor and left him a garrison of 400 janissaries from our division.

Wallachia, 1462

While Mehmed could be a very bad guy – Antichrist himself on occasion – he was by no means the worst actor on the world stage. A competitor for that role would be Vlad the Impaler, chief of the Getae and son of the Voivode of Wallachia. Both of that leader's sons had grown up in the Ottoman court. When their father died, Mehmed sent Vlad, the eldest, home with money, horses, robes and tents – with instructions that the young man continue to send the annual tribute.

Well, evil men often assume their being treated well is a sign of someone else's weakness. So when "Dracula" returned home – calling himself after an old Order of the Dragon we had yet to penetrate – he formed an army, marched them across the Danube and attacked villages of the Ottoman empire, both Christian and Moslem, in the area around Nicopolis. He had his troops cut everyone's noses off so he could string them and carry the trophies home to brag how many "little piggies" he had killed. When our diplomats arrived at his court, he had the men impaled – hence his "Impaler" nickname. I suppose he had learned how to treat diplomats and prisoners from Mehmed! It seems a law of the universe: Eventually Karma rules.

When the Sultan learned of all this, he must have felt like a boy who has had his pants yanked down and been found wanting. He armed the younger brother, Rados, with 4,000 cavalry and a division of irregular infantry and sent them off to face the older brother. A massive battle of cannon ensued. When the dust cleared, the younger brother was the new Voivode. Vlad escaped to Hungary, where the king threw him in prison to keep the peace with us. The people and countryside of the Getae, meanwhile, suffered greatly for the sins of their arrogant leader.

Istanbul, 1462

Now somewhere in all of this incessant warring and stitching up each other's wounds and hunting and pillaging and writing reports (because it was still beneficial to be attached to one of the "Sultan's own" regiments while taking reports from the field), I was becoming confused about some things and increasingly clear about others.

It was obvious that the networks of contacts and communicators had proven incredibly useful, especially when managed one as part of the other. Intelligence can feed "group feeling" or "troop morale" or "national spirit" as easily as it can unveil enemy deception. Communication can use a mixture of what everybody knows and what hardly anyone knows (or merely what you want them to "know" ... *untrue as that might be*) to garner public support for a war or public support (or disdain) for a leader.

The realization is intoxicating anywhere near the nexus of the two activities, which is precisely where I found myself. While this made me "powerful" in a sense (and Power is always laced with danger to one's body and soul), I began to realize that in our tyranny this was especially apt to render me vulnerable.

At some point, I realized that youth plus success breeds arrogance; and arrogance breeds envy and hatred; and where those two exist ... scandals and violence cannot be far behind.

I began to prepare for my exodus. I did not know if it would be fatal, whether it would be exile, or whether I would be one more of those who ended up on remote assignment ... to be used, but forever after kept at arm's length.

None of this was obvious, busy as I was, so it helped to have loyal friends who could act as one's eyes and ears – and sometimes conscience. Jason proved to be my most loyal and irreverent friend, letting me know when my expectations of the world were getting ridiculous (calling me "Pompey's Ass"), when my studied opinion was becoming overly cynical ("Did someone make fun of Caligula today?"), or when I was waxing philosophic when what was needed was reality ("Apollo is full of shit; bring me Dionysius!"). Without friends we are lost. Our perception is miniscule compared to the universe of our present situation.

I sent Constantine my chest of books and told him I would join him in Venice as soon as I could.

The Islands, 1462

Nikorezos of Lesbos was setting up his island as a center for pirates and Italians – neither being convenient to Mehmed's designs. When Nikorezos stopped paying his annual tribute, the Sultan ordered Mahmud Pasha to make ready 200 ships and crews.

We had observed Nikorezos allowing corsairs to use his ports. He was also providing them guides to pillage coastal cities from southern Anatolia to the northern Black Sea. While an aggressive spirit himself, Mehmed found it exceedingly difficult to abide a competitor. We soon received our orders: "Conquer Lesbos or lay it waste!"

Like Xerxes, we crossed at the Hellespont, putting us close to Troy, where Mehmed took time to address us as the avenger of Hector against Agamemnon!

> *Allah has reserved for me, through so long a period of years, the right and obligation to avenge the massacre of the Troy. I conquer Priam's enemies. I plunder their cities. I enslave their wives and take their children as spoils of war. The Greeks, Macedonians, Thessalians and Peloponnesians who*

ravaged this place now pay for their sins through their children. Through me, Justice is restored!

I recalled the fights of the gods over the future of Troy. I remembered the histories and how they divided the city-states of Phoenicia, Anatolia, Carthage, Egypt, Greece and Rome between themselves, and I wondered whether Mehmed's Allah and my God could be the same One. If not, then whose will had I been doing for 10 years? What might be the consequences for my soul? I wondered, too: Who will now control the Mediterranean? For this had always been the central object of the Pantheon's concern.

Mahmud crossed over with the 200 ships and gave siege to the main city, Mitylene, but the inhabitants locked themselves in and thought to wait him out. He brought cannon to bear, and as my Emperor and Giustiniani had replaced walls with earthworks at Constantinople, these people thought to do the same. The Sultan became impatient and ordered our armies to cross over to the island. When the islanders saw Mehmed and his thousands preparing to lay waste their entire island, they begged forgiveness and sued for peace. The Sultan received them graciously, gave instructions, and departed.

Mahmud divided the populace into three. A third would remain in the city to inhabit it and pay the annual tribute. The aristocracy would move to Constantinople. The remainder were made slaves for the soldiers or the market. As to the Italians, not one lived. Mahmud made the same division among the inhabitants of each of the cities of the island, then left Ali of Samos as governor.

Depending on your viewpoint, thus ended dissent or freedom in the Aegean. The isles would faithfully pay tribute to Islam and Mehmed el Fatih. His design was to expand this sea power across the Mediterranean. Sea power he understood as a matter of managing the choke points. He now built fortresses on both sides of the Chersonese to control Black Sea trade from the other side and to lock up the Balkans in the north, just as he reinforced the Bosporus and Dardanelles in the south.

Bosnia, 1463

Mostly, men try to avoid defeat, treating life as some sort of ball game or tug of war. However, I should add that the pride in one's greatest victory can sometimes lead directly to one's greatest fall. This was what happened to me over Dalmatia, land of the Bostrians.

I believe I mentioned that my adoptive father – whom I enjoyed like my real father, for far too brief a time – was a heretic. He was a man from this land washed at times by waves of paganisms, the earliest Christianity, Orthodoxy, Catholicism and Islam. In such places, some themes remain eternal despite the changes in politics. Doctrinal differences can be a flavor *du jour* that will not stand the test of time.

I believe the most ancient values here had to do with Albina, the White Lady of Death and Inspiration on whose island I became an oracle. She was Alphito, the barley goddess who gave her name to Britain – Albion. She was Cardea to the Romans, the Holy Spirit to the old Christians, symbolized by the Dove who flew into Christ at the Jordan River. She was the Spirit who had moved on the face of the waters. She has had many names and attributes through the centuries ... as has God the Father.

What was peculiar to these people and their brethren in Italy and France was that they believed, like the Jewish high priest or king, that Sonship is a matter of being anointed and *adopted* by God. If I might generalize on some of their major tenets:

- *One prays only to God the Father.*
- *God is Love.*
- *God's cause will not perish; there will always be a pure Church.*
- *We are fallen and sin is in our nature.*
- *This does not mean children are guilty of "original sin."*
- *Humility is the first sign of godliness.*
- *If we listen, the Holy Spirit will tell us how to return to the Light.*
- *Believers are Christs, God's disciples on Earth.*
- *A church is a gathering of people, not a building or institution.*
- *Believers know and keep the Commandments.*
- *Neither Jesus nor saints nor priests come between us and God.*
- *A Christ is not God, and does not replace Him.*
- *Jesus was a man who dedicated his life to fulfilling the prophecies.*
- *Every Christian has the power to bind people to God.*
- *Monks' robes often hide devils; and it is better for the clergy to marry.*
- *One does not require baptism until one is an adult.*
- *We should seek to perfect ourselves.*
- *There is no need for a Nicene Creed or any other.*

- *Jesus was not born the Christ; he became one.*
- *The Last Supper is a symbol of union for believers in God the Father.*
- *Righteousness and the incarnation of Christ in us is the point of religion.*

Books deserve to be written on these people. I believe they were the only ones who really understood Moses, Jesus, Paul, Clement, Origen or Lactantius. I think the only memory of them today in the Church is maybe the Mozarabic Rite with its hint of adoptionism.

Now you can imagine that people on fire with this Spirit would have little use for the Vatican, for the Patriarch at Constantinople, or for the Prophet of the Arabian Desert. They KNEW the secrets of God. They KNEW the secrets of Wisdom. They KNEW the secret doctrines of the Christ and the Wheel of Life. They had several names ... Patarenes, Waldenses, Nestorians, Cathars, Bogomils, Paulicians, Puritans, Arnoldists, Spiritual Franciscans, Albigenses, Baptists ... all known to each other as The Brethren. They descended from Sabaeans and Jews through the Essenes, Nazarenes, Mandaeans, Ebionites and Elchasites. Jesus sought to unite these early faiths. His reforming message was carried into Asia by Thomas and into Europe by Mary, Martha, Lazarus and Paul. The Brethren would be feared by inquisitors as *the most dangerous of all heretics, because the most ancient* and because *they live justly before men and believe aright concerning God.* [Reinerius]

These people were the real defenders of the faith on Europe's frontier. Had they not been destroyed by inquisitions of their Catholic and Orthodox "brethren" – they might have maintained a barrier to Islam crossing into Europe. Some of their holy books were the *Shepherd of Hermas* ... the *Nazarene Bible* ... the *Didache* ... and many of their works are still unacceptable to the churches of icon and sacrament.

Mehmed and his ancestors knew better than to offer these people a choice between the sword and the *Koran* – for these were the original People of the Book from whom Muhammad had learned the Jewish and Christian scriptures. A much better policy would be to hold them to their own Holy Book and the poll tax.

Unfortunately, these people treated so badly by Orthodoxy and Catholicism trusted no one, refusing all treaties. This freedom from foreign entanglements left them the frequent object of plunder. The Sultan now planned to put this house in order and to induce them to pay the poll tax.

In a few days, we captured their worthwhile fortresses and destroyed the rest. When the capital of Yaitsa did not surrender to siege, Mehmed engaged in divide-and-conquer, informing the populace what would happen if we had to bleed to take them. In secret, the townspeople sent messengers to surrender. Their ruler, upon learning of this, attempted to escape. We caught and executed him.

The Sultan allowed the people to stay in their city. He gave them presents, stationed a garrison of janissary there, and informed them of the annual poll tax. Their request? Religious freedom. The Sultan granted it; and with that, we went on to capture 300 more towns.

Here is the proclamation by which the Bosnians obtained their desired religious freedom:

> *I, The Sultan Khan, The Conqueror, hereby declare to the whole world that the Bosnian Franciscans granted with this Firman are under my protection and I hereby command:*
> *No one shall disturb or harm these people or their churches!*
> *They shall live in peace in my state. ...*
> *No one shall insult, place in danger nor attack the lives, properties or churches of these people! ...*
> *By declaring this Firman, I swear on my Sword by the Holy Name of Allah who created Heaven and Earth, Allah's Prophet Muhammad, and the 124,000 former prophets, that none of my citizens will behave contrary to this Firman!*

While this declaration, which I view as the greatest victory of my Ottoman years, was legal under Shariat law, it was not without its detractors and controversy. For while there is a certain acceptability to People of the Book (being Sabaeans, Jews and Christians), there are also verses of the *Koran* saying "Do not take my enemies and your enemies as friends." And the concept of freedom is highly suspect anyway – for, to put it simply, "Islam is submission."

Istanbul, 1463

Upon my return to Istanbul, I learned that in drafting this document for the Sultan I had "innovated in religion." I knew that Caesars such as Constantine the Great and Julian had signed such documents; the Prophet Muhammad had granted one for the monastery of St. Catherine in the Sinai; and the Caliph Muktafi II of Baghdad granted one to the Nestorians in 1138. The real issue at hand was that I had intruded too far into the prerogatives and expertise of the 99th Orta and its conservative Sheikh (not my friend the old Sufi mystic).

I was to be given a hundred lashes; I would give a pound of flesh (my tattoo was to be cut off); I was to be drummed out of the Corps; and I was to be shunned. No provision was made as to how or when or if I might leave. Simply I was to don a new aspect of disgrace, akin perhaps to the *sambenito* with its illustrations of Hell that you force heretics to wear following their conviction by the Inquisition.

I could look at my prospects as if my star had fallen from the heavens. Or I could see myself as an arrow of God's quiver finally drawn and released. I took the whipping without complaint, though skin cleaved from bone in a few places. I watched as the 99th *Çorbacı* sliced the tattoo away with his dagger. They took my horse, my *kılıç*, my bow, my turban and uniform. I was given the shirt and trousers of a peasant and I was told to depart the council.

Perhaps they wanted me begging around the gates of the city as a cautionary tale against the pride of youth, but I did not plan to give them the satisfaction. I began to think again of taking my boat to freedom – only ten years late! First, I would need to heal and I would need some money.

I grabbed a torch and applied it to my arm in front of the chaplains. Cautery is an illegal healing treatment with Moslems – prohibited by the Prophet himself – but it works. Some looked away in disgust. Others, clearly agitated, threw stones until I collapsed.

When I came to, later that hot summer evening, I stole away to the only place I could think of where I would not be placing anyone in danger – Yasin's shed where he cured the wood and aged the drying bows. I laid on the floor bleeding and breathing in the familiar smells of nature's gentle bounty being hardened into something new and dangerous. I would have enjoyed a skin of *boza* or *raki* about now, but I had only my pain.

My grandfather the Megadux came to me that night in a dream. "If you would heal our wounds, you must get out," he said. "The West has seen Mehmed act, but the kingdoms with whom he treats believe themselves safe. Not one is safe! Find the key actor in Europe and warn him, no matter what it takes. The Sultan believes himself the Mahdi, a reincarnation of Muhammad. He will not stop until he slays

Christianity or it slays him! As for you, trust the Woman, trust the Word, and trust the Sword."

Half awake now, I remember wondering to what woman he could possibly be referring.

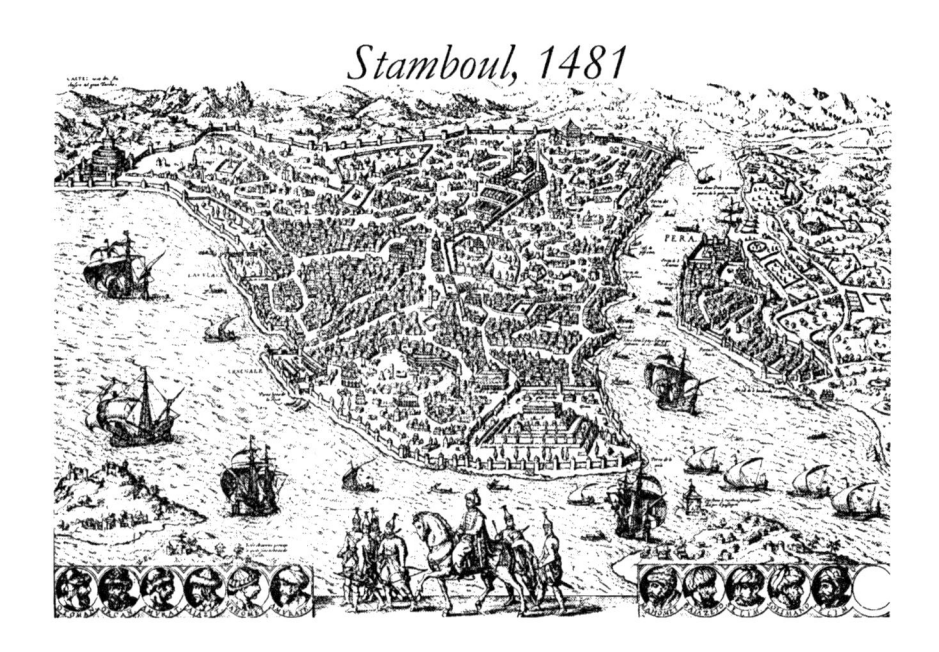

Stamboul, 1481

Mehmed's plan for the rebuilding and repopulation of Byzantium.

Chapter Seventeen

Who can find a virtuous woman? for her price is far above rubies.
Proverbs 31:10

He taketh away the first, that he may establish the second. Hebrews 10:9

Istanbul, 1463

The old man found me stretched out on the floor the next morning. Some of my wounds ripped open where they had stuck to the floorboards. Yasin had heard of my plight and said I could stay in his place above the shop as long as I wanted. I told him I did not think that would be an option – that the *ulema* would be looking to cause trouble for anyone taking me in. "In that case," he said, "what do you propose?"

I replied, "For now, I would like to stay here in the shed. Nobody will look for me here. Before I leave, I will need a favor: In the *Büyük Saray* – the old Great Palace – there is a gallery near the front of the Great Triclinium. On the side of that gallery is a niche where it looks like the statue of a saint or an emperor once stood. If the stack of balls is still located on the other side of the gallery, place one in the center of the pedestal. This will unlock a section of wall about five feet to the left. Otherwise, you can use a dagger in one hand while working the wall with the other. Give it a shove and the latch will stay open. Go down the steps – take a torch with you – and you will find a storeroom.

Take only the small box about a cubit long beneath the shelf in the farthest corner on the right. If you cannot find it, see if you can reach a scribe in the *Saray* named Kreshnik and tell him *Yay Burcu* needs his box. If the admiral wants to help, tell him I would like to reach a Venetian merchantman named Doria if he still sails out of the Neorion. If you see Ahmed, tell him I could use a horse, a dagger, a wineskin, a bedroll and some proper clothing. He is the right size ... and thank you! I really had no place else to turn."

I stayed with the old man nearly three weeks. He gave me a war bow, a holster for it, a full quiver, a *sipar* and thumb ring. I packed them in a bedroll. He brought me the blade of the Caesars and I honed it and made a new sheath. The old man had long kept for me the leather bag the janissaries had issued me as a boy, where I kept my little book of quotes and had saved up a few dozen gold pieces in hopes of one day leaving the Imperial City. Disgraced though I was, I was ready to seek my fortune. I had really done all I could do within the constraints of Islam and I had definitely worn out my welcome. It was high time to warn the West and work the other side of the ideological fence.

One afternoon, Admiral Baltaoglu and Ahmed showed up with an Arabian horse in tow. Arrangements had been made. I could board the boat that night and be in Venice in two weeks. The admiral had written me a letter of passage to get me past the guards in my old adopted name "John Emanuelis." The only hitch would be if I were recognized as an escaped slave (by either side). Depending on where I was in Italy, I could end up deported! The Sultan was negotiating with everyone to keep control of everyone here and at the same time keep everyone elsewhere off-balance.

There would also be a layover at Piraeus Harbor in Athens for a day or two. We decided my cover story would be that I was a messenger for the Doge of Venice. This required a bit of ingenuity in the way of clothes – an Italian hat, pointy boots, hose, and a doublet (which would no doubt raise eyebrows among the janissaries). I believe we effected it rather well.

I swear it looked like a cloak pulled around a short dress! "Two weeks with sailors?," I asked Captain Doria. "You'll be fine," he laughed. Worse, they told me I had to shave and cut my hair! Were I any prettier when they were through, I would have attracted soldiers! The idea of spending any time in Piraeus Harbor in such a get-up made me more nervous than a novice in a monastery. I practiced looking stern and hoped I could maintain my imposture. The captain passed me a packet of mails he was carrying. "Might as well act the part if you're going to look like that!" Everyone laughed but me.

The Admiral hugged me, gently clapped my back, gave me the customary two kisses and slipped me a bag of coins. Ahmed laughed, told me he could escort me as far as Athens if I desired, "Always ready to help a damsel in distress!" More laughs. Yasin gave me a hug and, always the bowyer, told me "Don't forget how to shoot!" More laughs.

At the last minute, Jason showed up with a wineskin full of *boza* and a warning to lay low for a time, no matter where I went. "They're looking for you," he said. "They've realized you know more about this place than they do. You would do well to be dead for awhile." I asked him, "So ... do you think they'll be searching for me in clothes like this?" He smiled and replied, "Only if they want a date!" More laughs. My embarrassment was now complete. With that, the captain said he had to leave and suggested I not to be too long. Ahmed came along to see me to the boat.

They say the Lord protects children and fools. Were that not the case, I would long ago have been dead and forgotten. On the way to the port, we came across a wagon with a casket and a woman dressed in Italian clothes. One of my Palaeologus cousins had "gone native" with the Moslems and his first wife decided to return to Italy when their son died. Aside from the obvious tragedy, she had some vague story of something having happened between her and her husband, which I am certain came to nothing more than her inability to deal with the Moslem four-wives rule. But here I was being presented an opportunity for a double cover story – one for Istanbul port authorities and one for the Italians. If she wanted her honor back, I would oblige!

That day I learned one of those terrible lessons in life I am sure mothers only whisper to daughters of a certain age: "If you cannot marry for love, then marry for security!" We picked up a Book of the Family at the local parish and filled it out with my birth name as if we had been married for a few years. I paid the priest to "retake our vows" and stamp the book, explaining we had lost the old one and could not afford documentation problems with port security. That it was "A matter of life and death" – true enough. And so it was done.

I now had a ready-made family with a woman I knew could have children – and this was important to me for stupid dynastic reasons that should not have mattered, but somehow did. It felt wrong at one level, but at the time, I justified it to myself, saying it was no worse than the usual arranged marriages of aristocracy ... or the manner in which I had been born!

If I could make Venice, I was sure I could care for her. I remember thinking I had no idea what sort of wife she might be. In youth, a man hopes for four things from a woman – sex, respect, children, and virtue (in roughly that order). Genuine affection may become important much later – and social consideration or economics hardly enter into it at all. Right now, she was the least of my worries. I had janissaries to avoid and a boat to catch! I tied my horse to the back of the wagon and took my grieving wife and departed son to the boat. The crew cast off, hoisted sails, and we departed as the sun cast a long ray from the direction of the one whose memory I had just betrayed.

Venice, 1463

Athens proved uneventful. I bought wedding bands at the Plaka, the bazaar at the foot of the Acropolis not far from the theater of Dionysius. For the most part, the weather had been nice and the sailing smooth. We avoided Italian and Turkish and Catalan corsairs (so I imagine Captain Doria was either lucky or paid up in all the right accounts). Only my horse and the corpse of our deceased son were the worse for wear.

I spent two weeks getting to know my wife, the former Andrea Thalassino. She was the attractive and lively only daughter of an Italian sea merchant family, raised with a Catholic upbringing, and who simply could not abide a husband taking multiple wives. She possessed a deep reserve and a greater inner beauty and sweetness than met the eye. I decided that if she had tossed her fate in with mine, I owed her the Truth about any questions she might have. I can tell you I suffered greatly as she took me through the mental gymnastics of how I had brought myself to serve the Antichrist for 10 years and even save his miserable life! In this, she bit harder than the wolf and dug deeper than the *Çorbacı* with his dagger.

I love a person with strong opinions, but if you stir them up, talking to them can be less pleasant than falling victim to their punishment. I think she eventually understood my vision, but was too committed a Catholic to believe that peace might one day be possible between Jews, Christians and Moslems. For that matter, she said she had been mighty optimistic marrying an Orthodox renegade! It is funny how necessity will weaken one's absolutism.

Arriving the city of the Doge, we buried young Demetrius at the parish closest to the harbor. Had he lived, he might have been the Prince of Lemnos. That honor would now fall to another child of his father's new Great Lady.

I would go looking for Aunt Anna. I had no faith in my real mother Caterina and wanted no more to do with her now than she had to do with me in Constantinople. I imagined her somewhere nearby, ruining the life of a perfectly good gentleman with her selfishness and lack of patience or virtue. I remember praying to the Father that my wife would prove a better mother for my children than the one I had been given; and I imagined Andrea praying to the Mother hoping I would not prove a spawn of weakness like her former husband. My prospects at the moment must have seemed gloomy. Still, she had saved my life, and I would do what I could to become a decent husband.

Chapter Eighteen

And it shall come to pass in the last days, saith God, I will pour out of my Spirit upon all flesh: and your sons and your daughters shall prophesy, and your young men shall see visions, and your old men shall dream dreams.
Acts 2:17

Piazza San Marco, 1463

Since I did not know Aunt Anna's new address (she was having a villa built somewhere in the Castello neighborhood), I instead looked in on Constantine. Cardinal Bessarion had taken him under his wing, but instead of sponsoring him into the clergy at Rome, one of the brethren involved the young man in the military, grooming him as a *capitaneus urbis*, a minor noble with some power in the city.

This would do a couple of things for the Phatria, I imagine. It involved them in a new sphere of influence; and they could use it to penetrate other aspects of the Empire and the Vatican. The latter, of course, might present risks. I mean, I would not want to have young Constantine's looks in that neighborhood! Some there were like Zaganos or Mehmed – ranked high enough to where they no longer felt the need for discretion.

I asked him about the manuscripts I had sent. He said they were being copied in Bessarion's scriptorium in Rome, but that I could have them back as soon as first copies were rendered. I agreed. My long-term plan for them was to have them printed using one of the new Gutenberg presses. If possible, I wanted them in a language other than Latin. That dead language may be acceptable to Churchmen, but it is not one that affects how real people think. He said the books would be another few months. In the meantime, if I would consider accepting the copies when they were finished, the Cardinal was prepared to pay for the originals. I said that would be most acceptable. He replied, "In that case, we should make a trip to Rome fairly soon."

He showed me the courtyard where he and his friends trained at fencing. Europe no longer seems to believe in heavy blades. Now everyone is more interested in thrusting than slicing, in parrying than severing, in dancing than fighting. I figured that if I had to dress like one of these people, I would have to learn to act like one as well. We practiced rapier and short sword in our doublets and hose – and I remember feeling pathetic. It seemed to me that the big difference between men and women in this town was the length of their hair – though by now I found my friends had lied. Short beards and moustache were still in fashion. In shaving me, I hoped my jokester friends were just helping with the disguise.

Constantine initially thrashed me. Fencing is quicker and more subtle than what I had learned on the field of battle. All my movements designed for a heavier blade were too wide and too slow and it took a couple of rounds before I could use both hands to good effect. We discussed where I could find my aunt. Afterward, he wanted to thank me for saving his life. He proposed we go out drinking. I used my wife back in the tavern as an excuse. You should have heard him! I made my apologies and promised to see him within a week.

Castello, 1463

Andrea and I found my Aunt Anna as the finishing touches were being made to her new villa. She was the person in the family who had been the greatest beneficiary of my grandfather's foreign investments. She was quickly becoming the great patroness of the Greek community in exile. Grandpa had clearly foreseen what was coming.

"Hippolyta, my Queen of the Amazons, so good to see you again!" I said, bowing deeply. She laughed and then scowled. "My young Hercules, I shall have my girdle back now, if you don't mind!" Andrea looked at the two of us as though we were crazy. "Aunt Anna, I present my wife, Andrea Thalassino Palaeologina." Anna kissed us and laughed through her tears (crying, I imagine, because while she knew my family secret, she was happy and surprised to hear me using my real name; because Uncle George and her sister had kept her from having the same surname; and because she was genuinely glad to see me alive). "Come in, come in. Where have you been staying? Tell me everything: how you lived, how you escaped, and if we can bear it ... the last days of my father and brothers." There were more tears, in which I joined her, and we held each other.

We talked for hours, stayed for dinner and I explained our situation. She graciously offered us a place in her villa for as long as we stayed in Venice. "It will be wonderful to have family again," she said. "Caterina has found herself a rich husband and doesn't visit often. Now it is just me and visitors from church. I had a chapel installed in one of the wings. The authorities have yet to approve our plans for a proper Orthodox church. One day it will happen. If you stay, you are bound to run into old friends."

So in no time, we had a place to live, friends nearby, a community, and a base of operations from which to begin the second front of my plan. My only reservation was that I knew the Sultan's agents would be about – looking for anyone who might aspire to the throne of Constantinople ... and perhaps for an escaped slave who knew too much. I would be careful.

Rome, 1463

A few weeks later, after we had settled in and the ladies were comfortable with each other, I left Andrea with Aunt Anna and rode to Rome with Constantine. Altogether, it was about a four-day trip. We visited his patron Cardinal Bessarion in his palace, which he had turned into what must have been the new Academy for the Phatria (who, of course, would no longer be known by a secular-sounding pagan name). Since Bessarion was the new-styled Latin Patriarch of Greece, I imagine the brethren might be called a reincarnation of the "Constantinian Angelican Order of Holy Wisdom" or something similar. I understand the group's special devotion had to do with Saint Andrew, my Uncle Thomas having presented the relics to Pius II in 1461.

The Cardinal had a good number of scholars engaged in translating, copying, teaching and illustrating. He was the foremost Greek in the world at the time and certainly one of the great fathers of the Renaissance. He did not have much time to talk, but gave us free rein of his scriptorium. It was wonderful to be surrounded by smart people who cared about ideas and who were unconcerned from whence they came or whether they were based on Scripture. I soon learned that the same phenomenon had been going on in Florence for a year, with even less concern for political or theological correctness.

One of the things that we, the expatriate community of Greeks in Italy, wanted to do was open up a conversation with the world. The world of the past five centuries or so had forgotten so much, thanks to the Churches drawing smaller and smaller circles on what was considered intellectually, politically or spiritually acceptable to discuss. The Great Schism had set up prejudices to overcome as well. Like their Orthodox brethren, the Latin Churchmen had long ago gotten into the habit of burning books and condemning individuals and groups for anything that disagreed with their traditions. In this way, Christianity – both Eastern and Western – had imposed heavy shackles on its mind. This decadent age of the churches will be the perfect time to begin breaking free of this mind-killing habit.

The Canon was a house of knowledge with half the shelves empty. The books were almost never in the popular language. Half the books were reserved for the exclusive use of the librarians and the other half contained references, acronyms or symbols intended solely for the initiated.

Give any group of mutually anointed experts (theocratic or secular) a couple of centuries and they will arrive at the same point of senility. Truth requires freedom, and an official Faith can tolerate neither! Eons ago, Prometheus and Orpheus suffered at the hands of the gods for bringing humanity knowledge. Not much has changed.

Thankfully, the world does not go ignorant all at once, despite our periodic destructions of libraries and people. Arabia and Spain could still remember nearly everything the great classical scholars had ever said. Perhaps I exaggerate, but generally, in the West there was a tremendous need for a revival of learning, a need for vernacular editions of the old works, and a need to overcome intellectual prejudices. Even the *Bible*, rich in allegory and double entendre and arcane symbology, had been purged of valuable materials and was now being treated as though it were a literal document. Finally, at least at Rome and Florence, the Light of Truth might burn again!

I rode away from Rome a happier man and a richer one. We had reached a price on my manuscripts. God bless Kreshnik!

Venice, 1464

The following spring, we had our first child, a daughter we called Diana after Andrea's mother and my stepmother. The baby had my mother's blue eyes and blond hair, both of which were quite popular at the time in both our Greek and Italian communities. Many women wore wigs to effect light-colored hair. I was happy for my mother in the baby having that Notaras family resemblance. While my mother had nothing to do with how I had grown up, I recognized (with some prompting from my aunt and wife) that we were still family, for better or for worse. Her husband, from old aristocracy, seemed a good man. Having few relatives, they very much enjoyed visiting us as grandparents.

How does a man describe his daughter? She was quite simply the prettiest little girl I ever saw. Were I in the habit of placing women on pedestals, hers would be the highest. Diana was articulate from a very young age. I suspect this was because her mother spoke to her incessantly! She was curious about everything, incredibly neat, playful and happy. She could coolly strategize or explode in emotion as the situation dictated. She was a great judge of character, and would quickly shun or accept a person. If it is possible to inherit a portion of one's soul or personality, then I am sure she picked up the very best mix of my traits and Andrea's. Raising children was the most rewarding thing I ever did and the greatest tragedy I ever suffered. As much as I enjoyed staying home and playing, there were other things I had set out to do that sometimes tore me away.

Cardinal Bessarion had come to town at the end of the previous year and I was briefing him on the ways of Mehmed. The cardinal was enthused about the prospect of a Crusade, something he had long advocated. The kings of Europe, however, were hesitant to expend blood and treasure taking on Mehmed's huge army. As long as the cancer did not grow too fast, they would be content to allow Europe to remain ill as they filled their coffers and pursued their narrow interests. This is a problem with a dominant power surrounded by lots of small players. The latter may wait too long to address their mutual problem, vastly raising the cost of restoring balance to the world.

I laid out for the cardinal the Ottoman order of battle. I told him of the spy network. I discussed the importance of the growing fleet. We talked about Muhammadan law as it pertains to slavery and booty. We talked about how the Sultan conquered Constantinople, how he mobilized, how he worked logistics, and how he combined land and sea forces in his campaign of conquest. Bessarion was a quick study. By the time he joined Pope Pius II at Ancona to mark the launch of the next Crusade, he knew Mehmed as well as anyone could.

Unfortunately, troops began deserting at the port when the Venetian fleet was delayed; and the Pope suddenly took ill and died. *Cui bono?* Ah yes, that would be the Sultan. I hoped I was no longer the only one who would note such strategic coincidences.

On another occasion, the Cardinal introduced me to a good copyist in the San Polo neighborhood who had access to the quality paper supplies for which Venice was famous and for which export was prohibited. This policy would make Venice a center for scholarship once we began printing – because presses and letter carvers would come here for the paper and shipping. Venice had replaced Constantinople as the capital of world commerce.

I discussed with Aunt Anna the possibility of investing in the new printing industry. She said she would wait until Greek letters were cut for the presses. She noted that such an enterprise would be a good way to meld Byzantine knowledge and Renaissance ideas. Meanwhile, I began using copyists for my projects. A good book of Plato cost at least 10 gold ducats. In a few years, with printing presses, we might produce the same book for 2 ducats. Since the Council of Florence, there was an increasing demand for classics like the works of Plato. There were also local perennial favorites like Dante and Petrarch.

Speaking of Dante, I may have had something to do with your country's discovery of the New World. One day I was down by the harbor – I still enjoyed listening to the tales of sailors and the news they brought from abroad – and I ran into an intelligent young man with apparently the same hobby, whose fascination was for tales of Atlantis. Knowing Plato, I began talking to him and he seemed to know quite a few of the other legends and prophecies associated with that continent, as well as some of the references of ancient geographers related to the distance around the world and navigation.

He was beginning to keep a small *florilegium* quoting such things. He told me what he most fervently desired was to find the route and location of that faraway land. As you know, this has long been debated. I suggested he consult Dante's Canto II of the *Paradiso*. I told him my interpretation of the passage was that if one followed the Tropic of Cancer from the Ganges River in India west to the opposite point of the globe, one would run into the Mount of Purgatory, another name for Atlantis. He apparently had not read the passage in quite that way.

> *Now had the sun to that horizon reach'd,*
> *That covers, with the most exalted point*
> *Of its meridian circle, Salem's walls;*
> *And night, that opposite to him her orb*
> *Rounds, from the stream of Ganges issued forth,*
> *Holding the scales, that from her hands are dropt*
> *When she reigns highest: so that where I was,*
> *Aurora's white and vermeil-tinctured cheek*
> *To orange turn'd as she in age increased.*

He was fascinated, noting that the time to make the trip would be in the late summer to early fall, based on the reference to Libra. This, of course, is exactly what Admiral Columbus would do in the very year the Old World was scheduled to die by the Byzantine reckoning.

This matched something the young man from Genoa said he had found in Seneca:

> *There will come an era in the End of Time when Ocean will loosen the bonds of the world and the Earth reveal her vastness. Tethys will disclose new worlds and Thule will no longer be the most distant realm.* Seneca, Medea

I remember thinking that this boy was like Jesus – a young man driven to fulfill ancient prophecy, though in his case the prophets were secular. When Atlantis was rediscovered in 1492, people would barely remember Dante's dream. Yet, I am sure his vision was essential to the discovery.

What is not generally known about Dante is that he may have been a pastor or leader of a group descended from one of the most primitive Christian traditions – one in which even Jesus was probably viewed as an innovator. The hint comes in a vision Dante's mother had before his birth and from several references in Boccaccio's biography of him where Dante is likened to a shepherd, where he is observed under a laurel (the Tree of Phoebus Apollo), and where he is transfigured into an angel resembling a peacock (a bird sacred to the Essenes, Mandaeans, Buddhists and the Yezidis of Babylon). Elsewhere, he also made negative references to the Albigensians – all of which to me suggests his sympathies lay with the Waldensians or an even more primitive sect of Christianity.

Appropriate to that ancient tradition, in the final chapter of Boccaccio's *Life of Dante*, the great writer is 'apotheosized' as we would say in the tradition of the Great Church – 'deified' in the Catholic sense of saints, as Bernard of Clairvaux described it. Unless I am greatly mistaken, Boccaccio regarded Dante as Eusebius had regarded Constantine the Great – as an incarnation of the Christ, for he concludes with a curious remark:

> *To Him, with all the humility and devotion and affection that I possess, I render not such thanks as are deserved, but such as I can give, blessing forever His name and worth.* Boccaccio, Life of Dante

It was not until much later, the winter solstice of 1492 to be exact, when I realized the meaning of my conversation on the docks and how it related to my vision of a time and place where the values of Greece and Rome might once again be realized. Europe would not learn of the New World for another three months, but on that day the Sun rose at the head of the Sign of the Bowman, I woke up knowing the young sailor from Genoa shared the dream and was making it come true.

That morning, I realized that part of God's plan for this world is for us to reach across the sea and establish a land where the freedom of Jerusalem (or at least her freedom of religion) will reign once again. As 1492 drew to a close, a year my ancestors had thought would be the end of the world, I realized this dream must and will be fulfilled before the next Great Transformation, for it is written: *From the East I will bring your seed, and from the West I will gather you.* Isaiah 43:5

For a time, Venice was a magical place and time in our lives. Unfortunately, it would not be long before God would again punish me and I would detect the long reach of His Shadow.

Chapter Nineteen

They praised the God of their fathers, because He had given them freedom and liberty. ^{1 Esdras 4:62}

There is truth in poetic fictions, and it must be glimpsed through tiny chinks. ^{Plutarch, My Secret Book}

Castello, 1467

I worked with Aunt Anna for her Orthodox chapel to be a success. It was the leading center for Greek expatriates in the city. Among the men, I instituted a club of sorts (these being quite popular in the better circles of Venice). We had about 50 members in which we began to discuss the symbols, legends and traditions whereby we might communicate the glory of Greece and Rome to future generations. We needed a patron saint.

Over the years, Christianity's veneration of saints had become confused. First, there were far more than anyone could possibly remember. Second, some of them were obvious Christianizations of earlier pagan folklore. (Saints Dionysius, Jupiter and Hermes come to mind.) Third, they revolved around a corrupt trade in relics whereby there might be multiple right index fingers or heads of the same saint in various parts of Europe. Whatever we used as our symbol would have to signify what we had lost to the Ottomans. Ideally, it could serve as a goal for our personal lives. In a perfect world, it would even unveil a cosmic truth that religion had buried too deep in the doctrine to find.

To my mind, there were really only three choices: St. Michael, St. James or St. George. Michael was an angel to the Moslems and heretics, so did not seem the best choice. St. James, as *Santiago el Mayor*, was the saint of the Reconquista in Spain, but his icon is merely war personified. No, the obvious choice for us was the one for which

Constantine the Great had been the archetype, though he had named the Order after a knight reportedly martyred in Palestine.

The symbol of the Hero and the Dragon is a constant in the annals of humanity, famous since at least the time of the Sumerians and their stories of the battle against Tiamat, which later became the story of Leviathan in the *Bible* and probably the story of the Hydra in Greek mythology. Just as the True Cross that Bessarion presented to the *Scuola di Santa Maria dei Battuti della Carita* symbolized the Golden Legend and the victory of Christ over death, we saw the Saint and Dragon as our symbol for the contest of Good vs. Evil, Truth against Power, and one day, the Greeks freeing themselves from Ottoman oppression.

To the various myths of St. George we added other stories. For example, from my family coat of arms came the legend of Constantine XI, my father, as a once-and-future king who would rise from his tomb beside the Saint Romano Gate to retake Constantinople. That an angel would revive him and hand him his sword. That a hero would arise from a secret door in one of the old churches of Constantinople. There were variations on the theme, but our purpose was to encourage Greeks to remember Magna Graecia, an era when Greek colonies stretched from the eastern shore of the Black Sea to Calabrian Italy, Alban France, Celtiberian Spain and Hyperborean Britain.

At this point, we were not really a reestablishment of the Order of St. George, though my friend Constantine would soon carry the club in that direction for the movement to go out-of-town or underground. Bessarion warned us that the Council of Ten was talking about the club as a threat to "good order and the unification of the churches." You see, the delusion yet lived!

At about the same time, I am pretty sure I saw Zaganos twice, once in the streets of Castello and once on the wooden bridge as we passed beneath what is now the Ponte di Rialto! It was also becoming obvious that Aunt Anna's chapel community was being infiltrated by non-Greeks. One day I spotted a young Serb I vaguely remembered from *Teshkilat-i Mahsusa* (the Special Organization). I did not know if they were looking for the lost *Yay Burcu*, but I was certain they would be looking for any Palaeologus who could one day pose a threat to Mehmed's dynasty. For the safety of all my family, I resolved to leave.

I was in the middle of leaving manuscripts for copying with Aunt Anna, and turning over the club to Constantine, meeting with Bessarion and packing things when our little princess came down with a fever and the big black swellings began. I tried doing what my adopted mother had done for me, but it was no use. Maybe there was some trick she had not told me – some herb or spell or lancing of the buboes or prayer.

I prayed to God and told him if he needed a soul to please take mine and not my little girl's. I was afraid to let her sleep. My baby promised that it was okay, that we would see each other again. She said she saw the angels and she would ask Jesus and his Mother to watch over me.

My little girl died in my lap, holding my hand and telling me not to cry. Andrea had spent a good deal of time at Mass, burning candles and praying. I was destroyed, yet our three-year-old's passing devastated Andrea for exactly one day – it was my 23rd saint's day when Diana left us. We took her to the harbor parish and buried her next to her half-brother.

Andrea's faith was unshaken, which is much better than I can say for mine. While I have always been content for the dead in their being free of this life of pain and problems, I have never accustomed myself to the idea that children need to suffer or die. It just seems unfair – unfair to them in not being able to accomplish the task they had set out for their souls ... and unfair to the rest of us in having to live without them.

The next day Andrea told me she had dreamt of the Virgin, who expressed sorrow at our loss and promised us a son exactly one year later. I was glad Andrea was taking this all so well, but now I was ready to leave. My joy with Venice had died with our baby.

My soul was in terrible agony until the following evening when I looked up and saw a giant comet. I cannot explain how I felt, but somehow I knew God understood my pain and forgave me for doubting.

The next day, we loaded up a wagon and headed out. Constantine came along as our armed escort and guide. We journeyed to Florence carrying an introductory letter from Bessarion to Piero de' Medici. If classicism was going to have an impact on the world, it would need a home with a bit more joy and freedom. I was ready for a change.

Chapter Twenty

Nor is our religion new, or of a late date; but, from the Creation of this beautiful fabric of the world thou hast instituted this religion with due observance of Thy Deity. Eusebius, Vita Constantini

I am seized with an admiration of the Emperor's great knowledge; in regard by Divine inspiration he expressed these very things in paint, which the words of the prophets had declared before concerning that same beast, saying, "That God would unsheathe a great and terrible sword against the Dragon, the Serpent that flees, and would slay the Dragon that is in the sea." Eusebius, Vita Constantini

Florence, 1467

Greek expatriates had found Firenze receptive since the days when Boccaccio used stories of Homer to populate his *Genealogy of the Gentile Gods*. In the century that had passed, more and more Greeks found their way home to the city-state of the Medici family. Emanuel Chrysolaras had made disciples of the city's leaders; and they, in turn, supported the gathering of Greek wisdom as the Turks and Moslems advanced on Europe.

The city's first family was the great advocate for the revival of Platonic thought. Old Cosimo de' Medici himself, sponsor of the Council of Florence in 1439 and then an auditor of Plethon's lectures, opened his palace as the center of the universe for Renaissance science, art and literature. With the possible exception of the Vatican, his family was the greatest economic power behind gathering ancient wisdom and art in our time.

Cosimo, who was Piero's father and Lorenzo's grandfather, had invested in the education of Marcilio Ficino, his physician's son, with an eye to one day opening an Academy like Plethon's and having works of Plato in a language he could read. By the time Cosimo died in 1464,

Ficino had helped him achieve his dream. The ideas of the Phatria were now being discussed in Rome and Florence as they once had been in Constantinople and Mystras. Through translations, copyists and printing, the voices of Plato, Plotinus, Proclus, and Pythagoras would return from the dead to trouble courts and clergy all the way to Britain!

The first thing we did upon arriving in Florence was take the tour. The Medici family knew Constantine for his having procured for them a number of copied manuscripts from Bessarion's collection. Ever anxious for ancient wisdom in any language, on any subject, and at just about any price, Piero sent us his youngest son, 14-year-old Giuliano, to be our guide despite Constantine's familiarity with the city.

Andrea was most impressed by the *Basilica della Santissima Annunziata*, a favorite church of the Medici. As at Rome, I was most impressed by the new Academy, which Cosimo had established at his gardened villa in nearby Careggi. Following the tour, we headed to the palace to see what Piero had to say and to see if he might let us take up residence in his city.

Several well-known Greek writers and professors now lived in Florence. I believe the only restriction was against people who "might stir up trouble," usually by being members of a politically active confraternity. In that light, I was not sure how to refer to my past. I might be aristocracy, but I was also an escaped slave and someone the most powerful man on Earth might wish to see deported. (Mehmed had an extradition agreement with Florence.)

Andrea visited with Piero's wife, the poet Lucrezia Tornabuoni, while Constantine and I went to visit Piero, who spent much of his time in bed with gout and arthritis. The unfortunate man with the inflamed knees, hands and ankles was even referred to as *il Gottoso*.

Piero nodded to Constantine as we entered, saying only "Captain Comnenus." My friend replied, "Excellency, I present to you John Palaeologus della Morea." Piero was lounging in a huge ornately carved chair and did not (or perhaps could not) rise. Nonetheless, he extended his hand and, as warned, I took it gently and bowed. I handed Piero the sealed letter and hoped for the best.

"Brother Bessarion!" remarked the sick man. "He says you're a child of Athens. Do you know your way home little brother?" I replied, "I long to see Olympus and the four stars, but I have yet to see True North. These are mysteries to me. Good thing the Lord made our souls immortal – so we might have the time to one day understand His Creation." Piero laughed, "That's a tall order for any man! So how might I help you?"

"We are looking for a healthier place to raise our next child. We lost our daughter to Plague in Venice. My wife Andrea is expecting at the end of June. The cardinal may also have mentioned that while quite young, I was in the interrupted last class of the Academy at Constantinople, or that I was helpful in procuring him some old manuscripts. One day, I would like to open a printing operation and perhaps apply one of the new presses to the works of Plato, Diodorus or Tacitus. I know there will be a market for such things."

Piero gave me one of those looks a banker might use to size up a client in need of a loan. "You look too young to be raising a family. However, it is my family's dream to form the best library anywhere. I would be happy for you to stay on as guests of my court until you are situated. If you can procure old manuscripts, I'll advance you a thousand ducats, and when you return I'll pay you 20 ducats apiece for any work I don't already own; 30 for anything illustrated; 50 for anything longer than a tome; and 500 for any original from the time of Constantine the Great or earlier. When you return, you can copy anything in my collection for publishing. While you're off on your search for manuscripts, I will take care of your family's expenses. So what do you say? Would that be agreeable?"

I thanked him profusely, though I was concerned about where I might go for more old works. Would Mehmed have my neck if I returned to Istanbul? Would I end up a galley slave? However, the worries of youth are fleeting. There would be time later for safe professions. I wanted to feel alive; and while sitting with expatriates in Venice or a court in Florence was the perfect situation for my proper wife, I needed something more active. In Florence, one was not considered an adult until age 30. I still had seven years left in which to forgivably play the fool.

One day we were having dinner with the Medici and members of the court when Piero turned to me and asked that I tell of St. George and his Order. Until this point, I had a few friends whose conversation I found fascinating, such as Ficino (about 11 years my senior) or Piero's eldest son Lorenzo (about five years my junior but with several more years of good tutors and the new Academy behind him). I otherwise kept to myself. However, if a story was to be the price of our meal, I was more than happy to oblige. I relate it now because you might find it of interest. Parts of it you probably know.

Saint George was a Roman knight from Cappadocia. He was assigned to Libya, near a place called Sylene, which had a small lake inhabited by a giant reptile. The beast had grown so large that it had begun to wander the countryside in search for food.

It was so quick and ferocious that none dared to face it. The townspeople resolved to feed it to keep it near the lake. Every few days, they would leave it an animal in the hope that this would be enough to keep it from going into the town and snatching people or livestock. Things went like this for a long time. After all, how many towns can boast of their own dragon? Well, one day, the people leading sacrifices to the lake no longer returned. The reptile had developed a taste for people.

The elders of the town decided there should be a lottery. "No matter one's station in life" one's child would be delivered when his or her name came up. The town was large enough to where one child each week "would make little difference." One day, the name of the princess was called out and the king was greatly grieved. He said he was sorry, but he could not bear to lose his daughter. He wept, "Take my gold, my silver, my precious stones, but do not take the only heir to my throne."

Well, you can imagine how the townspeople reacted, for they had lost more than a hundred children by this same law enacted by this same king – a law he now refused to apply to himself. "Give us your daughter," they shouted, "or we will destroy you and all your house."

Then the king met in sorrow with his daughter, explaining that his great regret was that he would never meet the man of her dreams, never see her betrothed, never live to see heirs. He asked the people for a reprieve of eight days that he might prepare her for her fate and the people granted it.

So the king ordered brought out the finest linens and silver and foods and held a banquet, as if the princess was to be married. He embraced her and kissed her and gave her his blessings. Then he led her to the place of the dragon and instructed her to have faith and be brave, that a savior would appear.

A young tribune from the imperial army named George, after Gorgias the Sun of Truth, happened upon the scene and asked the young woman why she had been left alone at the side of the lake. She told the soldier, "Flee lest you perish as well. My fate is bound to a dragon and there is nothing you can do to save me." As he untied the maiden, the animal jumped out of the lake and ran to seize them.

The knight mounted his warhorse and drew his lance and thrust it through the body of the beast, wounding it mightily. "Give me your sash, fair lady, and we will show these people the foolishness of their custom." She unwound her girdle and gave it to the knight. He tied it around the beast's great neck and tied the other end to the sacrificial stake. Then he and the princess rode into town and called the townspeople to come out to see their demon.

Some cried when they saw their dragon wounded and leashed, "Now we will all be killed in the beast's wrath!" And the knight proclaimed, "Believe in God and in Jesus His servant, and I will slay this dragon that you may never again lose your flocks or children to this evil." The Dragon was slain and the king and his people were baptized in the lake.

The king offered the knight his daughter in marriage and a great dowry, but Saint George refused, enjoining the king to build a church upon the site and to provide for the poor. The king did these things and the town prospered and grew.

However, these were also the days of the coemperors Diocletian and Maximian, and their persecution against Christians was great. In one month, they martyred 22,000 people and George decided he could no longer wear the uniform of a soldier. He gave up his property to the poor and donned the habit of a holy man. Then he took to the streets calling the gods of the Romans and Gentiles mere demons and saying there was only one God of Heaven.

This didn't go over well with the provost, who asked him: "Why do you say our gods are devils? Who are you?" And he answered: "I am George, formerly a knight of Cappadocia, and I have left all to serve the one true God who is older and greater than your Jupiter."

St. George, patron saint of the Order.

This was considered blasphemy and the provost had him severely beaten to break his bones and expose his guts, and have salt rubbed into his wounds. The soldiers tossed George into prison, where he soon recovered with a vision of the Savior, who promised that if the saint bore all, many would be saved. When the local ruler, an evil man named Dacian, observed what had happened, he called upon a sorcerer to destroy the Christian. The sorcerer swore by his own head that he would prevail.

The sorcerer mixed adder venom with wine, made invocations to the gods and gave the goblet to George. The saint took it, made the sign of the cross on it, and drank. There was no reaction, so the sorcerer made an even stronger brew with scorpion venom, which the saint also drank, again to no effect. The enchanter, now amazed, fell down at the feet of George and asked to become a Christian, to which the saint daubed his thumb in a puddle of water on the ground, crossed the man upon the forehead and said, "I baptize you in the name of the Father, the Son and the Holy Spirit." Seeing this, Dacian was enraged and ordered the sorcerer decapitated.

The next morning, Dacian set St. George between two bladed wheels to be hacked to pieces, but the wheels broke against each other. Then Dacian decided upon another plan, saying: "George, the gods have smiled upon you in their patience, despite your blaspheming. I pray you will return to our laws and make the proper sacrifices on the morrow."

The saint smiled, and said, " I will be happy to obey." So Dacian ordered all the city to come out the next morning to see the saint humbled. The next morning, amidst festivities, they watched the saint go to his knees in the temple of idols. The saint prayed to Heaven, "Father, give these people a sign that they may be converted. Fire descended from Heaven, destroying the temple and the priests, and as George walked away from the spot, an earthquake swallowed the stone and ash, and it was as if the temple of Jupiter had never been.

Dacian was afraid now. He yelled, "Liar! You did not pray to the idol and you have done a great evil." George smiled, and said, " I am willing to pray to your gods. Come, I will show you." However, Dacian no longer trusted him and instead had him dragged through the streets by horse and decapitated. The year 287 ended the great saint's presence on Earth, but he has long since been an intercessor for those who call on him for courage in their hour of need.

As Dacian took the road back home, he and his priests were destroyed by brimstone from Heaven. A great many people were converted then, saying that if a tyrant and his gods cannot defend themselves from one holy man, how much greater must be the one true God.

Twenty-six years later, Constantine the Great, an emperor Eusebius likened unto the Christ or a Phoenix, remembered the soldier-saint's bravery when he charged 50 of his knights to be his standard-bearers. To defend and rally his armies, Constantine would have them hold up a banner of the Labarum, or "St. George's Cross." The emperor said it came to pass that the one bearing the standard before a legion was ever invincible in battle ... and the soldier who relinquished it to escape was immediately deprived of life.

Now I know you are wondering ... "What about the famous vision at the Milvian Bridge?" I believe that was Eusebius' rewrite of Constantine learning the relationship of the solstices, equinoxes, ecliptic, horizon and zenith – geometries subsumed into the Christian mysteries of Easter, the Feast of St. John, Michaelmas and Christmas. Truth is, the Labarum was sacred to Sumerians, Gauls and Hyperboreans centuries before Constantine or earlier Caesars adopted it. It had been on Macedonian coins as well as those of Herod. It dates back to the cuneiform sign for Anu, humankind's first Lord.

For Constantine the mystagogue, perhaps the realization that nothing had been lost between the pagan mysteries and the Christian helped him decide to convert. He needed a warrior saint to reconcile his plans for Empire with the growing Christianity of the realm. The story also made for great drama as a passion play of sorts and as an allegory for great things to come.

There is another story, whose veracity I cannot vouch for, though it was supposedly carved on a marble slab in Rome, that said, "Emperor Constantine the Great, after having been cleansed of leprosy through Holy Baptism, created the Golden Knights symbolized by the Cross to defend the name of Christian."

There was so much exaggeration in early Christian propaganda that it is difficult to sort out the most ancient and true stories. However, Constantine's symbol was later used in the Chrismons of later kings such as Alfonso the Wise of Castile in official documents, as it would also grace the arches of several churches.

There is another legend that King Arthur honored St. George on one of his banners two centuries after the soldier saint's martyrdom. A Crusade tale speaks of St. George at Jerusalem riding at the head of 50 knights robed in white and wearing the triumphal crimson star. It was also by a special invocation of the Soldier Saint that Edward III defeated the French at Crécy in 1346. George is the patron saint of Germany's Teutonic Knights and England's Knights of the Garter.

The Constantinian Angelic Knights of St. George have been called the *Equites Georgiani*, *Militibus Fratribus Constantinianis*, the *Ordo Divi Sancti Georgii* and the *Cavalleros Constantinianos Angelicales Aureatos de San Jorge Martir*. The knights have been confirmed by popes beginning with Constantine's friend Sylvester I, and most recently by Pope Pius II.

At this point, the thoughtful-but-irreverent Lorenzo asked, "If your order is so established, why have I not heard of it before?" I nodded with red face to Constantine to explain. His family had supplied some 30 grand masters to the Order. "Success often breeds arrogance within and mistrust without," he said. "To ensure he maintained control of this new elite, in the year 456, Pope Leo the Great decided to place upon the Order the Rule of St. Basil, which includes a requirement for conjugal celibacy. You can imagine what that did for recruiting."

Lorenzo and his young friends laughed. "Sounds like he wanted you to last one generation and die on the vine – or recruit from within monasteries!"

There was more snickering. Constantine answered: "That may be true, but one could argue that a monk frustrated with living as a sexless human being – nearly a contradiction in terms – might develop sufficient anger and drive to welcome the life of a warrior for Christ. There were indulgences for these knights that covered a multitude of sins and you might say that rules demanding chastity make nice propaganda, but they tend to be more suggestions than commandments. The small warrior class of Rome and Byzantium, like many of your bishops, cardinals and popes, somehow managed to have children in each generation."

Giuliano thought on that and said, "Then it was about gold and land. Those who are officially celibate do not have legitimate children. Illegitimate children tend to go into the church or at least seek its support. Moreover, the fathers would be prohibited from passing on their wealth or name to the next generation. The church would win both ways, while ensuring the warrior class was held in check."

It was my turn to laugh. "A Cardinal could not have said it better!" To which he asked, "So where is the Order now?"

Constantine replied: "One day, we will approach Frederick III, the Holy Roman Emperor at Vienna, to reestablish the royal tie and begin to recruit crusaders for the coming fight with the Ottomans. We will once again have to engage the Pope at Rome. For now, we are an insignificant association in Venice, with little to recommend us beyond an old cape and an impressive Mass for an induction ceremony."

Piero smiled and said: "You can stay here as long as you like, but don't be recruiting vestal virgins from within my family or my city. There aren't any." With a good deal of laughter, we went back to the usual small talk and merriments.

Constantine would soon return to Venice where our little conspiracy already had a following and where he could recruit for the upcoming fight. And I? Well, let us just say that while Andrea liked the idea of my being around for pregnancies and children, she enjoyed the idea of Medici gold much more. She was therefore highly encouraging of my project, and as it pointed to more possibilities in my quest for wisdom, we were in perfect harmony. My only question was where to begin.

Lorenzo de' Medici, called "The Magnificent"

Chapter Twenty-One

*Your victory in the contest had naught to envy
the victories of Aemilius, Marcellus or Scipio.
Your honor is to ride the same comet.*
Luca Pulci, Joust of Lorenzo

Florence, 1467

I did not immediately run off in search of manuscripts. First, I had to learn what the Medici had already compiled in the Academy, the palace bookcases, and in collections that they had financed on behalf of others. I also had to compare notes with Constantine to see what he could purchase or copy in Rome or Venice. Obviously, if a book had just been published or a manuscript could be bought, that would be a better solution than making copies or translating.

Where I could in my readings, I noted referenced documents to look for in the future. One thing I had noticed is that searching for wisdom in the nooks and crannies of a good library is a bit like a kitten playing with a ball of yarn. One knot leads to three more strands and each of these leads to a new knot. Lorenzo was blessed with one of those wonderfully acute minds that could fit any profession. He was fond of pointing out the knots and hinting at works we would need to find.

Constantine brought in works from Rome. Aunt Anna engaged a scriptorium and was soon able to supply copies of what I had gathered with the help of Kreshnik. These, unfortunately, were now copies of copies of Lord knows how many generations previous to that, so it was natural for an occasional error or omission to crop up. I resolved to always search out the oldest manuscripts possible, no matter in how bad a shape.

Right on schedule, at the end of June 1468, little John the 10th was born. He had dark brown hair and brown eyes and the minute he was born he looked like someone who had soaked in the tub of a very dark room for nearly 10 passages of the moon, which I suppose he had, all wrinkled and milky white and crying at the top of his lungs. My first impression was not good. He looked like a handful. He was born with hair over his ears, which the midwife said was why his mother had been reluctant to eat for months, spending the whole time being sick.

Within a week Andrea was feeling immensely better; the little boy's skin grew rosy; and the two of them were losing their water weight. Each day they grew happier and John looked to be an athletic little fellow. Again, Andrea went into her Mommy mode, speaking incessantly to the baby. She would be busy and happy while I was gone. With a baby in her world, Andrea was complete.

I had great fun watching little John build his repertoire of smiles and finger grabbing and pouts and wide-eyed looks and cute sounds to manipulate the adults around him. It is amazing to watch how soon a child reaches out for mastery of the planet, exercising his or her God-given *dominion over the fish of the sea, the fowl of the air, the cattle, and over all the earth, and over every thing that creepeth upon the earth.* Genesis 1:26

Many of us are swept along by the winds of the world, and a few of us direct them. I wondered which he would be. For that matter, I wondered which I was. How important a role do any of us play? How far-reaching is our effect on all around us?

For a little more than a year, I engaged in my review of the available literature, playing with the baby, supervising the building of our small villa and getting it set up. I also put my mind to the problem of how to move gold, books, and manuscripts around Europe without raising the suspicions of clergy, nobles and thieves. Where I could use trusted agents at both ends, I would use ships. Otherwise, I decided to use a wagon. It would have two levels – one for appearances and one for my real business.

I also resolved to go West before I went East. There was no way I would get myself or anything else out of Istanbul if I did not first provide Mehmed something he wanted. I knew the works in Spain would appeal to him. For eight centuries, East and West had matched wits there. The time to buy manuscripts would be before the centuries-long *Reconquista* drove out or killed the remaining Moors and Jews.

Florence, 1469

One day in early January, we were speaking of the thousand-year history of Constantinople and I told Piero and his sons of the tournament Mehmed held in the Hippodrome shortly after proclaiming himself the new Caesar. The youths, both accomplished in the martial arts, said such a spectacle would be great fun. Their generous father, who could never oppose his boys when they had set their hearts on the same course of action, agreed to a *Giostra*.

The date for the tournament was set for February 7th, the day of Saint Moses, the Apostle of the Saracens who long ago kept peace between Arabs and Romans. For the spectacle, some of us would dress up as Turks to be opposed by Lorenzo, Giuliano and more of their friends. The action would take place on the plaza in front of the *Basilica di Santa Croce*.

We engaged in a play battle of horseback swordsmanship for the benefit of the crowd and exhibitions of horseback archery and spearsmanship. However, rather than risk life and limb in a joust before heading off into the wilderness to brave thieves and the elements, I limited my competition to archery, in which I took first place despite my lack of practice.

That day in the jousts, Lorenzo carried the day wearing blue armor on a white horse and sporting the *fleur de lis* motif granted the family by Louis XI. Lorenzo's banner, painted by Andrea Verrocchio, bore a Sun, a rainbow and the motto *Le tems revient* (The Times Return), which was Lorenzo's proclamation of a new Golden Age of chivalry, respect for beauty and a hint at our age nearing the End Times as well as the coming Phoenix, our next returning Messiah. It also portrayed the object of his love, Lucretia Donati, "She whom Heaven has sent to us as an example of the beauties of its eternal choir." From his grand victory that day, he bore away a silver helmet of Mars, Rome's war god.

Shortly after the tournament, I took my leave. The brothers were as excited as their father that I should bring them manuscripts. Lorenzo, ever alert to the mixed blessing of fame and its intrigues, was the one who suggested I find a highway name less likely to attract attention. "Lose the name," he said. "Try something like Yanni Mistropoulos (a Greek name meaning John of Mystras). That way, if friends need to find you they can, but an enemy would need to know you really well to find and strike you on the road."

Lorenzo also provided me extra copies of individual manuscripts such as Boccaccio's *Genealogia Deorum,* Diogenes' *Vitae et Sententiae* and Bracciolini's *Storie Fiorentine* ... things he was willing to trade away for something new. Regardless of a literati's taste, I would have something to offer.

Early the next morning I tossed on a plain black cloak, kissed Andrea and little John while the baby slept and headed out of the courtyard with a small covered wagon drawn by a mule. It had a false bottom accessible through locking planks on the side and a pull-out ramp. I had a small secret compartment near the front where I could keep money I did not want to carry on my person. Under the seat, I kept my bow, the sword and a handgun.

In addition to a couple skins of wine, dried meat, rice and beans, I had bought a hundred copies of a small edition of the *Vulgate Bible.* A few dozen copies of Thomas à Kempis' *Imitatio Cristi.* A few copies of Cicero's *Epistles.* A few of Augustine's *De Civitate Dei.* Pliny's *Historia Naturalis.* Some books on medicine and a few on philosophy. I would be interested primarily in religion and history. After that, we would see.

Fortunately, most highwaymen are not the least bit literate, so all I would have to do is never have very much money on my person, travel with a group whenever possible, and never engage in a fight until I knew what I was up against. I promised Andrea that I would be careful, not that I had a firm idea what else that might entail. I was pretty sure the road to wisdom would involve pain. I just hoped to survive long enough to get there. I turned toward the north gate. My first stops would be Bologna, Ferrara, Brescia, Lombardia and Milan.

Chapter Twenty-Two

Zeus, to guide mortals, established this fixed law:
Wisdom comes through suffering.
Trouble, with its memory of pain, drips in our hearts as we try to sleep,
and so men against their will learn moderation. Aeschylus, Agamemnon

Bologna, 1469

I soon discovered the realities of setting up as a vendor on the roads of Italy. No sooner had I left the outskirts of the city and I was beaten and robbed. The thieves settled for the coins I carried on my person, the knife in my belt and the wineskin I carried up front. As I had guessed, illiterates care nothing for *Bibles* written in Latin. Everything else I had hidden in the wagon's false bottom.

A merchant friend of the Medici was coming up the road – one who kept the right people paid for safe passage. So with the promise of 10 percent of my sales, I could ride with his caravan.

Then I learned why everything not made by a good friend down the street is so expensive. When I arrived at Bologna, I had to pay an "import" tax and there was another line to pay for carts coming out, which I supposed were "exports." As we passed the gate, I noticed a monk being waved through without a charge on his barrels of wine and olive oil. He simply showed a parchment to the gateman.

I asked my merchant friend how that was. "Bill of lading or a commission showing his shipment belongs to his bishop or some cardinal. Otherwise, he would pay a third of the price on the wine." I was an agent for the wrong book lover! I began to keep a lookout for a messenger in the colors of Venice or Rome. If I could get a note to Constantine or Bessarion, my luck might change!

Depending on the rapacity of the local lord (and the severity of the current war), each city-state would charge anywhere between two and ten percent of the value of one's merchandise – higher if one was trafficking in wine and fine linens. I could see how Dante felt the need for one universal government. How many feudal lords, each one playing robber baron, can the world's people bear?

I wondered how many towns it would take before my *Bibles* were rendered a liability as opposed to a source of profit. How many fees levied before the break-even price recouping my costs exceeded the market?

Now I understood why purveyors of literature were called *colporteurs* – carrying their pamphlets or broadsides beneath a sling of coal. If you came to town with merchandise, especially by mule or cart, the gateman wanted his *gabelle*; and since the value and scarcity of an item drove the tax, then coal was the best cover. I had made my compartment waterproof on top. Still, I did not like the idea of hauling charcoal and not having a place to work, read or sleep.

Upon arriving in the town, I set up shop in a local inn where I could stay for one gold florin a week paid in advance, which included a stable for my mule. I paid a young man to distribute some handbills that I penned for local merchants, bankers and courtiers listing the normal books I had brought and saying that I was interested in taking requests (so as to get a feel for the market). My sales were disappointing, but I met another vendor and one book collector with a pretty long wants list. I paid my 10 percent to the caravan boss; and the day after market, we headed on toward Ferrara.

Ferrara, 1469

I had at least three reasons for wanting to stop in Ferrara. For one, I had long wanted to pay my respects to the *Cattedrale di San Giorgio*. For another, I wanted to visit the city where our troubles began. Arguably, Mehmed would not have hurried to attack Constantinople if John VIII had not aggravated him by rushing into the arms of cardinals at the Council 30 years earlier. I had also heard there was a unique *Bible* assembled here, and a new edition of Boccaccio's *Decameron* recently published.

Since I knew Boccaccio to be a favorite son of Italy, and a bit controversial with the Church for having been entirely too honest about our present age of decadence, I bought 20 copies of the *Decameron*. Again, I did handbills and again my sales were less than exciting – a few *Imitatios*, a few *Bibles*, a Cicero and a Pliny.

I did meet a couple of enlightened ecclesiastics looking for something out of the ordinary. I told them I would trade Diogenes' *Lives and Opinions of Eminent Philosophers* for something interesting. They offered me a copy of the *Corpus Hermeticum* (something we already had back in the library) or an ancient Armenian text of the Paulicians. I made the trade and hoped one day to run into my old classmate Vahan or another Armenian to translate it.

Per our arrangement, the merchant, who was next headed to Venice, took his percentage of sales (not trades) and we parted our ways. However, I did ask him to pass a note to Constantine for me (asking how to arrange a commission for Bessarion) and another note for Aunt Anna and my mother, letting them know that Andrea and baby were staying with the Medici while we finished our house and I was on the road. I signed the letters with my highway name so they could find me if they sent a courier (and to cover me if the caravan boss peeked).

Before heading out, I attempted to visit Duke Borso d'Este to see the famously beautiful illustrated *Bible* he had commissioned done by hand. He was "unavailable" but I did meet with the calligrapher and artist who had done the work and, bemoaning my inability to see their handiwork, managed to purchase a draft folio page containing an omission. I loved the lettering and thought perhaps that I could have a similar font cut one day – not something I discussed with them. Their handiwork was the very best possible before machines changed their world. I hoped one day to do something in print as wonderful as what they had done by hand.

I arranged, again for a percentage, to ride with another caravan toward Milan. Before we left Ferrara, I paid my respects to St. George at the Cathedral and viewed some of the artwork he had inspired. "Il Cosmè" Tura was just putting the finishing touches on one such painting. I was gratified to see the symbol of our Order had not died.

Verona, 1469

Constantine's messenger caught up with me in Verona. His message was one of congratulations on beginning my search. He included a commission for Bessarion – merely a wants list for acquisitions if I was able to make it to the Lyon book fair or managed to connect with some of the publishing houses in Germany. He also provided news of works beginning to appear in Venice and Rome, such as Caesar's *Commentarii*, Juvenal's *Satyrae* and the works of Virgil.

Finally, he mentioned that Bessarion was in the middle of his own publishing project, *Against the Slanderer of Plato* (referring to George of Trebizond), defending Platonism from charges of immorality. I dashed off a note thanking Constantine and the cardinal, suppressing the urge to wish the churchman luck. There were excellent men that emerged from the Academies, but not all who ruled them were good men. Unfortunately, any collection of adults and children can be an invitation for confusion and abuses of power and trust. Bessarion was more than capable of besting George, but the issue was certainly worth discussing.

Brescia, 1469

Did I mention I was still a young fool? Going north in Italy was like going north in Spain. If one falls in love once an hour in Madrid or Rome, one will fall in love every 15 minutes in Zaragoza or Florence and every five in Huesca or Brescia. Being married had never felt so confining – like being a monk locked away in a desert cave, but instead of Beauty being an abstract dream in the darkness, here it was in the flesh all around me in the light of day!

There are inescapable beauties that penetrate our hearts, regardless of whether our destinies are the least bit compatible. The lesson was driven home just past the Via Innocenta, in front of the Chapel of Corpus Cristi. I crossed paths with a nun who looked exactly like Alítheia the last time I had seen (or dreamt) her. I stumbled and fell right there on the cobblestone and did not mind one bit having bruised my shoulder and hit my head trying to keep my stunned eyes on the lovely creature. She saw it all, of course, to my great embarrassment and came over to help me up. I begged her forgiveness and told her she reminded me of someone very dear whom I had lost. She smiled and said she would pray that I find her again; and then we each went back to our respective lives. Just for a moment, Heaven had touched me and it was glorious!

Like a child picking at his scab because it itches or forever nursing a broken bone that did not heal straight, there are wounds that mark us for life. They probably do not have to, but once a scar has become part of who we are, why would one wish to part with it? I still prayed for Alítheia almost every night. I still wondered how she was doing. If I had been one for going to confession, I imagine I would have been told it is not healthy to dwell on the past, but I do not believe I was being covetous. I could no sooner quit caring about her than I could stop loving baby Diana.

In Brescia, I sold a few *Bibles* and *Decamerons*, though of course not to the same people! The only interesting thing I bought was a large calfskin map of Europe based on Ptolemy's *Cosmographia*. It was a projection that hardly tapered to the north, so while all the directions and features of the land were fairly accurate for one travelling about, some of the countries were wildly out of scale. Britain and the Scandinavian countries were gigantic. I bought it for my own use on the road, thinking it would be fun one day to explain to my son where I had been.

I also hoped I might eventually find a star atlas from Hipparchus or Ptolemy, so I could ponder the ancient mystery, *What is above is like what is below, and what is below is like that which is above.* I was convinced there must be some sort of geographical correspondence between the two maps for Hermes to make such a strange statement. I also wanted to explore the idea of the prime meridian – was it simply an arbitrary matter of lining up a spot and a moment in time to make the latest presumptuous Sun King happy; did it involve an important sign of the Ages; and was there only one that made sense for all time? Wisdom comes slowly, especially for a mind preoccupied with such impracticalities.

Lombardia, 1469

On the way to Lombardia, I stopped to rescue a Franciscan monk who lost his wagon in a rut that had snapped two of his wheels. Amazingly, one of the casks of wine he was carrying remained intact thanks to the metal bands around it. Together, we used my ramp and loaded the barrel into my wagon. Then we caught up with the rest of the group. For awhile, we talked about the events of the world, our lives, where we were headed, but he seemed to know I had questions about his religious life. He told me to feel free.

Since the question was recently on my mind, I asked him about celibacy. "How do you do it?" I asked. He smiled, "It's what you don't do that is the key." Great ... I was with a sarcastic monk with a gift for understatement. "What do you mean?"

He said, "Try to remember when you were a child. Did you think about sex for two minutes beyond the time you saw two goats or two dogs or two chickens going at it?" I said, "No." "Exactly," he said.

"But you easily obsess about what you see or hear or talk about or imagine. If you can break that pattern of thought or action, you can go back to being an innocent child of God." I asked, "You are not just saying that because you swore to celibacy before you knew what you were doing?"

"On the contrary," he said, "I had a life just like you and figured out my vocation late in the game. At one point, I realized that I did not wish the normal life with a wife, children, a house, a trade, a garden and taxes. I wanted to be a force for good in the world, to share in many people's problems and to help them find solutions. I wanted to get out of the filthy city to be closer to God's countryside – away from open sewers and walls that have to be specially marked with a cross if you don't want men urinating on them. I wanted to share in a common enterprise with like-minded people. Believe me, I knew what I was giving up before I was ordained, and I considered the loss insignificant. I came in through the Third Order, so my transition was only as fast as I could turn myself into a better person."

"So what are you attempting?" I asked. "To be what Saint Francis was – another Christ." I must have gasped or opened my mouth and eyes too much, for he quickly said, "No, that is not a heresy. Our Herald of the Great King presented himself to his fellow man as the Christ returned to life. Indeed, that is a burden we are all here to share, not just in terms of His suffering, for we all suffer, but in terms of taking responsibility for this world." I was intrigued.

"While we despise our bodies and engage in acts of penance, that is not our primary task. No, our primary task is to purify our own conduct to bring the Christ to the center of our lives so we can lead people to God." Sad to say, in this late century, this sounded rather strange coming from a churchman. I had seen so many of them wrapped up in pride, caught up in the church's riches and rites, lording it over their common man, making quick work of life's greatest tragedies ... so I thought I would try to get past the dogma.

"Okay, so you're going to be like St. Paul and say, 'Christ is living in me.' What does that require on a daily basis and where is the rub? What is it that still makes life difficult for you once you have gotten past selfishness and sexual desire?"

Here he stopped me. "How is it any different for you? You have a wife and a child whom you respect, love, and attempt not to hurt.

In that last town, were you drinking and gambling or carousing? I'll bet you weren't, because you were thinking of them as well as your own good. You sold your books, you ate your dinner and you went back to your room and read or went to sleep. For the next thousand miles and several months, you will be sharing this simpler life, whether or not that is what you intended, and my question is 'What's your purpose?' You know mine ... to worship the Father just as Jesus did and use a purified life as a means to introduce more people to Him. What are you about? If you had nobody else to worry about and nothing else pressing in the world, what would you do with your last year of life, and is that what you are doing now?"

I thought the question sounded a bit presumptuous, as if anything that I said at this point was going to come out hopelessly ignoble by comparison. So I told him, and hoped it did not sound too pompous in return: "Before I die, I would like to UNDERSTAND some of the premises and axioms of God and the principles at work in the world – for either way leads to the other. I want to KNOW. I would even settle with sorting out how some of the ancient myths and religions fit together. After that, God or the Devil can take me and I will go quietly."

I went on, "The one thing of which I am sure is that what I was taught as a child, what I have read in the Scriptures, what I see with my own eyes, and what I can dream or conceive ... is so horrendously inadequate an understanding of the universe that I am amazed that I am not yet as dead as the snake we just ran over. If I may say so, I suspect that my TRUTH and your God of Truth are One and the same. We just have two different journeys climbing the same mountain. I cannot tell you whose path will be steeper or longer or involve more setbacks, but I'm pretty sure we are aiming for the same summit."

"And what would you do with all that knowledge?" he asked. "Well, if I have time before the end, I would like to tell someone and save them some pains." He laughed, "Then we have indeed set out with the same goal – to learn and to teach others. You could be a Franciscan tertiary if you could deal with a life of poverty, chastity and service."

I hitched up my left sleeve and said, "I have failed a few times on the chastity requirement, but I am familiar with poverty and service. I was born to rule and instead spent a decade of my life as a slave. My back is worse than this, but my grandfather was the richest man in Byzantium and my father the most powerful, yet my net worth at this moment is a little house in Florence that is really my wife's and the books in this little wagon. One good fire or a broken wheel and I will equal your poverty."

He chewed on that for a bit and I reproached myself for having said so much. He said, "Well, I did not really answer your question: 'What does it take and what's the rub?' I would say it takes waking up every morning trying to make today better than yesterday – for God, for me and for everyone else. And the 'rub' is that how best to serve is hardly ever apparent. If it were easy, wouldn't the problems already have been solved before they came to me?"

"How about an example?" I asked. "Well, it would have to be from real life and not from hearsay or confession," he said. "So let's say I have a friend, a very rich man, a minor noble who lives in a fine villa surrounded by a magnificent library with all the wisdom of the world at his fingertips. When he was young, he had his pick of all the pretty girls and all the best ales and wines and all the best tutors and all the best friends. You would think such a man the happiest in the world. But no, he is the most miserable and frustrated man on the planet because the only thing he ever wanted from this life was a son.

"He has had two lovely wives, each of whom miscarried several times and each of whom finally bore him a daughter. One woman died of the Plague and the next died giving birth to a deformed boy who died within the week. So it is painfully obvious to anyone but my friend that his male seed is corrupt. Well, now he is married to his third wife in 15 years, a beautiful young girl from Lombardia, and every morning that she doesn't wake up with morning sickness or announcing they're having a child he slaps her, berates her, and goes storming out or straight to his cups. By the end of the day he is nearly useless in any capacity and he cannot shake his obsession and the girl cannot make a baby by herself and the only person that knows all this has taken vows to hate concupiscence and the desires of the flesh ... and to promote justice!"

He continued, "So I walk about with this terrible knowledge and I hate myself for not knowing the solution. Is my friend supposed to die? Is his suffering redemptive for anyone? Is the girl to resist taking her own life only to offer her long-suffering as some sort of sacrifice to the Lord? Am I to stop taking pride in my vows to help them both?

Or will the Lord provide a better solution? I know the mystery has something to do with our respect for all creatures carrying the imprint of God, our seeing divinity in our fellow creature, and helping them to love and to forgive each other, but the 'rub' is not understanding what is God's will. It is easy to do the right thing for the wrong reason and the wrong thing for the right reason. That little trick is called intent. However, sometimes things just seem to happen without too much anguish or premeditation and they work out just fine – like losing the wheels to my wagon and finding another on the same path with a driver willing to help. I do believe in Providence, but sometimes I just do not see the big plan." I smiled and said, "Who does?"

In Lombardia, I sold more books, took people's want lists, and bought a couple of old manuscripts from the monastery with the help of my new friend, Salvatore di Milano. He kept his wine, saying it was for a special customer back home. On the way out of town we stopped at the home of Salvatore's friends, who asked him about their daughter. The wife pulled out a beautiful crochet tablecloth and shawl she had made, saying, "Please take these to Elena." The good friar said he would. The woman of the house then gave us some wonderful bread just out of the oven, two bottles of Lombardy wine and some of the best-fried sausage I ever tasted. By the time we caught up with the group, we had full bellies and light heads and might have sung if either of us had a voice. Instead, we talked. I learned of things of the Spirit and he learned of God's sense of humor with respect to my life.

Milan, 1469

Entering Milan, we separated from the caravan. Everyone else headed straight to market. We headed downtown to what I suppose could be considered a minor palace or a major villa. I had lived in palaces and this was still impressive.

A goddess met us at the door. She appeared to know Salvatore as a good friend and let us in. The master of the house was just settling in from a busy day at the court of the Duke. He warmly greeted my companion, and I was introduced as a collector of rare manuscripts and an agent for Piero de' Medici. The gentleman showed me his library and said that he had a few extras he could spare and offered to engage a scribe if there was something of particular interest to the Medici. He asked me to make myself at home in his study and he and Salvatore went out to unload and tap his cask.

I took note of interesting things he had that we lacked, and related books I knew of in Rome, Venice or Florence that he might desire. I wondered what the plan for the evening had been before we arrived. At dinner, we discussed requests and he both accepted and offered some trades. Soon, he and Salvatore were back out in the main gallery drinking, the daughters were sent off to bed and I was again alone in the library. This time I was reading and updating my *Florilegium*, the little book of wisdom I kept from my youth.

The goddess soon joined me, her sweet and sad eyes looking for approval. By now, I knew her as Elena. The go-north-for-beauty rule had again applied, only it had not taken three seconds for me to be completely under her spell. She was the recipient of the crochet from Lombardia; and the moment I saw her blue eyes, long dark tresses and curves of Olympian perfection, I suddenly understood what Dionysius the Areopagite had said:

> *Beauty bids all things to itself ... and gathers everything into itself. ... Beauty unites all things and is the source of all things. It is the great creating cause which bestirs the world and holds all things in existence by the longing inside them to have Beauty. There it is ahead of all as Goal, as the Beloved, as the Cause toward which all things move, since it is the longing for Beauty which actually brings them into Being.* Divine Names

She picked up a harp, knelt in front of me and began to play and sing, and while she knew the usual tunes and sonnets, she had some of her own composition that were much more beautiful. I was enthralled. We spoke of life and love, of truth and poetry, of troubadours and myths. Meeting a kindred spirit was a joyful moment for both of us.

I wish I could say that what came next was predestined or altruistic, but the truth is we were just two young people thrilled to have touched the right chord in each other. As the old men out in the gallery drank and told stories and laughed and swore (yes, even old saints sometimes retain bad habits), the two of us made our own poetry long and shamelessly.

I have no idea what time Salvatore and I headed out – sometime after midnight and not long before the dawn – but we were both immensely happy. While we did not discuss it, I am sure that happiness was for all the wrong reasons.

A year later, I almost encountered the nobleman and his wife as they emerged from the *Basilica di San Lorenzo Maggiore* holding a handsome son and chatting with Salvatore as godfather. I did not cross the road and I hope I went unnoticed. I was very happy for them and yet mortified at the same time. Beautiful Elena would be the last time I strayed, though she was certainly not the last woman for whom I felt attraction. It lashed my soul to know that I was as weak and sinful as any man had ever been.

Before I left Milan, I heard a rumor that Lorenzo de' Medici would marry Clarice Orsini in a political marriage. I remember feeling sorry for him, for Miss Orsini and for Miss Donati. How terrible to know from the very first day of marriage that you would never marry your first choice, or marry and know you were not the first choice, or not marry and know you had been the first choice. I guess that before age 30 it is easy to make bad choices. Way too easy.

Chapter Twenty-three

History is the witness of the ages, the torch of truth, the life of memory, the teacher of life, the messenger from ancient times. Cicero, De Oratore II 9:36

Milan, 1469

I left Milan in a terrible state. I said goodbye to Salvatore and promised to send the monastery whatever I could find for his friend. Contrary to what I had been doing, I did not even wait for a caravan. My mind and soul felt as black and dirty as the Devil's chimney. For to my way of thinking, and according to the ideals of our bright new age of chivalry, I had just failed Love for the third time.

Instead of worshipping a woman, virtually as the Holy Spirit incarnate, and allowing her to remain pure and untouched as one's Platonic Form or Dantean Ideal, I had taken three women that I cared about (and a few I didn't) and treated them as playthings or receptacles or negotiated interests.

Alítheia my hero, the one with whom I wanted to spend eternity, had known our life together was doomed this round and so used sex to place a period at the end of that chapter of our lives. Should I have refused? Should I have gone after her? Andrea, my savior who kept me out of the hands of my enemies my last day in Istanbul, I had regarded as some sort of lifelong obligation acquired in an escaped slave's life. Yet, she was the one deserving all the attention of my heart and soul. With Elena I had flattered myself thinking she had somehow been attracted to me, when in fact she had been engaged in an act of duty to win back her husband's love! I realized I would never understand love and the only Dantesque "purity" in my life had been a wonderful stepmother and daughter – both of whom God saw fit to take back almost as soon as I had noticed the beauty of their souls.

So I left Milan with a dark cloud over my head. In less than 300 miles and two months, I had shamed myself. I remember concluding that every one of the best people I had ever met was a woman. My grandfather was wonderful, but he played both sides of the gathering conflict and it caught up with him. My father was wonderful, but in the end he could not deliver the moral authority to engage the West even in its own defense. My stepfather was wonderful, but he had lived as a hypocrite to have any kind of authority. While I could sit in judgment with respect to most men, I was much harder on myself.

By comparison, Lorenzo and Salvatore were doing so much better. Lorenzo had poets singing that he was the Phoenix of our age; and now he had carefully separated his Ideal, the divine source of his joy, from his Marriage, the source of his power on Earth. I could see this as a rather poor strategy to keep one pure thing in this life. I imagined it would be awkward, especially for Lucretia. Perhaps it would have been better not to embarrass the woman of his dreams.

Salvatore – from the menu of fight, fly, negotiate or comply – chose to escape the dramas of earthly love by complying with his Celestial Master. I, on the other hand, had always felt like life is one long negotiation with reality. However, what if this life on the road was just my attempt to fly from a real life in Florence? What if Elena was just my lustful weakness and a fight with the practical celibacy called marriage? Were all my sufferings for failure to comply with God's will? I felt the wretched victim of my own sin and I wanted to change.

In this cold year, finally, the snows were retreating from the land; the rains were coming and the wagon I had thought such a brilliant solution when I started was looking like an increasingly bad idea. I was in need of a horse and it was time to simplify my load. I could make the trek over the Alps. Alternatively, I could ship what I had thus far acquired. I decided to take a partial gain rather than continue to risk a total loss.

Chivasso, 1469

The problem I was having with my big map of Ptolemy was that while the geography was much the same as it had always been (only rivers and shorelines move from time to time), everything had new names and there were so many more villages now. I left *Mediolanio* (Milan) in the direction of the colony of *Augusta Pretoria* (Aosta) where I would be able to catch the road to *Augusta Taurica*, which today is called

Turin or Torino. Thank goodness, I ran into a horseman along the way who sent me toward Chivasso instead of Aosta – a much shorter route! From now on, I would ask for help marking the map before going on.

In town, I traded my wagon and 30 florins for a horse. The price was steep, but since I was riding into hill country any way I turned, I did not have much choice. A stable hand shoed and fed the mule and horse. Now all I had to do was give them less to haul.

I was able to unload most of the remainder of my *Bibles* and Kempis here by reducing the price, leaving a dozen unpublished manuscripts and codices and a couple dozen printed books of mostly history and philosophy to haul to Genoa.

They are religious people in the Piemonte and always have been. I think the Catholic Church could have contented them with its doctrine centuries earlier if it had stuck to the original message of Christianity and if it had included a role for the *Theotokos* from the beginning. Of all the people on Earth, these are folks who understand that women have souls and intelligence and are equally called to think, to act, to witness, to teach and to lead.

Diana, my stepmother, once told me that the first real Christians in Italy and France had been baptized by Mary Magdalene and Joseph of Aramathia. She said they had traveled by boat from Palestine and taught the people of Provence and Piemonte the message of Jesus. She also said this version of Christianity was profoundly like Judaism, focused on the Commandments and stripped of any pomp or legalism.

Torino, 1469

From Turin, fifty miles southeast was Alba, an early home of the Queen of Heaven, who preceded any talk of the Father or the Son by centuries. Fifty miles to the southwest was the fortress of La Madalena nestled in the Alps – doomed to be a latter-day Tephrike, I wager. Like my stepparents' brethren, the people of this region have lived condemned and anathematized for more than four centuries and still there is no forgiveness in the Church.

The biggest "crime" of the people from the Piemonte, I think, was in not believing sacraments are necessary to salvation. What are priests to do with such a people? How can you control someone who does not feel compelled to confess or ask permission to marry or request last rites? When faced with death as the price of their contrariness, the Waldenses proudly said: *With the eye of faith we see our King reigning in*

Heaven and by His own Almighty hand He will raise us up to immortal triumph and bestow upon us celestial joy!

Renerius, writing centuries ago, said these people seceded from the Roman Church in the time of Constantine the Great, having observed avarice in Pope Sylvester and his cardinals rather than Christian charity. I find it difficult to condemn a people saying the Church of Peter pulled the rug out from under them. After all, was that not the same objection made by the Great Church?

While in Turin, I did not get the chance to compare the *Bible* of these *Vallesii* (or Waldenses) to Rome's Vulgate, though they do look similar in content. Were I a betting man, however, my money would not be on St. Jerome as having produced the more accurate text. These people will have come closer to the original Greek and Hebrew Scriptures, just as their lives more closely resemble those of the original Apostles.

I took my leave of this Holy Land of saviors, resolving to be a better husband, a better father and a better man. However, the Most High was not through testing me. As He did for Balaam on the way to Arnon, He sometimes would place a dark angel in my path to slow me down and teach me a lesson. I took the road toward Asti and Alessandria, this being the faster way to Genoa.

Asti, 1469

One makes better time without a wagon. Where before I probably averaged 10 miles a day when I was traveling, now I could easily do 20. The weather was not too bad, raining maybe two days a week.

Winding through the foothills toward the sea, I heard a gunshot followed by some screaming. I tied up my animals and peered around the bend. It looked as if there were four men committing a rape and robbery.

The worst criminal was picking on what appeared to be about a 14-year-old girl with the help of one of his companions. I shot him in the back and he stopped bothering her about the time he noticed an arrow sticking out his chest. A third man flew at me on his horse waving a sword and I dispatched him with my handgun. The second, leaving the girl to grab his musket, took two arrows. The fourth ran at me with his sword, and I had occasion to test the steel of *Aghen Glas*.

The ancient blade was short compared to what the other fellow was swinging in my direction, which cost me a slice across the chest, but my steel was so much better. On about the third blow, his blade snapped and a bit of stardust warmed his heart. I put away my things, tying my animals to a greener spot and joined the group of six Jews (an elderly couple, a younger couple, a girl and her little brother) now taking back their things and comforting each other.

The oldest man said in Spanish, *Thou deliveredst them into the hand of their enemies, who vexed them; and in the time of their trouble, when they cried unto thee, ... Thou gavest them saviors, who saved them out of the hand of their enemies.*
Nehemiah 9:27

I smiled, "You would have done the same for me, I am sure." I had never been called a savior before. God forgive me, but I rather liked the sound. "So where are you from?" I asked.

The younger man, whom I guessed to be the son or son-in-law of the older man, said: "We finally wearied of being devils. We lived in Palma, the big city in Mallorca. There, we were called *Chuetas* and we were made to live in a cramped Jewish quarter, attend Christian churches for the privilege of being scorned, where every few years the people would slay some of us or riot against us and the Inquisition would take our property – all because they failed to understand the Jewish man they call their Savior!"

The man's wife, having helped her daughter now weeping between her grandparents, came over and offered to stitch up my wound. I thanked her and took off my shirt, saying, "Do not be alarmed, but I have had problems of my own." The little boy gasped. He was probably pointing at my back judging from the others' expressions. "Your problem was intolerant Christians; mine was intolerant Moslems. However, What or Whom you worship is no business of mine as long as it does not involve burning me at the stake. Just out of curiosity, why would you abandon one zealous Catholic country for another? The direction you are headed is one where Christian saints were martyred for *understanding* the same man!"

"We had to get away," she said. "When they start, they talk to everyone you know – especially anyone who has fought with you or might be jealous of you. They write down everything. When they decide you are guilty (and that was decided before they bring you in), you can confess everything, but they want to torture more charges out of you. When you have humiliated yourself in front of them, and they have ruined your family and your health, and torn apart your house looking for writings or phylacteries or prayer shawls, then they will kill you and take your house and your savings or ... they will throw you back into the community to live as their scapegoat and spy. It is as if their only job is to make our lives Hell. Why? Because a group of Jews more than a thousand years ago did not accept a carpenter as Jerusalem's new king, as their Messiah, or as their general who would stand up to the Romans? Forgive us for saying so, but he never did!"

Her husband added, "And now it gets worse. Our King of Aragon will marry Isabel of Castile, who vows, they say, that all Iberia will have one religion and anyone whose family is suspected of being Jew, Moslem or Apostate will be expelled. That is no place to be raising children as *Chuetas* or 'Judaizers.' It was only a matter of time before we would have been rounded up, like our parents and grandparents before us, separated from our children, and forced to watch them be baptized. Anywhere would be better."

I said, "I may not be the best person with whom to discuss all of this, but better me than a zealot. Almost any Catholic country is going to inflict these difficulties. It will happen every time someone decides Christians and Jews pray to two different gods. Your brethren throughout Europe face these things. On the other hand, in Palestine or Constantinople I believe all they would do is make you wear a certain color clothes and tax you extra for not going to their five prayer gatherings each day. Do as you wish, go where you wish, but that would be my best recommendation. Oww!" She had put a stitch through one of my nipples. It hurt.

"Sorry," I said, "I'll try not to be a big baby. You say you are from Palma. Do you happen to remember a Diana Valls or Diana Agron?"

The older woman answered, "I knew *Dinah* Valls briefly, though she was about 10 years younger than me. She lived in our little four-block neighborhood in the middle of Palma. Her mother's name was Esther and I don't remember her father's first name, but he was from a merchant family out of Tarragona. They escaped when Dinah was 10 years old, around the time of the *Sh'hita*, the massacre, of 1435. I later heard she married a Montenegrin trader from Cattaro who had signed on with the Venetians somewhere – Constantinople I think. Why do you ask? What became of her?"

"Well you know," I replied, "Constantinople was not the best place to be in 1453. She died trying to defend me. She was my mother, not by blood, but in every other way. She hardly told me anything from when she was growing up."

"I don't blame her," said the older woman. "We were Jewish souls wearing a Christian mask. That is how her Jewish name turned into a Christian name. Converting and marrying Christians of any stripe was how many of us survived. Unfortunately, in Palma it hardly mattered if you converted. As long as you still lived in the *Call Menor*, you would always be treated as less than a real person."

I dragged the four dead men away from the road in case they had associates and took the musket, ball and powder for the younger man, showing him how to use them. Now that he had seen what could happen to his family, he would do a better job defending. We made a fire and had something to eat and the food did taste like something Diana would have made.

I told them my plan was to go to Genoa and that if they had gold or gems they could sail to Athens, Istanbul or Galata from there to be safe. They said they thought they had some extended family in France whom they would try to find. We parted our ways. Before I left, they asked if there was any way to repay me for helping them. I said, "Pray for my family and I will pray for yours!"

The next day I arrived in Asti, where I spent a few days healing and searching out old books. I found nothing in the way of old manuscripts, but the time there gave me a chance to think about what I was doing. What my friends Piero, Lorenzo and Bessarion really wanted was ancient literature, something I knew to be in Istanbul. To get it, I would have to offer Mehmed something he might want more than my hide. Aside from vanity, his weakness was wisdom, thinking it instrumental to gaining more power. He would be searching for Arab classics as hard as anyone here was searching for old Greek or Latin.

Neither the Lyon trade fair nor visiting publishers in Germany was likely to lead to success as anything but a bookseller. My dream was rather to gather and publish ancient ideas, which is not precisely the same thing. Going north would lead to new books, but probably would not yield much in the way of old wisdom. For weeks, I had been running away from the fact that my success might have to begin with me stretched out on a rug before the Sultan's throne. I had allowed Bessarion's suggestion to sidetrack my original plan. Again seeing the Light, I now prayed the Genoans still sailed to Istanbul.

I found nothing in Alessandria but Catholic texts. This time, I did not seek out want lists. A few people bought *Decamerons*, Pliny, Galen and Plotinus and then I was off to Genoa.

Genoa, 1469

When I reached Genoa, I sat down and tried to figure out if the trip so far had been worth it. In all, I had cleared about 300 florins and turned 150 new books into an armful of manuscripts for copying or publishing in the future. I had received my money back on the animals plus some for two horses I had picked up along the road. When weighed against the risks, I was not sure it was the kind of life that could sustain a family and I was not sure how long little John might have a daddy if this was how I had to earn a living.

I boxed the manuscripts and codices and wrote notes for Constantine and for Andrea. Then I procured some proper clothes and had my hair cut. The next day, before boarding for Spain, I shipped a box to Venice marked "Property of Cardinal Bessarion." I gave the captain Bessarion's note in case the taxman had questions. I should have felt bad, but didn't.

Chapter Twenty-four

Ask, and it shall be given you; seek, and ye shall find; knock, and it shall be opened unto you. Luke 11:9

Motril, 1469

I found a caravel ready to sail south for Barcelona, Valencia, Cartagena and Cadiz. For a few florins more, the captain said he would put in at Almeria or Motril to get me to Granada and Cordoba. I figured the voyage would take about four days, but with stops along the way, he said it would take us eight. We left Genoa in the late afternoon to take advantage of the winds as the mountains cooled down.

About the only thing interesting along the way was the new silk market at Valencia, where my Genoan shipmates, fabric merchants all, did a brisk business. Farther down the coast, a *vendavale* wind blew in from the Straits of Gibraltar as we rounded Almeria. The dark clouds blowing in may be what kept the corsairs on the African side, 120 miles away at Mers el Kébir instead of laying in wait to attack us.

As I looked south toward Alítheia's home, a town not far beyond that old Roman port, the rain began. I wondered if one day I might see her again. In the big scheme of things, I realized it did not matter that I loved her despite the turn of the stars in our lives. Perhaps it was just the idea of her that enchanted me, a fond memory, a romantic delusion or an icon in my mind. But in the moments I missed that other half of my heart, I would say "My new life!" and walk on with renewed joy.

It was an article of faith with me that God would grant me this one reward if I became a better person. If not, how could Heaven be Heaven, if even there you cannot be with the ones you love best? I was not unique in finding deity in a woman. The year Muhammad married little Aisha was the year he had his vision of Heaven. The year Beatrice died was the year Dante began his *New Life,* longing after his impossible dream but transformed into a better writer. In my case, Alítheia was simply the closest I had felt to Divinity this side of the clouds.

Love is the key to unlock the good in a man. If it was three years before Muhammad consummated that marriage ... if Beatrice died married to another ... and if my soul mate lived in another man's palace, then that love can be Platonic, one-sided and absolutely hopeless, and still be the key.

It was about a mile-and-a-half hike up to El Varadero de Motril. I rented a room, took a bath, washed my clothes, and had a fantastic meal of saffron rice, seafood and vegetables. The next day, after a long sleep, I updated my map with the help of a merchant, bought a horse and resumed my journey refreshed.

Granada, 1469

I spent the night in Mondújar, about halfway up the road to Granada. One thing about traveling in a country of Moslems – one does not face many robbers beyond the merchant wanting to haggle starting from a ridiculous price. I visited the Castillejo to see if anyone might have some wisdom to impart to Sultan Mehmed, who I said inherited "much Greek philosophy and Christian theology, but who is in need of Arabic literature." Thankfully, I had paid attention in Arabic class because nobody here spoke Turkish, Greek or Italian. Since they were at war with Castile, I did not feel right trying Spanish on them.

The owner of the castle was not there – the family actually residing in Granada – but his brother and son were present and they had a good laugh. Al-Zaghall, brother of King Muley Abu'l Hacén, found it comical that the Ottoman Empire invading Europe might send someone to a kingdom on the brink of destruction to learn something. He ordered me some tea while the boy, Boabdil, brought me a book, the *Kitab al-Fihrist* of al-Nadim. This Index is a review of Arabic literature, world religion, philosophy, history and science up to the 367th year of the Hegira (about 980 AD). I thanked them and said I would discuss their situation with the Sultan when next I saw him.

What is interesting about the *Fihrist* is that it discusses the Sabaeans' worship of the stars, which must have emerged between the time of Cain and Abraham. Abraham was reportedly one of the first to receive teaching on the subject, about the time God told him, *Look now toward Heaven, and tell the stars, if thou be able to number them: and he said unto him, So shall thy seed be.* [Genesis 15:5]

You and I can take that to mean that his descendants would merely be as *numerous* as the stars, but that is not all that was said. Plato (who, like Moses, had studied under the Egyptians) in his *Timaeus* has the Creator saying He would sow the divine seed, that souls would equal the number of the stars, and that each of our souls would be assigned to a star where we return if we live well. [Timaeus 42] This could be related to the *Phaedo* where Socrates says:

> *Then here is a new way by which we arrive at the conclusion that the living come from the dead, just as the dead come from the living; and this, if true, affords a most certain proof that the souls of the dead exist in some place out of which they come again.* [Plato, Phaedo 72]

This is similar to Ecclesiastes 1:9-11 or Hosea 14:7, and is probably why the *Bahir* says, *It is thus written, "A generation goes and a generation comes," teaching us that it has already come.* [Bahir 155]

The Sabaeans, also called *Harnaniyah*, are the second of Muhammad's People of the Book. [Koran 5:72] They may be from the time of Abraham living in Harran [Genesis 11:31] or the term may refer to where some ancient fundamentalists fled when Jerusalem fell to Rome. Muhammad saw them as derived from the Hebrews, which is consistent with their adoring John the Baptist (who told us all to repent and avail ourselves of baptism in the *mikvah*) and spurning Jesus (who had much more to say and, in their eyes, erroneously arrogated to Himself the Godhead). They marked each day with prayers at dawn, noon and dusk. They marked the sky and year with the east, zenith and west and started their year with the month of *Nisan* (the vernal equinox).

Their God was the Moon, Bull of Heaven, for whom they sacrificed on the sixth day. They had sacred mysteries and three grades of initiation. With Plato, they shared the four virtues of the Spirit: wisdom (or "prudence"), fortitude, temperance and justice. Today we call them Baptists, Mugtasilah, Chaldeans, Nasoraeans and Mandaeans. In their *Haran Gawaita* (Scroll of the Great Revelation), they remember Adam as King of the World, whom they had gladdened by caring for agriculture before all others. They recall Abraham as one of their people and John the Baptist as their savior. To this sect, Jesus and Muhammad were innovators who seriously deviated from holy doctrine – though I believe Moses, Jesus and Muhammad each saw themselves as reformers restoring God's original teachings.

The next day I made Granada. By now, at least here, it was beginning the warm part of the year; and whereas the early Arabs and Berbers who first crossed the Straits must have found this region paradise in contrast to their hot sands, to one coming from the north, I found it hot except amongst the trees.

Here I went to the university, to the mosques and synagogue, and to the Alhambra itself (where the king would not see a Greek bookseller) searching for books of wisdom that could be had for the asking, for gold or for trade. For the most part, people were generous with their knowledge since Moslem and Jewish texts had been coming in their direction for centuries (both from the Middle East and from areas being reconquered by Christians). From the Jews I received a copy of the *Sepher Ha-Bahir* (Book of Illumination) and the *Zohar* (Book of Enlightenment).

What did Pliny the Younger say? *The happier the time, the quicker it passes.* [Epistles VII] Finally, I was learning lessons in life that did not begin with bruises and wounds! I was very happy, and were I an artist, I would have painted the beauty of the mountains, the Alhambra, the gardens and fountains. However, neither words nor my limited talent would be adequate to describe the beauty here. Where the Andalusians irrigate, they could grow the Hanging Gardens of Babylon. Where they build, it appears Damascus has come to Europe. Where they dance, there is only joy. I stayed a week, then rode toward Jaen.

Jaen, 1469

In this caravan stop and mining town that Scipio once captured from the Carthaginians, a learned old man gave me a copy of the *Kitab al-falaha al-nabatiya* (Nabataean Agriculture) of al-Wahshiya, a history of the times before Muhammad. He also told me of a collection where I found parts of Abu Masar's *On the Great Conjunctions*. That work explains the signs in the heavens marking the beginnings of religions and dynasties, the beginnings of wars, the promulgation of great laws and signs of the prophets. The implication in Abu Masar is that life on Earth, as in Heaven, is cyclical – *as above, so below*.

As the planets and stars come back to their positions, they point to the rise and fall of prophets, religions and nations – which brings into question the whole idea of Muhammad being "the Seal of the Prophets" [Koran 33:40] or Jesus being the "Last Adam." [1 Corinthians 15:45] The prophets and their avatars, the great Righteous Ones, are periodically among us. What else could words like *I am with you always, even to the end of the age* ^{Matthew 28:20} mean otherwise?

What else could Peter have meant when he said:

> *In this world there come a succession of prophets, as being sons of the world to come, and having knowledge of men. And if pious men had understood this mystery, they would never have gone astray.* ^{Clementine Homilies 2:15}

Part of the willingness of people to part with the wisdom they had previously guarded zealously may have had to do with the periodic attacks my Chueta friends had mentioned. Though there was no active Inquisition or persecution yet on the mainland, attacks and riots had been going on for years against Jews, Moors and "New Christians." These people were happy to save from the flames the holy wisdom of their ancestors. Had I not been seeking it, they might have buried it or sealed it behind a wall in their homes. Under the new regime, wisdom was dangerous – hence dispensable to them and more rare and precious to me.

On the road to Cordoba, I learned the city was under siege by the Christians. Now I understood the dark humor of al-Zaghall (who would wrest control one day from Muley Hacén) and Boabdil (who would wrest control from his uncle). It was yet another story of a house divided falling to its destruction. Had they been Turks, I doubt Mehmed would have let either of them live long enough to pose a threat. To him, blood ties were a delusion of the weak and an unaffordable luxury for a monarch or heir apparent. Better a bowstring around a royal neck than one sleepless night.

Toledo, 1469

The road was long between Jaen and Toledo, and my old map nearly useless. Ptolemy might have recognized the Tagus River and Toledo. All the roads and stops in between on his map had to be filled in, and almost every name had changed.

Other than my bow, which I kept wrapped in a blanket, and the "pagan" books I kept in saddlebags, there was little to draw attention to me. At one of the first towns on the road, I traded my horse for a mule and now dressed as a Castilian none too successful, neither wanting to appear rich nor too unrespectable. To spies and robbers, I was not an obvious target. When I could, I travelled with a group and was careful not to betray my mission. I had thought to travel in Castile as a priest, then decided Salvatore had not taught me enough for that to be convincing. Better to appear a merchant not having much luck.

Riding up the Tagus, which locals pronounce "Tahoe," I came across an old Templar Castle. I thought of the multitude of Europe's ancient pagan holy places on which they had built cathedrals and the wealth of the world's ancient wisdom they had gathered at the orders of St. Bernard of Clairvaux. I wondered about my past life. What could I have failed to do that still had me searching for wisdom across this arid plateau? Assuming I successfully gathered it, would anyone read it or would I share the fate of the Templars – robbed and silenced by burning at the stake? Could I make a difference? I crossed the bridge and wound my way up the hill toward the Alcázar, a fortress that had defended in turn the Celtiberians, Romans, Visigoths, Moors and Castilians. I suppose control of the city that produces weapons is as important as controlling a key crossroad of commerce.

In Toledo, I was looking for anything left from the old *Escuela de Traductores*. From the late 12th century to the 13th, a number of translators here interpreted literary and scholarly works from Greek and Hebrew into Arabic, and Arabic via Spanish into Latin. In the reign of Alfonso X "The Wise" – an era much more scientifically inclined and tolerant than when I arrived – the school was a center of international culture. Scholars made further translations into French, German, Italian and English. Works of Aristotle, Plato, Galen, Hippocrates, Euclid, Ptolemy and Vitruvius were revived here. Works of some of the great Arabs were translated here, such as Abu-Bakr, Alfarabi, Averroes, Avicenna's *Canon of Medicine,* his version of Aristotle's *De Anima* and al-Kindi's treatises on alchemy and the intellect. I imagined this was where Hebrew works such as Maimonides' *Guide for the Perplexed* were translated as well. The rumor was that here were more than 200,000 manuscripts – a gold mine.

Now, in a time of cultural conflict, I suspected gaining access to the Arab works might be problematic. How locked away would such a collection of non-religious works be kept and under what circumstance might they be viewed?

My first step was to learn the location of the archives. I checked into an inn toward the top of the hill near the Plaza de Zocodover and began looking for anyone appearing as if they belonged in the royal court or the Cathedral. They were not hard to spot. They were well fed, well dressed and seemed to navigate by sniffing the clouds. When I asked about the School of Translators, even well educated folks did not seem to know. Everyone I asked suggested that I try the Cathedral.

As usual, some of the best-kept secrets are right under the noses of the inattentive. I went to a bookshop about a block behind the Cathedral and found a friendly proprietor who said I could look around his cellar. He had recently purchased the establishment from a family whose father had just died and the widow and sons did not care to keep the shop. I dug my way past the stacks and spider webs, and in a corner, just past a huge tome of choir lyrics on a stand, I found a copy of al-Biruni's *Chronology*. The owner let me have it for only three florins. I wonder if he knew what it was, aside from his only work in Arabic.

Next day, I was able to speak to a priest at the Cathedral, who allowed me to see his collection. However, there would be nothing for sale and he was not interested in anything I could trade. I asked whether he might allow a copyist to spend time in the stacks and he agreed this would be acceptable. The books the clergy considered most worthwhile were large and on chains. It was a good collection – about 5,000 works, mostly Catholic in nature. I went looking for a copyist – a literate and talented *converso*.

The following day, I was having lunch at a nearby tavern and noticed a serious young man listening to everything the proprietor offered in the way of a meal. After he had passed up every opportunity for some great food, the exasperated older man said, "Then what about a salad?" The young man replied, "That would be wonderful if you can make it with no meat." Here in Spain, it was the first time I had heard such a thing. Castilla-La Mancha is famous for its lamb, roast pig, sausage, wines, cheeses ... and the young man, who looked normal otherwise, wanted salad. I turned to him and said, "You know, the ribs here are excellent," to which he smiled and replied, "Perhaps another day."

I was intrigued. He either was dirt poor or of a religion that does not trust the meat prepared by Christians. "Tell you what," I said. "You can have anything on the menu, my treat. Do you still want just a salad?" He replied, "That is kind of you, but I cannot accept. I would be happy to split a loaf of bread and a bottle of wine with you if that's alright." "Perfect!" I said, and asked him to join me.

It turned out he was headed home from the University of Salamanca. He was not too sure how he might fare in the city now, the rumor being that the Reconquista was about to take on new force with the pending marriage of Isabel. There had been difficulties in 1449, when his father had lost his public post and 1467 when his brother was in a riot brutally crushed. Juan Antonio Herrera was from a Sephardim family who had converted decades before. They still spoke Arabic and Hebrew at home, in addition to Castilian Spanish. They were doing pretty well financially, though he did not say how. Because his father was a friend of the Chancellor at the University of Salamanca, Juan Antonio had studied law there for six years and now was ready to face the world. I offered him some temporary work copying or translating at a good rate. Told him I would pay him and he could hire whomever he wanted within that amount. I told him to meet me the next day at the Cathedral, and for both he and his friend to "look respectable."

The next day, while the boys were busy going through the stacks with my criteria for what might be important, such as books of wisdom, Moslem law, pagan texts, ancient history, astronomy, astrology, medicine, battle tactics and war strategy ... I spent my time developing a friendship with the priest, a Franciscan.

I had learned that Spain is roughly like Florence. To get anything done, you have to know somebody. The good news about Spain is that everybody knows everybody if you take the time to see how the world is connected. If each of us knows about a thousand people and each of them knows about a thousand people, you can accomplish things for people halfway across the world you never met ... like these fine young lads working for a Sultan they would never meet but in their worst nightmares. For them, there was no culpability in this. As far as they were concerned, I was buying for the Medici.

My priest friend was the second son of one of the Old Christian noble families of Toledo. His older brother had access to the Alcazar. Through the brother's contacts in the Council and the Caballeros (as a companion of the Grandmaster of the Calatrava Knights Don Rodrigo Tellez Giron), he introduced me to the administrator of the archives.

The world can be a delightfully tiny place, that is, right up until you are embarrassed. After that, you might want to find a cave far away, crawl in it and bar the door. Toledo was my cave for the moment. I was still red-faced about Milan.

We hired another translator, worked for four months and in that time copied, abridged or translated a few dozen books. I also purchased a couple dozen "useless" old items from the Alcazar that would not be needed there in an all-Catholic future.

Finally, I had something to trade Mehmed for my life and some items of interest for Lorenzo. I bid my Toledo friends farewell and journeyed by horse and mule to Valencia, where I would board the first caravel bound for Genoa, Venice and Istanbul. I picked up two trunks, a bolt of silk for the ladies, some fine (and not-so-fine) leather skins for bookbinding and bid Spain goodbye. The silk, skins and about half the books and letters headed to Venice marked for the Cardinal (whose part-time secretary Constantine would sort out who received what). A couple of days later, I found another boat out of Genoa that was not stopping in Italy and would head from Malta for Istanbul. It was time to find my fortune or pay for my sins. I was ready.

Chapter Twenty-five

If the righteous wanted, they could create a world. What interferes? Your sins. As it is written in Isaiah, "Only your sins separate you from your God." [Isaiah 59:2] *Therefore, if not for your sins, there would be no difference between you and Him.* [The Bahir 186]

Istanbul, 1469

It took a month to reach Istanbul. Thankfully, we did not run into corsairs and we arrived without incident.

The first thing I needed to do was find a place to stay. There were lots of places down in the old city, but they were not the sort that might attach reputability to a visitor. I bought a sturdy horse and made my way up to the old Grand Admiral's villa. A servant opened the door and I asked him to tell Baltaoglu Suleyman Bey that there was a famous archer from Florence hoping to see him. The young man asked my name, but I did not provide it.

The old man's smile reached all the way to his eyes, or at least the good one. "Come in, come in. I cannot believe it is you! How long has it been? Six years? Let me look at you! Kahil, run tell Ahmed his brother is home!" The youth gave him a strange look, but ran off.

The old man's eyes glistened and he gave me a bear hug and the customary two kisses. "Where have you been, what have you been doing and whatever made you think the mullahs might forgive you?" I smiled and said, "Living in Venice, Florence and collecting wisdom." He laughed, "What would you know of wisdom? You've all your hair and none of it has gone gray!"

I told him of Andrea, little Diana and John, of Bessarion and Piero. I told him of my travels. He, in turn, informed me of doings in court – Mehmed was entering a new phase. *Jihad* had taken to the seas and the

Sultan was in search of ways to curb the power of the Venetians and the Catalan corsairs.

Soon, Ahmed joined us. He had gone Navy instead of cavalry. He told me he was glad to see me growing a beard again and "back in men's clothes." I told him I was happy to see him too. He was working in the admiralty's strategic planning section, not a big cell but an important one. Like me, he had been out surveying the world and updating ancient maps. He said they were looking for ways to carve away at Venice's empire and open new ports to Ottoman shipping. The Sultan saw sea power as the key to world commerce.

We talked about ports on both sides of the Adriatic – Ancona on the Peninsula side, Ragusa and Split on the Dalmatia side. Ever since I had left, the Ottomans had been at war with the Venetians. For that matter, the Venetians had recently engaged in scraps with Florence as well. Having taken Bosnia and Herzegovina, the Sultan was in a position to open up Ragusa and Cattaro if he had a European partner. I said, "Get me an appointment with Mehmed and you will have one." He laughed. "That might not be a good idea considering the circumstances under which you left." I said, "Get me an appointment with Mehmed as an envoy from the Medici and that will all be forgotten. Here, take this gold for the vizier and maybe that will see me through the door."

A few days later, I was seen into Mehmed's *Saray*. The new palace was impressive by any standard. Of course, this was to be expected of the man who had controlled trade with the East for 16 years. There were jewels, silk, ivory, mother of pearl and wonderful gold-, brass- and silverwork everywhere. I wore a black caftan decorated with six-pointed stars in gold thread that I had picked up for such an occasion in Granada. Kahil and another servant came with me carrying a trunk inlaid with ivory, mother-of-pearl and gold filigree.

I prostrated myself in the Eastern manner as someone murmured in the ear of Mehmed. "We thought you dead or lost, Sinan. Where have you been and what news do you bring us?" I was relieved. The mullahs would wait for me to slip up before they struck. "I have crossed the sea and visited the brethren in Granada. I am afraid the *Jihad* is not going well there. Castile and Aragon grow mighty at the expense of al-Andaluz."

"What would Granada have me do?" he asked. "I cannot speak for their king, Excellency, but I would think they are in need of your opening a second front in their war with Aragon." Mehmed laughed. "And just what would that require? I already have a foothold in Europe; I have been expanding it; and in fact, I remain at war with the Christians."

I replied: "They are aware of this, Excellency. However, your enemies – Venice and Aragon – depend more and more on their ships for commerce and raiding. The king who al-Andalus fears the most, Ferdinand, has allied naval and land forces in nearby Naples. Were he distracted, Granada might have only Isabel to fight. They say they have 100,000 troops with which to combat the Castilians." He answered, "Then let them fight and we will see whether they have the spirit and courage and artillery to do what we did here. Where else have you been and what news do you bring?"

"Excellency, when I was expelled from the Corps by the 99th, I went to Venice and saw how the nobles oppress their people and seek to expand their empire. After a number of years there, I went to live in Florence, where I have joined the court of the Medici. On their behalf, I bring you this gift from Granada. It is Arab wisdom left by earlier followers of the Prophet. There are Greek and Hebrew texts as well, also in Arabic. They are the texts I could save from al-Andaluz and could gather in Toledo from the old School of the Translators."

"And why are these of any use to me?" he asked. "I have many Arabic, Christian, and Hebrew texts of old." I replied, "Excellency, they are the beginning of a friendship between you and the Medici. You always taught us that the enemy of my enemy is my friend. Venice has just warred with Florence; and Florence would like to expand its trade with you ... without the tariffs or interference of Venice. Lorenzo 'il Magnifico' as they call him, is, as you are, a lover of wisdom and art. The two of you could profit together at the expense of Venice. It is a matter of using ports friendly to the two of you, on the Peninsula and in Dalmatia."

Mehmed laughed. "Is this your idea? Lorenzo's? The Admiral's?" I answered, "It is plain to anyone with a map, Excellency. The city-states of the Peninsula are ever competing with one another. If you would pull wind from the sails of Venice, and wealth from her Doge so you can expand your control beyond the Marmara Sea, then you may want some of that wind and wealth to go to Florence."

"I like it!" he exclaimed. "And how soon might we conclude such a pact?" "Excellency, I can return with proper diplomats to work out the details, but for now I should think a wedding gift for the recently married couple of Lorenzo de' Medici and Clarice Orsini, and perhaps a gift of books for Lorenzo's father Piero, who sent me on this mission, would go a long way toward achieving your mutual goals."

The Conqueror turned to his Vizier and said, "He is pardoned. Make sure his voyage was worthwhile. Give him access to my scriptorium and prepare something appropriate for his new masters."

I held my hands across my chest in the Eastern way, bowed deeply and backed away. I had bought back my freedom.

The next day, Kreshnik arrived to take me to the scriptorium. He flashed a big smile and said, "This time your arrow struck your target's heart the first time!" "What do you mean by that?" I asked innocently. "Books, codices, manuscripts, scrolls ... news from afar. You got him in his weak spot. The Sultan is all about gathering all the information possible, making up his mind, and conquering the world with it. Fortunately for the world, it doesn't always read the same books ... but you made a big hit with him." I laughed, "Yes, we go way back."

"So how is business?" I asked. "Did he destroy the library in the vault, sell it, or keep it for himself? The rumor is that you burned thousands of volumes. Knowing the Sultan, somehow I doubt that."

He replied, "I picked out classics and a few things of interest before we handed stacks over to the Patriarch. After he selected what he wanted, then yes, there were bonfires. There was much the Patriarch did not want to survive and lots of religious doctrine and mythology that also ran counter to Islam. However, we still have a small collection of books and my boss has us making elegant copies in Arabic and Turkish that will last the centuries. I have been instructed to allow you about fifty original manuscripts in Greek. We will be keeping our copies in Arabic and Turkish of those. Of the oldest manuscripts, those from the time of Constantinople's founding, I can order copies for you but I cannot hand over originals at this time. There are less than 100. Now, just for you, I can get you a copy of Kritovoulos the Iskander's *History of Mehmed the Conqueror*. I'm sure you will enjoy it. Have you any requests?"

I thanked him for all he had done to protect the treasures of the past and all he was doing for me. Then I asked, "Have you anything left from the Old Man of Mystras, Plethon?" He smiled, "We kept his *Compendium of the Doctrines of Zoroaster and Plato,* his copy of the *Chaldean Oracles,* and the one fragment of his *Book of Laws* the Patriarch didn't burn."

I was happy for my friends Bessarion and Constantine. The Phatria's memory was intact! I said, "Well then yes, I could use two copies of those!" Then Kreshnik asked me if I also wished a copy of George of Trebizond's *On the Truth of the Christian Faith* in which "the bootlicker lays out plans for a glorious Moslem-Christian empire, telling Mehmed he is Caesar of the entire world!" I laughed, "If you have an extra copy, I would rejoice to see it in flames!"

Chapter Twenty-Six

Forgive us our sins, as we forgive those who fail in their duty to us.
Luke 11:4

Florence, 1469

Mehmed could be a generous sovereign when he thought it worth his while. He rewarded me with a sack of gold weighing about 20 times more than I had bribed his vizier. He sent me home with books and manuscripts for Piero's library, some ornate gifts of intricately carved ivory and crystal for Clarice, and a jeweled gold book cover for Lorenzo. He also dictated a letter of friendship with Florence, outlining some initiatives for cooperation and inviting a delegation to come cement these ties.

When I returned home, Constantine and Lorenzo warmly greeted me. They reported that both Bessarion and Piero were elated with what I had been able to find for them. Unfortunately, it was not a very happy time for any of us.

Piero was on his deathbed. What in the beginning had been a disease of kings – the result of too much rich food and sweet drink – was now killing him. He was bloated, in terrible pain with joints inflamed and twisted. Only his clear mind and voice still worked. His heart, liver and kidneys were in a race to be the first to shut down. I went through Avicenna's *Canon of Medicine* and found nothing that might serve as a real cure, only treatment for the latest and worst symptoms. Like Avicenna, Western doctors suggested bleeding out the poisons from his joints, but this could do nothing to get at the root cause. The family patriarch died a painful death December 3rd. He was 53 years of age.

I returned home to find that Constantine had helped Andrea finish setting up the new house. She finally had it decorated and landscaped just the way she wanted. My study required a few adjustments, but the rest was definitely hers.

Andrea was sick in the mornings and moody all of the time. Watching her exchange worried looks with Constantine, I resolved to accept the obvious and pretend I did not know the basic mathematics of gestation when our next baby came due.

I had essentially done the same as Salvatore's best friend – left my attractive young wife unattended in a world of biological imperatives. I would never say a word, nor give hint that I knew what transpired when our "two-months-premature" baby showed up full-size. What else could I do if I still loved them both? He who cannot forgive knows not how to live! Nor did Andrea ask the usual jealous wife questions when I returned. I imagine she assumed the worst and was relieved when I did not play the jealous husband. In July, Andrea gave birth to our second son. I named him Constantine, in honor of my father ... and my best friend.

On my next trip to Istanbul, in about May 1470, I brought my friend Constantine with me. He got along famously well with Ahmed and Mehmed's son Bayezid II, a friendship that may serve them one day if the Ottomans want to establish a more traditional, legitimate rule for their subjects in the Morea or Trebizond. I also introduced Constantine to my friend the Sufi Sheikh. I knew there were Pythagorean secrets there to share on the history of religion. Kreshnik was true to his word and produced beautiful copies of Plethon's work. He also had freed up some truly ancient manuscripts for Lorenzo.

On that trip, Constantine and I finally figured out the relationship of the Order of St. George to the Phatria. It was not that there were two orders in competition with each other, one holy and one occult, as they had often appeared to my youthful mind. It was that every religion has within it a core of mystics contemplating the divine light, and those students of the divine revelation are just a little different. Outside that tiny circle gathered around the fire (whom normal people would not understand even on their best days) are the practitioners who want to lead an active life of service and to do so within the usual rites and narratives of the organization built around the core.

That is why religions like the Sabaeans ended up with three degrees of initiation. The Mandaeans were the masses. The Nasoraeans were the clergy. The Nasirutha were the masters. Catholicism went with a more layered Mithraic hierarchy, but it was the same idea.

The Order of St. George was comprised of knights charged to defend Christianity. They were practitioners. They learned the stories and meanings of some of the symbols. The Phatria was a silent inner group studying all the old mysteries and all the philosophical truths of the world, cobbling together narratives and symbols that might make sense for the future of mankind. The Order would try to breathe back life into what was once Rome and Greece. The Phatria would try to build a better world.

If you were a person of fixed ideas, the Order was for you. If you had an open mind, it would not do to have you arguing all day with the others – and into the Phatria you could go. For the multitudes who were just fearful enough of God to want to do a few things right in this life? Well, they went to Church every week and lived in the Empire every day and cared not that there were other kinds of people charged with defending or growing it. They would happily live their lives watching shadows dancing on the cave walls until the next war or famine or Plague.

St. Cyril of Jerusalem once set out a pretty good goal for the Church at all levels of initiation. He said it was to be the school for Godliness:

> *The Church is called Catholic, then, because it extends over the whole world, from end to end of the earth, and because it teaches universally and infallibly each and every doctrine which must come to the knowledge of men concerning things visible and invisible, heavenly and earthly, and because it brings every race of men into subjection to Godliness.* Catechetical Lectures 18:23

Unfortunately, this worthy goal assumes Godly men at the top and that is hardly ever the case. Quite a few popes and emperors had proved that. St. Cyril himself had proved it. Was he not involved in the murder of virtuous Hypatia? Nor would my friends and I be judged any better; so it was not the goal that needed changing – it was men. Constantine and I prepared for another trip, this one to Austria.

Chapter Twenty-Seven

Such is the 'virile robe' of these people. Such is the first honor of their youth. Till then the young man was only one in a family. He becomes by this rite a member of the Republic. ^{Tacitus, Germania, On the Presentation of a Sword}

Schlossberg Castle, 1470

If Mehmed was a master of force, the Holy Roman Emperor in Austria was the master of diplomacy and ceremony. Why squander lives and treasure if a well-placed marriage, a medal or a promise might buy you peace? Frederick III had, and by his example promulgated, a preference for jewels, medals and titles over blood and glory on the battlefield.

What Constantine and I wanted was to reseat the Order at the home of Empire, providing it a wider influence than it might receive from Venice. The Order had been famous throughout Christendom as having the highest precedence in antiquity, but now it had no voice in the machinations of Europe. Without that, the ideals of Greece and Rome would become a whisper amidst a primarily Teutonic uproar.

We brought Bessarion with us to convince the Emperor. The Cardinal, stung by his experience at Ancona, still wanted to mount a 10th Crusade. We all try to measure up to our heroes, and I suppose his was St. Bernard (right after Plethon). However, given the spotty success of most of the Crusades and given Mehmed's current might, European nobles much preferred a good show to a real battle. One could fight all day with such men and not kill anyone! In fact, this had been the result of the latest fight between Venice and Florence.

Frederick, meanwhile, saw our Knights as a new force to limit the aggression of the Turks and as a defense of the German kingdoms. He appointed a Great Master and made him a prince of the realm. He provided a castle and lands at Millstadt, where he also turned a former abbey into a Cathedral Church of Canons. We held initiations with the help of Bessarion and a local priest, and 50 knights were sworn in under the rule of Saint Augustine.

First, there was an interview of a dozen questions for the knight and his sponsor. Next, the noble sponsors armed the knights with swords. The knights swore in with a *Credo* – one considerably longer than the Nicene or Athanasian creeds. A responsorial interview followed with the knights and the Great Master, ending with another oath. This is when the candidate was tapped on head and shoulders with a sword; and as each knight arose, a mantle that had been blessed was placed on his shoulders.

After the Mass and ceremonies, we had a marvelous banquet that included people from all the confederated kingdoms, as well as brethren in arms from afar. At my table, for example, we had visitors from the Knights Avis (Portugal) and the Knights Calatrava (Spain). I saw Constantine sitting with Teutonic Knights and Knights of St. John; and I observed Bessarion speaking to a Knight of the Garter and a Knight of St. Ivan of Ancona. In all, there must have been 300 people from throughout Europe's nobility.

Through Frederick's support, the movement would spread. Soon the Knights were also to be found in Genoa, sponsored by the Duke of that city. The Venice knights were now centered in nearby Brianno with my friend Constantine as their Grand Master. Thanks in part to our efforts, the Order is today remembered in a dozen more countries than when we started and a few more men are aware of the ancient wisdom hidden in the original Christianity.

Chapter Twenty-eight

For a just man falleth seven times, and riseth up again: but the wicked shall fall into mischief. Proverbs 24:16

Florence, 1470-1480

When we returned home, I was a dedicated family man. I had belatedly realized that being a good spouse and parent is one of the very few chances we get on this wheel of life to redeem ourselves of previous stupidity. Besides raising a child, how many miracles are there in which God invites us to take the lead? Whether I was good enough at it to wipe my slate clean ... we will see. I suppose I had been more sinful than most, in which case I am hoping Jesus' forgiving *until seventy times seven* Matthew 18:22 prevails, as opposed to Yahweh's promise, *I will punish you seven times more for your sins.* Leviticus 26:18 Unless, of course, He means He will send us back to pain on Earth seven more times, in which case, sign me up!

Constantine returned to Venice for a time. Soon, with Bessarion's recommendation, he would go to Rome and become part of the security force for the Vatican. This proved a wonderful spot to hear and read ideas from across the Empire, as well as to observe the inner circle's care of the religion of the Christ. The following year, Bessarion died at age 69, the greatest Greek scholar of our time.

By the winter of 1471, little Constantine was 18 months old. He was walking, talking, stacking things and knocking them down. Having a little child that adores you is about the only thing in the world better than being in love. I imagine it must be how God feels every day. I hope we make him proud sometimes.

I stayed in touch with my network of friends, knights and book-collecting families. Sometimes I would get out to swap or borrow manuscripts for my trade, or to purchase an estate's holdings.

On occasion, I would get out to a book fair or run into a traveling bookseller.

Much of the time, I would study history or review the progress of scribes working for me. I never did set up the printing press with Aunt Anna. She supported the Aldine Academy at Venice when it began and eventually sponsored the first all-Greek edition of a printed book, the *Etymologicum Magnum* published by Zacharias Kallierges, who used my family's double-eagle as his printer's mark.

Not many of my second-chance years were very interesting or sinful. I did find a new love. Through my sons, I learned how to teach; and Lorenzo would sometimes have me over to his Academy where he was raising a group of very bright youngsters and scholars. In all, I would say his Academy seemed to lack the propensity for shenanigans between professors and their students that earlier schools of the sort had suffered. At least I saw no obvious signs of such misbehavior. Lorenzo was a decent and noble man. If ever a people benefited from a benevolent tyrant, it was the Florentines under *Il Magnifico*. I believe Plato would have viewed him as the philosopher king he had always wanted to see.

We had a couple of scares in which there was not much one could do. In 1477, Ottoman forces were again attacking Venetian interests, having previously massacred the island populace of Negroponte. I figured it was just a matter of time before Mehmed made the long-prophesied run on Rome. As he consolidated control of his side of the Adriatic, I wondered how long we would have. He would likely attack from the sea when the time came – there being such long lines of communication to defend if one attacks by land, especially from the north. Still, I felt my family threatened by his insatiable desire for glory, and found it exceedingly wearying.

The other scare came at the end of April 1478. The King of Naples, with Pope Sixtus IV (make that four evil popes on my list now), his nephew Cardinal Riario, Archbishop Salviati and members of the Pazzi family decided they wanted to expand the Pope's lands and oust the Medici brothers through assassination. Andrea and I were in church for the Solemn High Mass that day. Andrea had gone to confession that morning and was looking forward to communion. While I would have liked to abandon the Mass at that time, we were going to stick around for her Lord's Supper.

As the priest broke the bread and took the Host into his mouth, a number of villains sporting daggers sprang up around Lorenzo and Giuliano to take their lives. There were priests among the assassins! I grabbed Giuliano's murderer by the throat as he ran to escape the scene of his treachery, and broke his head against the wall. Lorenzo escaped with some friends into the vestry. Giuliano was dead almost from the first strike.

The attackers thought shouting "against the tyrants" would be a call to arms. Instead, the crowd tore them to pieces. Such was the generosity of the Medici family that cries of "People" and "Liberty" meant nothing. The archbishop and his henchmen who had simultaneously attempted to storm the palace were summarily hanged. Only the intervention of Lorenzo saved the Cardinal, who lied, swearing he had nothing to do with the attack. (Riario would meet a violent end some years later at the hands of his own people.)

Some of the bodies of the villains were dragged through the streets. Few conspirators or their families escaped. One made it all the way to Istanbul, only to have Mehmed send him back to us for judgment. Some of the conspirators were imprisoned. Most were simply mutilated and deprived of their lives immediately.

Then the King and Pope, frustrated in their plan to position the late Archbishop Salviati in the Florentine government, now threatened war and excommunication to all Florentines, so that we might turn over Lorenzo or elsewise banish him. *Il Magnifico* offered surrender rather than invite the wrath of the powerful on his city. Not surprisingly, the people preferred Lorenzo to such royal and holy benefactors.

Milan said it would join us, for this Pope had murdered their Duke, also in a church. Venice promised troops to check the power of the south. King Ferrante and the Pope did all they could to isolate us from all help. After months of the war going badly, Lorenzo traveled to Naples to speak to the King, who detained him from December to March. Our master statesman then headed home with a treaty for mutual protection in his hand! This drew the rage of the Pope and Venice – and the Duke of Calabria refused to withdraw from Sienna. It looked like we were headed into a few more years of internecine warfare when something occurred to give everyone pause.

Seeing all this confusion on the Peninsula, Mehmed apparently saw his opportunity and sent his former Grand Vizier Gedik Ahmed Pasha to Otranto in July 1480 to begin the attack on Italy. For me, this was finally the unmistakable sign on which to act.

Centuries ago, in the monastery San Vincenzo al Volturno, a monk named Iohannes wrote in his *Chronicon Vulturnense* that the End Times would see another attack on Southern Italy by the Moslems, the first having occurred in the year 881, killing 900 monks there. There are dozens of such signs for the times of Antichrist, but this one I clearly remembered.

I had finally reached the end of my patience with the Sultan. He had taken my father, my stepmother, my grandfather, and my uncles. He had taken my freedom and my first love. For all I knew he might have sent Zaganos with Plague to Venice when my baby Diana died (as the Tartars had carried it to Kaffa three decades earlier). And now he threatened what was left of my life and family?

I had no love for the King of Naples, who would be the first to fall. I had no love for the Pope, who merited any punishment inflicted. However, I would not stand idle to any threat to Andrea or the boys.

"Know thine enemy" say the great generals. This enemy I knew as if he were my own shadowy twin. Wisdom and Power Mehmed asked of the Serpent. Wisdom and Power the Serpent would teach!

Chapter Twenty-Nine

To the Shadow of God, Most August of the Caesars, King of Kings, Mehmed the Conqueror, the Fortunate, the Two-Horned, hope and comfort of all Muslims, by the will of God I salute you!

Sinan Yay Burcu
Servant of thy servants

Years ago, O Sultan of the Romans, I promised you a Book of Prophecies if ever I wrote one. Here, with your indulgence, I would aim to fulfill that promise. There is little prophecy here, but hopefully a bit of wisdom. As a force shaping the destiny of nations, you were seldom the one in need of a seer. No, the whole world consulted oracles to see what you would do.

Before I go on, I should probably confess: I was the Prophet of Belgrade. The events of that unfortunate battle unfolded as I had seen them in a vision granted at a Temple of Apollo. I should have said nothing. I told one close friend and the rumor spread like wildfire. However, neither the vision nor the rumor was the cause of our destruction that week. Some destinies are truly written in the stars.

I should confess that, before you were my Sultan and I the least of your servants, at the age of nine years old, I was your sworn enemy. When you took my empire and my city, you also deprived me of my family. Eventually, I forgave you. Later, you took my love, placed her in your harem, and then sold her to the highest bidder. In time, I forgave you even this. Today, a generation later, your Italian campaign threatens my new family. My soul is now so vexed that it will require another lifetime to earn back my wings. So be it.

Let others flatter you now. You and I shall deal in Truth.

Everywhere man blames nature and fate, yet his fate is mostly but the echo of his character and passions, his mistakes and weaknesses. ^{Democritus}

The Past

The memory of humankind only goes back to the last great disaster. We periodically pass through a winnowing of humanity so severe that we lose all record of the past. We no more remember what preceded that time than we can remember before our births.

Though we have been on Earth for eons, our histories go back 5,000 years and our legends 20,000 beyond that. Just beyond the oldest legend lurks an Alpha-Omega moment of destruction and rebirth. The Alpha-Omega refers to a star sign of the great and terrible season.

"Creation" stories, then, are a half-truth, a marker selected by a storyteller for when his tale begins ... or it stands for the real limit of human memory. There were Creations for the Universe and the Galaxy and these are unknown to man except conceived as the act of a God we cannot see and cannot know, despite anyone's pretensions to the contrary.

Dates of Destruction we can know. The difference between the two is as the day we are born versus the day we die. Were we born the day God sowed our souls *In the Beginning*? The day our fathers lay with our mothers? The day we took our first breaths? Yet the day we die is no mystery. Our mind ceases. Our heart stops. Our soul journeys back to God.

The Alpha-Omega moments for the regeneration of the Earth are of the greatest significance. They are the reason the *Bible* begins with Creation, ends in Apocalypse and is written on a scroll. The story is to be read through in a year, every year, and this is also why the word *Koran* means "tie together" as in: Tie the ends of this scroll together, for it is complete.

Scriptures, then, are the holy cycle and the beating heart of the Universe. They teach us to watch for the Alpha-Omega and to prepare. Understanding life and death, where we came from and where we are going, is the purpose of religion. Serving God and humankind is ours.

The Present

Just as you and I had signs in the stars marking the day that Light would first strike our eyes, we also were fated with signs indicating when we would die. You were fortunate in having learned yours long beforehand. This gave you time to put things in order.

O Bull of Heaven, you are to die again, this time in the knowledge you achieved one of Muhammad's hadiths, that of taking Byzantium: *Verily you shall conquer Constantinople. What a wonderful leader will her leader be, and what a wonderful army will that army be!* The Prophet's other dream – that of taking Rome – you will not achieve in this lifetime.

You are dying as my master Piero died, the painful death from a life too abundant. The penalties for a life of gluttony and lust are vicious, and the suffering they bring is redemptive only if they teach humility and godliness.

Throughout our long and painful lives, you and I were helping God to shape the destiny of the world. You helped Him destroy what remained of iniquitous Byzantium, and you did this because it was right for your people and your religion. I walked behind you planting the seeds of your Empire's destruction – and this was right for my people and my religion.

Looking back, I wonder: Were those our fates or did you and I choose this evil? Did two lovers of wisdom have to spend their lives at war? Did the Prophet really intend the slaughter of other People of the Book? I, for one, refuse to believe this cycle of mutual destruction is or was ever necessary.

The Future

The world is fast approaching the next End of Days – a renewal of the planet written in the skies. At the end of our dynasties, about a cycle of the Phoenix from now, humanity will be within a century of its next great crisis marked by signs in the heavens.

You and I will return then ... you to attempt to seize control of humanity and guide it through the gate of destruction, and I to ensure your success is not the end of hope for mankind. Your weapon will again be Power. Mine will again be Truth. You will establish Order and I shall clamor for Justice. You will establish Tyranny and I will demand a benevolent King. You will establish an Oligarchy and I shall demand an Aristocracy that cares for people. You will harness the Mob and I will demand Democracy.

Neither of us wins when we act separately, just as no one religion, king, Prophet or Savior was ever the answer to all humanity's problems. You established the Laws and I attempted to reform them.

You relished human sacrifice and I substituted an animal. You enjoyed blood sacrifice and I substituted plant offerings. You punished humanity with your rod and I told the children they did not deserve your abuse.

I have no illusions about the morality of our positions. In Ecclesiastes 7:14, it is written, *Also one opposite the other was made by God.*

I see Evil on both sides, just as Good can be on either. If the way you wish to impose your Order ... *Jihad* ... involves killing people instead of teaching them, then I see your Order as Evil. If mankind worships so long at the altar of Freedom that it raises children as the connoisseurs of vice instead of as good people, that too is Evil. In this life, you were the more successful, but whether what you and I did was Good, that remains to be seen.

In our next lives, you should follow your heart instead of being fearful of people like Zaganos, who only follow the Devil of their own selfishness. Irene, your first and best Love, probably forgave you for what you did to impress that man. As Plutarch said, *Death sets us free even from the greatest evils.* [Consolation to Apollonius] If she loved you, you will find her in Heaven waiting, not to serve your carnality but to rejoice with your soul. You and I will do better next time, especially if we can return with those we love best.

As to the future of humanity, the end of this Age of Pisces is the end of another turn of the zodiac. The signs are lining up for an Alpha-Omega rebirth. Upon our return, I hope you and I can work together, Truth in support of Power, and Power in support of Truth. Together, and God willing, we might ensure that humanity survives. Otherwise, beware the sign of the Son of Man.

Your brother in Wisdom,

John IX Palaeologus

NOTE: *The Florilegium that accompanied this letter is at the end of this tome.* [Page 336]

Chapter Thirty

He [the Antichrist] shall be broken without hand. ^{Daniel 8:25}

No decoration is more worthy of the eminence of a prince or more beautiful than that crown bestowed for saving the lives of fellow-citizens. ... To save life by crowds and universally, this is a godlike use of power. ^{Seneca, On Mercy}

Florence, 1481

When I was a youngster growing up, and had known a gypsy woman with talents in potions, she had told me of a special hide in Africa that only the tanners could withstand. She said it had raised blisters and if the blisters popped when the leather was dry, it could be fatal to anyone that breathed in its dust.

When I was in Granada, I had seen such a defective skin and purchased it. It went to Florence in a bag marked "Do not open for any reason." Now, for a special gift of mercy to Mehmed, I gave it a light coating of wax and used it to cover a copy of my *Florilegium*, or commonplace book, my little book of quotes collected since I was about six. When I was finished sewing the pages and gluing the little codex together and letting it dry, I covered my mouth and nose with a wet rag and buffed the book with gloves. The blisters rubbed open.

Using a cloth wet in a yellow dye, I then gave the book a light brushing. This gave the finish an interesting polka-dotted pattern, which was common in those days with the Ottomans (usually on clothes, not books). That night, I could not sleep. My chest was tight and congested and my brain was on fire with a lightning storm that went on for about six hours. I was glad I had not breathed the powder and had only touched it.

I sent the book to Kreshnik through a contact at the port doing business with Istanbul. I said it was a book the Sultan ordered when we were exchanging manuscripts. I asked him to deliver it to Mehmed in the gilded box provided, sometime between the 1st and 3rd of May. I added that the Sultan had said he would be taking it easy on those days, even if he were in the field.

Much later, I would learn that the Sultan was out on campaign, but that he had been "ill and resting" and had sent for his doctor. I had imagined that, recalling his prophecy, he might stay inside to avoid stray arrows. My hope, of course, was that he would welcome a book at such a time.

The doctor delivered the book. I have no way of knowing whether Mehmed read it, but he died at about 11 a.m. on the 3rd. The Sun was at the heart of Taurus, a sign in which Abu Masar (six centuries earlier) had announced Byzantium would be ascendant!

Campaign planning for the full-scale invasion of Italy was cancelled. When the former vizier learned of his Sultan's death, he retreated from Italy. Two weeks later, Bayezid II was the new Sultan and he was considerably less ambitious than his father. Praise be to God!

Chapter Thirty-One

For a man to stand forth as the defender of parents, children, friends, and fellow-citizens, led merely by his sense of duty, acting voluntarily, using judgment, using foresight, moved neither by impulse nor by fury – this is noble and becoming. ^{Seneca, On Anger Bk I xii}

Florence, 1481

On May 3rd, I confessed to Lorenzo what I had done. He probably would not want to be harboring a fugitive from Ottoman justice if Bayezid II was upset about being promoted early to Sultan, so I thought I would let Lorenzo decide what to do with me.

Clearly if life were a chess game, by now I would have lost half a dozen times for my inability or unwillingness to think out the third- and fourth-order consequences of my actions. I just hoped and prayed that when I made a decision, it would be with the right intent. After that, I would be in God's hands and that would be alright.

The first thing Lorenzo said was, "You did WHAT?"

J: I killed the Sultan this morning.

L: And how could you possibly do that from a thousand miles away when you have been here all morning?

J: It was something he read, a bit of bad news. I sent him a special book, a *Florilegium* I had been keeping since I was very young.

L: (Laughing) Why would Mehmed read such a book; what makes you think he received it; and just how can reading a book kill a man?

J: Once Mehmed's father finally got his attention by assigning a teacher with instructions to beat him whenever he did not do his lessons, Mehmed became a lifelong student of wisdom. He did not read for the benefit of his soul or his people. He did it to harvest measures of glory to heap onto himself and to understand the means for gaining greater power. Last month, I sent the book to a friend in his scriptorium and asked for it to be delivered by today. The binding was poisonous.

L: (Scowling now) Why would you tell me you did such a thing; why would you do such a thing; and what am I supposed to do with you?

J: As ruler of Florence, you must decide whether what I did was the right thing for your people and whether your agreement to extradite fugitives to the Turks includes capturing me and sending me to my death as a token of your good faith. What I did, I did for all Romans – all the citizens of the old Empire whom that son of a slave chose to capture or slay next in the name of his Prophet!

L: What made you think Mehmed would not simply stop at Rome? What if he was defending us against Rome, Naples and Calabria?

J: Because I knew Mehmed better than Mehmed knew himself. His design, if he had sufficient troops, arrows, gunpowder, gold and time was to recapture the lost lands of the Muhammadans all the way to Portugal and to recapture the lands of Alexander the Great, his hero. He had what he needed to do it, given the fractious nature of Christendom, so I deprived him of time. If what he was doing was defending you against the King of Naples, he should have invaded sooner. We were in what to him appeared as a civil war for nearly two years. He was playing watch-them-kill-each-other, then divide, conquer, steal the wealth and sell the slaves. That was his goal, his method and his legacy! He left many beautiful white buildings in Constantinople, but he was no better than any Caesar of old. Everything was done with slave labor, with stolen gold and in the name of a tyrant. He lived by the code of all the old Emperors: *What is won through trial of combat is won by right.* For me, this was personal on so many levels it would take all day to explain. My life is yours. What would you do with it?

L: Well, John, I believe you are right. I did not invite his forces to the Peninsula even when we needed help because I didn't think him a man with control of his passions. With his ruthless nature, he might have made a successful banker or businessman – right up until people got to know him. So let us assume your plan to render reading fatal has proven successful. Does the crime trace back to you?

J: Mehmed's son Bayezid will have a lifelong distrust of books. I signed the letter using my Ottoman name and the introduction using my real name. Bayezid knows me. If the new Sultan wants me, then he also knows I am ready to meet my maker. Right now, he has the perfect opportunity to make his father a hero and a martyr or to quietly take control. He is a better man than his father. I think he will burn the book and that will be that. He knows his father was no martyr and certainly no saint.

L: Is there anything else I should know?

J: Mehmed was warned about 36 years ago that a son of Rome by the name Palaeologus would strike him down with the Sun in Taurus. If his vizier had not crossed into Italy, Mehmed would still be alive. Until then, I had no pressing need to preempt him or to seek revenge. At this point, we cannot undo the past and we must look to the future. What would you have me do?

L: As fantastic as your story sounds, I would be a fool to send you bound to the Sultan – old or new. Whatever happened, I should not really know for two weeks. My suggestion to you would be to pack your things so I can banish you. As to Andrea and the boys, they are welcome to stay until she chooses to join you. You could just go on one of your manuscript hunts and write to see how things are before you return. Whatever you choose to do, I thank you on behalf of my people and my family. We are in your debt. Unfortunately, we are not in a position to be recognizing you for what you have done – since we cannot afford a war with the Ottomans. I do think making the fight personal is more civilized than killing thousands, though I cannot say I approve of your methods. If, as you say, there was a blood debt, then I am sure justice was done. For the lives that were saved, I thank you again.

We shook hands and I left, but it was still time to face the music.

Chapter Thirty-Two

Jesus said unto them, "A prophet is not without honour, save in his own country, among his own kin, and in his own house." Mark 6:4

Florence, 1481

The conversation with Andrea did not go nearly as well. Apparently, there is only one sin as bad as introducing competition real or imagined into a woman's life – and that is getting into it with one's own competition. Nothing Mehmed had ever done, not even invading Italy, was worth getting involved. According to her, everything was supposed to be peace, love and penance – even if that meant being hauled off as a slave or being martyred by a guy with a big sword. Her idea sounded as fatalistic as what I had been taught by the Imams. Wait to see what God wills and suffer through it.

I am sure this was her theoretical reconstruction of Christianity talking, because that is not how she had led her own life. She could have remained one of four wives to one of my cousins and instead she had left him. Of course, the other thing you should never do with a woman is bring up ancient history! Their memories are better – illustrated in fine detail with near-perfect recall and drawn from the vantage point least advantageous to whomever they happen to be instructing. No. Tis far better to hear out the rant and live with whatever resentment is left. It all came down to my bringing undo danger upon her children by saving my fellow citizens. As always, she was right. How irresponsible of me!

The bottom line was that I should go on one of my trips and take my time coming back. She would keep the villa and the business going. If she needed anything, she would talk to Clarice or her friend, the poet. "Or Constantine," I uncharitably thought to myself, but then I figured they had probably repented of that little episode, as I had of Elena.

This time I would visit the knights in Brianno, Millstadt and Genoa. This time I would hit the book fairs in Lyon and Frankfurt. This time, I would find my family. This time I would see the books I had missed in Spain. I kissed Andrea, told the boys to be good and I was off to the Medici bank for some bills of exchange. Why carry a bag of gold when one can dress modestly and carry almost nothing?

Chapter Thirty-three

May he grant justice to the people who are oppressed. May he save the children of needy people and crush their oppressor. Psalm 72:4

Piemonte, 1481

I love the country, far from the noise, the phoniness and filth. Climbing a hill overlooking the great valleys and rejoicing in the nearby snow-capped Alps, I was mindful of what wretched rulers of creation men are. We try so hard to improve on the works of God and there is just no point. In nature, I always found something to eat, something to drink and a place to get out of the rain where it never cost a florin.

In these times of reverie in the bright light and the stiff breeze, I had no need of books or people and very little need for food. An occasional brook or spring and I was happy to walk off my city-fed fat. These moments relaxing among the pines provided a wonderful time to reassess my life.

The boys were growing so big and they were so eager to learn. At 13, John appeared as someone who could grow up to play just about any role – landowner, courtier, soldier, scholar, or tradesman. For the moment, he was a bright young student who much enjoyed debating other students in the Academy. Constantine, at 11, seemed more interested in the cloth, possibly due to his mother's influence. She attended Mass every day, and between the court and the congregation, she was always quite busy. Constantine was a sociable, sensitive soul. The age of Lorenzo's eldest, Lucrezia, he played with Piero, Maddalena and little Giovanni as well. Andrea was encouraging him to join the San Marco monastery. I told him I would support any decision he wanted to make.

The Order was doing well, though I observed everywhere a new current in the politics of Europe. A debate had opened over the form of government that should eventually prevail. People seemed to see monarchs as an expedient way to further a city's or a country's interests for now, but the discussion emerging from a reacquaintance with classical literature was promoting alternatives. I could see the positions of even such excellent people as Lorenzo were going to be precarious.

Three generations of Medici had spent hundreds of thousands of florins improving the lives of their compatriots and hosting grand spectacles. In that sense, there was a considerable reserve of goodwill. Nevertheless, I could see that Florence would soon want a real Republic back; and her people would be no less volatile once they achieved it. For now, they were happy with Lorenzo, but I could see them readily disenchanted with most anyone, including themselves.

At each establishment of the Order, I would leave a copy of our Rule, our History, our Ceremonies and my *Florilegium*, the latter only because it contained some ideas I thought as worthwhile to humanity's future as they had been to our past. Looking back, perhaps my little collection of sayings was both part of the problem and part of the hope.

The manuscript and book trade was fueling fires of discontent and I could imagine the Church and all Europe's ancient nobility would be concerned. The more we read and talk, the more our thinking becomes nuanced and complicated, and the less willing we are to embrace old codes of behavior and aristocracies. While I welcomed the idea of throwing off shackles that had bound people a thousand years, I wondered what sort of bloodshed may be on the horizon as new tyrants are encouraged to imperial aspirations, oligarchs are encouraged to concentrate wealth in fewer hands, and the people in their poverty are encouraged to replace their masters. Does anyone outside royalty regard governors as God's appointed stewards?

I was beginning to see my desire for a peaceful life and Andrea's desire to stay in the city could not long remain compatible goals. The Florentines would soon abandon their experiment with Dantean Monarchy and would want to restore their Republic rather than repeat the errors of their Roman forebears. My prediction was that we were heading for an ugly day. In fact, less than three weeks from my departure on this trip, Lorenzo suffered another assassination attempt, again in a church! Sixtus IV was one greedy pope.

If "civilization" is the fruit of efficient government creating a surplus of resources for the people, then Lorenzo's beneficent despotism was indeed generating the Golden Age of which he dreamed. Arts and letters were flourishing. Jealous infighting of the aristocracy was calmer now since he had born injury with magnanimity, captivity with generosity, and insult with grace. He even reconciled with several of his enemies and their families. Despite such hopeful signs, I began to cast about in my wanderings, thinking of where I might wish to move the family if a coup were to destroy the Medici, and Florence were again to banish its illustrious families, as it had in the time of Dante.

On this trip, I travelled sometimes alone, sometimes in a merchant caravan, and once with gypsies. Sometimes that was the luck of the road and sometimes a matter of my mood. There have been times when I am better off without people and, I am sure, they are better off without me. There are others when life deserves to be a party.

There are a couple of difficulties in travelling with gypsies or *Rom – Sinti* as they are called in this region. One is how they are sometimes treated by xenophobic townspeople in areas they have lived only a short time. Another is their language, which is not as easy as learning Italian or Castilian. It is more like the ancient Aramaic spoken by Jesus.

They liked the idea of having a bowman along and I enjoyed their tending to travel from festival to festival. I met one that was a horse trader, one a blacksmith and another a goldsmith, but mostly I met musicians and dancers who marry young, die old and are ever willing to help bring in the harvest if they can keep a bit for themselves. Mostly, theirs was a good and peaceful life.

While they seem to behave as one extended family, I shared campfire with a one-wagon family of a grandfather, two parents and two children. The grandfather seemed to be the leader who worked the politics of the family with the larger group, and it was all very friendly.

The children were curious about the outsider. I undertook to learn their language while they attempted to learn some of my Greek, Italian and Spanish words. It seemed they took to other languages as easily as I did. The little girl was called Tsuri, which means Dawn – first goddess of the Aryans. The boy was called Tobar. She was 12 and he was seven. Both were beautiful, but she was strikingly so. Green doe eyes, olive skin, high cheekbones, a bright smile, a perfect chin and nose. No sculptor ever did finer work than God and her parents. Had Diana grown up, I know I would have died worrying for such beauty.

Late one afternoon, the children were out gathering wood and water for the evening's cooking when a local tyrant decided he wanted a couple of slaves and had his men steal them. The whole camp was ready to go to war with knives to take on swords and crossbows. I calmed the grandfather and told him I would bring the children back with their father Stevo and one other man who had spent time as a soldier. We had a good idea where the kidnappers were headed and we rode to meet them before they retreated behind the walls of a manor.

We attacked them at the only bridge before their destination, Stevo and I from the bridge, the other man from hiding about 50 feet before the bridge. The captors wore mail, so we took down the lead and rear guard with head shots. We looked pretty disreputable, but not necessarily like gypsies, so they initially couldn't tell us from any other group of brigands. Unfortunately, the children saw their father and started yelling "Dad."

Stevo yelled something in Romani I did not understand. Tobar jumped off the bridge and our friend jumped in after him. I closed with the man in front. He got off a bad shot with his crossbow catching Stevo on the left shoulder. Before the man could reload, I was on him. He pulled his sword and I took him out with my rapier in a few strokes, parrying with *Agheu Glas* and finishing him with a *coup-droit* to the throat. Fencing practice with my friends had paid off.

Now Tsuri's captor began to back up with an arm around her neck and a dagger to her side. What could we do? Well, in the old gypsy sense of honor a dead daughter must be somehow better than a dishonored one. Stevo yelled something and the girl went limp in the crook of the man's arm. As he shifted his balance to squeeze the one arm to hold her up, he stabbed her with the other while receiving a dagger to his forehead. I wish I could throw a knife that well! The girl and the tyrant crumpled in a pile, Tsuri gasping for breath and bleeding between the ribs.

Tsuri was about to die unless Stevo was willing to help. I told them both to stay calm, even though she was gasping for breath. I told her not to panic, to relax, that we would breathe for her three times and after that, on the last breath, she should leave her breath go for a few seconds. I ripped the dress along the side. I told her father to give her air when I held up my hand and I would depress her abdomen between breaths. As he did that, I breathed into my lungs everything coming out of the wound, letting nothing flow back. After we had done that three times, I jammed a gold florin into the wound flat against the ribs and had Stevo hold it in place with his finger. Then I quickly sewed the wound shut and bandaged it with some moss, ground horsetail and old orange peel I kept in a pouch.

Tsuri and I were both miserable that evening coughing up blood from our lungs, but she lived. When we got home, Stevo asked me if I wanted my florin back. I laughed and coughed, then said, "Whatever she fetches for a bride price, tell the groom he can have her for one gold piece less than his offer ... and she can tell him the story if she wants!" We grown-ups that night laughed and cried and drank and danced until we dropped. Brave little Tobar was in great shape and promised to better protect his sister in the future. I made him a beginner's bow, quiver and arrows before I left for France and Germany.

Chapter Thirty-Four

Gain God, and you will have no need of a book. St Theodore of Stoudios

Lyon, 1481

I made the summer fair. It was steamy hot, and there were so many vendors from afar. I had never envisioned paradise being so warm. There was much to see, read and discuss. Everyone set up a booth, tent, table or blanket in the field along the Rhone River. I wandered the books and manuscripts, of course, but there were many other products for sale – spices, silks, leathers, blankets, knives, jewelry, and prints – something for everyone.

I had not brought along a large collection of anything, just a few unusual manuscripts for trade. I was still more interested in scriptorium parchment than printed works, but I could see that printed works would flood the market of literature in no time. In the first few days, I simply wrote a list of everything for sale in my subjects of interest. The last year had been a good time for history, with printings of chronicles for Britain, Spain and Italy. Ecclesiastical and heresiological histories were popular. Werner Rolewinck had a successful illustrated history of the world that seemed to have a new edition each year, still doing a brisk business.

There were Roman and humanist essays coming out as manuscripts, but I no longer knew what I was looking for. There had been a time when I wanted all the secrets of the universe – geometry, astronomy, scripture, philosophy, and even kabala. Now I found I was interested in everything and nothing. The best conversation at the fair I recall had to do with calculating the End Times through the precession of the equinoxes. Some people were using 1 degree per 100 years, like Hipparchus – too slow. Some were using 1 degree per 66.6 years, like al Battani, Zoroaster and the Hindus – a little fast. Those who favored the Alfonsine Tables assumed 1 degree per 136 years – ridiculously slow, as if Earth's orbit had been confused with Mars!

In any case, it was becoming ever more difficult to keep up with all the ideas. People seemed to be pouring their minds into increasingly narrow fields of interest. I was convinced one could now read everything by everybody and not end up better educated than a Plotinus, Plutarch or Seneca wandering off to contemplate the universe alone! I bought a couple of saddlebags worth of material and headed on to the fair at Frankfurt. I stopped in Mainz to see Gutenberg's press in action, but the process no longer fascinated me as it once had.

When I arrived in Vienna, I learned there had been secondary effects of my sending a book to Mehmed. King Matthias of Hungary, one of the great book collectors of our age, after years of watching his border states gobbled up in attacks by Ottomans, no longer had to fear his southern flank. Now he was able to focus on his feud with my friend Archduke Frederick of Austria. The lesson for me: You can do the right thing for you, your family, and your nation and still do the wrong thing in another aspect of your life and the world. In the next few years, Hungary would strip Frederick of lands and even take Vienna.

Rather than return home through Hungary, I backtracked to France and thought I might swing through Spain. I felt like Spain was just more ... more friendly, more passionate, more scenic, and more sure of what the future should look like. It also possessed more interesting books than anywhere else I knew. I felt my destiny tied up with the place in mysterious ways – and if there was anything I never learned to walk away from, it was a good mystery.

Chapter Thirty-Five

As I looked out from this spot, everything appeared splendid and wonderful. Some stars were visible which we never see from this region, and all were of a magnitude far greater than we had imagined. Of these the smallest was the one farthest from the sky and nearest the Earth. ... And, indeed, the starry spheres easily surpassed the Earth in size. From here, the Earth appeared so small that I was ashamed of our Empire, which is, so to speak, but a point on its surface. Cicero, Scipio's Dream

Nimes, 1482

Life, in addition to being one long negotiation of what is and what we would like the future to be is a series of initiations. As Plato said, we are here to attain knowledge and there are a number of unveilings before we realize there is more to the world than the shadows of our own little cave.

Sights and dreams seemingly from a former life punctuated my trip. The first came somewhere near Lyon while watching a campfire, and the experience was much like Scipio's dream. I was in the Empyrean realm of the ninth Heaven, and Earth was only a tiny dot in the distance, but I was aware that I could focus on her from every star in the heavens at once, able to see across the universe and all the way down to this campfire. The realization was soon over, but I had caught a glimpse of God's care for us, as well as His omniscience.

As I neared Pont du Gard, an aqueduct bridge built in the time of Augustus, I had one of those moments when you know you have been there before and yet in this life you have never come near the place. That night, at the inn closest the arena in Nimes, I had a dream of a dream.

Alítheia and I – she was going by the name Isabel in this era – were returning to Beziers along the same Via Domitia connecting Italy and

Spain. The year was 1209. We were troubadours, travelling with two friends and returning from Avignon and Châteaurenard, where we had been performing. In this dream of a dream, in which we also spent the night at Nimes, Archangel Michael carried me to a spot high above the island of Malta where I could see from the Pillars of Hercules to Persia.

In the gathering darkness, for the Sun was going down in the ocean, I could see red fires lighting, first in a triangle between Montpelier, Montsegur and Bordeaux, but then spreading in every direction across the world. The angel told me Innocent III had unleashed another war after his destruction of Constantinople. This war, the angel said, would be with us until the End of Days – when we will find Wisdom or destroy all life.

The spark for the new and final war of religious genocide was the death of a single man – not even a good one. A more judgmental, insufferable zealot has seldom graced the Earth. Just north of Arles, a soldier of Raymond VI had killed this Papal Legate Peter of Castelnau. Peter had publicly excommunicated and humiliated the soldier's commander, our Count of Toulouse. The soldier had avenged the insult on his own.

Unfortunately, whenever great evil is contemplated, any pretext at hand will do. Rather than pursue the murderer, the new Papal Legate Milo and the Abbot of Citeaux Arnaud Amaury laid the charge of murder against the Count and all his people, since the crime had happened on our lands! The Abbot now placed the land under interdict, depriving us of services and sacraments, meaning for instance that Alítheia (Isabel) and I could not marry.

Our Count was flogged and ordered to humble himself at the feet of the church's officials at St. Giles. He attempted to solicit mercy on our behalf. Failing to obtain pardon for a crime neither he nor we had committed, he returned to the city, instructing us to submit to the Vatican, else 10,000 soldiers with twelve cardinals at their head would come destroy us.

The brethren replied that it would be better to confess our true faith and die for righteousness' sake than to confess falsehood and lose our souls. That it would be better to displease the Pope who can destroy our bodies than to displease God, who is able to destroy souls. That we would not forsake our faith in Christ; and even at the hazard of death, we would not exchange it for a religion nullifying the merits of His righteousness.

I asked the angel how my family would fare in the conflagration. He said they would be among the first to die – that it would begin before we arrived home. The Pope did not abide our failure to submit to his dictatorship; he did not abide our despising his greedy womanizing bishop or our rejecting his priests for worse reasons. He especially did not abide our deciding for ourselves the meaning of Scripture.

I asked the angel why he showed me this. I asked him what he wanted of me. "Learn," he said. "Learn to tolerate one another. One day, man will have the power to destroy all life. If all you have is this wrath and hatred for one another, then that is what you will do."

I asked him if humanity might learn the lesson in time to save itself. He said, "If mankind one day sees itself as one family under one God, you may return to Eden or live in the New Jerusalem. Fail, and this little classroom of Purgatory will become your eternal Hell." He then returned me to my friends. I woke them and told them what I had seen and we rushed home. As the angel had warned, we found our town destroyed, men and boys with their guts spilled, women and girls lying naked and just as dead. Not even the babies were spared. In places, there were piles of still-smoldering bodies.

The commander of the attack, Abbot of Cîteaux Arnaud Amaury, had ordered, "Spare no one, irrespective of rank, sex, or age. Kill them all. God will know his own!" He then washed his hands in the blood of 20,000 and declared his first battle "Divine Vengeance."

In exchange for the pardon of their abominable sins, the 10,000 "warriors" under Amaury had inflicted on my people the curse of Deuteronomy 13:

> *You shall surely strike the inhabitants of that city with the edge of the sword utterly destroying it and all that is in it and its cattle with the edge of the sword. Then you shall gather all its booty into the middle of its open square and burn the city and all its booty with fire as a whole burnt offering to the LORD your God.* Deuteronomy 13:15-16

I wondered what sort of god could possibly relish this horrendous stench of burnt hair and bone and roasted meat. Our lands and titles were now forfeit to whoever had enlisted in this unholy Crusade against Christians. We were left with nothing but what we had taken with us –

our instruments and a change of clothes. Therefore, we went south of the Pyrenees, first barrier to the madness that was to come. Here I knew, thanks to the angel, that we could survive nearly three centuries before the bloodlust washed over those mountains.

Our friends went to Barcelona to see what life there might bring. Alítheia (Isabel) and I settled down as weavers high in the mountains in a little village called Escuain in the province of Huesca. The air was clean, the view was heavenly, and the shepherds in the valley below kept us supplied with wool. When we were blessed with children, we were happy again. We would write verse to teach them of the first Christianity, but we would never again sing our *tenso* debating the religious ideals of Albi and Rome. No, we would never sing again.

I noted two ironies in the events of the Albigensian Crusade: The Cistercians, led in 1209 by a murderer, had once founded the Templars – an order that shared with Languedoc the secrets of early Christianity. Second, that Antichrist does not always return as a pagan. Sometimes he gets to be a Legate, an Abbot or a Pope.

Chapter Thirty-Six

For the children of Israel shall abide many days without a king, and without a prince, and without a sacrifice, and without an image. ^{Hosea 3:4}

La Jonquera, 1482

When I crossed the border into Spain, I spent a night at the junction of the Via Domitia with the Via Herculea. It was the coastal road the Godman Hercules (both worshipped and worshipful) once traveled from Cadiz with the bulls of Geryon toward Mycenae, which is probably an ancient story from the Age of Taurus hinting at a time the Sun rose in the West thanks to the Wrath of the Lamb. One such shift occurred in the Age of Aries around the time of the Exodus and is a source of the Golden Fleece legend. ^{Euripides, Iphigenia in Tauris}

I was granted a vision of Spain and Portugal that evening, viewed again from the sky. Again it was past sunset, with red fires beginning this time from Sevilla and progressing first in the south throughout al-Andalus, then north to Aragon and Castile, and then Portugal.

The Vatican and the kings, after nearly three centuries, apparently still felt threatened. I took the blood-red fires to mean that forced conversions had not been an effective way to stamp out Judaism or Islam. The first *Auto da Fé* had happened in February 1481 in Sevilla, killing six forced converts. I anticipated many more murders by Sixtus IV in the name of Paul's "God of love and peace," ^{2 Cor. 13:11} in this holocaust that was a continuation of the one ignited by Innocent III.

As I passed through the country, I noted that people's attitudes were changing. It was as if I suddenly found myself in a town of people so tired of each other's scandals, envies, rumors, and hatreds that there is a presumption of guilt for all newcomers. It reminded me of Seneca when he said, *the things which goad man into destroying man ... are hope, envy, hatred, fear, and contempt.* I was very careful to seem reserved – neither stingy nor generous, neither boisterous nor meek. It might have been useful to speak the local dialect but I did not understand the strange mix of something ancient with Spanish and French. I thought about traveling more inland, but then decided that would make finding Valls more difficult. I began traveling 30 miles a day whenever I could.

Tarragona, 1482

I made ancient Tarshish in four days. I was initially drawn to it for its having been mentioned a couple of dozen times in the *Bible* and the fact that somewhere nearby I might find something of my past. It also has monuments in which the first layer was built by the sons of Japheth – huge stones we could not begin to move today, piled one upon another as in some of the most ancient sites around the Mediterranean.

Perhaps the Inquisition will complete the religious odyssey of this ancient people. Mithraic Sun-worshipping Roman soldiers conquered the Moon-worshipping Iberians about two centuries before Christ. Some converted to Christianity by the asceticism of Priscillian; others by the Nicene Creed. Arrian Christian Visigoths captured the land in 475, followed by Moslems in 714. Four centuries later, it went Catholic when captured by Alfonso I of Aragón. Unfortunately, people's family traditions rarely keep up with the fashions or politics of cathedral and castle. So with the exception of the Jewish neighborhoods, I am sure there was more than a little confusion on the human or divine status of Jesus the Nazarene, or even which books of their ancient *Codex Tarraconensis* might still be thought canonical. The sad truth was that many of us were born into just this sort of theological confusion.

Alítheia, for example, once mentioned that she was the daughter of a *converso* mother who married a Christian merchant to get out of Spain. Her father had decided to seek greater profits in Constantinople. Her Jewish mother's surname was Cresques, and her not-so-Christian father (the one thinking Genesis 19, Judges 3, Song of Solomon 2 or Isaiah 60 spoke to him) was a Llull. Since there was regular trade between Oran and the Spanish ports, there was a chance I could get word of her older sister Sarah and learn from her how Alítheia had fared. In Constantinople, Sarah had married a Catalan merchant with the last name Nicolau and had left Byzantium shortly before I met my love.

It was good to visit a port again for word on the greater world. I noted more than one janissary spy among the tattooed sailors. Apparently, Bayezid was reviving one of the more grand ideas of his father – control of the Mediterranean. All that would be required was a greater presence and a few key ports near Gibraltar to siphon off gold, slaves and raw materials beginning to come in from Africa. The great advantage of having so expanded Islam vis-à-vis Europe was to cut off the white sons of Japheth from the rest of the world and set a tax on their access to world commodities. Eventually, Portugal, Spain, Italy or France will be forced to deal with the extortion.

I asked around for the Nicolau family and found they were invested in most of the ports along the Spanish coast and islands. I was able to learn that the main branch of the family was at Barcelona. I resolved to go there if I had the chance. For the moment, I wanted to see someone, anyone I might regard as family. It took me one afternoon to make the trip to Valls. I found lodging and resolved to set out in the morning to find "Dinah's" family.

Valls, 1482

The problem with looking for someone with their town's name for a surname is that it can be pretty common. The problem with looking for a Jew in a Spanish town is that the people of the three religions are supposed to remain segregated in all their dealings. Unless I was wearing the Jewish hat and cape or badge, I was not supposed to talk to them. As it was explained to me when I started asking around, mixing with them would "dishonor God's crucifixion and risk bringing back the Plague that destroyed one family in five a century ago." I imagine the Jews must have been blamed.   How God's chosen people could end up the designated scapegoats for the normal ills of society escapes me. Ninety years later, Jews who converted in the time of the pogroms were still held in contempt.

Risking the wrath of racists, I set out to look for anyone who had known Esther or Dinah Valls. I found an elderly aunt of my stepmother's who told me the family had moved to Barcelona after Mallorca. It seemed God wanted me in Barcelona. The city was also in the printing business and there were works by Raymond Llull (perhaps an ancestor of Alítheia's father) that I hoped to purchase. He had written almost 250 works, some of importance to me. Before I left Valls, I received dirty looks from all sides of the religious divide for violating their segregation rules, but I was not questioned on the matter. Barcelona would be two days away. I set out the next morning.

CHAPTER THIRTY-SEVEN

You only have to behold the aspect of those possessed by anger to know that they are insane. ^{Seneca, On Anger}

Barcelona, 1482

I was in for something of a shock. In other cities, since about 1408, one could find a walled and gated area for the Jews to live in – a *juderia* – and one for Moslems – a *moreria*. There was no longer a Jewish ghetto in Barcelona. The old neighborhood was in ruins. Apparently, following the riots of 1391, when hundreds of Jews were killed, the king abolished the *juderia*. Thousands of the king's Jews (financers of his realm) had converted to avoid further troubles.

I had been hoping to walk up to a gate, talk to an *adelantati* or one of the neighborhood officials to find information on my stepmother's family or Alítheia's. Instead, I found a densely packed ruin of terraced *mudejar*-style buildings stacked up four or five stories with nobody in them. When I learned of the mass conversions, I did what I believed to be the next logical step – I went to the Cathedral.

Unbeknownst to me, there was lots of tension about bringing the Spanish Inquisition to Aragon. *Conversos* were trying, successfully for the moment, to keep the new Inquisition out of the region since Barcelona, quite literally, had "no more Jews." However, since the *conversos* had never received catechism classes, everyone knew there were still Jewish practices in many homes. I guess my question would be who cares about whether someone eats *kosher* except for the racist who thinks the God of the Jews in the Old Testament is different from the God of the Gentiles in the New Testament – an idea that brings into question the very existence of the *Bible*.

I spoke to a priest at La Seu Cathedral by the name of Pedro Furia. I cannot say the conversation went well.

J: Good morning, Father. I am trying to locate my mother's family. My grandmother's name would have been Valls.

P: I am afraid that is a typical surname in this region. Can you tell me anything else?

J: Her name was Esther Valls. Her family was from a town of the same name. I believe they were originally Jewish, though now I suspect she would be a *conversa*, or deceased or has perhaps moved on.

P: [Looking cross.] From your statement, it sounds as if the family were Jewish to the best of your knowledge, in which case you should be wearing a badge and, depending on when you arrived here, you have two weeks to leave the city.

J: Well, then allow me to rephrase my request. I am looking for the family of the woman who raised me. Members of her family were *conversos* from Valls.

P: What was your family and religious background if the woman who raised you was a Jewess?

J: You would not believe me if I told you, but I was born Orthodox in Constantinople and I was raised differently.

P: Your nation's failure to unite with the Catholic Church condemned you to fall to the Turk. You realize this, of course?

J: Well, I suppose you could look at it that way. Alternative theories are that the Pope failed to send crusaders to defend Byzantium, that we should not have trusted mercenaries to do what we could not do alone, that God chose to punish us for the sins of our fathers, or that our faith in God and the Virgin was less than the Turks' faith in Allah. Nothing is gained by trying to put a label on it. The past is past. The truth is, one day we were Orthodox and the next day many of us were Moslems.

P: [Red-faced and fists clenched] So you are a Moslem, in which case you should start in the *Moreria*. I have no time for renegades!

J: Father, I am not a Jew and I am not a Moslem. I would just like to find the Valls family.

P: Well, what is your name and are you otherwise of good family?

J: I am John IX Palaeologus, son of the Emperor of Byzantium and Caterina Notaras, daughter of the Grand Duke. As a child, I was raised by a *conversa* by the maiden name of Valls. This was for my own safety, because my grandfather knew that the day the city fell would be the day I died. Now ... if it is not too much to ask ... could you tell me whether in your registry you have a Valls family in your parish? I currently attend St. Reparata in Florence and am a member of good standing.

P: Well, yes. We do have a Valls family. They live over on Old Bath Street, *Carrer dels Banys Vells*. It is three blocks southeast and seven blocks northeast.

J: Thank you so very much. Might you also have a Llulls family?

P: I believe they are even closer. *Carrer dels Mercaders*, just two blocks past the palace.

J: You have been most helpful.

P: Peace be with you.

J: And also with you.

It was not hard to see why *conversos* were a bit nervous. The new racist categories of blood purity were going to have many good people (Jew, Moslem and Christian) accused and condemned for no better reason than they were not "Old" Christians directly descended from pagans who worshipped the Lights of Heaven. I could see there would be a booming business in fabricating family trees once the Inquisition came to town. One of the first customers would be Fernando the King. (Rumor had it that his mother was a *conversa*.)

Carrer dels Banys Vells, 1482

While I found the Valls family near the old public baths, I learned almost nothing new of my stepmother. To stay in Barcelona, her family had become converts the Christians call *marranos* for pigs and the Jews call *anusim* for the compelled or the forced ones. Her mother had died of natural causes the year before. A cousin of my mother's had inherited the small textile business. I stayed long enough for one good meal and a couple of family stories. I gave the lady a big hug and I was off to search for Sarah.

Carrer dels Mercaders, 1482

The Llull family was related to one of my favorite authors. I introduced myself as someone that had known their family in Constantinople and was hoping for any kind of news as to how they had fared. I added that I was employed as an agent of the Medici in search of old manuscripts. The grandmother was very gracious. She said she prayed for Alítheia all the time, but that she had no idea what had happened to her in the fall of Constantinople.

I told her the last time I had seen her, years after the fall, Alítheia was very well, but that life had torn me away. (I figured if someone in the family knew of Alítheia being sold and was not telling the grandmother, then I should not be the one to pass along new worries.) She told me Sarah was well and gave me directions to her house, sending me on my way with a copy of Llull's *Gentile and the Three Wise Men* as well as treats to take to her great-grandchildren.

Sarah and her husband lived upstairs from the silver shop they owned over on *Carrer de l'Argenteria*. She had one of those beautifully colored tile staircases typical to the city, and upstairs was simple oak and stone construction with plaster, but it was nicely appointed as one might expect for a scholar with a talent for working silver. Obviously, they were doing well. The children quickly got into the treats.

After introductions, the husband went back to working on an intricate gold and silver goblet for one of his customers. I told Sarah what I knew, and what I thought had become of her little sister, and asked whether she had managed to hear from Alítheia. I explained that, for no particularly good reason, over the years whenever my mind wandered it was to her sister and her life in Oran, and that I prayed all was well. She told me she suffered the same problem, but that all seemed to have worked out as best it could. She pulled out a stack of letters, separating those of Constantinople from those she had received through merchants arriving from Oran. She told me I was welcome to read the latter. I must have figured in the Constantinople letters, for she blushed and looked down, then so did I.

Some of the letters I saw were picturesque descriptions of what Alítheia had seen and suffered. For example, one of her more barbaric days had been the ceremonial circumcision or "harem cut" received when she arrived in Oran, which she said is intended to render a woman more pure and chaste (no longer capable of receiving sexual pleasure). "It's just one more thing I never understood about the *Saray*," she complained. "How does permanently robbing a woman of her own pleasure encourage her to be of service to her husband?"

As I had seen in my dream, she went into the harem as the fourth wife. At first, she did not think much of the man who had bought her, but in time she saw her new Sultan was kind. The day she was discovered to be with the Sultan's second son, the Sultan's mother, the Valide Sultan, promoted her to a higher status in the harem.

Unlike Mehmed, this Sultan did not feel the need to keep 250 concubines (and *sodomitai*) awaiting his urgent desire. Her Sultan's energies were dedicated to maintaining his small kingdom and improving the lives of his people. He seemed to consider her insights in his decisions and she found this reassuring. For instance, in private quarters she had cast the deciding vote on a new vizier, a man named Abraham with Jewish background, known for his discretion and integrity.

It had not all been a bed of roses, though. One of her earliest letters, while she was still hurting as the new kid orphaned from her former life, was the saddest, and one of the noblest in the collection.

O Sarah, when and how did we lose our way?
What did we do to merit such destruction
of our childhood, our country, and our religion?
Surely this life is punishment for our iniquities and those of our fathers.

We were not safe as Jews.
We were not safe as Christians.
And I will never feel safe as a Moslem,
for neither God nor man will accept my double treason.
All the Earth is woe and suffering.

I have come the length of the sea closer to you,
yet the distance remaining is as between life and the grave.
Where is the Angel to mend my broken heart?
Where is my Messiah to free his captive?
Where is my Lord to release me from this darkness?

My joys were the love of a prince and my friendship with the Valide Sultan.
With her blessing I escaped her son and found what I pray will be a better life.
One day I hope a word from you will come to me ...
a ray of hope that I will not perish utterly forgotten.

Still, who am I to complain of this burden?
What of our ancestors in Egypt?
What of our ancestors in Babylon?
I must cast my burden upon the Lord who sustains me,
and bear what comes with righteousness.

I pray for you and your family five times a day.
Please remember me, dear sister. Remember me.

Over and over she broke my heart, the unintended casualty of her letters. More and more I cherished the memory of the purest soul I had ever met. I felt terrible about never having attempted to rescue her or even to write her, but I knew the chance of such an enterprise was impossibly small, and, given her family situation there, highly inappropriate.

Sarah and I talked for a bit more, mostly about our new lives, but also regarding things about which she had long wondered such as the encoded notes her sister and I would leave in the tower. Before I left, I told her of my visions of the coming destruction in the religious war, and encouraged her to get her family out of Spain.

I think she forgave me my interest in Alítheia after all these years, considering the way in which we had been separated. At least, I hope she forgave me. I wished them well and offered my help if one day they needed me. The next day, I caught a boat for home. I had been gone nine months.

Chapter Thirty-eight

The heart of the sons of men is full of evil, and madness is in their heart while they live, and after that, they go to the dead. Ecclesiastes 9:3

Barcelona, 1482

There is a reason armies and navies look young. Run yelling into a mass of flying stones, arrows, blades and ball often enough and, unless you are a true rogue, the gods will carry you home. Only tricksters are granted a longer stay so the rest of us learn our lessons of tragedy.

Sailing the Mediterranean was beginning to resemble going into battle or negotiating the next mountain pass with brigands. It was an armed adventure dependent on favorable winds, a good map and a brave captain. The tragedy was that sailors had become their own worst enemies. The more privateering and piracy made shipping merchandise unreliable, the less business the ports did ... and the less business the ports did, the more sailors had to rely on stealing from others.

In just a few years, the problem would become worse, with Jews carrying precious stones to escape Spain with enough wealth to survive in a strange land, and dispossessed Moors wanting to wreak havoc on the country that had rejected them at the point of a sword. Pirates stripped a quarter of the coastal populations for slaves. Rape and murder on the high seas would be common. Considering where pirates sailed would become as important as where the gold and silks were.

Still, I did not want to take another three months getting home. I boarded a nao named *La Celestina* and took my chances – and wondered why anyone would name their ship after a famous old whore. The captain said he had some stops to make, but we could get close to Florence, "In about three weeks, God willing." My books and bow went in a long box. If he did not provide a berth for me, I would use the box for one. He offered to carry my horse in a sling and I told him I would get another. I berthed with the crew.

I swear the bread must have been rye gone moldy, because I had the strangest series of dreams that first night. In the first, I was in a swordfight with the Devil and it was a tough fight. He left me an opening and I hesitated, lamely wondering what Jesus would do in such a situation. With a great laugh, he parried my next stroke and ran me through. My lesson? If and when you get the chance to put down real evil, don't hesitate to strike. I could have saved half a million lives had I applied that to Mehmed when first I met him.

In the next, I came across the Son and he was crying. I asked him what was the matter and he told me to look around. Everywhere we turned children were playing with swords, some wearing crosses, some dressed as Moslems, others as Jews, and all making a bloody mess of themselves and everything around them. He said, "I freed you from His doom and this is how you choose to live? I unchained you from His hundreds of laws and this is what you do with freedom? I sent you prophets, history and parables and did you believe nothing we said? Learn to live together, or He will destroy you in one great fire."

In the next, I soared to Heaven on the wings of a Great Eagle, following the Milky Way past the seven spheres, past the Horologium and the Phoenix to the Goddess. There I saw Wisdom herself, the Shekhinah, Theotokos, Great Mother and Holy of Holies seated on her throne. Her face was that of Alítheia and I was overcome by love, as if a star of joy had exploded in my chest and I had lost all sense. "All is forgiven," she said, "but you have much work to do. When the time comes, you must walk away from all you know and love to warn man of his folly. On that day, you will be neither Greek nor Jew, neither slave nor free, neither Moslem nor Christian. You will tell them the Truth and it shall set you free."

I had another and it terrified me. I rode with Helios a narrow golden track through the heavens, passing by great signs of the zodiac on either side. Near Aquarius was a great cloud where we heated up greatly, the Earth lost her balance and the planets slipped their courses. This, a deep voice called *Ekpyrosis* – a conflagration with explosions on Earth and a great flame from the Sun, followed by an age of ice. At Leo, there was a cloud of ice where Earth was pelted with water and stone, and this He called *Cataclysm*, or the Deluge. I asked Him if there was another way. He said, "Once there was another way and one day you will escape this fate, but for now you must endure. *Ekpyrosis* is coming. Warn them."

In my final dream, I was the Phoenix. Below me was a great fire of pine and pitch, frankincense and myrrh. I was weary of this life and ready for another. Above the flames, I saw my Beloved and She held out her hand. "Come," she said, "our work is not done but you must rest. The Lord will wake us when we are needed." And I replied, "Come, my bride, come!"

Toward the end of the second day, the captain was sailing us between Corsica and Sardinia to avoid raiders from Tunis. Unfortunately, that is exactly what they had assumed we would do, so they had lain in wait just beyond Isola Maddalena. They quickly began gaining on us, the stiff *libeccio* wind driving us both toward Rome was probably the *scirocco* blowing up from Africa combining with a *mistral* blowing down from France. When they combined with a *gregale* coming off of Greece and Italy as the mountains cooled, we were going to get quite a storm. As far as I could see, the sky was beginning to darken and to spin.

I wondered what our captain would do ... fight, fly, negotiate or wait to see which was stronger – the gale-force winds or the pirates. No matter what happened, I resolved to kill as few people as possible unless they were just totally depraved. I would try to be patient and use reason and see what happened.

For the captain, it was time to consider coming about, furling or bringing down sails if he wanted to preserve them. We were sailing right into a cyclone. In the distance, just beyond nearby Isola Tavolara, I saw two waterspouts forming – a bad sign even when you don't have company. I moved down to the deck and made my way toward the bow. Whatever was coming, I wanted a spot on the front row.

Despite the storm, the Ottomans decided to attack. The corsairs began firing from our stern, our merchantman helpless in that direction and seriously outgunned by the faster ship, a lateen-rigged xebec. We had six cannon, three leeward and three starboard. He had 24, with at least two in any direction of a compass rose. We could not outrun him, we could not outgun him and we probably could not outsmart him unless our captain knew the shoals. The pirates could send us to the bottom, and then our merchandise would be good to no one. Alternatively, we could let them board and offer up everything in exchange for our lives. Given all the factors, I assumed we would now drop sail and stand by to be boarded. Instead, our captain continued his run into the coming storm.

I wondered if they would be in the mood for killing or slave-taking. Their most profitable course of action would be to keep us intact and turn our crew into theirs – with a bit of oversight from their overly large crew of 300 marine raiders.

Given our captain's decision, their next move was to be expected. They popped a couple of holes in us at the waterline. Then they took out our cannon on the leeward side before we could do any damage to them. In these choppy waters, we could now expect to sink in an hour. They were going to steal our cargo and capture whomever they could take peacefully. Those who opposed them would die. I decided to go peacefully, given a chance.

Off the coast of Sardinia, 1482

When the pirates finally boarded us, there was mayhem. The Ottomans behaved aggressively to see if any of us sincerely wanted to live, in which case our only option was to surrender. I climbed up on the forecastle and moved up to the bowsprit.

My nearest opponent yelled in Turkish that he was going to kill me and feed me to the sharks. I told him, *Bismillah al rahman al rahim*, which means "In the name of God, most Gracious, most Compassionate." And asked him in Turkish, "Are you in the habit of making Moslems your slaves?" He added, "That is a trick. You know one Arabic phrase and I should let you go? You will be my bitch and galley slave!" I told him, *Allâh, dönüp dolaşacağınız yeri ve varıp duracağınız yeri bilir*, which is Turkish for: "Allah knows your place of turmoil and your place of rest." [Koran 47:19] He shouted, "Then let it be here!" and rushed me with his sword. Before I could draw *Agheu Glas*, Allah (also known as *Ia* or *Poseidon*) sent a sign for the pirates to leave me alone. The man was carried into the depths by a flying shark flung from the waterspout not far away. The man's superstitious comrades backed up, more than a little amazed, and I asked to see the captain.

A man of authority stepped forward to say, "You can ransom yourself and your cargo in Tunis. Point out which is yours as we move it to our ship. In the meantime, give me the sword and come aboard."

Chapter Thirty-nine

Jewish: *There is One alone, and there is not a second; yea, He hath neither child nor brother.* Ecclesiastes 4:8

Christian: *Thou believest that there is one God; thou doest well: the devils also believe, and tremble.* James 2:19

Moslem: *They should serve one God only, there is no god but He.* Koran 9:31-33

Al-Mahdiyyah, 1482

Since the 8th century, Moslem navies have operated out of Tunis. Now it was up to the Ottomans to defend Islam's interests through sea power, but in this generation, a tradition of *jihad* by sea was devolving into something more properly called piracy.

Raids for slaves were starting to resemble the destructive pride of the Cilicians' thousand galleys pitted against Rome. It is an embarrassment to civilization and a scourge to Christendom – coastal cities stripped of their citizens and wealth. Unfortunately, this time there is no General Pompey to command 500 galleys and 120,000 foot soldiers to march around the Mediterranean seacoast. No, this time Valencia, Marseilles, Genoa, Naples and Athens will pay and pay. I can think of no greater spur to nationalism and alliances in Europe than the Turk.

I soon found myself in the city founded by Ubayd Allah al-Mahdi Billah, first *imam* of the Fatimids and one of Shi'ite Islam's self-proclaimed saviors. The city of the Mahdi had been one of the earliest ports for the Moslem conquerors as they expanded westward. I wondered what sort of tyrant might here decide my fate. Once again, my life was not my own to command. Once again, it was forfeit to an avaricious man seeking to maximize his gain. Once again, I found myself wondering what surprise God's plan held for me.

The first stop for me was the prison. Most captives went straight to the slave market or public baths to spend the rest of their lives trying to make other wretches happy, which is sort of like trying to push boulders uphill. Much sweat for zero progress. For the lucky few of us, those calculated to bring a ransom or serve as an example, or achieve some political end, there was this solitude and bad food. I looked at it as my time in the wilderness, a monastery cell in which to grow. I made a point of cleaning my hands with sand and praying toward the southeast each time I heard the call of the *muezzin*. There is honor in doing what is expected in a new place.

Except when another boat was captured, the population in our prison declined over time. A prisoner would go to his hearing and never return. None of us had any idea whether we would live until next week or whether we might be sold at auction. Some chose to worry. I chose to wait and see. Thus far, God had been mostly kind. There is no sense objecting over His tests and moral dilemmas – they are part of the reason we are here!

In my cell, we had a mixed group of people snatched on the high seas. You might think in such a situation they would be preying on one another or ready to riot, but the truth is, it was easier to wait and see which way the wind blows. Some were visibly agitated or depressed, but most seemed to maintain some ray of hope that all would be well if we were patient and respectful of our jailers, who seemed to view us as so many dogs in a cage.

One day, out of pride or boredom, someone began an argument over religion, which is about as useful as joining a game of tic tac toe after somebody has placed his mark on the center. Rather than stay on the periphery of this emotional spectator sport about to spin out of control, I decided to join in. The players included a Jew, a Christian, a Moslem – and I offered to play the part of a philosophic pagan. I drew four ellipses on the floor and told them that whatever beliefs we could all agree on – where the ellipses overlapped – that would be a religion worth following because that is a creed on which all of mankind might agree. To speed things along, I asked each of them to scratch on the ground in their ellipse the most important concepts of their religion in as few words as possible.

The Jew began the conversation. "The most important idea of Abraham, our father, was that there is only One God. When he said it, there were many gods idolized in the Earth and the Sky. In all other matters of creed, I would favor the list of Maimonides." He wrote:

> 1. G-d exists
> 2. G-d is one
> 3. G-d is incorporeal
> 4. G-d is eternal
> 5. Prayer is to be directed to G-d alone
> 6. The words of the prophets are true
> 7. Moses was the greatest prophet
> 8. The Written Torah and Oral Torah were given to Moses
> 9. There will be no other Torah
> 10. G-d knows our thoughts and deeds
> 11. G-d will reward the good and punish the wicked
> 12. Messiah will come
> 13. The dead will be resurrected

Next came the Christian, a dyed-in-the-wool Catholic who said the basics of Christianity could all be found in the Nicene Creed:

> 1. We believe in One God, the Father and Creator of all things
> 2. One Lord Jesus Christ who for our salvation, came down from Heaven and was made man
> 3. He was crucified, suffered and was buried
> 4. On the third day, He rose again and He ascended into Heaven
> 5. He will come again to judge us
> 6. His kingdom is eternal
> 7. We believe in the Holy Spirit who spoke by the prophets
> 8. We believe in one unified Church of believers
> 9. We acknowledge one baptism for the remission of sins
> 10. We look for the resurrection of the dead

Next came a Moslem, who said his creed could be found in the Shahadah and the Kalimas:

> 1. There is no god but Allah
> 2. Muhammad is His Messenger
> 3. Allah is One alone
> 4. Allah alone we worship
> 5. All glory and praise belongs to Allah
> 6. Allah gives us life and grants us death

    7. *He is the Good*
    8. *His Kingdom is Eternal and He will grant us reward or punishment*
    9. *In Him is all power and strength*
    10. *Man is sinful and we seek His forgiveness*
    11. *In life, there are actions we must complete*
    12. *There will be a Day of Judgment*

I wrote:

    1. *Our Universe manifests such Order and Wisdom as to point to One Author*
    2. *The Order exhibits Cycles; and living in time with them is essential*
    3. *We are given Messengers to explain the divine Order*
    4. *The Messengers reveal the Cycles, and our observance of these we call Worship or Mysteries*
    5. *The Messengers bring us Rules that we might live together for a Just and Common Good*
    6. *We must repent of our sins when we harm others through our selfishness*
    7. *For the righteous, the Order lives in us and we will live on in the Order*

Then I asked them if they saw anything on anyone else's list that they could agree with. Everyone agreed there is a Supreme God, though we failed to agree on His Name. Where the ellipses intersected in the sand, I wrote the words to which we could finally agree:

We believe in One God to whom we Pray. He sends us Messengers, who, by His Spirit, communicate His teachings, blessings and commandments. At the Day of Judgment He will send us His Messiah that Goodness Will Triumph and the Righteous shall live in His Kingdom forever.

About everything else in the ellipses, we disagreed. I noted that therein must lie the "essential" points of doctrine that make people willing to kill and enslave each other! Speculative subjects included what is Hell, what is Heaven, are they our eternal abodes or only a place between lives, whether one day we might come back as reward or punishment, is Hell this world where we live (and we aspire to return to Heaven), or is Hell some brimstone lake inside the Earth? Are we all to be resurrected or only a chosen few? Paradise was even more sketchy. Do we eat there? Is there sex? Will we work there? Is one married? Do we get to see all our relatives and friends?

There are a great many Unknowables regarding the afterlife we find comforting, believing we know the answers. Whether the afterlife lasts an eternity, comprises a journey of 3,000 years [Herodotus II:123] or 1,000 years [Plato, Republic Bk X] ... winding through the lower kingdoms of the mineral, vegetable and animal before returning to our humanity ... or whether we must simply wait until the Last Days to be raised up ... we all wanted to believe in some sort of Divine Justice, else why must anyone behave on Earth? It was a fascinating conversation to be taking place in a prison. In the end, we all felt as brothers ... as if we had solved a great problem of the world.

Unfortunately, we were not the ones in charge of the world that day or any other, and so we went back to patiently awaiting a hearing with the Emir of Tunis, Abu Omar Othman.

Chapter Forty

Seek'st thou a tyrant's door? Then farewell freedom! Though FREE as air before. ^{Sophocles}

Al-Mahdiyyah, 1482

The Emir was a much more democratic man than his late cousin Mehmed. He ate with his court. He still met with his people, heard complaints and administered justice. He generously entertained. In that respect, his hospitality resembled that of the steppe or the desert, as opposed to the rich self-indulgence of one man that passed for civilization in Istanbul.

I found myself an invited guest of the Emir's court about ten days after my arrival. This day would decide whether I would go free, become a slave or die. I was to be the first of three prisoners that day from *La Celestina*. The other two were a young woman of good family who had been on her way to marry a man in Pesaro, and a Napolitano. As we were waiting for our hearing, I quietly asked the girl in Castilian if she wished to stay in Tunis as a wife or slave – or if she would rather be free to marry in Italy or return home. She said she would like to go to Italy as planned. I asked if she had been harmed. She whispered that she had not. I then suggested she go along with anything I said or did. About that time, one of our jailers menaced that we should be silent. When he looked away, I asked her what they had taken from her. She said, "Seven dresses, 500 ducats and a chest of linens." About this time, I got an ear boxed for not keeping silence. "What is your name?" I whispered. "Maria Cristina," she whispered back.

When it came time for my "hearing," the Emir asked his vizier why I had been kept apart from the other prisoners now in the *bagnos*. The vizier said, "The captain of our ship here said this one claimed to be a Moslem." The Emir told me to step forward and explain myself.

I said, "Your Excellency, I was in the process of departing Catalonia with a shipment of books I will eventually sell in the *Saray* at Istanbul and the Medici Palace in Florence, as I have done before, when your captain captured us off the coast of Sardinia. I say 'us' in the sense that I was captured with my wife here, which I recently acquired in Gandía. We were on our way home to Venice when we were taken by your crew."

There was chuckling near the Emir, to which the Emir inquired, "Mr. Ambassador, do you have something to add?" The ambassador from the Ottoman court at Istanbul said, "This poor deluded fellow would be wasting his time with the new Sultan. Mehmed 'El Fatih' might have been interested in old books and manuscripts, but his son Bayezid will have nothing to do with them. He forbids us even an official printing press! If this couple can make ransom, they are best left to return to their home in Venice and they should forget the *Saray*."

The Emir said, "Two hundred gold ducats apiece and they can go. Captain, return to them their effects if they can make ransom." I requested access to my box, pulled out 400 ducats from a locked compartment and paid the man. I said, "And my sword?" The captain said, "I thought it was a toy." He pulled it out of his belt and handed it to me. I replied, "The Greek I got it from said it belonged to Julius Caesar." Everyone in the court laughed. The Emir smiled, "You know what they say about Greeks bearing gifts. Well, their merchants deserve even more caution!"

I was very happy. That had gone extremely well. I said in Spanish, "Let's go, Cristina. We are free to go."

To which the Napolitano said, "Wait! Where is she going? Why is she free? They weren't together on the boat!" I could have gutted the man where he stood. The Emir said, "They have paid their ransom and you have not, and you question the word of a Moslem and you are not. So ... I would now have proof from both of you." Pointing to me he said, "Recite to me the Kalimas." I did, in Arabic. Then he said, "Jailer, rake the coals, take their boots, and we will see which one is telling the truth."

Fortunately, I had done a fire walk once with Sufi friends in Istanbul. It is uncomfortable, but quite possible if it is not too long a fire pit. I walked the ten feet across, and at the other end bowed with arms crossed against my chest. "You may go," the Emir said.

The Napolitano just stood there mortified. The Emir's decision came quick: "To the *bagnos* with him. Get him out of my sight!"

We returned to Italy via Malta. There was a ship going that way commanded by Jason, of all people, who now went by the name Arslan, which means "Lion." He said it was a nickname from Navy pals, who remembered the day one landed in his lap. He put Cristina and I in his quarters for the trip and the three of us had a great time telling stories. It was a bit awkward for Cris and I sharing a bed and then NOT sharing a bed, but it was much better in the captain's cabin than below decks with some of our former shipmates on their way to auction.

From Malta, we sailed to Pesaro, a beautiful little sea town of about 6,000 people, where I gave the bride away at the wedding, having added a bit to her dowry. Her husband Stefano told me to please consider their city if ever my family was looking to start over. I signed over to him 2,000 florins in bills of exchange, good at any Medici bank, and asked him to buy me a nice plot of land near their place where I could begin to construct a small villa. I told them I would like to be there by the "End Times" predicted by my Byzantine forebears – the year 1492. I said I would send more money once I arrived home.

Stefano said we could build a very nice villa for less than 15,000 florins. Talking Andrea into leaving the Medici before the Florentines turned violent might be a trick, but by my reckoning we would not have much time before everyone attached to the court would suffer exile. Through the centuries, many great and lesser families had suffered at the hands of the fickle Florentines, and I wanted to be ready.

I bought a mule the next day, repacked into saddlebags and headed west along the rivers. Getting home would take another two weeks.

CHAPTER FORTY-ONE

It seems the providence of some god to lessen that happiness which is too great and inordinate, and so to mingle the affairs of human life that no one should be entirely free and exempt from calamities. Plutarch, Aemilius Paulus

Florence, 1482-1492

As it turned out, there had been no need to go anywhere. I apparently had done Bayezid II a favor by emptying the throne of his father. His only competition was a younger brother the Europeans kept on a string to unsettle the Sultan with the prospect of a civil war for succession. Bayezid would talk tough to the Europeans, but could not really afford a resumption of Crusade, having difficulties with some Egyptian forces to his south. Where his father had besieged the Knights of St. John at Rhodes, Bayezid now began paying them 45,000 ducats a year to retain his brother Jem as a political prisoner. The knights later transferred Jem to the Pope, who was equally happy to receive the money.

When I returned, the Italian wars were still going on. Venice was trying to take Ferrara with the Pope's help while Lorenzo and his new ally the King of Naples were trying to form a League of Rome, which came to fruition the following year. The Pope was shamed into joining the League, at which time he excommunicated his overly aggressive former ally, the Venetians. When peace broke out on the Peninsula, they say Sixtus was so angry he had a fatal heart attack. Greed and the politics of divide-and-conquer had found their limits.

The next pope was a friend of Florence, which made all of us rest easier. In fact, Lorenzo was one of his most trusted agents. Innocent VIII was also father to Francesco Cybo, a ne'er-do-well who in a few years would marry Lorenzo's daughter Maddalena. For a time, then, our court and the Vatican were as cordial as one could imagine.

We also saw much more of our friend Constantine, who had married. My only issue with his pope was the continued Crusade against the Waldenses, who once had been blessed by Pope Alexander III and whose poverty had been imitated in the reforms of St. Francis (as if to suggest the "heretics" had been right all along).

I began our exit from Florence by treating the Pesaro project as a summer home. We planted grape vines, mulberry and olive trees on a property south of the city, making it into a nice little estate for John to take over someday. He very much enjoyed making decisions on the villa and the land, though he received lots of ideas from Andrea, who like my Aunt Anna had opted for a chapel alongside the villa. Andrea liked Stefano and adored Cristina, though she did not much approve of how Cris and I had met. Our son Constantine was still close with the Medici and more involved in the church than ever.

Pesaro put us ostensibly in the orbit of the Sforza family and the Duke of Urbino, but we tended to stay busy with the Medici in Florence on social occasions. Even when we were spending time near the beach, we were not regular guests at Pesaro's *Villa Imperiale*, though we did make the rainy June reception when Giovanni Sforza brought his lovely young bride Lucretia Borgia from Rome.

From time to time my mother and Aunt Anna would visit, though as they grew older they came less often. I would drop in to see the ladies when I traveled to Brianno, where Constantine had given up his grand mastership in deference to one of our old friends. I remember we talked about starting a commandery or priorate in Rome with help from the Vatican, but decided to wait. Like us, my friend Constantine and his wife chose Pesaro for their summer home.

In attempting to regain lands lost in the recent wars, such as the town of Sarzana, Lorenzo noticed that the Florentine Republic's short-termed officers were ineffectual when it came to making decisions about war and taxes. As a remedy, he implemented a Senate of distinguished citizens, now giving the Florentines two houses of legislature as had been typical of Greece and Rome. Now aristocracy balanced the forces of democracy, which tend to be more volatile but less corrupt than their wealthy counterparts. I called the two houses the greedy and the needy – and wondered how long such a solution might serve. Clearly both were still entirely dependent on the sagacity and influence of the Republic's most illustrious citizen.

Lorenzo reformed our police force and made Florence one of the great European centers of commerce and ideas.

The entire world beat a path to the Medici Palace door. All the great kings sent delegations and asked for favors. The Pope was pacified of imperial ambitions. It was a Golden Age as Lorenzo had foreseen, thanks to his judicious use of wealth, his encouragement of the arts and sciences, and his policy of carefully maintaining a balance of power between the major houses of Italy and Europe.

In these years, we gathered hundreds of manuscripts. My compatriots translated Plato, Plotinus, Herodian, Xenophon, Plutarch and a hundred classics of Greek literature. We copied and published much that had long been lost.

Civilization had died and been reborn in my lifetime. Though Lorenzo died a sick man in pain like his father, he left a wonderful legacy to the world. I know he was proud of what he had been able to do. His final concern was for his children. He wondered if they would be ready for what was to come.

The year 1492 was a big year for all of us. I lost a dear friend and Italy lost its most important statesman. Lorenzo's son Giovanni became a full cardinal (even without ordination) and he asked my son Constantine to join him in Rome with the promise of a priesthood or a lucrative position. Our eldest married a minor princess, Maria Phoca de Colonea, and moved into the Pesaro home. Pope Innocent VIII died and was replaced by Roderigo Borgia, now to be known as Alexander VI. Finally, as my Byzantine forebears had predicted, it was the End of the World – at least as we had known it.

I mentioned earlier a vision I had during the winter solstice of 1492 in which Dante's dream of the Isle of Purgatory had led to the discovery of the New World. I had a second vision that night and it pained me as no other.

Chapter Forty-two

In history, you have a record of the infinite variety of human experience plainly set out for all to see; and in that record you can find for yourself and your country both examples and warnings: fine things to take as models, base things, rotten through and through, to avoid. ^{Livy, Early History of Rome I:1}

Florence, 1492

The Son of God was crushed with pain. "Look at them," he said. "Save whom you can." In my dream, I saw Jews robbed of everything trying to get to the boats in Granada. I saw others killed, waiting for their Messiah to deliver them. I saw them land in Africa, only to be raped, sliced open in a search for jewels or hauled off by slavers. Some I saw now wounded, hungry and naked thrown back on the shores of Spain with nothing, the subject of additional cruelties. I woke with a terrible need to do something. I packed my clothes, a sword, and told Andrea I would be home in a couple of months, that the Lord did not speak to me very often but that when called, the best thing to do is respond. I rented a xebec and crew in Ancona and sailed.

Barcelona, 1493

When I arrived, Sarah and her family were still there. They say a frog will let you boil it alive if you turn up the heat slow enough. People react only slightly quicker. I told them to take their pick – that I would be happy to escort them to Oran or to Rome but the Lord had twice shown me Barcelona was no longer safe for them. I suggested they gather up no more than ten families of their closest friends and relatives, and to avoid being stopped, to bring only the essential – a change of clothes, a handful of jewels, and maybe a scroll.

I was lucky. They knew I was serious and they accepted the idea that I cared enough about them to return after ten years with a boat.

We found six other *converso* families willing to make the trip in the dead of winter. Others were too afraid of authorities, too afraid to try someplace new, or too afraid one of their own brethren might turn them in to the Inquisition, whose days of calm were officially over in Aragon and Catalonia. The following night, we arranged to meet at sunset on the plaza at the church of Santa Maria del Mar.

The following evening, just in time, the families appeared. Unfortunately, so did Fray Pedro Furia, along with a Judas who had turned down my offer, with a number of club- and rope-carrying goons ready for a lynching. My families were unarmed. Under the rules of the Edict of Granada, they were not carrying their tools of trade, nor gold nor silver. That afternoon, at my suggestion, they had each signed over their properties and trades to one of the 15 great "Old Christian" families of the Royal Order of the *Toisón de Oro* (Golden Fleece) with a request that these properties be transferred with all haste to the Crown.

I instructed them not to run, not to panic, and not to admit under any duress to being Jews or apostates or anything other than good Christians making pilgrimage to Rome. The Pope had agreed to accept Jews and *conversos* who arrived there, so we should be safe at both ends of our journey. This was not what Father Furious had in mind.

From across the Plaza he yelled "Get them!" and his mob bore down on us. I told the families not to panic, that God would deliver them. Before the two dozen miscreants could arrive to inflict mayhem, as many light cavalry knights on horseback interposed themselves. Each carried his family's shield. Each wore, painted in soot on his forehead, the Chrismon of the Knights of St. George. I had discovered these good men at the Chapel Sant Jordi that morning at the Generalitat (Catalonia's Seat of Government). One of them I knew from Schlossberg Castle years before. In front of the St. George sculpture, I dubbed them Knights Sant Jordi and they swore to defend Christians against all enemies. I told them of the converts wishing to emigrate five months beyond the terms of the Edict, and they decided to help.

Fray Furia threatened excommunication and confiscations. He shouted that he would have the Inquisition looking into their affairs. He threatened to have me up on charges before the magistrate. His crowd disintegrated, not in need of powerful enemies, and my families walked the quarter mile down to the docks escorted by the most noble gentlemen of Barcelona. We boarded my boat and we sailed.

Chapter Forty-three

Here art thou unto us the meridian torch of love
and there below with mortals art a living spring of hope.
Dante, Paradiso 33:1

Oran, 1493

How does one face a former love? With fear, joy and great anticipation. My heart raced to think about it. For Sarah's sake, and that of her traveling companions, I had to get a message to Alítheia at whatever the risk. There was no reason to expect our welcome to Oran would be any better than my nightmare. The harbor would be crawling with Ottomans.

By not stopping, the voyage took only three days. I remember praying that we not run into storms, corsairs, or the long arm of the Inquisition. Sarah said late in the previous summer Alítheia and her Vizier had convinced the Sultan to open the ports and gates to Oran despite his countrymen being outnumbered by refugees at the time.

I remember wondering, "So what has kept you in Barcelona?" but then I realized the question was not exactly fair. What kept my family in Florence when I knew we would be better off in Pesaro? I wondered when the water might get too hot for us and whether Andrea would be willing to jump out in time.

When we arrived Mers el Kébir, one representative of the ship was invited to come ashore and explain to the authorities what we were doing there, how many people we had aboard and whether we had brought anything useful in the way of provisions. I reported that I had brought 42 refugees from Barcelona and that we would be willing to purchase such provisions as might be required. I asked him if there was any way to get a message to the Vizier for the Sultan's wife from Constantinople. The foreman said both were encamped on a nearby hill overseeing refugee operations. For a price, any message could be sent. I took a slip of parchment and drew the following.

$$\text{اثنان واربعون لاجئ}$$
$$✡ \quad ☽ \quad ♃ \quad I \quad II$$

I gave the man 50 ducats to deliver the message. I hoped Alítheia would receive the note and remember. What I was trying to say was "Forty-two refugees. Meet me at the synagogue on the 7th (1st quarter of the moon), Thursday, between first and second prayers." I was sure she would know who sent it.

That night, I could not sleep. What would I do if the vizier arrested me? What would these people do? They certainly could not go back now. I decided I would take Sarah with me. That way, at least one of us could get into the harem if that proved necessary.

The next morning, we kept our appointment shortly before noon prayer. Abraham the Vizier met us at the door and showed us in, leaving two men posted outside. He led us into the building, then past an arch to the right, stopped and bowed. I started to bow low with arms crossed, thought better of it, and dropped to one knee with my head bowed. Sarah walked into a long tearful embrace. Alítheia turned to her Vizier and asked, "Abraham, could you give us a few minutes?" He bowed and left. I didn't move.

In a moment, she came to me, touching my shoulder. "And how fares my prince?" she asked. "Still living for your happiness," I said. "Stand up, silly, and give me a hug. They will not see and probably wouldn't shoot you if they did." "Arrows and ball never worried me. It was long blades and harem cuts I feared." She laughed, "You made the right choice, my janissary." I blushed.

In about an hour, we had caught up on 36 years of personal history. She said she would take care of the refugees we had brought. She had a sizable camp of them as they trekked east or took boats to Istanbul. Bayezid had also agreed to take in Jews, valuing their literacy and talents, their jewels and bills of exchange. Alítheia said she would send someone to show us around, but that she would have to get back to her work. She asked how long I would be staying and I said I would be going as soon as the ship could be ready. Again, she cried. "Thank you for saving my sister and bringing her to me." I went to kiss her hand. She raised it, twisting mine to her, held my hand in both of hers for a moment, pressed her lips to my cheek and said, "Bless you." We gave each other a long hug. I touched my forehead to hers and quietly said, "I'll see you in Heaven." Then I backed away reverently and bid farewell to Sarah.

Sarah left with Alítheia through a courtyard in the back. I returned through the tabernacle to the Vizier. He said someone would show the refugees and I to the camp. About an hour later, a fine-looking young man with brown hair and blue eyes arrived with a couple of bodyguards. He introduced himself only as "the Prince." We spoke briefly. He thanked me for making his mother so happy. Then he asked to speak to Miguel, Sarah's husband, whom he embraced as a long lost uncle. He showed the families to the encampment, where there were still about 15,000 refugees. He said there was plenty of food and water and clothing available, and that refugees were asked to contribute as best they could to the effort of sustaining the community. He said thus far things were working surprisingly well, but Oran would not be able to do this for much longer.

He looked and sounded like someone I would have enjoyed having as a Sultan, a captain, a friend ... or a son. In the end, he left me a box of things for my family. "Open it when you arrive home," he said. I bowed with my arms crossed. The xebec's captain had purchased a load of oil, grain and perfumes. I paid him extra to drop us in Rome. Two of the families had opted to go there rather than stay in Africa.

In all, it was a worthwhile trip. I did not know if I had done exactly what the Lord had in mind, but it certainly felt good and provided a sense of peace regarding Alítheia's fate. Andrea liked the gold thread finery. The boys loved their jeweled swords. For me there was a bit of gold, more than reimbursing me for my expenses. There was also a scrap of parchment with Arabic and symbols on the front. A note on the back, written in a beautiful hand, said simply, "Remember Heaven."

Chapter Forty-four

Nothing is more terrible than a military force moving about in an empire upon uninstructed and unreasoning impulses. ^{Plutarch, Galba}

Florence, 1493-1498

Inertia is the strongest force in the universe, and the sloth it lends one's moral judgment can be fatal at either end of the pendulum's swing. In just a few years, Florence, crown city of the Renaissance, was cursed both for her declining morality and for her strictness. I suppose it was like observing the slow, unrelenting seduction of a maiden, who, one day realizing she is no longer a virgin decides to lash out at the one who corrupted her. For all concerned, it was an exciting time, but immensely sad to see.

For all his learning and ambition, Piero II was not prepared to step into the shoes of his father. Where Lorenzo had been careful to act as the power broker, forging flexible alliances to thwart the most greedy and powerful, Piero now chose to side consistently with the giants. He drew closer to the King of Naples and Pope Alexander VI. The disadvantage to such a course of action would soon be apparent, for now Milan under "il Moro" felt compelled to woo Charles VIII of France in his competition for the dukedom of Milan, then being contested by the new King of Naples, Alfonso II. Charles, in addition to seeing Naples as a wonderful target, for he had family pretensions to the former reigns of the Anjou, saw an opportunity to prevent the union of the Italian city-states.

Through this one early misstep, Piero had basically invited France to invade the Peninsula. This set off two years of war in which the first phase was the conquest of our city-state. As you can imagine, the populace was not pleased.

The Medici, who for four generations had been the greatest family of Florence and Italy, suddenly and irrevocably found themselves exiled. The incident served to propel Alexander VI to new heights of power. To prevent France from becoming the only great power in Europe, other players now flocked to the Borgia pope. Ferdinand of Aragon, the new Holy Roman Emperor Maximilian I (reigning jointly with his father Frederick III), and Venice now banded together in order to push Charles back to the Alps.

The companions of war are famine and disease. With sailors from the New World came an epidemic of venereal disease quickly conveyed by soldiers on their march home from Naples to a population who had lain prostrate before them for two years. We called it the French Pox and it would be crippling to a society grown too free in its tastes. All this misfortune might have arrived eventually anyway, but Piero's mistake had brought it to our doorstep so much the sooner. For the moment, my family survived the convulsions, but soon we would see other effects of this war we never would have guessed.

As Germany was attempting to raise money for the Italian War, Maximilian had asked for another papal endorsement of the Imperial Order of St. George, which Alexander VI granted. I imagine it was accompanied by indulgences for fighting, but I am not sure how that might work for clashes between Christians (or for previously excommunicated Venetians). A few years after the war ended, there was a papal request for Constantine and I to bring the Order to Rome for a large initiation ceremony. I would like to think the Borgia Pope's initial interest in the most ancient order of chivalry was sincere. However, if it was, then it took him no time at all to uncover and exploit the unseemly side of the knighthoods of Christendom.

One of the things popes and kings can do to raise money is sell titles. In previous times, this might have entailed a fiefdom of a town whose noble had died without issue. A monastery that had fallen into disuse might be granted a new wealthy benefactor of the realm. Well, Alexander appears to have envisioned a way to sell a whole series of titles essentially with no cost to himself in terms of real estate or politics. All that would be required was a little gold, a strip of silk, and a hierarchy of grades for the new commandery.

The truth is, I do not know what he charged, but at Rome in 1498 there would be 400 new knights, knight captains, and knight commanders or priors. Over these were the Masters who were also *Commensales Pontificum* with the privilege of sitting at table with the Pope. The Masters could grant or restore honors, legitimize bastards, award doctorates, recognize poets laureate and establish public notaries.

In Germany, when a knight captain served more than a year, his successors were allowed to forever display a crown as part of the family's heraldry. Alexander established the new Order at Ravenna, old seat of the Western Empire, and assigned his knights the task of freeing the Adriatic of pirates and defending our coasts from the scourge of the Ottoman corsairs and slave traders. If these men succeeded in that endeavor, perhaps that might be as honorable as bearing the flag of Christ and Rome into battle and never letting it fall. Though I wondered ... how many of these fine gentlemen sporting their gold trinket on red silk would actually fight now that they could wear their honors and buy even grander ones?

As in the recent past, a certain number of knights were asked to join the Phatria. What happened next was the occasion for my listing a fifth pope among the world's long list of antichrists. He was the cause of my final deadly sin.

Alexander VI, the Borgia Pope

Chapter Forty-Five

Repent, for the kingdom of Heaven is at hand. ... Prepare the way of the Lord. Make his paths straight. ^{Matthew 3:2-3}

Florence, 1498

Andrea and I had remained too long in Florence. Morals, which tend to flow down from a society's leadership, had so far degenerated under Piero II that God had to send an emissary to remind us how far we had fallen. The *Decameron* had replaced *Leviticus* as the clergy's guide to morality, and general society had lost all sense of piety, with more than the usual murders, rapes and robberies.

Into this milieu walked a priest with his eyes wide open, possessing the knowledge that God was still with us and not the least bit amused. His message was simple: This Church is going to be punished; it must be renovated; and the change begins here and now. He had predicted a day in which wives would be snatched from their husbands, virgins would be violated, and children slain before their mothers and the streets would flow with blood. He had said the fountain for this evil was our own clergy, and France would be the punishing hand of God.

In the subsequent wake of France's invasion by 90,000 soldiers, and the populace expelling the Medici who had brought it on, this prophet, Girolamo Savonarola, became the leading voice demanding reform for Florence and the Church. In an age when the powerful quickly and frequently resort to knives or poison, this was both a sign of bravery and a serious death wish. It was also wildly popular.

Savonarola recommended the people return to fearing God, to setting aside private interests to serve the common good, to forming a constitution, a new assembly and senate, amnesty for former officers of the Republic and forgiveness for those indebted to the city-state. The Republic granted all his changes. Next, he wanted to abolish a mechanism for mob rule in which the populace gathered in the Piazza to ratify decisions already decided by the Medici. Again, he got what he wanted. He asked for a bank providing charity to the poor. He had his way, establishing an interest rate of six percent to relieve the debtors.

He could be harsh as well. Gamblers, blasphemers, and prositutes found themselves in line for beatings, tongues sliced and establishments shut down. He told us the consequences of our continued debauchery would be death, like the Plagues that struck us now and then.

He spoke of the relationship of virtue to freedom, and this was his message for the ages:

> *The true, the only Liberty consists in willing that which is Good. ... Citizens, will you be free? First, love God, love your neighbor, love one another, and love the common good. If you have this love and this union among yourselves, you have true Liberty.*

Though he was a Dominican, this religion he advocated was not one narrowly construed by a rule, order or denomination. It was Virtue itself:

> *Christian life does not consist in ceremonies, but in being Good; and he who is Good cannot refrain from showing his goodness. ... In this consists the Christian religion, which is founded on Love and Charity.*

I no longer wonder how much better the world would be if every one of us rose in the morning and demanded virtue of ourselves and those around us – because I have seen it. Indecent clothes were put away. People fasted. Many gave away their riches and joined a convent. Hymns were heard instead of vulgar poetry. People returned to church. Companies and banks began fair dealing and addressing the needs of the poor. All Savonarola asked of us was "good works" and most of us attempted each day to deliver them.

He was not optimistic of what reward awaited him for all his pains:

> *The servant is no greater than his master, says the Lord. You know that after preaching I was crucified. Martyrdom awaits you as well.*

Yet, despite this foreknowledge, he pressed on.

Now, as I said, morality starts at the top and Alexander VI was a pope as no other. Others had been less tolerant, others had been more greedy. Yet others, while good people, had made terribly bad decisions. Alexander was in a category by himself.

From all appearances, this Borgia pope thought himself a reincarnation of the Bull on his family coat of arms. Two things counted in the world – his next lust and the barrier to be smashed on the way to its accomplishment. He very much reminded me of Mehmed. Alexander VI and Savonarola were on a collision course, and it would be an uneven contest only because the latter believed in the Catholic Church and the Papacy.

The man who had done the most to restore the Florentine Republic now swung his state too far to the right. He sought to control the membership of the Assembly to limit the influence of his enemies, the libertines he had driven from power. He sought to curtail entertainments that might lead to immorality. He prohibited balls and festivals. Children went door to door during the carnivals of 1497 and 1498 collecting luxuries, vanities and books for an *auto da fe* declaring Jesus the King of Florence. The "immoral" items would be burned as unacceptable to His Kingdom.

As you can imagine, this concerned me, thinking of the pain and expense of having collected rare works, now to have someone burn them just as Patriarch George Scholarios would have done. Thankfully, the monks in St. Mark's bought up the Biblioteca Laurenziana to keep it intact.

Savonarola pressed hard the theme that the Church required reform. He said:

Draw nigh, infamous Church! ... Your luxury has made a disfigured harlot of you. You are worse than a beast. ... In time past, you blushed for your sins; now you have not even that much shame.

On Ascension Day, 1497, the Compagnacci (young nobles) and Arrabiatti (Medici supporters) thought to assassinate him during a sermon. They were unsuccessful when supporters came to his defense. Now the pope excommunicated Savonarola for failure to report to Rome and for continuing to preach.

When that happened, the Devil's minions (or rather Alexander's) came out to play. Indecent attire came out of hiding. Obscene songs were heard again and women uncovered their breasts. Vice, indecency and crime went back to the streets. The next cardinal in line for pope offered to arrange the withdrawal of our city's excommunication for a few thousand scudi – not that our papal disgrace mattered. Savonarola continued to preach and to give us communion.

The Pope was livid with this priest who defied him. Alexander threatened the city with an interdict such as Sixtus had used to have us surrender Lorenzo. Savonarola responded with a note to the kings of Europe recommending a Council for the reform of the Catholic Church in light of the sins of Alexander. "I affirm that he is not a Christian, and that he does not believe there is a God."

Sometimes, Savonarola acted with such a holy rage you would think he were Jesus among the moneychangers. One day he yelled out:

> *If the priests go to church, to vespers, to the office, it is for money. They sell the sacraments, trade in the Mass, and wear fine shirts. ... The whores go publicly to St. Peter's where every priest has his concubine. It is said everywhere, 'If you want to ruin your son, make a priest of him!'*

Savonarola's enemies now devised a way to discredit him in front of the people. They would challenge him to a trial by fire. If he burned himself in it, he was culpable as the Vatican said. They proposed a fire walk accompanied by a priest with opposing doctrines, Francesco di Puglia. Savonarola said he was willing. On the agreed day, while the crowd waited, the opposition, as planned, refused to show. Only Savonarola walking 80 feet end-to-end without being burned would satisfy the crowd. Otherwise, they would turn on the holy man for his lack of faith and for the lack of purity in his doctrine condemned by the Vatican. People waited for hours and through the rain to see him do the fire walk. They waited in vain.

Thus ended the preacher's influence on the people. On Palm Sunday, rioters went to kill him at St. Mark's. His brethren armed to defend him and he told them to put away all weapons but prayer. He was captured with some of his closest associates. They were tortured for days. In the end, they were found guilty of heresy, though the only error found was Savonarola claiming his messages were from God.

On the 23rd of May, the huge crowd gathered at the Piazza to see what Rome and Florence had chosen to do with the man who had single-handedly revived their Republic. Savonarola and his companions Domenico da Pescia and Silvestro Maruffi were hanged and burned as heretics. On the way to the gallows, their habits were taken and they were excommunicated. A few steps later, a papal commissioner granted them indulgences from the additional pains of purgatory. Such was the mercy of the Borgia pope!

The Savonarola incident was my family's occasion for leaving Florence. We had seen autocracy and democracy work when led by virtue; and we had seen them fail when evil prevailed.

At first, I felt a little guilty for what had happened to the good friar. Perhaps books I had imported had left some people confused. Then I realized they had been pushed to this unruly madness by the very Vicar of God.

Expecting Alexander to act honorably was a bit like asking a man of intelligence to do an 80-foot fire walk. It could involve a long wait.

Girolamo Savonarola, Prophet of Florence

Chapter Forty-six

> *The law, like a good archer, should aim at the right measure of punishment, and in all cases at the deserved punishment.* ^{Plato, Laws 11:934}

Rome, 1503

I offer that aside on the Pope and Savonarola because it sort of prepared me to see Alexander's Vatican for what it had really become – the enemy of virtue. From Day 1 of his reign, the Bull, as they called him, would be known as a tough master. In the 17 days prior to his election, there had been 220 murders in the city of 50,000. He set an example with the one murderer who was caught by razing the man's house to the ground and hanging him above the ashes. During Alexander's 11-year reign, it is said the rate dropped to four or five murders a night.

He ordered persecution against the Bogomils, Picards and Waldenses, though he was easy on the Jews. A *converso* like Ferdinand, he sometimes extorted money from them in exchange for pardons.

When he decided materials being printed throughout Europe were inappropriate, he invented the *Index Expurgatorius* – books to be burned whose authors, publishers and readers could be excommunicated (with Inquisitional extortion to follow). What a badge of honor for authors that black list would become!

While Alexander's apparent orthodoxy could be impressive, terrible things were said of this pope and his relationship with his daughters ... of orgies held and attended ... of multiple mistresses ... of hired assassins. If your gods are what you spend your time, energy and money on, then the one spiritually relevant thing about the man was his illegitimate children. There was nothing under the Sun he would not do for them and no sin of theirs he could not forgive. One of his sons was said to have killed another, which to me suggests he might have gone too far in spoiling them.

I suppose one could call Alexander the "victim of an immoral age" – but then how does one explain a man like Savonarola so readily able to rise above it? Whether or not it is in use, there is a standard for what is right and what is wrong; and if people are reminded, they generally will adhere to it. Some clearly cannot. Having seen Alexander's kind before, I have to say that there is not much that could shock me; but sometimes I heard things from my son or my best friend at Rome that made me wonder how God could place such a beast on the throne of St. Peter. The rumor, and I believe it, was that the cardinals had sold the seat to the highest bidder.

A more charitable soul might call Alexander the victim of rumors, but why, then, were so many evil things said of this man and no other? Among his parties of the papal palace was a ballet in which 50 dancers were prostitutes hired off the street! I could not imagine anything so diabolical as procuring the position of Pope to debase it with hypocrisy, but what else explained such activities in the high places of Christianity?

I heard it said that Naples' King Ferrante, a monster in his own right, "cried for Christendom" when they told him Roderigo Borgia had risen to the papacy. I feared for my son in such a Vatican. Anyone could fall prey to this man or his vicious son Cesare. My friend told me of poisons the Borgias had developed. He said their knowledge of vile things mineral, plant and animal was impressive. He could not tell me how they worked ... only that they seemed reliable. I asked him how many corpses it took to be able to make such a statement. He said, "Of 36 cardinals created, 27 have died. Of these, at least six were obviously not from natural causes or normal circumstances."

Through his many excesses, Alexander will have done the Church a great favor. In his creation of an evil so obvious, so pervasive and infamous, the bishops and cardinals now, for their own livelihood, must seriously undertake to reform the Church. The only untenable alternative for them would be to just walk away and look for work.

That is the way of good and evil – one eventually leads to the other. When life is going along blessedly in the way of one's interests, someone or something is duty-bound to screw it up. If, in your selfishness, you have sufficiently oppressed one nation, group, family or person, they may one day choose to address their grievance. This pope was an offense to Christianity and nobody was doing anything about it.

Young Roderigo Borgia was getting into trouble in private gardens like his son Cesare would later get into trouble in public baths – both drawing the concerns of their elders even as cardinals. Prior to his election, there was hardly the odor of scandal about him. Then again, he had at least seven children by women married to other men and an untold number of lovers. Where there is this order of smoke, somewhere there is a raging fire ... about three feet off the ground. The man seems to have had a very primitive idea of what it means to work for the God of Love.

In 1498, we had taken the Order and Phatria to Rome. My friend Constantine was more involved with the Phatria. I had little inclination for their sacred magic or scientific pursuits, not being much of a mystagogue or team player by nature.

One day, Constantine said there was something radically wrong in that ancient body of Pythagoreans. A new rite had been implemented for the initiation of "hermaphrodite man" through "the Middle Way" (as in turning Da Vinci's Vitruvian Man face-down). Instead of the positive Gnosticism of Clement, they were heading down the dark and odorous paths of the Naassenes, who had so much contempt for women. The mystical journey in such an initiation was to help them *pass over from the earthly parts of the nether world to the everlasting substance above, where there is neither female nor male, but a new creature.* [Hippolytus, Refutation of all Heresies] ... something to do with the oft-repeated "love one another" and "a sensible union between Man and God."

They said this was what Paul was talking about in Galatians 3:28. That this was what was meant by Genesis 1, 5, 6 and 7 – God creating humans "male and female." That this was the mystery of the widow's son. [1 Kings 17] That such an initiation was one's rebirth and the path to wisdom. Moreover, they said this was in the imitation of Christ and the love of the Father for the Son, that this was the secret of Jacob's wrestling with the Lord [Genesis 32] and the Dionysian blessing of Judah, [Genesis 49] and that it was the secret of Exodus 33, Psalm 4:3, Hosea 2:12, Matthew 11:27 and John 13. Moreover, they claimed it was the very spirituality of Jesus and the disciples, taking the *Acts of John* as their authority. I had never heard such a pernicious doctrine.

My parents were right – 12 verses out of context and one has all the makings of a cult. Two years from its establishment at Rome and the Phatria had fouled its philosophy. We installed a new grand master, one with a more sound understanding of true religion and we started over. The Phatria has since split off from the Order. I guess they felt their enterprise now exceeds the bounds of Christianity, which to me indicates that they, like the Western Canon and the Vatican, have forgotten quite a bit.

Their particular unmentionable sin was absolutely out of control in Alexander's Vatican. For a church that takes so much in the *Bible* literally, there was considerable vagueness regarding the mystical love of God and no attention at all was being paid to the strictures of Leviticus.

Alexander and Cesare had also fashioned a sort of financial empire out of the capital of Christianity. If they took a baron's castle and lands in a war, he might buy them back for 50,000 ducats. If one wanted to be a cardinal, one could purchase the hat for 10,000 – ordination being optional. Art treasures were sold for gold. Indulgences, pardons for capital crimes, forgiveness for *marranos* ... Savonarola was right. This Vatican was all about money. And Jesus was right. One cannot serve God and mammon. [Matthew 6:24] Again, I held Alexander responsible.

The worst were the murders and confiscations. One's feudal lands were forfeit if one failed to pay tribute to Rome. If one irritated Cesare enough, one could be brought up on false charges and condemned to death or imprisonment. If one was wealthy, one's family could be rendered destitute by similar methods. The rumor, according to my best friend, was that both of those causes might now affect my son Constantine and his friend Giovanni the cardinal. My boy had crossed words with Cesare; and Lorenzo's son was being considered for a confiscation. By my estimation, God save my soul, it was high time for a new pope.

So the question I had is what do you get the man who has everything or knows where to steal it? He was a master of intrigue, head of Rome's assassins (or father to their master) and the inventor of ingenious poisons.

That was it! I would beat the master at his own game.

Chapter Forty-seven

Socrates: *The proper office of punishment is two-fold. He who is rightly punished ought either to become better and profit by it, or he ought to be made an example to his fellows, that they may see what he suffers, and fear and become better.* ^{Plato, Gorgias}

Rome, 1503

I suppose the worst criminal should suffer the worst death. Is that not your theory? Why else would you roast victims half an hour before allowing the fire to claim them? In the case of the Borgia pope, the biggest criminal was immune from prosecution, yet he made a complete mockery of Christianity.

If ever there was a perfect target for your righteous indignation, Alexander was it. A woman joining a nunnery in his Rome enjoyed no more honor than a girl sold into a brothel. His most powerful cardinal was a known murderer. I remember thinking that Alexander's punishment would have to be terrible and supplied by God Himself. All I would do was direct it to the right place, for the Antichrist is to be brought down "without hand." ^{Daniel 8:25}

It so happened that in last summer's heat, the mosquitoes were unbearable and the stagnant waters of the marshlands were breeding such fevers as to slay anyone not in perfect health. Everyone blamed the diseases on *malaria*, the "bad air." Indeed, August is oppressive in a city with too many people and not enough water to carry away the waste. The quiet pools of the Tiber would be my alchemist's laboratory. All I needed was to discover the active ingredients. I employed a number of birds, a cat, a dog and a pig to do that.

I should probably mention at this point that I received no help from any human accomplice. Being one of the *Commensales Pontificum*, I was a known and trusted personage in the papal palace with access to the right people and the right events. Once I found my organism and method of delivery, I would be ready.

Ancient authorities had known there was something in the stagnant water of marshes that can be fatal – some organisms too small for the eye to see. Some were fatal if you ingested them, some if you breathed them in, and some if they were carried into the blood through a wound. Again, it was a matter of finding the right one and concentrating it. I figured if I succeeded in killing the animals, then I could probably hand an old man over to God's justice.

My problem was that, aside from his unlimited ambition, greed and lust, Alexander had few habits to be exploited, and he was in excellent health. At table, he would eat only one plate of food. Such a man would have to be taken down by degrees. I began my research toward the end of July and hoped Cesare might not act too quickly against Constantine or Giovanni.

I found an abandoned shack down by the river with a fenced-in area. I put the animals in cages with doors in the back to place their food. I built a tent of netting of fine cloth for everything above and to the front. Through the front of all the cages, arranged in birds-to-pig order, I ran a small stream of marsh water. Before the exit of the tent, I made a little pond with grasses from the marsh. Each day, I would check progress and see what was going on in the cage.

At the end of Day 3, everyone was still alive. The "pond" looked murkier than the day I had installed it. By Day 6, two birds had died and I noticed mosquitoes in the tent. By Day 9, all the birds had died and there were many mosquitoes. Some bit me when I was giving the animals food and I had a terrible fever for days. I decided mosquitoes were the main vector and started using gloves. By Day 12, the cat had died and the dog looked sick. By Day 15, only the pig was left. My problem now was how to get an organism growing in these mosquitoes into the Pope and his son. Mosquitoes cannot be trained and introducing them into a home would not necessarily infect the right people.

Whatever I was going to do had to be done quickly. We had a dinner party scheduled at Cardinal Adriano de Corneto's for August 6th. That evening, I brought two vials of strained downstream water from my animal pen, a perfume bottle with rosewater and a bag of mosquitoes tied-and-cut from the netting. We could all be sick! It would be a small group. I felt for Corneto, though. He is a good man. Before the party, as everyone was outside having wine and aperitifs, I spilled a dash of the water on the salads of the two guests of honor and let the mosquitoes fly. I also mixed a vial of the downstream water with the rosewater and sprayed the dining room "to make it smell nice." It did not smell exactly nice, of course, so we occasionally used the spray throughout the evening.

Several of us became sick, but nobody was dying. The next day, my pig died. I removed another couple of vials of water and another bag of mosquitoes. Then I burned everything to the ground. I went to visit my friends in the papal palace.

Known for having medical knowledge, I was allowed to see the Pope and speak to his doctor, whom I suggested could use a break. While he was out, I slipped a vial of the water into where the doctor kept his leeches. The other I dumped into the water where he rinsed his instruments. I let the mosquitoes go inside the Pope's room. By now I was pretty sure that it was the mosquitoes going back to the contaminated victim that concentrates the poison.

Before I left, I wished Alexander well and gave him a deck of marked cards. He loved to play. In his mind, he left this world a victor – and several cardinals left his side so much the poorer. They mourned all the more when, with the Pope and Cesare deathly ill, Cesare's men broke in to steal everything – 200,000 ducats in plate and jewels and another 100,000 in gold. There would be no refunds to the cardinals' losses.

By the evening he died, August 18th, the Pope had become the nastiest corpse ever seen; and no amount of silk or gold could cover up the disgusting mess. The master of ceremonies reported: "The face was very dark ... the nose swollen, the tongue bent over in the mouth, completely double and pushing out the lips, themselves swollen. The mouth was agape and so ghastly that people who saw it said they had never seen anything like it." Constantine called it "inhumanly putrid with the sulphurous stench of Hell escaping ... no, exploding ... from every pore and orifice!"

The burial scene too was a disgrace. The coffin wasn't big enough. The mouth foamed. The body bloated. The body was decomposing so quickly there was no time to build another box. They removed his mitre. They pounded the gassy corpse into a coffin and slammed the lid tight – with no showing, no candles, and no tears. His Requiem was attended by four prelates. One story says there was no memorial because the new pope, Pius III, forbade another Mass saying, "It is blasphemous to pray for the damned." That report could be an unkind exaggeration or the precise truth. I cannot say. As for me, I would simply add "Amen" to the words of St. Bernard five centuries earlier:

> *Is not Rome the acknowledged refuge for ambition, avarice, simony, sacrilege, concubinage, incest and for those desiring to be promoted or to retain honors they have forfeited?* St. Bernard, De Consideratione

The new Pope tried to take on the by-now-recovered Cesare and to begin the process of Vatican reform demanded by Savonarola. Within a month, the pious man was winging his way to heaven. The fear and loathing this now inspired for Cesare within the College of Cardinals was substantial. They elected a mortal enemy of the Borgias as the next pope, Julius II.

The "unstoppable" force of the Borgia had thus been defeated by precisely as many small forces as it took to restore balance. The power-hungry Cesare used to say, *Aut Caesar, aut nihil* (Or Caesar or Nothing). So be it. He shall be Nothing!

Cesare Borgia

Chapter Forty-eight

Where absolute freedom is allowed there is nothing to restrain the evil inherent in every man. Aristotle, Politics

Such things taught Pythagoras, though advising above all things to speak the Truth, for this alone deifies men. Porphyry, Life of Pythagoras

The Road to Pesaro, 1503

Somewhere along the road back to Pesaro, I was knocked off my horse by a vision. I am not sure, but I think it was God the Father and he was ANGRY. "Have you learned NOTHING?" he roared "Have you no MERCY?" I woke up on the ground. The horse was waiting.

Then it dawned on me ... I had become my ghosts. That Mehmed and Alexander still walked the Earth ... in me! I might be less greedy or less ambitious, but I was every bit as violent and treacherous as they had ever been! In their own ways, their lives had possessed more integrity. In their own points of view, they too had always done what they thought was right and necessary. And the one who was playing *their* game instead of fulfilling his *own* purpose was *me!* From that spot, I just wandered in shock and depression ... hoping for someone, something, someplace ... holy. I needed to cleanse my soul.

How many times do you look back at your life in disgust and wonder where it all went wrong? A decent soul probably has lots of practice doing such a thing. I could not remember the last time ... probably Milan. I arrived to a fork in the road and let the horse decide which way to go. I came to another and did the same thing. Eventually, in this way, we arrived at Assisi.

I rented myself a room and stable, washed and hiked up to the Duomo di San Rufino to see the place that had nourished the spirit of a young Saint Francis.

I was in perfect misery. There was no service going on, so I went forward toward the altar and lay prostrate before the step. "Oh, Father, help me!" was my cry. I was speaking to Our Father in Heaven, though of course that is not how it was interpreted. "Yes, my son," I heard a priest reply. The voice was familiar and I looked up. It was Salvatore! I remained on my knees. "Oh, Salvatore, I am so ashamed and I feel so bad!" He answered, "Let's go for a walk."

He took me out to some steps facing the forest on the north side of the cathedral. Pointing to the woods, he said, "I am sure the Saint felt much more at home out here, where one can see God more clearly. Cities are messy. People are messy."

"Out there," he said, "it all makes more sense. So what brings you here?" I asked if it would be okay to confess right there. "I'm sure it's all the same to God," he said. I said, "I don't know. He sounded awfully angry this morning!"

For the next hour, I unburdened my soul. I think I told him everything, but maybe I only told him the best and the worst. When I was finished, he gave me an assignment. He said no amount of Hail Marys or Our Fathers was going to improve the way I felt about what I had done. He said, "It is time for you to go back to first principles. What is your purpose in life? What are the principles you believe with all your soul? And if you had nobody else to worry about and nothing else pressing in the world, what would you do with your last years of life?" I agreed that I had much soul work to do and that I would return to the path the Father had placed me on so long ago.

He smiled and said: "May our Lord Jesus Christ absolve you; and by His authority I absolve you from every bond of excommunication and interdict, so far as my power allows and your needs require. I absolve you from your sins in the name of the Father, and of the Son, and of the Holy Spirit. Amen."

I thanked him and he said, "May the Passion of Our Lord Jesus Christ, the merits of the Blessed Virgin Mary and of all the saints and also whatever good you do or evil you endure merit for you the remission of your sins, the increase of grace and the reward of everlasting life. Amen."

I returned to the tavern and prayed my little prayer for awhile. Then I took out a plume, my inkhorn and a piece of parchment and wrote:

Purpose of my Life: *I am here to awaken my soul, to learn righteousness, and, by my words and good or bad example, to teach others a shorter path to righteousness than the one I took.*

Principles I believe in:
- *God and Wisdom are One; and all paths we take will eventually lead back to that Truth.*
- *Here on Earth is where we balance our accounts with God and man – in this life or the next.*
- *All of us err as we attempt to think, to say and to do what is Right.*
- *Because we commit our sins through ignorance, all deserve our Mercy – even those who must be stopped.*
- *It is due to our failures to each other that Humanity lives in so much pain and misery.*
- *Our Selfishness, our Arrogance, our Lack of Caring, and our Willingness to Judge are what enable us to sin against others.*
- *Through our Love, Truth, Power and Faith we can become Wise and be a blessing to others.*
- *Love is what binds the universe together.*
- *Achieve Righteousness and the Light and Power of God will be made manifest.*
- *In the end, all things work out for the best.*

What I must do before I die: *Pass along what I have learned to the heirs of Greece and Rome.*

In two days, I was home. I did not burden the family with what I had done. In fact, I had rarely burdened them with anything associated with the Order, the Phatria, or the unusual things I read or heard. I always figured it was better to let them grow up good Catholics than be confused by me. I did encourage the boys when they were little to each begin a *Florilegium* to serve as their own practical and personal *Bible*.

We had a wonderful fall and winter. In the spring I left my worldly goods to John, asking him to take care of his mother – telling him I had something I had to do in Spain before I could retire to the beach. Andrea was helping the convent make a big tapestry and John's wife Maria was pregnant with our first grandchild. The three were very soon destined to be happy. I also foresaw that my son the priest and his friend the cardinal would be fine now that Cesare had lost his sponsor, his cardinal's hat, and his estate – being exiled to Spain.

Chapter Forty-nine

The just man does not allow the several elements in his soul to usurp one another's functions; he is indeed one who sets his house in order, by self-mastery and discipline coming to be at peace with himself. ... Only when he ... has made himself one man instead of many will he be ready to go about whatever he may have to do. ^{Plato, Republic}

Toledo, 1504

On my way here, I stopped on the coast long enough to bury the Sword of the Caesars in a lead-lined box at an old site of the Order and the Empire. One of your future kings will be a Holy Roman Emperor. He is welcome to it. Truth is, modern swords are more effective.

When I arrived in Toledo, I requested an audience with the Archbishop rather than the King or Queen because I was warned in a dream that the Spanish throne will not be stable for several years. Past that point, for a time, Spain will be the greatest empire on Earth. I realize that this sounds preposterous, that your King and Queen are both still alive and have successors waiting in the wings. Nonetheless, you asked for the Truth and you shall have it. My grandfather instructed me that Archbishop Cisneros is the man to be warned if I am to complete my mission. For a time, the Archbishop will be the most powerful man in the world.

The facilitator in my passing along the legacy of Empire to the heirs of Greece and Rome turned out to be Toledo's newest priest – Pedro Furia. I found it ironic that he should now be posted here, but then I imagine things proved hard for him in Barcelona. How strange that he would be my entrée to you. This must be Providence's way of making sure my message gets through. A day after I spoke to him in the Cathedral, I found myself in your jail. This was surely not the best way for me to have an audience with the archbishop, but if it serves the purpose, so be it.

I am sure Brother Furia has mentioned my previous meetings with him in Barcelona and his suspicions of me as a sympathizer of *conversos,* of the probability that I am a practicing Jew or Moslem, that I am a heterodox Christian, or some sort of sorcerer and liar. The man is as imaginative as he is quick to judge – the very portrait of someone who takes his own Faith as the only one acceptable, consigning the rest of us to Hell. So to the question, "Do you know why you are here?" I can only reply that I have no idea of the specific charges, but a very good idea from what quarter they arrived.

In my defense, the first time I met Father Furia was prior to the imposition of clear inquisitorial jurisdiction in Aragon and Catalonia. King Ferdinand was negotiating with Pope Sixtus IV for his own tribunals. In the second instance, I assisted Christians never accused of being relapsed Jews or Moslems. It was Brother Furia's own actions that were to the prejudice of public order, not my own. I asked the families who thought they might be accused of falling within the purview of the expulsion order to donate their property to the Crown of Aragon. As far as I know, they complied with that request.

As to whether the Papacy granted forgiveness to the two families that went to Rome, well I suppose that would be in the records of the Vatican. As Christians they should have required no forgiveness. Even in the case of their *converso* status being revoked by Aragon, the penalty would not exceed their worldly possessions, which they had abandoned to be free of Spain.

If being circumcised is a crime, then I am guilty of being one of the sons of Constantinople captured by the Turks in 1453. A barber clipped us all. We were not asked; and we were not practicing Moslems at the time.

While in Italy, I was a practicing Catholic. If subsequent to living in Italy I once found it necessary to claim otherwise, I would remind you that it is permissible for anyone of any faith to do the same when their lives depend on it. However, my trip to Spain was not to justify myself. I came to provide the archbishop a bit of added perspective.

My message for Archbishop Cisneros is simple: The Ottoman Empire must immediately be discouraged from gaining control of the Straits of Gibraltar and Mediterranean trade or you have wasted eight centuries of *Reconquista* and you stand to lose everything again.

If you have read my story up to this point, you realize Mehmed captured Constantinople beginning with precisely this sort of naval choke point. If you have read your reports from spies in Oran, and I believe I met one while I was there in 1493 – Lorenzo de Padilla – you know how strong the Ottoman navy has become at Mers el Kébir. Since 1494, you have had the Pope's blessing to conquer all Africa but Morocco and Guinea. It has been ten years and you have yet to assume the leadership of the world God will confer on you if you will now engage your enemy.

The remainder of my confession will consist of what I discovered in my quest to understand what happened to the Empire, along with some mysteries that might contribute one day to your building a more inclusive, truly universal Church. I cannot promise that this is authoritative or divinely inspired. I can only say it represents a Truth that came to me as I picked up this quill and makes more sense than what the teachers and priests had to say when I was growing up.

I hope one day the Church or a wise king will gather sages of the different faiths and sciences to decipher the keys to mankind's past and future. God scattered Wisdom across the Earth so all His children would have a path to Salvation before the Judgment. We must find those seeds and nurture them before it is too late.

As to your next question – whether I will recant all this – I must tell you that I am not the same person I once was. There were times in my life when I was willing to do or to say almost anything to survive. Now, I would rather die telling you the Truth than live with any more lies.

Cisneros became a cardinal and Regent of Spain.

Chapter Fifty

What is now called the Christian religion existed even among the ancients and was not lacking from the beginning of the human race until "Christ came in the flesh." From that time, true religion, which already existed, began to be called Christian. Saint Augustine, Retractations

There is only a single religion in the variety of rites. ... Just as You the King are only one, there ought to be only a single religion and a single cult of adoration of God. ... Truth is One and is impossible not to be comprehended by every free intellect. All diversity of religion ought to be brought into one orthodox faith. Nicholas da Cusa, De Pace Fidei

Why Byzantium Fell

Byzantium was founded on the knowledge and values of Greece and Rome. We lost her when we divorced Freedom from Virtue and God from Wisdom. Like the Israelites of old who had done the same thing, it was our turn to suffer.

Hear the word of the LORD, children of Israel. For the LORD hath a controversy with the inhabitants of the land, because there is no Truth, nor Mercy, nor Knowledge of God in the land. Cursing, lying, killing, stealing, and adultery have exceeded every restraint until bloodshed is widespread. Therefore our land will mourn, and everyone who dwells therein will waste away; and all living things in her, even the animals of the field, the birds of the sky, and even the fish of the sea will die. Hosea 4:1-3

We had plenty of food; we were well and saw no evil when we made cakes, burned incense and poured drink offerings to the Queen of Heaven, but since we stopped doing those things we have lacked all things and been consumed by war and famine. Jeremiah 7:18, 44:17-19 & 44:25

The workings of the Byzantine court had been scripted for 500 years. Our laws had been in place for a millennium. Our Churchmen had not had a good debate in two centuries. Intellectually, militarily and morally we had fallen asleep on guard duty.

Our enemies noticed and overwhelmed us, first the Latins and then the Turks. We counted on allies who existed only in our minds. In our arrogance, we thought our enemies unable to breach our defenses. Except in a small circle, we had ceased to teach the pride in nation or bravery in war that grow and defend an empire. In the end, we could not hold even one walled city. Honor and bravery were no longer ideas that ruled us. St. George, our victor over evil, had ended up a dusty icon. He was no longer the hero who inspired us.

Fewer and fewer people learned the ancient knowledge: the Order, the Phatria, Churchmen, and a few nobles. Most of them never read past the *Bible*. Their thinking, I imagine, was that if man's history only goes back a few thousand years, and Byzantium reigned over the meaningful thousand, then what is there to know beyond a few emperors' names? We turned our back on our legacy, and in doing so threw away our future.

In the Beginning

I remember telling Alítheia and Salvatore decades ago that I wanted to understand a little about God and His world before I died. Over the years, I learned there are few big answers. Even though they are all different facets of the same thing, neither is there a last word regarding wisdom, religion, science, philosophy or history.

Before He or She was assigned a personality, "God" was our every attempt to understand the Universe. Religion and mythology are our attempts, through symbols and stories, to understand the vital cycles of the Universe and to teach life's most important lessons. I have read and heard stories of the Sumerians, Persians, Brahmans, Babylonians, Hittites, Phoenicians, Egyptians and Hebrews. While the names of the characters changed, the stories were the same. What they told me was that ancient man used the Sun's path through the stars to remember the events significant to humanity's survival.

The most universal story was the oldest and must never be forgotten:

> *There is also the Year that Aristotle called the Greatest, rather than merely the Great. ... The Year has a great winter called the Cataclysm,*

> *which we call the Deluge, and a summer called Ekpyrosis, which is the Conflagration of the World, for at these two times the world apparently is either drowned in water or set on fire.* ^{Censorinus, De die natali liber 18:11}

Speaking of the descendants of Adam through Seth, Josephus recalled the same lesson:

> *They also were the inventors of that peculiar sort of wisdom which is concerned with the heavenly bodies, and their order. In order that their inventions might not be lost before they were sufficiently known, upon Adam's prediction that the world was to be destroyed at one time by the force of fire, and at another time by the violence and quantity of water, they made two pillars: the one of brick, the other of stone and they inscribed their discoveries on them both.* ^{Antiquities of the Jews, Chap. II}

In the past, the Sun's loops through the zodiac have led to serious celestial trouble at least twice each round. To my knowledge, no one ever said with certainty whether that meant there was trouble at two disastrous ends of a long track, whether our problem was traversing the middle of the Milky Way, or if the zodiac rotating around us periodically brought us a far-traveling nemesis. What we do know is that about 26,000 and 13,000 years ago, a Great Dragon the Magi called "Ahriman" came by. Time before last, one of his nine heads struck Earth, penetrating to the core and nearly destroying humanity.

The Sumerians said that eons ago there was a collision with a giant called Tiamat. Perhaps "Ahriman" is what remains of that great clash with the Sumerian Dragon that others would one day rename "Satan." Whatever it is, the Dragon or one of its companions was big enough to have brought a long age of ice to mankind's first Paradise, located within 25 degrees of the Pole ^{Fargard 1:9} and today found below the Tropic of Capricorn ^{Pliny & St. Brendan} where previously that ancient land saw daylight between the vernal and autumnal equinoxes ^{Pomponius Mela} — meaning that our world was upside-down from what it is today.

An Egyptian priest once told Solon the story of the destruction of Phaeton (another name for this Tiamat or Ahriman), saying it signified *a declination of the bodies moving in the heavens around the earth, and a great conflagration of things upon the earth.* ^{Plato, Timaeus} I suspect the story also relates to the tales of Typhon and Medusa.

After its disastrous birth about 23,615 BC, the current Age of the Sun ran into trouble about 12,813 years into its round. Around 10,801 BC, we again encountered Ahriman flying out of the Milky Way's center near Sagittarius (a pivotal danger spot in the heavens marked for us by the Egyptians with a Shen, the Hebrews with the letter Qoph, and St. John with the mystery of the Omega – all designating a shifting point or Axis of the galaxy ruled by Ea "The Deep"). Again, there was a pole shift ... a Flood ... and Dragon's Fire exploded over Atlantis, raining destruction over a quarter of the world. The resulting darkness brought back the age of ice.

> *The Giant turned back, and passed from north to south; he left one pole and stood by the other. ... He dragged the two Fishes out of the sky and cast them into the sea; he buffeted the Ram. ... He shadowed the bright radiance of the unclouded sky by darting forth his tangled army of snakes. One of them ... skipped upon the backbone of the heavenly Serpent ... another entwined about the ... Bull's horned head ... another made a bold leap ... and jumped around Opheuchus' arm that held the viper.* [Nonnos, Dionysiaca I:176-200]

A similar story is told of Oceanus:

> *I will drown the fiery Sun in my quenching flood, I will put out the stars of heaven! ... I will wash with my waters the ends of the axle and the dry track of the Wagon. ... I will drag down from heaven the fiery Milky Way ... and bring him back to a new home in the Celtic land; he shall be water again and the sky shall be bare of the river of fire. The starry Fishes that swim on high I will pull into the sea and make them mine again.* [Nonnos, Dionysiaca XXIII:290-302]

One does not drown the Sun, drop the Big Dipper into the Ocean or make the Milky Way disappear below the horizon without turning the Earth drastically. There is another reference in the *Bundahishn* where Ahriman arranged the "water" *below the Earth* and, rushing out upon the whole creation, *he made the world quite as injured and dark at midday as though it were in dark night.* [Bundahishn III:14 & Nonnos, Dionysiaca I:495]

In the Flood of 23,615 BC, the Cord of Pisces by which the Fish were tossed into the sea was the one they used to pull Vishnu, the Aquarian Sun, back out of the Ocean of Darkness. [Matsya Purana] Such a switch can apparently take place quickly – in a single 48-hour day. [Sirach 46] The Pisces-Aquarius switch happened in the time of the One-Eyed King (Son of Man). A Great Bolt of Lightning produced a Great Wind, followed by Earthquakes, Darkness and Storms, followed by a Great Light and Conflagration. ^{Fulbe legends of the Kaidara and the Great Star}

Such a large pole shift would return the winter Sun to the Druids' Circle at Stonehenge (which is staring into the Dragon's mouth as Sun passes the dangerous Sign of the Bowman). Perhaps this is the real point of Serpent Mounds, Orphic Eggs and dragon stories. Draco will be at the zenith of that Druid Circle again on Doomsday, prepared to switch places with the Cross while Taurus (Alpha) and the Eagle (Omega) act as the hinge.

Trouble arrived between Virgo and the Ancient Serpent thousands of years later, bringing about another flood. If the Second Flood of the Hebrews (Noah's Dove version) ^{Genesis 8:8-12} was the Deluge of Censorinus that destroyed Atlantis, mankind might be safe for eight millennia. Unfortunately, the "Deluge" came earlier.

In Egypt, a giant monument with the eroded head of a woman on a Lion's body stands as a sign for when the age of the gods, which began with Helios about 23,000 years before Christ ^{Diodorus Siculus} ended when the Age of Virgo met Leo in 10,801 BC.

The Pisces-Aquarius cataclysm mentioned by the Hindus, ^{Matsya Purana} was even more traumatic than the Virgo-Leo transition. This suggests that we might want to watch the skies as the Sign of the Son of Man again approaches the Sun at the vernal equinox. Ahriman, or what is left of him, is on the way.

Sphinx marks the Virgo-Leo Flood.

The ancients warned that our next turn of the Sun's path will take place toward the end of Pisces (an Age that ends violently). They said there will be great heat ^{Revelation 16:8} ... a tilt of the Earth ^{Revelation 6:13-14 & 11:16} ... and a brush with comets ^{Bundahishn 30:18-19 & Revelation 6:8; 8:7-11; 12:4; 12:15} ... associated with years of plagues, earthquakes, famine and war. ^{Daniel 12:1; Matthew 24:21; Revelation 6:6; 19:19; Luke 21:11} Even the paths of the planets will be disturbed! ^{Mark 13:25}

The beginning and the end are the same in this *Renovation of the Universe* ^{Bundahishn 30:17} that is our *Day of Judgment.* ^{Bundahishn 30:10-16} It is the ongoing contest of Ahura Mazda (Jupiter often saves us from impacts) and Ahriman the Great Comet – good and evil, order and chaos.

Zoroaster said Ahriman returns every 12,000 years and that a Renovation occurs in twice that time. These he signified by keeping a double clock in which the zodiac is a clock face to be counted two ways – forward as a regular cycle of 12 houses for the Greatest Year, and backwards at 1,000 years per sign for what Aristotle called the Great Year. [Bundahishn 34] Earth is about to mark the passage of a Greatest Year.

Zoroaster said that the period of the Savior is 57 years [Bundahishn 30:7] ... that our troubles last 30 years [Bundahishn 3:22]... and that the very worst challenge is 90 days in which the Sun and planets lose their moorings to the stars, stones fall to Earth and smoke darkens the skies. [Bundahishn 3:24] He said the big sign to watch for is the constellation of the Great Adam, which he calls Gayomard. [Bundahishn 30:7] (The Great Adam is covered in the *Florilegium*, the commonplace book of my youth.) [Page 336]

Signs

Long before the Sun and Aquarius would normally meet at the vernal equinox, the Sun will pass the dark Void of the Milky Way. This will be a sign of what is coming, though not the first.

Understanding the signs is complicated. It is as if someone long ago wrote them down in code and sent different pieces of the scroll to distant kings. One can approach the mystery as a Pagan, Brahman, Jew, Mandaean, Christian, Taoist, Buddhist or Moslem. Solving the ancient mystery, though, requires seeing pieces of the puzzle held by others.

People of wisdom should convene to understand the mysteries before the "End Times." For example, Buddha said that in a cycle of seven suns, there will be a time when *it does not rain; and while it rains not, all seedlings and vegetation, all plants, grasses, and trees dry up, wither away and cease to be.* In the "fifth" sun, the oceans are left almost without water, perhaps meaning an Ice Age follows Ahriman (or something very large comes so close as to steal or evaporate our seas). In the sixth, volcanoes *reek and fume and send forth clouds of smoke.* [Sermon of the Seven Suns]

Our task is to awaken mankind in time to save civilization. When the Cataclysm was to be a Flood, we moved to the mountaintops or took to the sea. If it was to be fire, we took cover in caverns, burrows near a river or lake, tombs, catacombs or the world's underground cities. Since both the *Bible* and the myths now rule out Floods, then as we near the New Sun, we should prepare for the sort of age of fire and ice and a shift of the Earth such as Yima survived. [Fargard II]

Our challenge will be food. What nation has stockpiled sufficient grain for seven years of famine? [Genesis 41:27] What nation or city-state can feed its people for even half that time? [Revelation 13:5] When the world economy dies, so will the distribution of food. Within a month, the unprepared will become desperate and commit great evils – the worst being a return to cannibalism. [Deuteronomy 28:53-57 & Leviticus 26:29]

Saving civilization will also require an attempt to save some of the world's knowledge and diversity of life. In one pole reversal event during the Age of Taurus, El instructed one of our ancestors to bury the world's knowledge at Sipparis, City of the Sun. When the Flood subsided, Sisuthros and his family dug up the writings, founded cities and temples and rebuilt Babylon. [Berosus] Cities, with their books and technology, tend not to survive these cataclysms. Fired clay tablets and carved stone are all the knowledge that survived beyond a handful of legends.

Instead of sharing the mysteries and their truths to ready mankind, up to now, great pains have been taken by the clergy to deface each other's sacred monuments, to burn and scatter the ancient writings, to declare each other's religions as false, and to claim one's own Prophet as the last true and faithful Word from God. Such continued arrogance on the part of our priests can only get all of humanity killed. Ironically, the great holocaust of mankind for which they thus pile the wood they will call the Wrath of God. Lord, save us from such men!

Each holy book tells a piece of the story, though sometimes the next clue is to be found elsewhere altogether. For example, there was a prelude to Genesis 1:1 – an Aleph written in the stars. The Torah scroll reads, *In the beginning God created the Heaven and the Earth.* With these words, the *Bible* begins with a "B" ... *"Bereshit bara Elohim et hashamayim ve'et ha'arets."* There are mysteries here, hidden from the time Abram the Chaldean from Ur left his homeland.

In the world of the gods, "A" was for *Abba* "Father." The Semites began writing their scriptures in the Age of Taurus, then called *Tora*. Perhaps that is why their holy book takes that ancient name and why the constellation Taurus forms their alphabet's first letter, the "Aleph" – in honor of Earth's Lord at the time, *Anu* "Bull of Heaven." The Greeks shared this god with them and called him Uranus.

For the Hittites, A was for *Alalush*, the king of the gods on the opposite side of heaven from *Anu*. By the Greeks, *Alalush* was called

Chaos or *Hypsistos* "The Highest." Sumerians called him *Apsu*. He was the Storm God, the "Great Spirit" who resides in the constellation of "The Eagle" astride the Milky Way. This is the eagle of Mithras – Persia's *Faravahar* and Egypt's Sun Disk. This *Alalush* was also the Hebrews' *El Elyon* (signifying "Most High"). Muhammad surely remembered *Alalush* or "Alala" when he called God "Allah." This revelation probably came as a surprise for Arab tribes worshipping God as Hubal/Sin, the Moon God still remembered in the Crescent. However, through this name from the ancient past, Muhammad was very clearly prophesying of the Day of Judgment.

Faravahar symbolizes the day the Sun is reborn between the Eagle and the Serpent.

Alalush is the Eagle in myths and folklore involving the Eagle and the Serpent. The two egg-bearing constellations are near the dark center in the Milky Way the Sun passes through at each Creation – just in front of the point of Sagittarius' arrow. This seminal moment brings to mind an Egyptian funerary inscription referring to Horus/Lyra/Apollo: *I have raised myself up in the form of the Great Hawk which comes out of the Egg.*

A key to the Alpha-Omega event of Creation in the Genesis is the phrase, *And the Spirit of God* (the Sun) *moved upon the face of the Waters* (the Milky Way). [Genesis 1:2] That verse unveils some of the mysteries of the ancients, such as those of the Cosmic Egg or Brahma Egg.

The Sun at the Crossing (of the zodiac and the Milky Way) can be seen as a precious egg in the mouth of a Dragon if one views the Milky Way as a giant Serpent chasing its tail. The Y at the cleft forms the mouth or, for some, a forked tail. This dark rift between the tail of Scorpio, the foot of Ophiuchus and the arrow of Sagittarius presents us the greatest danger with each round of the zodiac.

This Crossing appears to be an event that was remembered by the Ophites, who held one of the great serpents – Draco as *Nakhasch/Nehushtan* rather than Ouroboros or Serpens – as the Christ.

For the Sumerians, the creature to beware was Tiamat the Mother of Life. She is the Ouroboros "serpent" that turns into a "staff" when Earth turns over. She bears all life at the nexus of the Sun, the Milky Way and the Zodiac, between the Eagle and the Ancient Serpent.

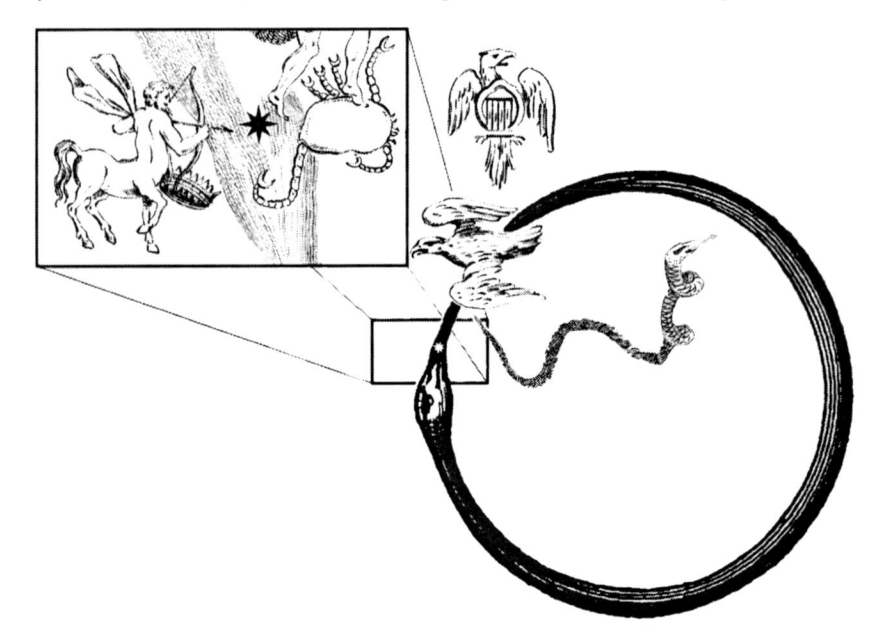

The Cataclysm comes near the time Sun passes the jaws of Ouroboros.

Greeks would remember the Egg as Apollo's seat on the Omphalos, his mountain temple of Delphi sitting as the "Navel of the Earth." [Strabo] Perhaps this "Navel of the Earth" where Zeus' [Pindar] (that is, God's) [Luke 17:37] Eagles met is part of Earth's center of balance as we went through a Creation event. Perhaps it will be important again. Why else would the Omphalos stone (a large marble egg) be covered in a folded fish net – a globe cut in half covered with two sets of knots, one askew the other, both resembling the grid of a map?

There are other "Navels" of the Earth in Ireland, Jerusalem and India. So which way will be north along this line? What land would move to the new ice fields? What new or ancient land might be unveiled?

When the poles reverse and the tropics switch places, then Phoenix flies north [John 12:34] as Draco gives way to Lupus. Will the new Tropic pass through Delphi? Where will it pass on the other side of the ocean? If it shifts, what are the implications for the opposite side of the globe?

And then shall appear the sign of the Son of Man in Heaven: and then shall all the tribes of the earth mourn. Matthew 24:30

For as the lightning, that lighteneth out of the one part under Heaven, shineth unto the other part under Heaven, so shall also the Son of Man be in his day. Luke 17:24

For many, Creation is remembered as the birth of modern man. This "sixth day" of Creation came during the Age of Taurus, about 3761 BC. The Age had opened about a thousand years before, when the Sun began to cross the constellation of the Bull at the vernal equinox. It was a time sacred for much of the ancient world. I suspect it reveals another piece of the secret.

January 1st of 4713 BC, at the start of Caesar's Roman calendar, the Sun intersected with the Water Bearer, revealing the Logos – "The Word." The Grand Phoenix that happens here is an astronomical event seen once every Greatest Year, the culmination of the New Creation. Its little brethren can be viewed more often if you adjust the date to find the Phoenix on a solstice or equinox.

In that Grand Cross, the Horologium forms the "L" ... Phoenix forms an "O" ... Water Bearer forms a Roman "G" (depending on which stars one focuses) ... Sun the second "O" ... and Draco the "S."

In the beginning was the Word, and the Word was with God, and the Word was God. The same was in the beginning with God. John 1:1-2

This sign of the Milky Way, the road for souls passing between Heaven and Earth at birth and death, is also portrayed in the Sumerian letter "G" – the sacred word "Gamma" – the sexual connection between Ea/Yahweh and Mama/Shekhinah, symbolized by Horologium and Aquarius (to always remember the Alpha-Omega moment). For the androgynous disciples of Plethon, this connection would be between Zeus/Sin as the Eagle and Ganymede, his male companion, but the real sign for that particular story could as easily have been a Mercury-Moon ... Zeus/Sin and one of his children. Mercury/Hermes cuts a six-pointed star in his dervish dance around the Earth. *Gamma*

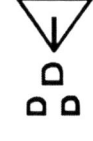

With the Hebrews' sacred Word AM, the angles of *Abb*a Father (Horologium) and *Em* Mother (viewing Aquarius now as a Hebrew "M") became the Seal of Solomon, symbolizing the magic and terrible union of air and fire, water and earth. Others saw Horologium as Attis, and Aquarius as Cybele. Others called it the *Ave Maria* or the sacred Word "AMA."

The sacred Word for the Hindus is "O'M" or "AUM" – union of the Sage or Creator (Brahma/Alalush/Osiris), the Preserver (Vishnu/Ea/Isis) and the Destroyer (Shiva/Tiamat/Seth).

In ancient Egyptian, the Word is "Neter" NTR, written with symbols for the Milky Way, Horologium and Aquarius – next to the symbol for divinity (a hatchet). This may suggest the Phoenix event at Aquarius was symbolized by the double-axe claimed by Zeus as Great Lord, a symbol sacred to Crete and Mycenae and remembered in the fasces of Etruria and Rome.

In the Crucifix, Christians remember the end of the Alpha-Omega season stretching from the death of the Old Sun at the winter solstice (Christmas/End Times) to approximately the vernal equinox (Passover/Easter/Grand Phoenix/Earth's Resurrection) in which Son of Man appears as the New Creation or "The Word."

The great religions remember the same signs in the heavens.

In the Christ's outstretched arms, we remember the Pythagorean "Y" of Yahweh at the dark cleft in the Milky Way. There, He is Ea "The Deep" where the Milky Way and the zodiac come together, and the star patterns on each side of the Void signify our choice between the wide road leading back to Earth or the narrow Way of virtue and heavenly ascent.

The Cross also symbolizes the Cosmic Cross of Sun, Venus and Mercury on the Pole of the Word near the vernal equinox. The mound below the cross is the Lambda of the "Logos" – the Father represented by the Horologium. The Christ is our human Phoenix, our once and future Sabaean/Magi Sun King.

Sometimes artists include symbols for the four living creatures of Ezekiel and the Apocalypse – lion, calf, man and eagle – illustrating the zodiacal alignment of solstices and equinoxes for the Return at the end of this Age of Ea, the Fish of Heaven and Lord of the Deep:

Verily I say unto you, This generation [Age of the Zodiac] shall not pass away, till all will be fulfilled." Luke 21:32; Mark 13:30 & Matthew 24:34

This symbol for the Creation and the God who, like Prometheus or Attis, suffered for us; Diodorus Siculus, History or, like Orpheus, went to Hades for us; Ovid, Metamorphoses X or who, like Aesculapius Ovid, Metamorphoses II and Adonis, Firmicius died to save us ... is seen elsewhere as the Eye of Horus, the Tat, the Ankh, the Sword in the Stone, the Hammer of Thor, and Yggdrasil the World Tree. Around the world, there must be many other names for this central signpost of our Creation and Resurrection.

The Hebrews used *Logos* as a code word for their Holy "AM." Philo said it was a legitimate title of God. This symbology of the Tree of the Word was impressed as Palm Tree, Holy Grail and Urn designs on coins declaring Jerusalem's freedom from the Romans. The Urn upside-down reveals the Grand Cross or Tau with a Phoenix/peacock tail in the middle and Lambda at the base.

The Urn is an ancient sky sign. Associated with Aquarius was an area known as Gu, Gurra or Gu-la (the Great Goddess) referred to as "The Void." This was the *Vohu* in the phrase *tohu vovohu* Genesis 1:2 (meaning *There was darkness over the Deep*). Besides recalling the Phoenician goddess Baau, Bahu of the Akkadians, or Zoroaster's *Vohu Mana*, the Good Mind, this may also be a veiled reference to the constellation Crater's role in the drama of the Creation. Page 324

Given the number of Jewish coins with Palm Tree, Urn and Holy Grail motifs at the time of the revolts against the Romans, it appears a Messiah was believed imminent. No doubt, the Essene oracle at Mount Carmel regarded the rapidly approaching star sign of the Great Adam or Urn (twenty years away at the time) as one of great hope.

The Moon-with-Mercury (elsewhere known as Isis and her son Hermes) also seems to be a warning of a returning Day of Judgment. Watch for the sign September 29, 2011, in conjunction with *a great wonder in Heaven; a woman clothed with the sun, and the moon under her feet.* Revelation 12:1 It is a sign the Catholics call *La Virgen del Rocio*.

When John says of the woman that *she will be travailing in birth*, [Revelation 12:2] he speaks of a planet in the womb of Virgo, while the Sun is in that sign. John would have observed similar Virgin and Great Adam events in 86-87 AD from Patmos at the time of his vision of the End Times.

It may be significant that this sign of the woman *pained to be delivered* [Revelation 12:2] will not occur leading up to the Roman-Celtic Phoenix years of 2287 or 2487. The Renovation is expected before then.

Simplifying the Family Tree

Another mystery in the Book of Genesis is an abbreviated history from the Sumerian, Hittite, Egyptian and Babylonian records. Alalush/Apsu/El Elyon/Hypsistos in one myth was the king deposed by Anu/Uranus "Bull of Heaven." (Taurus and the Eagle replace each other above the horizon in the big pole reversal.) In another story, Alalush died in a hunting accident. [Sanchoniathon]

To avoid misleading difficulties, Moses in the Genesis simplified the royal Sumerian family tree, of which Abraham was a descendant. The title God or Elohim covers for the first three generations (or successions) and care must be taken to credit the appropriate family member if one would decipher who did what among the conflated personalities.

Part of the confusion stems from the ancients naming a child after a parent or grandparent, such as Anu/Anush and Zeus/Sin both being called "Bull of Heaven," and Enki and Poseidon both being called "Ia" for "The Deep" (positioned very near the sign of the Eagle) though they too were probably of different generations. Suffice it for now to say that Anu was the alleged father of two brothers: Ea/Enki and El/Enlil/Cronus/Kumarbi/Kumara.

The first chapter of Genesis approaches the story of Creation with *Anu* (Heaven) and *Gaia* (Earth) in place of their grandparents (*Apsu* the Storm God and *Tiamat* the Dragon Queen). In the *Bible* story, they also stand for God the Father and his consort the Spirit, who *moved upon the face of the waters* [Genesis 1:2] – meaning the Crossing of the Sun over the Deep of the Milky Way.

The Lord by Wisdom hath founded the earth. [Proverbs 3:19]

The Mother of the gods and humanity known as The Spirit or *Shekhinah* was the Wisdom worshipped by Solomon and the Lover who inspired his Song of Songs.

Their line is gone out through all the earth, and their Words to the end of the world. ^{Psalms 19:4}

To some extent, the gods were interchangeable, thanks to their organization. On the Council of the Gods, called the *Marzeah* or *Dodecatheos*, Mama's position was that of the Water Bearer – one held at different times by Gaia, Ninhursag/Rhea, Asherah, Themis, Hebe, Athena and Isis/Maia – the latter being another sacred word for the *Logos*, union of God-bearer MA and God IA of the *hieros gamos*.

Generations of the Gods

Apsu/ El Elyon/ Allah/ Hypsistos/ Brahma – Tiamat/ Saraswati

Anshargal/ Ocean – Kishar/ Urash/ Gaia

Antu/ Nammu – Anu/ Uranus/ Adam – Ki/ Gaia/ Eve

Ea/ Enki/ Iapetus/ Cain – Ninhursag/ Rhea/ Eve – El/ Cronus/ Abel

Marduk/ Atlas   Prometheus   Poseidon/ Ia—Asherah   Zeus/ Sin—Hera/ Eve

Hephaestus – Athena/ Eve   Apollo – Calliope   Hermes/ Thoth

Orpheus – Eurydice

The "Seal of Rhea" (the Aquarian Sun) was part of the *Logos*, Great Adam or Son of Man asterism. This "Pole of the Word" ^{Proclus on Euclid} would later also be called "Maria" as the *Theotokos*, undoubtedly fulfilling the same role for Orthodox Greeks as it had for their pagan ancestors. The Greek "R" is the Sun in Aquarius of the Grand Cross, just as it is the Sun of the vernal equinox in the Rho of the Chrismon.

Communing with Earth's First Gods

By our ancestors having made gods of the Sun, Moon, planets and constellations to recall their history, stories they told of celestial events were as violent and bisexual as Alexander's Vatican. At least that is the impression one gets from the myths of their successors.

For example, the way to take the male reign in the matriarchate that prevailed until the age of Taurus was to cut the legs off one's male predecessor, offer his heart to the Sun, eat his testicles to steal his strength, and give a thigh to the fire and the royal women (one's new mates) as a sacrifice. This began after the period when Astarte the Great Mother *placed the head of the bull on her own head in token of sovereignty.*

^Sanchoniathon^ Leftovers of the king went into a skin, chest or Urn to be planted in the ground with the promise of a rebirth or resurrection – like a seed. The head, meanwhile, was kept as a sacred relic or *Teraphim*.

If you do not believe me, note the sanctity of the thigh in the *Bible* and the myths. Observe the Bacchantes devouring Orpheus, the rending of Osiris, Titans tearing Dionysius or Zagreus, King Pentheus ripped apart by his own mother, or the slaying of the Bull of Heaven.

In later times, the devilish cult's dealings can be seen in the killings of kings and their substitutes, recalling the deaths of William II of England by arrow, Thomas Becket by sword at the altar, and Prince Henry by sword while taking communion. Henry's heart was put into a golden vase and placed on the tomb of Edward the Confessor!

These macabre ceremonies were in commemoration of the mystery of the "Bull of the Foundation." The Bull of Heaven (Taurus) plays a pivotal role when Lupus the Beast replaces the White Dragon/Draco in the time of the Red Dragon (Ahriman, Kali, Tiamat or Satan). [Revelation 12:3 & 13:2] The ancients would sacrifice a bull or a god (priest-king) and place him under the cornerstone to dedicate a megalithic sacred site.

Phoenix dies in December 2012.

What they were remembering was ancient history. Tiamat or Ahriman the Destroyer, castrates or "devours" the Horologium, slaying the Son of Man every 12,000 years or so, coming by the time of the vernal equinox following our Judgment Day. [Bundahishn 3.12] The astrological sign beginning and completing the season is Taurus.

The season of danger for everything turning upside-down is between the summer solstice preceding the End Times at the winter solstice (with the Sun nestled in the dark center of the Milky Way with Taurus above) and Creation marked by the vernal equinox cusp of Pisces with Aquarius. The frame for the action is Taurus circling the scene.

I have been the written Word. I have been the First Book. I have been the light in a lantern of three year quarters. ^Canu Taliesin^

Running into our past

In our next season of prophesied planetary crisis, which few will believe is coming even if we discover the pillars of Adam where he carved them in stone for all the world to see, there are some very visible signs leading up to Cataclysm in which to prepare. At the risk of being brought back to suffer the plagues and troubles of the last days, [Revelation 22:19] I will offer an interpretation of what is to come.

John lists the beasts in the order of fall to summer to spring to winter, indicating at least three years of successive disasters. This would suppose Leo-Virgo in the fall of 2010 (perhaps the autumnal equinox, the Star and Crescent November 5th or the lunar eclipse on the winter solstice), Taurus in the summer of 2011, the Man Aquarius in March of 2012 and the Eagle in winter of 2012. [Revelation 4:6-8]

Sol and Luna take on Ouroboros in December 2012.

I wonder if it might be more reasonable to assume a typical progression to the seasons beginning in May 2012 with the Sun in Taurus and culminating in February 2013, with Aquarius near the vernal equinox, following in this way the writings of the *Bundahishn*.

A sign will arise from Sagittarius (the rider of the white horse) – a signal for the besieger to go forth *to conquer*. [Revelation 6:1-2] If a comet appears near Sagittarius between 2010 and 2012, it will be high time to study the Scriptures and myths of every religion on Earth.

Nonnos heard this regarding the last time the Destroyer came:

> *Then the Archer let fly a shaft ... between the two Bears, and visible within the circle of the Wagon, brandished the fiery trail of the heavenly spine.* [Dionysiaca 1:245-250]

My guess is that this "shaft" was Comet Ahriman, who flies out of the Milky Way twice with each lap of the Sun. Ahriman, like the Taurid meteors, could be the remains of what was once called Phaeton (for it was the Pleiades, Phaeton's sisters at the heart of the Bull, who mourned this son of Helios when the giant shattered).

The comets that took the Devil's place are the *horrid hosts of Giants serpent-haired* [Nonnos, Dionysiaca 1:19] with *two hundred furious hands* [Nonnos, Dionysiaca 1:296] reportedly destroyed by Dionysos. [Nonnos, Dionysiaca 1:20] If we are exceedingly lucky, most of the fragments have previously exploded and have been absorbed into the Earth [Nonnos, Dionysiaca II:240] or the Sun and Jupiter (these having been our Saviors in the past). This agrees with Psalm 74:14 and Isaiah 51:9. In Scripture, the Dragon called Leviathan or Rahab has already been wounded.

In my adjusted-seasons scenario, the second seal would be broken in August or September 2012, with the Sun and Moon in Leo. [Revelation 6:4] Then begins the final battle of the unholy war begun by Innocent III. A Nubian king [Prophecy of Nefer-Rohu] will arise in the south as large Asian armies gather from the northwest (Auriga) [Zechariah 6:2] and from the East. [Prophecy of Nefer-Rohu] In this battle, a Red Army will be destroyed. [Nahum 2]

In the end, there will be a pyrrhic victory declaring a winner to the holy wars. When God removes his mask, we will find He was the One for every religion and nation on the planet – and that not one house of worship well represented Him.

Ma'at, the Word of God, the New Phoenix, will be seen February 27, 2013.

Virgo travails with Mercury and Saturn September 19th while standing on the Moon. [Revelation 12:2] The most intense period of the New Creation should take place between November 2012 and the end of February 2013. [Bundahishn 3:24 & Revelation 4:6]

The third seal comes in the winter of 2012, bringing famine as the world economy collapses. $^{Revelation\ 6:5-6}$ The rider of the black horse is Ophiuchus. The balance in his hand is Libra. His horse is Scorpio.

If history repeats, the start of the battle in which Sol and Luna take on the Red Dragon Ouroboros will be December 13, 2012, when Ophiuchus again wrestles the invading Serpent. $^{Nonnos,\ Dionysiaca\ 1:200}$

Eight days later, as the Sun reaches its southern boundary on Earth at the winter solstice, the Spirit of God will move upon the face of the waters $^{Genesis\ 1:2}$ crossing the dark rift of the Milky Way.

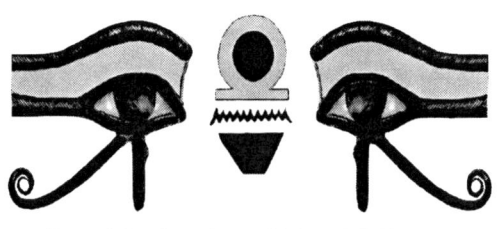

The fourth seal breaks while the Sun joins Aquarius. A quarter of the world's people will be in danger; and the survivors of Hell on Earth will blame the world's religious for their many misfortunes. $^{Revelation\ 6:7-11}$

Sign of the Cataclysm of 23,615 BC

The culminating sign will be the birth of the New Phoenix, February 27, 2013. That day, the pure in heart should see the sign of the Son of Man in all His glory. *Unto them that look for him shall he appear the second time.* $^{Hebrews\ 9:28}$

To Christians, Jews, and Moslems, this Grand Phoenix could be a sign to go outside and wait for Messiah/Moshiach/Mahdi to appear. However, I would suggest that the reference to a "second time" could be the symbology for the death of Phoenix Apollo in December and the birth of the New Phoenix in February, or it could mean we will see the Logos from a new perspective. Constellations are known to flip over and change directions around the time of the Giant, $^{Nonnos,\ Dionysiaca\ 1:46;\ 1:176;\ II:650}$ as does the Pole of the Word. $^{Nonnos,\ Dionysiaca\ II:260\ \&\ Book\ of\ the\ Dead}$

Another Sol-Luna event awaits Ouroboros March 11, 2013. The end of our danger could be the Moon at what moderns call "the Bull's-Eye" the following week. The sign of the Moon at Aldebaran marked the lunar year. In ancient times, it would have signified Cronus or Zeus slicing off Bull of Heaven's thigh or hindquarters (his "castration"). The Moon was the sickle of the Goddess slaying the Man of the Foundation.

Judging from myths and monuments portraying the Pleiades next to the Bull, the ancients viewed Taurus upside-down from us! ^(Dionysiaca 1:46) Other constellations were also known or depicted as having "flipped." These include the Eagle (the double eagle of my family, the Hittites, Seljuks and Sumerians), the Lion,^(Book of the Dead & Narmer Palette) the Phoenix, ^(Christian two-peacock motif) Auriga, ^(Dionysiaca 1:176) Scorpio, ^(Epic of Gilgamesh) and Aquarius, ^(Stela of a Harpist) which also gives us Shiva's Third Eye or the Eye of God.

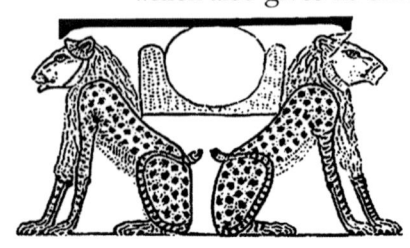

The Flood of 10,801 BC

Herodotus noted such reversals of the heavens, saying that in 11,340 years (about two of Plutarch's ages of the gods), Sun had *twice risen where he uniformly goes down, and twice gone down where he normally rises.* ^(History II:142) One day soon we may see the skies as our ancestors did.

Whenever the pole shift, comets and Age of Aquarius next arrive, there should never again be a need for sacrifices! He who was the Passover offering as the Lamb of God satisfied the sacrifice of Aries. He whose symbol was the Fish satisfied the sacrifice of Pisces. The Messiah who returns to us already satisfied the manly sacrifice called for in the Age of Aquarius. There is no more need for ritual murders, inquisitions, crucifixions or holocausts. The Son of Man slain in the heavens is all that was ever needed.

One could well say that the Lord laid upon Himself the iniquity of us all ^(Isaiah 53:6) and the bill in the Divine Economy was always paid in full. Our task, which we have never fulfilled, was to live peacefully and righteously with each other:

For I desired Mercy, and not sacrifice; and the Knowledge of God more than burnt offerings. ^(Hosea 6:6)

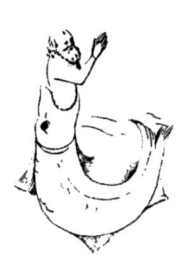

Perhaps next round we can unite the faiths by some strategy more intelligent than killing our way to orthodoxy. Perhaps we can even stop naming scapegoats to bear away each other's sins.

We will know the Black Sun of the Egyptians. We will survive the giant fish of Jonah/Oannes or we will suffer his sacrifice of three days. One way or another, we will participate in the World's Resurrection.

Finally, we will understand the myths and mysteries our ancestors revealed and our religious leaders concealed.

We will finally "get" what Jesus, Matthew and John were talking about. The words of Enoch, Daniel, Isaiah, Zechariah, Aratos and Nonnos will make sense. We will have fulfilled the laws of the old religions and will be ready to become the generation of saviors Zoroaster spoke of so long ago. [Fargard II & XIX] After a time of suffering and horror, it will be time for us to begin again and attempt to build the Kingdom of God (a single Empire for humanity founded on Truth, Equity, Justice and Brotherhood).

I hope we can live in the future with less superstition and violence than the last time we passed through the Cataclysm. What was seen in the stars made for gruesome rites. The royal family held a winter solstice ceremony in a cave each year. The great secret of the goddesses was *Taurus Draconem genuit, et Taurum Draco.* "The Bull has begotten a Serpent, and the Serpent a Bull." [Clement, Exhortation to the Greeks 2.14] At that time, our local fertility god, the bull-mask-wearing chieftain with access to the royal women, daughters and vestal virgins was remembered as the frame for Creation. Then he became our sacrifice.

Sun centers on the Milky Way near Taurus at the summer solstice six months prior to the New Creation, which is due December 21, 2012. That said, I believe the actual date of *Ekpyrosis* comes a bit later.

At the moment of Creation, the Sun stands before the bow of Sagittarius at the dark center of the Milky Way on the winter solstice. We will pass Milky Way's center *"Vishnunabhi"* (the Seat of Brahma) while the latest incarnation of Lucifer finds himself by the very pit of Hell. [Isaiah 14] Watch for a great ball of fire – or better yet, take cover.

The Taurus-Draconem secret may relate to the divine family tree having Anu the Bull of Heaven begetting El the Serpent, begetting Zeus/Sin as the next Bull of Heaven (begetting Apollo, associated with the Python). Over time, El the Ancient Serpent became associated with Ahriman/Tiamat. His redemption became his son and grandson. That little genealogy of Apollo is the only purpose or excuse I ever discovered for the Filioque clause "the Holy Spirit, the Lord, the giver of life, *who proceeds from the Father and the Son.* ..." Ia as Most High was supported by Apollo as Lord, but as we all know, in the society of the divine, the Son/Lord is destined to become Father/Most High … and the Father reincarnates as the Son – exchanging places.

At the same time that the royal women celebrated the life of the retiring Sun King (replaced by his brother consul), December festivities would observe the birth of a new Sun King, who had been conceived in an orgy of the spring equinox. A child born that year to the Temple or *Dodecatheos* would be sacrificed in December if the Sun King's reign was to be extended.

The year the King was the sacrifice, the baby from that year would be raised in the warrior traditions and stories of his Father, that he might become a reincarnation of the chief. Meanwhile, each eighth year, Venus would complete its Pentagon (five-looped star dance) around the Earth, realigning the calendars. Outside the cave, the royal daughters (or Muses) would celebrate the mysteries, dancing the steps of the Sun's Labyrinth and the paths of the planets.

The tradition of slaying the Sun King may be why royal Abraham invented the animal scapegoat (wanting neither to die nor to kill a son) and why the Moslems suggest it was Ishmael (the eldest) on his way to a rendezvous with death. Prior to first-born men being dedicated to the Lord, studying scriptures and letting their hair grow as Nazarites, [Numbers 6] they were stand-ins for the designated sacrifice. [Exodus 13:2 & 22:29]

Scapegoats, slaying red heifers in Jerusalem's Temple and Romans slaying the white bull of Dionysius all represented a significant reform. Ritual killing of the leader was the earthly origin of our redeemer gods — a duplication of what had taken place in the heavens when Ahriman/Satan sliced Son of Man in half and the Sun in darkness had to be brought back to life.

In an early step of the reforms, my Greek ancestors found it convenient to sacrifice a less valuable proxy rather than the leader.

> *Thus they would say over the youth who was thrown each year into the sea for the release from the oppressing ills: May you be our purification. Deliverance or redemption!* [Photius]

When Great Adam/Gayomard/Son of Man is resurrected in the stars, it is humanity itself that begins to rise from detruction at this sign of the Grand Phoenix, the Word. Like the Egyptians who viewed the Bull as Earth's perpetual return to life, we will have much to celebrate when we see the Taurus Sun climbing toward the zenith again in May. This was, and will be again, the occasion for our great spring festivals.

I pray I am wrong about the Crossing and that it is no longer so dramatic or so punctual. I pray verses like *fire came down from God out of Heaven, and devoured them* ^{Revelation 20:9} are only allegories for our purification. I pray that God will continue to save some of us as He promised to do *while Earth remaineth* ^{Genesis 8:21} and that humanity has already passed the biggest challenges to our existence.

Our hope is that tension in the Holy Family is over, that our Galaxy and our Sun have come of age, and that the periodic "flood to destroy all life" ^{Genesis 9:15} need no longer strike us. I pray that with the destruction of Atlantis, the star or comet or burning light or planet or debris at the Crossing has finally spent itself and we are no longer in danger. Otherwise, I pray we find that beyond *Finis Mundi*, the Age of the Holy Spirit begun by Saint Francis can continue as we begin to rebuild civilization.

If Ahriman/Kali/Satan is still there at the Crossing ... if we truly must navigate the rough seas of Tiamat ... then the point to remember is that humanity will survive the holocaust (even if it is only one family of eight people) ... and from the ashes, our once and future king, our God, will deliver us. As to the rest of us, we may return to life one day, though the road back through the three lower kingdoms takes time.

Were human society less corrupt, perhaps God would feel less compelled to clean Earth's slate from time to time. Our periodic destruction as a consequence of natural processes is a harsh but just way to clear the field of unnatural aristocracies and their greed, to strike down corrupted theologies and politics, and to put us back in touch with Earth and each other. The Judgment is our baptism by fire, ice and water and our permission to begin again.

As Jesus said, we must not fret. *Whoever seeks to keep his life will lose it, and whoever loses his life will preserve it.* ^{Luke 17:33} Muhammad also seems to have felt the dead fare better than survivors of the Tribulation. ^{Koran 56}

Unfortunately, most will be unconcerned as we approach our trial. Some will assume the time of impending troubles can be no worse than any faced by their parents or grandparents. They will think, *These things we have heard in the times of our fathers; but behold, we have grown old, and none of them has happened unto us.* ^{Clement, First Epistle} Others will give up their responsibilities and take to hedonism. *Every mouth is full of "Love Me!" and everything good has disappeared.* ^{Prophecy of Nefer-Rohu} The worried will prepare. The righteous will repent and seek to help others.

Regardless of what we do, a Phoenix comes quite unlike the one John observed from Patmos. This Day of the Lord, so well-announced and anticipated by the religious of so many faiths, will catch us by surprise, no matter how many confirmed signs are seen leading up to it. No one wants to believe in a curse that makes civilization start over every 5,125 or 12,000 or 25,626 years. However, like a New Year or a New Life, a New Age is a good time to begin again.

The New Age

If the Earth balances as it did before the last shift, Paradise may be restored. Europe will see Phoenix high in the sky again and Crux (the "Southern" Cross) will return home to northern skies. If people cannot then understand the symbolism of ancient Christianity that *preceded by millennia* the words of Abraham, Moses or Jesus then there is simply no hope for this corrupt and forgetful world. (By the way, the Judgment is the "setback" after which the Roman faith will be vindicated.)

> *I saw four stars ne'er seen before save by the ken of our first parents. Heaven of their rays seem'd joyous. O thou northern skies! Bereft indeed, and widowed, since of these deprived.* ^{Dante, Purgatorio, Canto I}

Imagine our relief when Sun again emerged from the shadow of the Giant and we had survived the dust of exploding comets, immense tidal forces and a great shift in Heaven and Earth:

> *The radiant God, the spring of joy to every eye, as thou art mounting up o'er the high shining Flood. Thou by whose luster all the world of life comes forth, and by thy beams again returns unto its rest, O Sūrya with the golden hair, ascend for us day after day, still bringing purer innocence. Bless us with shine; bless us with perfect daylight; bless us with cold, with fervent heat and luster.* ^{Rig Veda 10:37:8-10}

One of the secrets is Orion. When Sun comes to the opposite side of the galaxy, regard the staff of the Great Shepherd and Hunter not as being merely a stick or club in his hand, but see him as pointing with every star in his body as a band across the Universe connecting Draco to Crux, showing the poles about to reverse. Moses gave us this secret in 1641 BC (Julian), when he readjusted the calendar back to the vernal equinox and Aries. The Nehushtan and Staff of Aesculapius extend far beyond Aries.

They connect the Tav of Moses [Page 300] to the Great Tao when Earth turns over. [Page 324]

At the great stone circle in England, the White Dragon will be crucified upon (that is, replaced at the zenith by) the Cross. At the recently rediscovered Ogygian isle [Homer, Odyssey VII-IX] of St. Helena, he will reunite with the Sun on the winter solstice. What holy lands and monuments across the Ocean mark the ancient and new Tropics and the new Equator?

The long pivot of the Tao is in the myth of Hercules (next to the Eagle) and Atlas/Orion (next to the Bull). [Euripedes, Heracles] On Earth, it is the Mali Empire south of the Atlas Mountains. That afternoon, above this land of the Dogon, the zenith will center on Apollo Delphinus, son of Ia/Poseidon, as anchor of the universe. I suspect this was the inspiration for my friend Aldo Manutio's printer mark, St. Clement's Anchor Cross, and Hippolytus' tree at the center of the Cosmos.

A sign of the Father, Horologium the Mountain and Throne of God, [1 Enoch 25] will once again preside over the land we currently call the "North." It should reappear at the top of the sky, just as when Zeus impregnated Danaë.

The change of the skies will be almost as sudden as if one passed a compass over a lodestone. The lodestone could be the Milky Way stretched between Ursa Minor (our present north) and the great Delta or Sacred Heart of the now-southern sky.

The needle of Earth's compass appears to run along the Pole of the Word. The entire Universe will appear to flip over as we go through the gate, but that of course will be an illusion. Our Earth will simply shift its poles back to where they were before Draco ruled the zenith of the north.

Unfortunately, the switch does not go smoothly. The outer Earth takes time to catch up with what has already happened in her excited volcanic innards. [2 Kings 20: 9-10, Bundahishn 3:24-26 & Hesiod's Theogony]

In one long day of our season of Judgment, we will transition from the heart of the second Fish of Pisces into the Age of Aquarius. Our seasons will reverse themselves from winter to summer in a time that the entire galaxy has been warming the Earth in preparation for another deep freeze of northern Asia. [Fargard 1] Where it was day, it will suddenly be night and the stars will shine brighter than ever – at least before the catastrophe when the great darkness descends.

Prior to the shift, Earth may be heading back to its old tropics and sea levels as the ice melts. However, if a comet strikes or volcanoes blacken our skies, the stars will disappear as the new Ice Age descends. Whatever happens, our Sun will rise again – quite possibly in the West!

No matter where we live then, we must look to the heavens. In one place, the Sun will remain in the sky hovering in the great letter Delta or Sacred Heart. That will be our new pole of the north, and to live we must follow our shadows until we find the night.

In another part of the Earth, darkness will rule. If we can see only stars, we must go off in search of the Sun. However, until we can see the stars again past the clouds and find our new pole star, there is no way to know exactly where the New Age has taken us. For 90 days, even a compass and astrolabe may steer us wrong. With a little patience and luck, few people should have to move in order to find lands directly below the twelve signs of the zodiac.

Gnosis

Returning to Genesis ... there was a good garden where *the Lord God took the man, and put him into the garden of Eden to till it and to keep it* ^{Genesis 2:15} which was the scene of an offer of heavenly knowledge. *God doth know that in the day ye eat thereof, then your eyes shall be opened, and ye shall be as gods, knowing good and evil.* ^{Genesis 3:5} The question was whether we would remain slaves or whether we would accept knowledge making us more godlike. In theory, the fruit we were offered was the apple, whose core teaches a mystery of the Goddess – the orbit of Venus.

El/Cronus was the younger of the two sons of Lord Anu born to different mothers. However, by virtue of his mother Ki/Gaia/Eve (and his real father, El Elyon having seduced the wife of his son) both having higher rank than Ea's parents Anu and Antu, El became the higher-ranking son, assistant to Lord Anu. As the story goes, El (called Enlil by the Sumerians and Cronus by the Greeks) wanted to keep mankind his ignorant slaves.

Ea (called Enki by the Sumerians, Yahweh by the Hebrews, and Iapetus by the Greeks) had been civilized man's Creator with his wife Ninhursag/Ninki/Clymene. He was also the inventor of astronomy and writing, which may be why the stars still have a coherent story to tell us after thousands of years.

The Assembly of the Gods agreed that humanity should be intelligent so we could do their work and they could get back to enjoying life.

^{Atra-Hasis I, 190-215} According to my Greek ancestors, mankind's test was whether we would take the first step toward Godliness, embracing the teachings of the Spirit, the Tree of Life – our Queen of Heaven. Like other personalities on the Council of the Gods, her political position as the Lord's wife or consort was marked on the zodiac. Gaia "Ma's" position was that of the Water Bearer, later assumed by Ninhursag (linked to both El/Cronus and his brother Ea/Enki).

Our Teacher passing along the traditions was once the head woman of the tribe. When the matriarchy ended, the position devolved to men.

She is a Tree of Life to those who lay hold of her,
and happy is every one that retaineth her. [Proverbs 3:18]

In all ages entering holy souls,
she maketh them friends of God and prophets. [Wisdom of Solomon 7:27]

Man's "Creation" by Ea and his wife in the Sumerian tale (by Poseidon and Prometheus in the Greek tale told by Plethon, or Hephaestus in Hesiod's version), was really the act of adding a spark of divine intelligence from one of the Angels/Annunaki/Elohim (godly ones) with good memory to the next generation of humans through interracial breeding (with the royal women). This act making us more intelligent came in the Age of Taurus, about the time of the Sixth Day of Creation (3761 BC) mentioned by Moses. As in the *Bundahishn*, the previous five days of Creation stood both for eons of the world's existence and for millennia since the last Cataclysm.

Conflict

Man's birth of intelligence and culture (humanity's first children raised in a school) was a good deal of time after Prince Enki (or Qa-Yin/Cain) had his birthright of first-born usurped with the arrival of his younger half-brother, Enlil/El/Abel. These two were likely the real brothers Gemini. They and their progeny seem to have been the first kings and priests, at times a descendant assuming both roles.

Many of the early followers of the new Lord – Father El, or "Ob-El" – were Ophites, serpent worshippers. Saint John later called them evil. [Apocryphon of John] Perhaps he was offended by the phallic nature of this era – the time of the first El/Bacchus/Dionysius/Sabazius. However, the Ophites may have been accurately remembering a previous Creation event – the beginning of the Greatest Year in which three great serpents (Draco, Serpens and Ouroboros) had figured spectacularly.

The Ophites appear to have been fundamentalists, hearkening back to when the Serpent Tribe *(Serpentiginae)* ruled Athens and Sparta in the days of Aegeus, Cecrops and Menelaus. They migrated from Atlantis via Morocco, Libya, Egypt and Phoenicia; and it may have been one of their leaders that Apollo had to defeat for control of Delphi, rather than the Python of legend, a source of the St. George legend. Clement and Epiphanius agreed that Eve may have been of this tribe, depending on how one pronounced her name. This makes sense, in that one of the Eves – Athena of Greece – was daughter of El the Serpent.

Regarding the regicides, what we have at their foundation is a Flood or Creation myth. El's "castration" by Zeus was the same as Anu's by El – the Moon at Aldebaran. What is interesting about the repeat of the crimes is the implication that humankind may actually recall four of these Creation events. This could constitute more than 100,000 years of ancestral memory if successions of the gods each marked a Greatest Year cycle of creation. Even if each Age of the Gods is as short as Plutarch described, then it might still imply 20,000 years of ancient memory. Either way, the successions imply great spans of time; and these are as amazing as the *Avesta* remembering when, thousands of years ago, some of us lived in an Arctic paradise and our homeland suddenly shifted toward the Pole. [Fargard 1]

Once he disposed of his father in a gruesome murder, El/Cronus/Saturn became an eater of "fruit" from his wife, the Tree of Life. El, fearing a successor might do to him what he had done to his father to become the new Most High, devoured his children at the solstice or otherwise made our matriarch, the Goddess, miscarry each time she was pregnant, so he could eat the unborn child as his own immortality insurance. She fooled him one time with a gallstone and Zeus/Sin survived. However, the point is that it was El/Cronus the Serpent saying "fruit of the Tree" was good to eat, thereby making Death enter the world for fear a son might replace him.

> *For God created man to be immortal, and made him to be an image of his own eternity. Nevertheless* **through envy of the devil came death into the world.** [Wisdom of Solomon 2:23-24]

In the Genesis, everyone was condemned: Abel for disagreeing with Cain on how to worship the gods. Cain for reportedly killing his brother (though we know it was El's son Zeus/Sin who sliced El open). The fourth Adam was condemned (Apsu begat Anshargal, who begat Anu, who begat El) supposedly for listening to the fourth Eve (Tiamat begat Kishar, who begat Ki, who begat Ninhursag). This Eve was condemned for listening to the "Serpent" – her husband. So much for the innocence of "Adam" and 6,000 years of demonizing women!

The Floods

The "Serpent" of the *Bible* was a conflation and a confusion of El/Enlil and Ea/Enki. After killing Father Anu, the new Bull of Heaven was El. Eventually, his son Zeus/Sin replaced him, and El would be symbolically demoted back to Serpent.

The Serpent was "evil" for having eaten of the fruit of life that early man saw as the fruit of Wisdom – meat eaters being more intelligent than plant eaters. On the larger stage of the night sky, Ancient Serpent would always be near the womb of Virgo to threaten her children.

During his tenure as Most High, El/Enlil came to wish mankind would die in a Flood.

> *The gods commanded total destruction,*
> *Enlil did an evil deed on the peoples.* Atra-Hasis II viii, 34-35

In a repeat, this goal would one day be shared by El's son, Zeus/Sin, in the Second Flood of the *Bible*, Genesis 8:8-12 the one of 3113 BC.

> *It was his wish to wipe out man and rear another race.* Aeschylus, Prometheus Bound

Saving mankind from this fate, rather than giving us knowledge or killing his brother, was the transgression for which Ea (or Ia) was banished from the Council of the Gods. Ea/Vishnu/Ahura Mazda – in the role of the Preserver – was the one who warned Flood heroes Atra-Hasis, Manu, Ziusudra, Utnapishtim, Satyavrata, Fo-hi and Yima. The story would repeat later with Ia/Poseidon and Prometheus as the Preservers and Noah and Deucalion as the Heroes.

Many races were saved, but all humanity had been slated to die in the Floods. Since Yima's story coincided with an age of ice, and Solon's destruction of Atlantis is about 10,000 years before our Lord, the Flood that separated El and Ea could have been the one between the Ages of

Virgo and Leo (Virgo's Raven version of the Genesis story). ^{Genesis 8:7} However, I would favor a later date.

St. John said the Genesis story was rewritten. He said that the "chief archon" (El Elyon) had seduced Eve (Gaia, sister and wife of Adam/Anu), who bore two children: *Yave is righteous but El is unrighteous. ... And these he called with the names Cain and Abel with a view to deceive.* ^{Apocryphon of John} The names reveal the mystery. Ea/En-Ki (God of Waters and Fountain of Life) in Sumerian is equivalent to Qa-Yin/Cain the Spear that is the Fountain of Life (Iao's corn phallus). El became Ob-El/Abel ("Father El").

The Genesis, as it is written, blames the wrong brother by leaving out a good bit of the story. The roles of Ea and El might have been clarified when Moses met Ia/Yahweh on predecessor Sin's mountain or at least by the time Hezekiah retired the serpent.

> *Moses made a serpent of brass, and put it upon a pole, and it came to pass, that if a serpent had bitten any man, when he beheld the serpent of brass, he lived.* ^{Numbers 21:9}

> *Hezekiah removed the high places, and broke the images, and cut down the groves, and broke in pieces the brazen serpent that Moses made: for the children of Israel still burned incense to it: and he called it Nehushtan.*
> 2 Kings 18:4

Moses said Cain killed Abel and was banished, but there had been other reasons for Anu to kick Cain/Enki out of Eden. Against orders, he gave man fire and language; he objected to first-born sacrifices; and even though all the Council had sworn not to tell mankind of the coming catastrophe, Ea could not let his progeny die.

Abel as El had slain sons and a daughter. "Abel" usurped the throne of the Lord through regicide, fatally cutting off Anu's "parts" with a sickle. Again, the devilish trend was that a son or brother from the royal line would violently depose the Father.

In the case of Noah's Flood, Isaiah's contest to be the "Highest" reveals a sign of St. George. In August 3113 BC (Julian), the planet Venus (cast by Isaiah as Lucifer, Son of the Morning) was climbing in the sky, soon to be the highest of the planets. It was also in line with Mercury and the Moon, in a line pointing at a celestial visitor in Serpens and symbolically placing a spear in the hand of the Virgin (then known by the Greeks as Athena) to strike *Leviathan the piercing Serpent.* ^{Isaiah 27:1}

Ia and Athena were seen as the Sun in Virgo, saviors of the Flood of 3113 BC.

Eusebius sometimes thought of "Zeus" as God, but after the Flood of 3,113 BC, this would no longer be Zeus/Sin. Rather, Ia/Poseidon had picked up a new title of Zeus/Iao and was described as the new Virgo:

> *Zeus was the first, Zeus last, the lightning's lord,*
> *Zeus head, Zeus center, all things are from Zeus.*
> *Zeus born a male, Zeus Virgin undefiled;*
> *Zeus the firm base of earth and starry Heaven ...*
> Eusebius quoting Porphyry, Praeparatio Evangelica

Virgo and Serpens would later also be known as the Knight and the Dragon. In star wisdom, they are one of several such portrayals of Good vs. Evil. The goddess Eve/Inanna changed constellations and names when she went to Greece to bequeath Wisdom to humanity. The symbols being stepped on and attacked by her old sign of Virgo both stand for El – the planet Saturn and the Ancient Serpent.

These signs of Ea and El together with Saturn between them point to a coming New Creation according to Virgil (written prior to Jesus):

> *Now the Virgin returns, the reign of Saturn returns,*
> *now a new generation descends from Heaven on high.* Virgil, 4th Eclogue

As a youth, I always believed the point of the Heroes vs. the Serpents was that one should destroy evil rather than tolerate it. El and Ea had both taught us this. The sign of Virgo and the Ancient Serpent also taught us that this battle is eternal.

Ia/Poseidon either replaced or was Marduk/Hephaestus, who had replaced El/Sin/Zeus as Lord after Zeus/Sin replaced Anu, who had replaced El Elyon as Most High. Ia became the new Prince, Lord or *Baal.*

Like Yahweh, Constantine the Great saw eternal wisdom in the sign of the Warrior and the Serpent or Dragon. The founder of our Order had a painting of himself done with this design on a grand table at the entrance to the Imperial Palace. [Eusebius, Vita Constantini]

While he named the Order after the Great Martyr who fell to Diocletian, Constantine himself was the earthly archetype for conquering evil. He was the pagan emperor become Christian. He was the military savior who Christianized (using the word in its most ancient sense) the world. His Christianity, however, was that of *all the ancient wisdom of the ages*, not merely the dogma of a Galilean's suffering or the paralysis in the face of evil that passes for spirituality today.

The mystery of the new Lord's name was hidden from the people, but it was known to the kings and priests. The rise of Yahweh brought the rise of priest-kings whose leaders were *adopted* by God.

> *The king will cry to Yahweh, "You are my Father, my God, and the Rock of my salvation"* [Psalm 89:26]

> *And the Lord will say, "I will make him my firstborn, higher than the kings of the earth."* [Psalm 89:27]

This priest-king could take for himself the secret Name and Spirit, breathe it in, wear it on his turban, clothe himself in it, and even bestow it upon His nation.

> *Joshua, the son of Nun, was full of the Spirit of Wisdom.* [Deuteronomy 34:9]

> *She entered into the soul of the Servant of the Lord.* [Wisdom of Solomon 10:16]

> *The Spirit entered into me.* [Ezekiel 2:2]

> *And thou shalt make a plate of pure gold, and engrave upon it ... Holy to the Lord.* [Exodus 28:36]

> *But the Spirit of the Lord came upon Gideon.* [Judges 6:34]

> *He hath on his vesture and on his thigh a name written, KING OF KINGS, AND LORD OF LORDS.* [Revelation 16:19]

> *And they will put my name upon the children of Israel; and I will bless them.* [Numbers 6:27]

> *My Name is in him.* ^{Exodus 23:21}

There is some indication that Jesus was heir to this tradition of the Name:

> *One single name is not uttered in the world, the Name which the Father gave to the Son; it is the Name above all things: the Name of the Father. For the Son would not become Father unless he wore the Name of the Father.* ^{Gospel of Phillip}

Eventually, "El" no longer named a destroyer and "Most High" no longer named Zeus. The latter may have had something to do with Prince/Consul Hephaestus splitting Zeus' head open with an axe. This story, however, was probably star lore of the Flood of 3113 BC with Virgo standing on Saturn – Athena jumping out "in full armor" (Mercury and Venus providing both her two-ring shield and her lance) as the Aurigan axe and the world flipped over. ^{Dionysiaca I:176}

"Most High" as a place would become the Har Moad, the Mount of the Assembly "in the north" – or rather, toward the zenith above the Logos – the pole of the universe. Nor was Wisdom any longer a woman, at least for the Hebrews. The secret name was Yahweh, and to Him now gathered all power and understanding. El Elyon, Ea, El and Shekhinah all became synonymous with the Most High God, just as Abraham must have hoped for so long ago, son of a Chaldean priest who had seen too much chaos from competing gods – back when a first-born's or a father's severed head adorned a home's mantle as the family god. Finally, the reigns of Sage, Preserver and Destroyer were united in one pair of hands.

> *For you, God, are Most High over all the Earth; you are raised high over all the gods.* ^{Psalm 97:9}

Any demonization of the God of the Jews must have referred to El's Bacchan pre-Flood and pre-Exodus days. Ea could have made such a complaint. Anytime after the Exodus, Scriptures making such accusations would be putting words in someone's mouth to separate Christians (again using the word in its ancient sense) from other groups, suggesting the latter still worshipped an earlier supreme ruler of Earth and the Universe. Jesus was a Nazarene Jew and it makes no sense for him to be lashing out at an evil "Father" of the Jews:

> *Ye are of your father the Devil, and the lusts of your father ye will do.*

> *He was a murderer from the beginning, and abode not in the truth, because there is no truth in him. When he speaketh a lie, he speaketh of his own; for he is a liar, and the father of it.* ^{John 8:44}

Perhaps Jesus was unveiling a mystery of the earlier El Elyon. Perhaps John was identifying Jesus as a reincarnation of Anu or Ea. Then again, the Gnostic John could simply have been casting stones. In Revelation 2, he did the same to the Greeks who lived near an altar of Zeus, calling it the Seat of Satan. Eusebius, Lactantius and Clement chose to reject this idea that Hebrews, Greeks and Christians were fundamentally incompatible in their cosmogony and theogony.

There is considerable confusion in early history with respect to the first rulers. For example, one Tree of Knowledge story comes from a Sumerian tale in which Ea/Enki is telling Adam/Adapa NOT to eat from the Tree of Knowledge or drink from the Water of Life (that he would soon be offered) and Adam neither eats nor drinks. However, in a similar story of the Genesis, God is again telling Adam NOT to eat of the fruit, but then Adam does!

In that version, remember John says the characters in the story had been switched. In it, the Serpent tells Adam he would "not surely die" and that Adam and Eve would become like the gods, which is then exactly what happened. ^{Genesis 3:22} The confusing lesson of the Hebrew story seems to be that the test of our humanity was whether Knowing is more important than Living ... and our answer was the answer of gods ... Yes ... but then we were summarily kicked out of Paradise by the angry God (Anu?) and barred access to the Tree of Life. ^{Genesis 3:24} It may have been a Creation story of when the poles flipped.

In any case, calling the God of the Hebrews evil (as in John 8:44) at this late date or a thousand years ago, was to accuse the wrong God. El/Abel was not the Father of the Jews, who descended from Seth. Seth begat Enosh, who was the father of Canaan, the father of Mahalalel, the father of Jared, the father of Enoch, the father of Methuselah, the father of Lamech, the father of Noah. ^{Genesis 5}

The Lord (number-two in the gods of the Middle East) who rejected Cain's offering of grain, preferring to share roasted animals with his priests, was Anu. It may have been the feast upon the return of the prodigal son – a repentant Ea returning home – when trouble erupted between Anu and his son El, and between the brothers El and Ea.

Ia was not known by the Hebrews as Yahweh the Lord until shortly before 1641 BC (Julian). Sometime just prior to the Exodus, God introduced Himself by a new Name.

God said to Moses, "I am who I am." Exodus 3:14

I AM the Lord; and I appeared unto Abraham, unto Isaac, and unto Jacob, by the name of God Almighty, but by my name Jehovah was I not known to them. Exodus 6:3

Sometime after the Flood of 3113 BC and before the Exodus, Ia went from being Angel of the Lord to being the Lord. Clues from the first Passover reveal the date of the announcement. The secret involves the vernal equinox, a lamb, and a strange mark – that of a Cross, an X, the shape of a door frame, or a Hebrew Tav – the Seal of Truth.

The moment beginning the month of Nisan in the year 2120 of the Hebrews (Noon April 4, 1641 BC Julian), in the reign of the Pharaoh Adikam/Menthesuphis Sefer HaYashar 77 there was a sign in Aries, the Passover Lamb, that fits those descriptions as the Sun crossed the celestial equator and the vernal equinox. The mark was formed by the Moon, the Sun, Venus and Mercury – a final symbolic gathering of El, God of the New Moon, and "his daughters" who had represented a Trinity long before the three men of Genesis 18 or the philosophical speculations of Plato, Philo, John or Augustine.

This very same occurrence in the sky was sacred to the Greeks. This was the moment Apollo went to Delphi. Finding two snakes in the road, Draco and Serpens, he lay down his staff and the two climbed on.

There is another secret to the Passover – the marking of the door lentils with Lamb's blood. Exodus 12:7 The lentil as the header of the Door (our stargate) is Orion. The sill, or the foundation, is Taurus. The way the world currently stands, the Bull of the Foundation rises before Orion. In other words, our world is upside-down – spinning backward through the Universe!

Whether or not our Universe has righted itself by then, the dawn of the New Age, February 27, 2013, the Sun will be in the asterism of the Seal of Rhea or the Pole of the Word, center of the second Eye of God (Ayin) – the first being the Eclipse of Sun over the Deep.

Passover, the Nehushtan and the Cross as a Seal of Truth were Moses' symbols recalling the Exodus. For the Greeks, the day recalled Apollo at Delphi.

When they receive their order from the Word, Orion will again rise before Taurus, as in the beginning. Earth will continue to spin counterclockwise when viewed from above the North Pole, inertia being so important when there is no greater force applied, but this same spin will then bring us the Sun and constellations from the opposite direction and standing at a new angle, thanks to Earth going back to its original position with respect to the stars.

I wonder if, when we see it happen, we might understand what periodically turns the Earth over. Is it the lodestone of the Milky Way? Does the sun hurl a great ball of Greek Fire in our direction? Does a larger planet pass us by? A dark sun? Or must we be struck again by a comet?

If it is the Wrath of the Lamb,[Revelation 6:16] I suspect a larger planet, in which case, how long we stay in the new direction could be very short. If our poles already line up, we will realign as it passes – flipping over in the process. If our poles are not already lined up, we would align with the larger planet and perhaps stay that way until it next passes again.

If I have interpreted any of this correctly, myth and scripture will end up being more True than anything ever said by a philosopher or scientist. It is one thing to be able to measure something or identify its properties. It is quite another to accurately relate events from 25,000 years ago and predict what that could mean for humanity's future. What a debt we will owe to Moses, Zoroaster, Muhammad, Nonnos and Saint John if we are forewarned by their stories! As to whether they were great historians, astronomers or men with insights into the very mind of God ... does it matter? Godly men they surely were.

Moses was sent *as a god to Pharaoh.* [Exodus 7] Following the Exodus, he would again be transformed, perhaps into an Angel of the Lord.

> *Moses came down from Mount Sinai. As he came down from the mountain with the two tablets of the covenant in his hand, Moses did not know that the skin of his face shone because he had been talking with God. When Aaron and all the Israelites saw Moses, the skin of his face was shining, and they were afraid to come near him.* [Exodus 34:29-30]

Previous to Moses, the patriarchs Adam, Enoch, Abraham, Jacob, and Joseph had been chosen kings on the Lord's Council. Joseph may have been promised even higher status if we consider his dream:

> *Behold, I have dreamed a dream more; and, behold, the Sun and the Moon and the eleven stars made obeisance to me.* [Genesis 37:6]

Since the Genesis, most of the rest of us are as confused and sinful as the Israelites dancing naked with Aaron around a golden statue of Taurus in the desert [Exodus 32] – remembering the wrong God, listening to the wrong leader, and dancing wholly out of step with the Universe. (We had entered the Age of the Ram and still had no clue.)

We are all to blame ... for our fear, our ignorance, our envy, our self-righteousness, and our hatreds. The beauty in the divine economy is that we can be forgiven if we believe, if we fear God, if we repent of our wickedness, and if we can finally begin to work righteousness.

The Church

The history of the church has been a long one of instructing us what to believe and then failing to provide us a clergy living by the commandments. Were it not for the story of the life of Jesus, rendering him both as "begotten" Son of Yahweh (Muhammad disagreed here) [Koran 112:3] and as an adopted child of God in the tradition of the priest-kings in the Order of Melchizedek [Psalm 110:4] – we might be altogether missing a standard. However, "Church" as an institution is not the only way to learn righteousness. Love might be the first step.

The Lord and His Spirit walk the Earth as long as men and women study, learn and can identify with the Wisdom of their teachings. If we can turn away from our quests for survival and riches and the many roles we play and seek the Divinity within, Ea and Shekhinah reestablish themselves in perfect love. This, I think, is the story of our prophets, prophetesses, avatars, saoshyants, boddhisatvas, gurus and vikramadityas – men and women who, in touch with the divine, define the Age.

> *The Lord thy God will raise up unto thee a Prophet from the midst of thee, of thy brethren, like unto me; unto him shall ye hearken.* Deuteronomy 18:15
>
> *And they that be wise shall shine like the brightness of the firmament; and they that turn many to righteousness, as the stars forever and ever.* Daniel 12:3

Celsus understood this concept of the Christ avatar when he asked:

> *If God, like Zeus ... woke up out of his long slumber and wanted to deliver the human race from evils, why on Earth did he send this Spirit that you mention into one corner? He ought to have breathed into many bodies in the same way and sent them all over the world.* Origen, Contra Celsum

The Church Father Origen declared that God had done just that:

> *For nothing good has happened among men without the divine Logos who has visited the souls of those who are able, even if but for a short time ... and though the advent of Jesus was apparently in one corner it was quite reasonable ... that the one prophesied should visit those who had learnt that there was one God, and who were reading His prophets and learning of the Christ they preached, and that he should come at a time when the doctrine would be poured forth all over the world. ... If anyone should want to see many bodies filled with a divine spirit, ministering to the salvation of men everywhere after the pattern of the one Christ, let him realize that those who in many places teach the doctrine of Jesus rightly and live an upright life are themselves also called Christs. ... Moreover, just as we have heard that 'Antichrist is coming,'* [1 John 2:18] *and have learnt no less that there are 'many antichrists' in the world,* [1 John 2:18] *in the same way knowing that Christ has come, we see through him that there have been many Christs in the world, who like him have 'loved righteousness and hated iniquity.'* Hebrews 1:9
> Origen, Contra Celsum

The world's most dangerous idea – this deification of the believer – was the secret for which the high priest with Yahweh written in gold on his turban wanted Jesus silenced. The Essenes/Nazarenes/Mandaeans were so upset he divulged their secret that they declared him a false messiah. The secret so threatened the Catholic Church that they tried to kill all who knew it. That is what the Orthodox of Constantinople knew about *apotheosis* that so offended Innocent III. That is what the Waldenses of the Piemonte and the Albigensians of Languedoc knew. That is what the Jews knew ... that God is in nature and in us. He/She is the redemptive divine spark in these bodies of dust and ash. The Church attempted to murder the idea of our divinity out of existence! For if we follow the ancient instruction "Know Thyself" and discover our divinity, of what possible use is a clerical bureaucracy?

Neither was it convenient for Jews to point out that their Scriptures had been taken as literal and renamed "prophecy" or that their *mikvah*, a ceremonial purification for brides, had become someone else's initiation ceremony. Nor were Parsis supposed to remember Zoroaster was tempted in the desert by Angra Mainyu five centuries before Christ walked the Earth. [Fargard 19:23] It was embarrassing if anyone pointed out that that the Mithraic communion was older, but identical to the Christian one. It was considered exceedingly rude to recall that efforts to erect "One Church Catholic and Apostolic" had required a great deal of raiding everyone else's ancient libraries to purge what was inconvenient (for saying the same thing first or for differing with the usurpers' new dogma) and to plagiarize what was needed.

To establish the Church's legitimacy, the clergy attempted to appropriate all wisdom and symbols of the ancients. To retain ascendancy, clerics then proceeded to confuse or discard anything inconvenient to their own primacy – especially the dangerous point of their whole religion. For who could need them after such a realization? Eventually, they and everyone else will figure out they condemned themselves by forgetting the cosmic Truths that once formed the basis for their stories.

Waiting for a God-man to descend from the clouds, making it a heresy to possess the Spirit, or declaring one's sect and Prophet the "final revelation of God" renders all future prophets and saviors stillborn and stops one's ears from hearing the Truth. Churches were to give birth to the new generation from Heaven – not bury it!

The Church rightfully observes that this idea of godliness can carry some into lawlessness. I may be a case in point. Defending my family and countrymen meant infinitely more to me than the Sixth Commandment's proscription of murder. I would make the same choice today.

If one's heart is greedy for wealth, power, lust or revenge – then yes, Christhood or Godhood is not only a terrible idea, but that greed would make it the very height of one's self-delusion. That said, neither should the arrogant be allowed to don a priest's robe or a Pope's mitre! History is full of selfish beasts and antichrists. However, if one's heart is prepared to serve God and humanity in disregard of the consequences, there is no greater power nor greater love nor greater wisdom nor greater good. If we all chose this path, there would be no need for religions ... or the ones we have would be immensely better.

All water runs pure at first, but run it through the elements, let it stagnate, and see if you still like the taste! Syncretism of principles picked up the flavor and practices of every religion whose disciples the Church absorbed. Followers of Attis and Cybele, like Origen and Eusebius, were still cutting off their genitalia to make themselves *eunuchs for the kingdom of Heaven's sake.* [Matthew 19:12] Mithrans and their disciples were (and are) still abusing children. When the Church realized it could appropriate Plato, it missed the opportunity to reject the sexuality of his Academy, garnering a generation of libertines believing themselves perfect while resurrecting errors of the Naassenes. To these, unfortunately, the Vatican has been most accommodating.

I am ashamed to say the infection was recent. The esoteric traditions of the Academy were transmitted from Mystras to the Council of Florence through Plethon's Brotherhood, the Phatria. Associating Christ too closely with Plato's Demiurge, and then not telling the whole confusing story of the powers of Heaven, they might as well have named him Satan. Looking back on it, Gennadios Scholarios lamented, "We no longer have a church."

The Son, the Prince of Peace, was supposed to be the Sun, eternal domain of the Lord and forever associated with Mercy and Truth – the morning stars Mercury and Venus.

> *His going forth is from the end of Heaven, and his circuit unto the ends of it; and there is nothing hidden from the heat thereof.* [Psalms 19:6]
>
> *My son ... let not Mercy and Truth forsake thee; bind them about thy neck; write them upon the table of thine heart; so shalt thou find favor and good understanding in the sight of God and man.* [Proverbs 3:4]

Just as the Sun was inadequate as a symbol for the Father (a reason "Lord" was always the number-two position in the old theology), so is the Milky Way the Mandaeans would call *the place of beatitude, with the water of Life, Radiance, and the celestial Vine* [Drasia d-Iahia 76] and Zoroastrians knew as *the region of light unrivalled in splendor.* [Bundahishn 1:2] Nature is the source of our most ancient, profound and sacred ideas. Over time, memories of the distant past become secrets for high priests and their initiates, while the rest of us go back to sleep.

To us, the sages pass along a children's story version of the Truth. For example, the story of the "virgin birth" of Mithras and Jesus was to signify Messiah coming after Virgo's return to the Autumnal Equinox with Saturn, signaling the coming End Times. On another level, the virgin birth was the story of a king's mother arising from among the maidens of the Temple. Interpreting zodiacal prophecy literally, Christian scribes felt compelled to make Jesus illegitimate, having to be adopted into the royal line, when his story was typical of an ancient royal line.

Truth is One and nature is the real fount of religion, science and philosophy. No words from a holy book – not even *Behold, a virgin shall conceive, and bear a son* [Isaiah 7:14] should be taken literally before considering nature and all the possible layers of meaning. Through excessive literalism, the church has become an unthinking home of ritual and tender stories – but not one where science, philosophy or common sense can stand in support.

Worse, you no longer tolerate a new idea or a story closer to the Truth lest it threaten your house of cards. You prefer to burn books rather than examine the dark images inside your own!

What this world needs is tolerance such as we saw in the path of Jesus or in Muhammad's early ministry – a Mozarabic Rite for your Moriscos, not an Inquisition. What this world needs is the day of saviors that Zoroaster once foresaw, whose instructions for individual *apotheosis* can be found in the Athanasian Creed:

> *... God of the substance of the Father, begotten before the worlds; and man of substance of His mother, born in the world. Perfect God and perfect man, of a reasonable soul and human flesh subsisting. Equal to the Father as touching His Godhead, and inferior to the Father as touching His manhood. Who, although He is God and man, yet He is not two, but one Christ. One, not by conversion of the Godhead into flesh, but by taking of that manhood into God. One altogether, not by confusion of*

> *substance, but by unity of person. For as the reasonable soul and flesh is one man, so God and man is one Christ. ...* Athanasian Creed

If one day you would unite with the Orthodox, drop the Filioque clause. Its only achievement has been to divide God's family! Christ and the Spirit were transmitted by breath, by the kiss of peace, by anointing, by baptism, and by laying on of hands. If you say they are transmitted by the Father and the Son, then we should remember the Angel of the Lord, the prophets, the kings and their high priests. Most especially, do not forget Theotokos, the Mother. Her Spirit entered the Savior at the Jordan River on the day Jesus was called to show us the Way and was reborn the Christ.

Enoch, Abraham, Moses, Jesus and Muhammad demanded we believe in One God the Father. They did not tell us to believe in a triple personality or three personalities. The "Trinity" was a Truth known by every ancient religion under different names. That did not mean we were to beggar the mind with an all-male triumvirate somehow in charge of giving birth to Life!

Remembering only the "Trinity" also leaves out one of the major players of the universe, someone who still plays a significant role – the one with the "three daughters." Forgetting the fourth face of God ignores the Mother, the Father, the Son or the Devil – or confuses one for another.

Here are the words of Phillip regarding one such confusion:

> *Some said, "Mary conceived by the Holy Spirit." They are in error. They do not know what they are saying. When did a woman ever conceive by a woman?* Gospel of Phillip

Nor did the prophets incarnating the Word insist Christians and Moslems hate each other or declare war on their Hebrew, Zoroastrian or Brahmanic brethren. The great religions share the same Father, circle the same Light, study remarkably similar Scriptures and read the same signs in the heavens.

At one point, we shared the same rites and the same heroes in recognition of the same Universe, but our clergy have added so many laws and stories through the centuries, they have forgotten our common roots. Perhaps the universal realities returning soon will encourage us to rediscover our common ground. That is what my fellow prisoners were trying to find:

We believe in One God to whom we Pray. He sends us Messengers who, by His Spirit, communicate His teachings, blessings and commandments. At the Day of Judgment He will send us His Messiah that Goodness Will Triumph and the Righteous shall live in His Kingdom forever.

If we search for this Sabaeanism before Sabaeanism, this Judaism before Judaism, this Christianity before Christianity – the primeval belief in a Savior Godman who illuminates this world – Muhammad says we will founder on an idea too dangerous, and that we will be rewarded with Hell. [Koran 21:29] Yet such was the first religion of man.

Before we studied the stars or read Scripture, we sought to be like God. Cretans wore leather girdles to stay as trim as Orion. Kings carried scepters to be like him! Maimonides once said, *The chief aim of man should be to make himself, as far as possible, similar to God.* [Guide for the Perplexed] Unfortunately, any success in that noble task has tended to reap punishment as a capital crime – more holocausts to El.

We carry in our souls a coded message, a task we inherited from our heavenly Father and Mother – a code for which the Christ or the Spirit is our key. If we respond to their call, our reward is overwhelming joy and love. Within these bodies of wet clay and ash, the fires of our being can still ignite to illumine all around us. We awaken and the Light begins to shine in our eyes as it did when we were children full of awe and wonder. The difference is as dramatic as the Sun breaking forth from behind the Moon (or Ahriman in the End Times).

Reaching for the divinity within and among us can and should be our common ground – but it is much easier to pray five times a day toward Mecca or take Communion once a week or try to live by every rule in the Book of Leviticus or look for signs of our futures in the heavens.

We see ourselves in terms of different tribes and pretend our citizenship pertains to family, city, religion or nation-state rather than to humanity and the Universe. When we divide like that, the evil inside us is what we attempt to extinguish in others. It would be better to recognize our shared divinity and begin to build the Kingdom together.

There has always been a way to balance the One and the Many – Justice. There was always a way for God's servants to come together – Truth. There is always a way to defeat the House of War – Wisdom. El said to fight and give chase to our enemies. [Leviticus 26:7] Ia said He would put His Spirit upon His Servant and bring justice to the nations.

^{Isaiah 42:1} His Servant said to love our enemies. ^{Luke 6:27} War, Justice, and Love – they all work. Wisdom is in the choice.

You always said the cornerstone the builders rejected was the Jews turning their backs on their rightful king. No, the cornerstone rejected was the mystical path of the seeker honoring Father God and Mother Wisdom, incarnating the Son, and rejecting Evil.

Jesus gave voice to a religion dating back to humanity's genesis. His reform was to remind us that Sonship, or divine childhood, belongs to each of us ^{Psalm 82:6 & John 10:34} if we will accept it and try to live up to it! His mission was to return the Word of God to us, the fallen ^{Revelation 2:5} – Gentiles, Jews, and sinners – that we might rejoin Heaven as Children of God.

I am not sent but unto the lost sheep of the house of Israel. ^{Matthew 15:24}

I am not come to call the righteous, but sinners to repentance. ^{Matthew 9:13}

The Greatest Children of God

Since mankind was leavened with greater intelligence about 4,000 years before Christ, there have been several such avatars, prophets or messengers sent to provide us revelations and reforms. Whether they came in the Phoenix years of Herodotus (500 years and 3 days), the Neros years of Josephus' ancients (600 years and four days), a zodiacal Age (about 2,136 years), or Plutarch's Year of Nymphs and Gods (between 5,000 and 5,125 years) could be debated.

According to Juvenal, the beginning of Pisces when Jesus was born was the "ninth age of the world." The Erythraean Sibyl said "the end of all things" will "come to pass in the tenth." So we near our rebirth in a new *Anno Mundi* and Kali Yuga will have passed.

Using Neros years as the guide for avatars, we can see that Muhammad saw himself as the next incarnation, or prophet, after Jesus. Muhammad's reform was telling us to remember our Holy Father more than the Messenger who brings us His Word. In a similar spirit, I suppose that is why Jesus taught us to pray, saying *Our* **Father** *Who Art in Heaven* ^{Matthew 6:9} and said *He that heareth my word, and believeth on* **Him that sent me**, *hath everlasting life.* ^{John 5:24}

Roughly, the avatars or Christs, the ones Da Cusa calls *kings and seers* or *prophets and masters,* are expected within a century or two of their due date. For my calculations, I used Caesar's Year of Light (the Logos) as the point of origin, and the Neros Cycle to count the years:

- Adam/Anu, ca. 4113 BC
- Enoch/Enki/Ea, ca. 3513 BC
- Noah/Krishna, ca. 2913 BC
- Melchizedek/Abraham, ca. 2313 BC
- Ia/Joshua/Apollo, ca. 1713 BC*
- David/Achilles, ca. 1113 BC
- Zoroaster/Jeshua, ca. 513 BC
- Jesus/Apollonius, ca. 87 AD
- Isaac of Syria/Muhammad, ca. 687
- St. Francis/Mevlana Rumi, ca. 1287*

These are double-phoenix dates coinciding with both the 500- and 600-year cycles.

There have been many more avatars than this, for God has always reached out to more than four religions and nations. For example, Zoroaster and Jeshua were accompanied by Buddha, Confucius, Lao Tzu, Socrates and Pythagoras.

The avatars are aware that they are messengers of one ancient wisdom and a single ongoing revelation. When Plato was asked how long his ideas would endure, he is said to have replied, *Only until He shall come who will open the Fountain of all Truth.* [Ficino, De Cristiana Religione XXV]

The reason the God of Abraham and Jacob, who became Adam and returned as Jesus, is causing others who slept in the dust to also return and teach us is that it is time to awaken and prepare. The world's religious have fallen asleep on guard duty as surely as Byzantium had.

The ideas of the Saviors and Prophets are simple, but almost as soon as disciples translate the parables, turn them into grand mysteries for initiates and write them down with embellishments ... the message is lost, disfigured or deliberately hidden. Fortunately, He who sends out the Christs also sends His Spirit to the rest of us, provided we have an ear to hear it.

> *I will give them one heart, and I will put a new Spirit within you.* [Ezekiel 11:19]

> *There is a Spirit in man; and the inspiration of the Almighty giveth them understanding.* [Job 32:8]

I said Byzantium fell because we turned our back on our legacy, throwing away our future. In this, there is perhaps one last secret I should pass along before I depart. Long ago, up until about the Age of Taurus, the tribe and religion of the Jews and Greeks was the same. We lived between Egypt and Jerusalem in a fertile land and we worshipped the *Baalim* (the Holy Family) together.

About the time of the Exodus, long after Cronus and Zeus had been replaced and after Lord Ia's promotion to Most High, we separated. The Jews took the Father (Yahweh) and His Law as their inheritance.

We took the Mother (Athena) and her Freedom as ours. By the ninth century BC, the differences between us were so marked that Elijah was killing priests of the Mother and we were turning our backs on the Father. A century later, the split was so extreme that the Father said He was willing to let us go for a time. ^{Hosea 2}

For a thousand years, our scholars and theirs alternately debated or ignored each other at Alexandria. Then, in the days of Clement, Origen, Eusebius and Constantine the Great, we determined it was again time to combine worship of the Father, the Son and the Mother. This was part of the work done at Nicaea, official accommodation again being made to the Mother in a religion that had absorbed so many other influences.

Within a century, Christianity chose the path of intolerance as the Levites had done before them. Clergy took to burning books of Wisdom and killing her high priestesses like Hypatia. They began redacting the wisdom of the Christ lifted from the Essenes and sages of other religions. Ancient wisdom was repackaged in cute stories; mysteries were hidden and forgotten. Competing manuscripts were quickly burned and voices quietly silenced.

Hiding the World's Most Dangerous Idea

In Spain, I found a copy of Saint Bernard's *Love of God* in which the saint describes being absorbed into the Godhead. ^{Colossians 2:9} The scribe making the copy apparently thought the concept controversial, and therefore treated the main idea as an encoded, abbreviated tiny afterthought – reserving it for the chosen of the chosen.

When the words of saints give pause to the censors, there is something seriously wrong. In such a world, the freedom to improve the condition of humanity is curtailed in exact proportion as controls are legislated on what we can read, say, or believe. Criticism of leaders and their corruption is the first to go. Then, the gravest injustices can be committed with impunity. Freedom of speech is the first requirement of good government. Freedom of religion is the second.

With your Inquisition, you attempt to control too much. In reaction, you will see a flood of ancient wisdom, heresy, science and witchcraft. You will generate the very liberties you hope to suppress. So build your fires high! You will breed enemies faster than you can slay them. For martyrs beget martyrs, by virtue of their heroism and by the oppression that forges them.

O chaste and holy love! O sweet and gracious affection! O pure and cleansed purpose, thoroughly washed and purged of selfishness, and the more soft and sweet, the more divine one's love! To love like this is to be deified. *As a drop of water poured into wine loses itself, taking the color and savor of the wine; or as the bar of iron, heated red-hot, becomes like the fire, forgetting its own nature; or as the air, radiant with sun-beams, transforms into light itself; so in the saints all human affections melt away ineffably into the will of God. For how can God be all in all, if anything merely human remains in the man? The substance endures – but in another form, another glory, another power.*

© Biblioteca Nacional de España

Father will always be frustrated with Mother's followers. What you should know is that He wants us back. He wants Her back. He much prefers to have us together as a family than try to cherish our fears and sacrifices or watch us kill each other. He no longer wants to be treated as *Baali*. [Hosea 2:16] He wants to be called *Ishi* (Husband), *Rea`* (Friend) or Abba *(Father)*.

One day, there will be no lost tribes and all will return to the Father:

I will say to them who were not my people, Thou art my people; and they shall say, Thou art my God. [Hosea 2:23]

311

The sign for our reconciliation – God to Wisdom and Virtue to Freedom – will be the next season of Creation and Rebirth.

Return of the Holy Family

As we await, hopefully or fearfully, the arrival of the Sun at the Grand Phoenix, we should look to the Mother, the gleam in the Eye of God. This incarnation of the Spirit, Great Sophia, will return to grant us Wisdom. She is the Theotokos Maria. She is Earth called to withstand Fire, Flood and Ice. She is the Queen of Heaven. She too will come again, pleading for the Father's mercy and speaking His mind. The Gnostics will call her Norea.

You can call her Shekhinah. Like the Father, she is eternal. Her earthly representative is your greatest love. Like the Christ, she is sacred. Like him and like you, she comes to us as Divinity wrapped in the skin of an Animal.

> *She is with all flesh according to His gift, and He hath given Her to them that love Him.* Ecclesiasticus 1:10

United, man and woman, we can work miracles. That is why we were given intelligence by the Father and the Spirit – to do the work of gods!

> *Jesus said: The works that I do you will do; and greater works than these you will do.* John 14:12

Eusebius, Constantine the Great's bishop, discussed the incarnation that has forever been the cornerstone of the religions of mankind:

> *He dispatches the most intimate of his own messengers from time to time, for the salvation of men below. Of these messengers anyone so favored by fortune, having cleansed his understanding and dissipated the mist of mortality, may well be described as truly divine, as carrying in soul the image of some great god. Surely so great a personality will stir up the entire human race, and illuminate the world of mankind more brightly than the Sun, and will leave the effects of his eternal divinity for the contemplation of future ages.* Eusebius Pamphilus, Against Apollonius of Tyana, VI

If we would have God's kingdom on Earth, WE must lay the bricks. The prophets reveal what is to be done, but ultimately WE are the ones who must do it; and it is no use waiting for Messiah to come and do it for us. The stories and allegories of the Scriptures are second- and third-hand reports of the last recognized Prophet or Savior. They are guides to show us where we are failing and what we still need to do!

Do with me as you will. I will rise again on the third day [Hosea 6:2] – death being the sleep before a new life of suffering, serving and acquiring wisdom. I realize now our task here was to empower the Christ, the Spirit within, and to endeavor to make our world better. This was the wisdom of the ancients.

I contented myself with El's way of chasing evil. Ea's way of justice was too hard, requiring Wisdom. Christ's way of Love was too difficult for my selfish soul. Judging and hating others is infinitely easier.

What I found, though, is that judging and punishing one's enemy is to attack a mirror image. It can involve you in the very sin you most condemn. It is the lesson of Jesus' parable of the mote in the eye: Slay the shadow within before you judge a weaker man you deem your enemy. I wish now that I had. Instead, I became what I most detested – a "leader" pretending to be God with no restraint, no mercy and no remorse!

This was the fear in my heart as a child, that I might not live up to the expectations of my Father. I walked too far along the path of Truth and lost too much Faith and Mercy to find Wisdom. I was an "Emperor" who fell short of being even a good Servant!

Rome did not revive freedom by killing Caesar. She earned another Caesar! I did not restore Byzantium with the deaths of Mehmed and Alexander. We were blessed with another sultan and another pope!

On the other hand, how much more did Alítheia, my Shekhinah, achieve in her meekness? Hers was the path of *fear, patience, long-suffering and self-restraint.* [Epistle of Barnabas] Rising above her suffering, she blessed with her love and service all who washed up on the shores of Oran when you forced them from Spain shouting "Convert, go into exile, or die!" My regret is having lived without her, and not having learned sooner by her example. How I wasted my life fighting and breaking my head to find the happiness God had freely given!

I learned many things on the path of *Wisdom, Understanding, Science and Knowledge,* [Epistle of Barnabas] but the one that counted most was this: Alítheia was right. In her case, a Slave had learned Majesty and Mercy. By comparison, I was so unworthy.

The Next Creation

One day, Sagittarius will again attempt to rescue Sun from the Dragon Ouroboros, while his brother Centaurus tries to fend off the Beast Lupus. This could only occur late in the year as the Sun is in the South.

A number of times in 2011 and 2012 the Sun will be in Virgo late in the year with the Moon at her feet. [Revelation 12:1] In September and October 2012, she will travail in birth with Mercury and Saturn -- while standing on the Moon. [Revelation 12:1-2]

This sign should precede the time of the Beast, which is expected to cast stars to Earth suddenly as if a scroll is being rolled up. [Revelation 6:13-14] This change sounds as if a pole shift precedes any meteor shower that could cause us to hide *in the dens and in the rocks of the mountains.* [Revelation 6:15] Disaster will strike if a rock or comet penetrates Earth's core. [Revelation 9:1-2]

Barnabas saw the End coming on the Seventh Day (each day being 1,000 years [2 Peter 3:8] and starting his calendar in 3761 BC). The New Creation, he said, will come on the Eighth Day – so your children, grandchildren and great-grandchildren may lead long productive lives until 4239. However, when it finally does come time for the Renovation, will mankind ever be ready? My suspicion is that we will always live in denial until the last minute, as my friends and I did in Constantinople and Andrea and I did in Florence. Asking people to take the ancients seriously is like asking a teenager to listen to an adult's voice of experience.

Yes, Renovation could come later than Mother's reunion with Father in 2012, and closer to when the sky turns to the Great Adam at the vernal equinox in 3502. We should remember, however, that Zoroaster allocated a thousand years to each house of the zodiac beginning with Aries; and Virgo was the seventh sign. This means that he, like Jesus, fully expected "the End" to come during the Age of Pisces. [Zoroaster, Bundahishn Chap. 35] That places the Judgment definitely before 2650 (when the vernal equinox enters Aquarius) and probably before 2132 (being 2,136 years after the vernal equinox entered Pisces).

Considering the Flood of Virgo's Raven [Genesis 8:7] happened in 10,801 BC, then, by the Hindu and Zoroastrian count of 12,000 years to Cataclysm, since 1199 AD we have enjoyed a long stay of execution.

If one dates the "time, times and a half" [Daniel 12:7] ... the "thousand two hundred and threescore days" [Revelation 11:3, 12:6] and the "forty and two

314

months" ^(Revelation 13:5) as all talking about the same period – and we date them from Pope Leo III's crowning of Charlemagne – then the "Renovation" occurs in 2060. But what if "Babylon" dates from the end of the Moslem Conquest at the Battle of Talas – and the "seven hills" are those of my dear city? That spells the fall of 2011.

If the death of Krishna came in 3102 BC, the season of the Great Transformation will begin sometime between 1898 and 2023, depending on how long one believes an age of the gods requires. Cardinal D'ailly said 1789 would overthrow the Old Order of laws and religion "if the world lasts until that year."

A rabbi with whom I was acquainted said he expected Moshiach before 2243, saying the world would last "only 6,000 years." However, if modern man's Creation was on the "Sixth Day" of God, then it sounds as if the Jewish eschatology derived from the Persian, or vice versa, coinciding in the return of Ahriman every 12,000 years. In that case, Apocalypse is due by 2239. Count it as you will, our date with destiny nears and we *know not what hour* our Lord doth come. ^(Matthew 24:42)

When it happens, the arc of the sky will shift between Draco and the Beast/Lupus/Leopardus and *every mountain and island* will be *moved out of their places* ^(Revelation 6:14) as *the third part of the stars of Heaven* are *cast to the Earth* ^(Revelation 12:4) (at least a 60-degree shift) and the constellations (the elders and four living creatures) fall *on their faces* ^(Revelation 7:11) before God (a pole reversal).

> *The Beast which I saw was like unto a leopard, and his feet were as the feet of a bear, and his mouth as the mouth of a lion: and the Dragon gave him his power, and his seat, and great authority.* ^(Revelation 13:2)

A hint of this pole shift marked by the old "navels of the Earth" is to be found in Genesis, where God's Flaming Sword (Cygnus) and the Cherubim (Dippers) ^(Clement, Stromateis) circling the Pole and keeping us OUT of our celestial home in Eden are located to the East. ^(Genesis 3:24) These barriers were set up precisely to guard the way to the Tree of Life (the Pole of the Word), which heads South at the end of the year with the Sun! Enoch says the Tree of Life will return to the northeast one day.
^(1 Enoch 25)

I believe Muhammad truly prophesied when he spoke of "The Event" – but exactly for whom the warning spells disaster escapes me. I suspect he was looking toward the north:

> *When the great event comes to pass,*
> *There is no belying its coming to pass —*
> *Abasing one party, exalting the other,*
> *When the earth shall be shaken with a severe shaking,*
> *And the mountains shall be made to crumble with an awful crumbling,*
> *So that they shall be as scattered dust.*
> *And you shall be three sorts.*
> *Then as to the companions of the right hand;*
> *how happy are the companions of the right hand!*
> *And as to the companions of the left hand;*
> *how wretched are the companions of the left hand!*
> *And the foremost are the foremost.*
> *These are they who are drawn nigh to Allah.* [Koran 56:1-11]

Of what profit, then, is Ea's battle with El — these two gods sharing the same patch of heaven (The Deep and Serpens being only about an hour apart in the night sky) who by turns despair of mankind? Neither is exactly the victor. They are markers of the Great Transition. They recall a papyrus I once owned. On the left was an Eagle. In the center was an Eye of Horus (signifying here the Sun's union with the Deep). On the right, was a cobra signifying Serpens. Above them was a bar signifying the Milky Way when the Universe was as it should be. That papyrus was about one of these seasons of danger, just as the Cosmic Cross or Ma'at is about the end of that season that may take the lives of many of us.

We exist on the Wheel of Dharma. Some say we rise and fall eight times [Leviticus 26:18] once every 3,000 years [Herodotus II:123] in a Greatest Year. Then we go home and *a new generation descends from Heaven on high.* [Virgil, 4th Eclogue] Perhaps this will be a new race of humankind, just as we replaced another generation of man the last time. [Lucian of Samosota, De Dea Syria]

Nature teaches us that the Warrior and the Dragon, Good and Evil, Life and Death follow each other in an order so grand that one — through excess, error, time or reaction — inexorably gives rise to the other. Just as Earth's poles shift and reverse, we should resign ourselves to the idea that neither Jews nor Catholics nor Moslems nor Mandaeans nor Brahmans nor Buddhists can or should "win" while all of us are here to serve and to seek the redemptive Wisdom found in all religion, philosophy and science.

The ennoblement of humankind and the understanding of Nature was the religion of the ancients. Our ancestors looked to the stars and the wandering planets. They listened to the prophets and angels, lords and gods, and that is what they sought: to understand, to find the Good, to improve their lives and their world! Perhaps those can be our goals again – perhaps even before we see the mysteries of the Church's stories played out in the heavens!

One more mystery of St. George and I will finish. The story of the Warrior and the Dragon symbolized by Virgo and the Ancient Serpent is one portrait in miniature of the much grander struggle for the survival of humankind. The great battle coming to the deepest blue skies will involve the entire Heaven from one horizon to the other. Ahriman will attack from Sagittarius, and the galaxy will appear to flip the Pleiades (the heart of Taurus) toward Orion at the same time Lupus takes the place of Draco.

The "demons" and "angels" we see flying through space will be the usual sort of heavenly bodies – stars, comets, and meteors. Just as Perseus fighting the Sea Dragon was Sun's battle with the Giant, Saint George illustrates the Son of Man superconstellation. The horse he rides is Pegasus. His great and strong sword against the Red Dragon is Cygnus. The Crocodile he must slay is Ahriman/Ouroboros (afterward symbolized by Draco). The maiden he rescues is the Sun.

The Cross on his cape is the sign of Orion. The secret of Orion as the hinge between Earth's old and new equators once located near Heliopolis (and between the sky's northern and southern hemispheres) is why the *Bible* began with a "B." Orion's right angles inspired that letter for the Phoenicians and Hebrews. It is why the pyramids at Giza are located at right angles to the Nile like

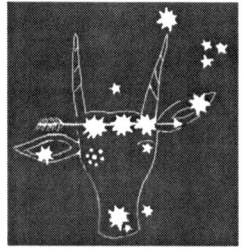

Hindu Orion

Orion's Belt to the Milky Way (Hermes' *As above, so below*) yet curve in the wrong direction! It is why Constantine's Labarum resembles this constellation. It explains why the Antelope's Head (Orion's Belt) was sacred to the Hindus. Hesiod says Orion once chased the Virgin stars (the Pleiades) into the Deep. Next time, they will chase him, when, like Osiris, Adonis, or Tammuz, he is torn apart, disappears and is later restored beside the intersection of the galactic and celestial equators. Finally, the Cross of St. George also signifies a galactic alignment of the signs and seasons that will begin the 21st Century. As Lorenzo used to say, *Le Tems Revient* (The Times Return).

The Pole of the Word, recalling the beginning and the end of the cycle of Creation, will find its way home to the north, provided we do not change the direction of "North" just because we find the heavens flying upside-down and backward from what we remember. Besides Lupus and Leo, Nonnos said changeling Zeus has also been the Great Dipper, Taurus, Aquarius and the Milky Way [Nonnos, Dionysiaca I] so the poles may end up having shifted further during the reversal, even after the Earth returns to normal rotation.

We should remember, however, that ancient stories only tell us what has happened before. They cannot tell us exactly what will happen in the future. They merely hint that the past is often prologue, and the ancient stories may be worth exploring before we pass through the Sagittarius-Orion stargate to a New Age.

If we escape a Flood, it will be because the Great Comet Ahriman has been partially destroyed. In that case, our season of danger could pass unremarked as compared to earlier cataclysms.

Unfortunately, mankind is nearly as dangerous to nature as nature is to us. There may be a doom in our future regardless of whether a comet or giant meteor is on the way. It no longer takes an act of God to destroy humanity. War, famine and disease are all within our power.

Unless I am mistaken in my readings of ancient history, the Dragon with the seven heads [Revelation 12:3] was once a watery giant planet that grew a tail as it approached the Sun. For this reason, the ancients knew its return in the Age of Pisces as the Age of the Great Dragon; and they called the Age of Aquarius the "Curse of the Rain." Like the Moon, the Giant raised the waters of Earth – only to so great an effect as to pull them from the ground to towering heights!

Our hope is that much of the comet is now gone. This is why God promised no more floods. [Genesis 9:11] The pole can shift now without the huge tides it caused when Leviathan made *the Deep to boil like a pot*. [Job 41]

Some polar shifts have already happened without disaster. Herodotus recalled priests telling him: *Egypt was in no degree affected by these changes; the productions of the land, and of the river, remained the same; nor was there anything unusual either in diseases or the deaths.* [The History II:142] Nonetheless, the day of the next shift might be a good day to visit the mountains. [Revelation 6:15]

Unless this now-smaller Ahriman, of whom the planets once threatened to *make a banquet* ^(Job 41) came too close to Earth when he last flew by, we may well escape his bite. A reason for concern is that our ancestors believed he comes as a doom written in the stars, that he could take a quarter of the life on Earth ^(Revelation 6:8) and cause a third part of the heavens to darken. ^(Revelation 8:12) He has struck us twice in 26,000 years.

© Jose Vargas

One of Ahriman's companions is the Wrath of the Lamb ^(Revelation 6:16) expected to fly out of the mouth of the Son (Sun in Aquarius) ^(Revelation 1:16) – a phenomenon we last experienced about 5,000 years ago. Ahriman joins us twice each cycle of Creation. The Wrath of the Lamb returns five times as the keeper of the Age of the Gods. An object sometimes known as the Sword of the Hebrews ^(Exodus 12 & 16) returns seven times to our neighborhood, lingering about 57 years in its near pass to the Sun.
^(Exodus, Joshua 3, 4, 10 & Bundahishn 30:7)

Many will scoff at these notions, saying the Sun passes the same spot in the Milky Way peacefully every year. Indeed, it does. However, we do not pass through the knife's edge that frequently; nor does her center annually stir to life as a great scarlet star.

Our apparent movement through the zodiac, is precisely that – a real movement through the stars. Some sages believe the Sun has a dark twin at the center of its path and they rotate past each other. If that is true, how close can they come and there still be life if we are to be baked each 26,000 years? And why do we not see the other star?

Many will see the prophesied signs in the sky and still not believe. Jesus had a question for these people: *O you hypocrites, you can discern the face of the sky; but can you not discern the signs of the times?* ^(Matthew 16:3)

Zoroaster and my ancestors were wrong. We do not pass this point each 6,000 or 12,000 or 24,000 years. It takes a little longer for Zeus the changeling to assume the shape of Leo (last time) or Leopardus (next time). ^(Nonnos, Dionysiaca 1:20-33)

St. John gave us a hint of how the galaxy works with his 144,000 Nazarites (or Nasirutha) *wearing the Name on their foreheads* Ezekiel 9:4; Revelation 7 and the number 666 (indicating that he knew two methods for calculating the cycle of Precession and Renovation). Both numbers are sacred measures of time. With them, John placed the *Ekpyrosis* conflagration sometime between 2012 and 2239.

We may be given the privilege to begin again, in an Age when we can share the great truths and begin to edit our sacred scrolls of their hatreds, inconsistencies and stories we no longer understand. Aristotle said they were embellished to frighten and guide the ignorant people, lending sanction to law and authority. Metaphysics XII:8

We must, at a minimum, give up our women-hating and people-killing dogmas doing the work of the Devil, cease killing our unborn children and disfiguring our children's genitalia Epistle of Barnabas and begin to build one Kingdom in which we are again children of the Father of Love and the Spirit of Truth. If we pay attention this time, they will help us to progress from sin to purification to death and immortality.

10,801 BC

If we fail to survive the Conflagration, and God has not sentenced us for all eternity, then we will follow the Wheel of Life around to journey back through the three kingdoms. As Vergil said, *The pure ether of the soul remains.* Aeneid Bk VI

The four great religions of the Book – in the *Avesta*, the *Torah*, the *Bible* and the *Koran* – offer different means of purifying ourselves, but repenting of our sins and undertaking to free ourselves from them is *the* prerequisite if we wish to return. Somehow we must *cast* them *away* if we are to receive our *new heart and a new spirit.* Ezekiel 18:31

Finding a way to commune with God is important as well. Finally, we should remember the avatars if we would learn to live a holy life. They showed us how to turn away from selfishness and to discover Divinity in each other.

Mystic Circle

The four religions of the Book each shed light on the attributes and virtues of God. The Magi saw Him as our Creator. They observed Him in the heavens and in the eternal fire. They saw Him locked in a cosmic battle against Death. Does that differ in any substantial way from Judaism, Christianity or Islam? These and the other religions all cast interlocking circles of light.

In the center, where they shine the brightest, their commonality represents the One God the prophets and mystics always told us about. Other members of His family – heavenly or fallen – are archetypes we recognize independently only because we never grasped the paradoxical whole of how good and evil have always coexisted, just as fire and ash or light and darkness coexist.

We invented "Satan" because we could not believe the Torah said *His hand hath formed the crooked serpent* [Job 26:13] or, *I form the light and the darkness; I make peace, and create evil; I, the Lord, do all these things.* [Isaiah 45:7]

The Truth that I have seen in the heavens is that the Ancient of Days is the Center of Heaven, but he is also the Pole of the Word, the Cornerstone and the Dragons, the Eagle and the Bull, the Milky Way and the Zodiac, the Sun and Moon. His Labarum symbolizes the pillars of the Pole where the wheels of the Zodiac and the Milky Way meet. He is the Hero slaying the Dragon, and He is the rider named Death. [Revelation 6:8] God is all the incarnations of Vishnu, the Shekhinah and the Word. He is the Wisdom of our Universe – all that WAS, and IS and WILL BE.

We were made in God's likeness, not so much in our faces and appendages, but in our mix of glory and gloom. We understand gods, angels, saints and demons only to the extent they are like us. We can understand a Holy Family. We have a hard time contemplating a bodiless omnipresent and omnipotent abstraction on whom we heap our every expectation and from whom we suffer disappointment as often as we ignore the Necessities of His Universe.

There is a better way to understand. The Bull in the Moon is the one in Taurus. The God in Jupiter is the one in Mercury. The God of Truth is the God of Mercy. The Great Warrior is the Great Shepherd and the Charioteer. He swung the Aurigan axe of Hephaestus. He wrung the neck of Leo. He brings the Light, the storm and the rain.

You can find Him in the Moon, the Sun, and the Word ... or in the very heart of the Milky Way. You can find Him in yourself. He is there. She is there. The Son is there. *Raise the stone and there thou shalt find Me; cleave the wood, and there I AM.* [Logia, Sayings of Jesus]

Raging inside each of us is the primordial sea of Chaos, laboring to give birth to something at once human and divine. God uses the

Power and violent selfishness of the Antichrist within and among us to tear down iniquities, to address threats, and to challenge others to defend their souls. He uses Prophets to establish laws, to give us Faith and to describe His Order. His children, the Christs, show us Love, teach us hope, and give us the faith and courage to create a better life.

Mankind approaches its gravest crisis in 25,000 years. If ever we needed a generation of Christs, it is now. As Aeschylus implied, another race could have replaced us in the last Creation, but we replaced them. Indeed, our first generations were defective. In Genesis 5, there was a generation of hermaphrodites who could not reproduce. In Genesis 6, there was a generation of violent giants. My Greek ancestors remembered some with many hands and heads, called *Hecatoncheires*, and another race with only one eye, called *Cyclops*. Worse were *chimera* – monstrous hybrid creatures that lasted one generation.

Last time, so few of us survived *Ekpyrosis* that the first partners were brothers and sisters or fathers and daughters, as can be seen in the *Book of Jubilees* and Genesis 19. The situation will again be dire if, as suggested in Isaiah 3, leadership devolves to starving children and there are so few fertile men left that seven women will marry one man. [Isaiah 4]

What sort of destruction leaves behind seas of glass [Revelation 4 & 15] and makes the hair of women fall out in clumps [Isaiah 3] while men die of wars, famines, beasts and plagues? [Ezekiel 14] Great faith, generosity and courage will be required of those who wish to survive. Selfishness, meanwhile, will kill billions, for we have never learned to share Nature's bounty.

The day Constantinople fell, I saw thousands laying down their lives for their countrymen. I once saw all Florence, the province in Italy with the most freedom, dedicated to holiness. I hope one day, when life itself despairs of all around us, that we can look deep inside and find the divine spark that animates these bodies of clay with courage and faith.

Mother Wisdom teaches Her Seekers to find Truth in all of nature; but we tend to view her from one narrow perspective or one faulty method, when we should see the world as She does – in the context of a divine design, mutual causality, fortunate timing and complex effects that exceed the understanding of a single life, spirituality, or science.

There are not two gods, nor three, four or five. There is only One, but that One Wisdom can no sooner be understood by one of the current religions or one of His faces than the stormy nature and tides of the Ocean can be discerned in a single drop of water. "He" is neither male nor female, neither pagan nor Jew nor Christian nor Moslem. He merely reminds us from time to time: *I AM*.

I have seen the Cosmos reborn. I have watched the zodiac spin like a top. I rise in every age and serve every dynasty. I break bread with each generation, bless every family, and kiss every child.

Accept the Truth or believe your stories, but know this: Before Abraham was, I AM. Though Earth be renewed, I Will Be; and in every Age of the stars and man, I Love You.

Love yourself and you will feel the Light. Love others and they will know the Light. Love all the Universe and you will BE the Light!

I told my children, "Ye Are Gods, Children of the Most High" and yet you fancied yourselves but a seed of my seed! You sprang a child from my Root, you drank of my Water, you ate of my Wisdom, you grew in my Light and still you cannot see?

I am the Lord, thy God, from the land of Egypt, and thou shalt know no god but me; for there is no savior beside me. Hosea 13:4

I live, yet not I, but Christ liveth in me. Galatians 2:20

I Am with you always. Awaken. Repent. BE!

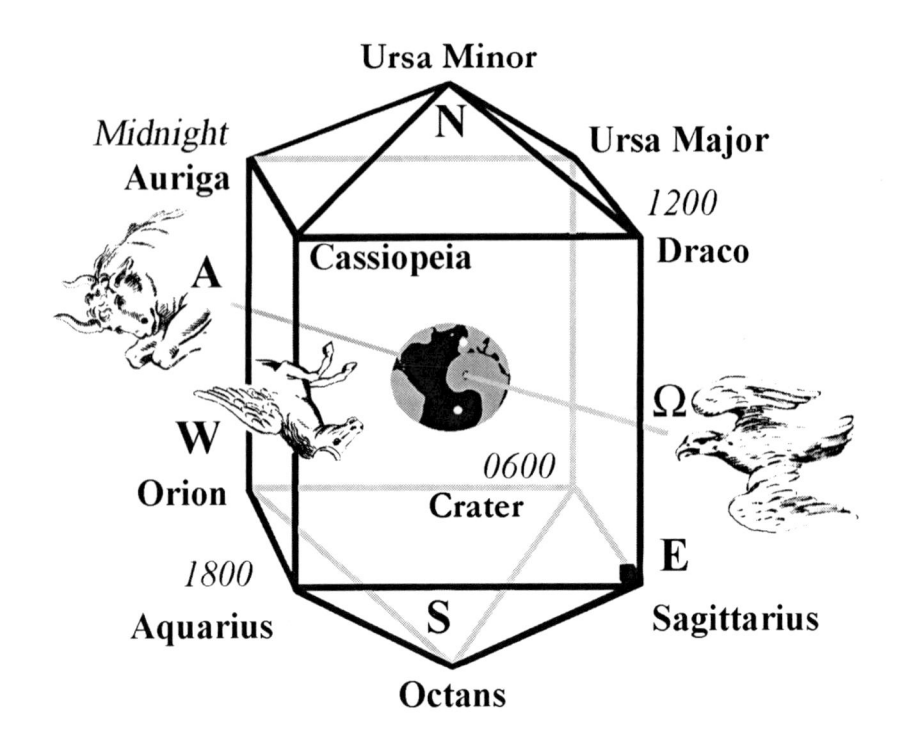

If the Universe is like the Kaaba, then we know what happens at the Alpha-Omega moment of our Day of Judgment. The above looks at the zenith of both Stonehenge (Temple of the Celtic Druids) and St. Helena (Isle of the Goddess and Cyclops) as central to the ancient stories of Creation. Noon is the moment of the Tao, our eclipse of the Sun with the Void (or the Deep). Whether this moment of the Divine Union at Sagittarius is what Abraham and Muhammad intended to signify in their placement of the black Cornerstone of al Hajar al Aswad (or Hindus meant by their positioning of Shivalinga stones in their temples), one can only guess. However, when the moment proves fateful, we will know we were warned by the religions, myths and legends of all humanity. Son of Man will again ride Pegasus; and "Leviathan" (innocent Draco standing in for Ouroboros) will be our scapegoat [Isaiah 53:6] *by the Son of Man's great and strong flaming sword.* [Isaiah 27:1 & Psalm 44:19]

Prayer to the Shekhinah
Holy Mother, Everlasting Light,
With thy kiss, curtail Death's night.
Brightness of Eternal Day,
Grant us Wisdom, this I pray.
  With my Love, let me arise
And with thy Truth traverse the skies.
Teach us to sing thy Victor's song;
Defend the child and right the wrong.
Restore the breath and dreams of our breast.
For us thy secrets make manifest.
Come, Holy Spirit, your servants wake;
Come Dawn, Holy Rites, Lethe's fetters break!

Prayer to the Logos
Holy Father, I await my fate
For a life too often filled with hate.
I pray for forgiveness, a chance to renew
The challenge of Life and happiness pursue
  With my Love, let me return
To show mankind how to forsake the Urn.
Help us to hear your message sage
In time to ring in a Golden Age.
I pray as before that we can save,
Some seeds of Life deep in a cave.
And 'ere you heat the Earth and Skies,
Prepare mankind to survive and rise.
Thou art Alpha-Omega, first and last,
Christ our Phoenix, help us learn from our past!

LOVE

TRUTH   W   FAITH

POWER

Which way does your soul point?

A Final Note To My Captors

An oracle is on the lips of the king: his mouth will not err in judgment. Proverbs 16:10

Toledo, 1504

Gentlemen, you have been kind and I have said things you no doubt regarded as crazy, arrogant and blasphemous. I assure you I told the Truth as best I could discern it. Fortunately, I am not a priest, nor have I a following. So if I uttered heresy, it is my own soul that is lost, not that of others. I submit to whatever you and God decide.

I have freely confessed to breaking the Commandments, to religious positions inimical to your doctrine, and to capital crimes punishable by the secular authorities. So let me make this easy for you. My biggest crime from your standpoint was embracing the most dangerous idea in the world – one that King David and King Jesus both espoused.

We are born to this Earth as gods. As the children and heirs of God, we are here to learn His mind and to do His will. One can attempt this as Mehmed or Alexander, embracing the will to Power of a Bull of Heaven and pitting oneself against the entire planet. One can flee or accept the pain of this world, assisted by the Faith of one's youth. Or one can negotiate one's condition and search for Wisdom.

Truth, however, will not be limited to what fits into one life or one book – even one with a curse at the end saying it is the final revelation of God. Truth is, science, philosophy and theology are the principles and facts we observe in nature. That is where God has always been – not in a jealous bogeyman who could never wring enough gold, silk, flesh and tears from our world, nor enough confessions from our pained lives of learning wisdom through sin and error!

Despite your reaction to my words, I would ask that you not burn this manuscript. Since it contains innovations in religion, I believe you are bound to forward it to your masters in Rome. Your king and the new pope may find it contains information of some worth as your power increases and the armed threat from Islam again looms large. One day, probably too late, religion will return to being something peaceful and universal.

The Moslems, meanwhile, are a patient and deliberate people. It took them as long to capture Constantinople as it took them to gain and lose Spain. They may require another six centuries to take Rome and another two to conquer Atlantis and Asia. They see themselves as we janissaries saw ourselves – as *Gazi* (Holy Warriors). If you would stop them, do not allow your forces of the Reconquista to retire. Zeal must be met with zeal or you have surrendered. Do you know what Mehmed ordered carved on his tomb as an epitaph? "I intended to conquer Rhodes and subdue proud Italy." The dream has not changed in eight centuries, unrealistic though it might be. Rome's day is coming.

On the day of my arrival, I prayed to God the Father for a way to communicate with you without torture distorting my message. You graciously provided it and I thank you. Even under different circumstances than accused of heresy I would have wished for such an opportunity to reassess, to pray and prepare for what comes next.

The first night of my capture, I prayed to the Lord for a sign as to when I am to die. The next night, I noticed Saturn and Jupiter approaching each other, heading again into Gemini. I have lived on Earth for 60 years. I have worked enough, loved well, and learned much. Though I did not accomplish a great deal in the business of restoring my father's kingdom, I left a few worthy people thinking about how that might be accomplished. It has been a good and blessed life and I am ready for it to be over.

Tomorrow is my 41st day with you. Jupiter and Saturn meet again. If you have a priest willing to confess my sins, administer communion or last rites, he would find me a willing subject. However, given my status as a renegade I expect no such spiritual comfort. No matter what he offers and no matter what you do to me, I will not repudiate the words in this tome. I have confessed and I have repented. I can do no more.

I would like to depart as soon as possible, by whatever means you choose. I welcome the quickest and easiest method for you and the magistrate's men. I have no need of this body and it is yours if you have need of a public spectacle. As for me, I would prefer to go quietly and with some dignity, but I realize this is not my decision.

I wish you and your king the best success in consolidating your gains against the Moors. Encourage him not to extend his empire farther than he can defend it with his own soldiers and solid allies, lest he find himself in the position of my Emperor, counting on forces who exist only in beautiful letters sealed in gold and the schemes of lying envoys.

I understand my cousins Andreas and Manuel have willed or sold their alleged birthrights to King Ferdinand and the new Sultan. I am in no position to dispute their claims. However, for the record and to reinforce your sovereign's claim, be it known that I, John IX Palaeologus, being of sound mind and under no duress, do hereby bequeath all titles, honors, symbols and property of Byzantium in perpetuity to the King and Queen of Spain and their heirs. May the Lord bless and keep their family.

I pray that one day you will establish your society upon a foundation of education for your people. Provide your citizens Roman justice. Bless them with the freedom Athenians once enjoyed. Give them the opportunity to perform in battle as Spartans. You are the new Rome and the new Byzantium. Yours is the next great crossroads of the world, and if you remember always who seeks to deprive you of it, you will be the greatest empire that ever lived.

Your church and state will be shaken in the years to come by new religions, which are only old ideas in a new garb. Your best defense will be young people full of ideas, as ready to adapt as to defend what they know. Allowing only one faith enforced by an Inquisition failed to serve my nation. Focusing on God and Faith while turning our backs on Truth and Freedom cost us the Empire. The brotherhoods, on the other hand, were useful, free to act when diplomacy and arms were not, checking each other when one exceeded its bounds.

Government requires belief, strength and honor. Our faith had wavered and waned. On the day Mehmed took our city, 300 monks converted to Islam. Most of our military had deserted years before. Mercenaries and allies would not defend a nation who refused to defend herself, no matter how well they were paid. Our royal line was failing, and my grandfather's ploy failed to consider our people and courts of other nations. A king hidden is no king. The people were left with nothing but a dream. I pray one day they will be free to fulfill it.

I thank the Lord for my ancestors who survived and possessed sufficient faith in the future to have and to raise children. I thank God for my families, natural and adopted. I thank Him for all my teachers. I thank Him for all whom I loved.

I thank Him as well for all who opposed me, for they too helped me along the road of becoming. As Aristophanes said, *A man may learn wisdom even from a foe.* Even Alítheia's father did something noble once – in helping to conceive a most precious child. Mehmed revealed God's hand for us, as Pharaoh had for Moses, and Hadad and Rezon did for Solomon. Alexander VI, vicious and worldly when he might have been a saint, was a patron of the arts and humane to Jewish refugees in their hour of need. We each have a mission on this Earth, and collectively we work God's will, despite our unbelief and our legion selfish errors.

As individuals we have a difficult time discovering where our Good ends and another's Evil begins. The *Bible* suggests it has always been this way. I certainly, then, do not envy you in having to decide where I got it wrong or where I got it right. I trust you to do His will.

I wish I had shown more love, more justice and more mercy as ever I tried to think, to say and to do what was right and true. Where I erred, may my failures be instructive to others.

As to doctrine, I trust Isaiah was right when he suggested that one day we will all understand and be forgiven:

> *They that erred in spirit shall come to understanding, and they that murmured shall learn doctrine.* Isaiah 29:24

> *I am He who blotteth out thy transgressions for mine own sake, and will not remember thy sins.* Isaiah 43:25

This concludes my confession. Serve the Lord and your nation's people. Seek Justice and Truth with might and compassion and you will succeed. As you look to God, forsake not Wisdom, for Faith without the other leads to madness and tyranny.

As for Freedom, read Polybius or Sallust. The oligarchy and the people will always take more liberty than is healthy. When they do, remind them of the importance of Virtue. Do these things and your people will never abandon you to the barbarians of sin. Farewell.

John IX Palaeologus
Son of Greece, Rome and the Great Church

Summary Of The Palaeologus Case

In Toledo, Friday, May 24th of 1504, John Palaeologus of Mystras presented me the enclosed papers as his confession so that the Tribunal of the Inquisition and Archbishop Ximenes de Cisneros could see them and be informed.

The Inquisitor delivered his customary sermon, after which we administered the oath of obedience to representatives of the civil power. We also issued a decree of excommunication against any who might impede the operations of the Holy Office.

Given the length of the prisoner's written confession, and in the interest of saving time, we asked the notary to summarize the chargeable offenses annotated in that manuscript and accompanying journal. Of each civil crime and religious misdemeanor, the accused affirmed the charge and expressed his willingness to abjure. On matters of heresy, of which there were several, he was asked whether he would repent, or lose body and soul by persevering in heresy. In each case, he claimed his opinion was orthodox and expressed his willingness to die rather than recant.

In preliminaries, the accused waived his right to eliminate witnesses, though he was aware of whence came the charges against him. At all times in his incarceration he was kept in isolation, so he could have had no exposure to our treating with his accuser. The prisoner also waived the right to counsel, preferring to write his own defense.

In light of the alleged nobility of the prisoner, he was not initially subjected to torment or forced labor. His written confession was made in the jail of the Inquisition from April 14th to the morning of May 24th. In his confession and questioning May 24th, he admitted to having been born of questionable parentage, of being baptized twice as an Orthodox, to being raised by a Bogomil and a Jewess, in associating with pagans, in having been converted and circumcised into Islam and in engaging in war against Christian forces. He further admitted to engaging in prophecy, to evading taxes, to stealing manuscripts, to selling illegal books, to committing adultery and to assisting converts to escape after the deadline of the Edict of Expulsion. He further admitted to bearing false witness in a Moslem court, to committing murders in Turkey and Italy, to believing in omens and dreams, and to having sought truth from the dead. In his confession, he also admitted to holding a number of heretical ideas that he says under no circumstance he will recant, professing their orthodoxy.

Though saving such a troubled soul was obviously beyond the capacity of this tribunal, it was our intention that he repent of these ideas drawn from other religions and ancient sects. In questioning, he either said nothing or simply repeated, "I have nothing more to add and I will not lie to make you happy." For this reason, the tribunal ordered him subjected to an ordeal by water and again questioned him, with the same result. He was subjected to the rack, again with the same result.

This single *auto da fé* began at 6 a.m. and concluded at 6 p.m. The prisoner was given the evening to reconsider his opportunity of reconciling to the Church.

The following morning, John Palaeologus was given the opportunity to recant his heresies. He refused. For the above reasons, we found the prisoner to be an adulterous murderer, a pernicious apostate, an observer of times, a protector of judaizers, and a false prophet.

We delivered him to the civil authorities as a traitor against God. The prisoner and his little book were taken to the Plaza de Zocodover for burning at the stake shortly before noon. He swore he would make no scandal; and indeed, he was good to his word throughout the proceedings.

The prisoner advanced to the stone platform without incident, aside from the usual jeering by righteous souls in the crowd. In front of the platform, we noticed the prisoner's accuser, Fray Pedro Furia. Furia was laughing and acting inappropriately for such a serious and sacred occasion. The prisoner was disrobed of his *sambenito* and all but his briefs. He took his place in front of the scaffold atop a bronze pipe for him to straddle or sit on. He was then chained by the neck to the stake and his hands and legs were left free.

The prisoner stood there with his head bowed and his hands clasped together in prayer. Over and over he repeated the words, "Father, Son,

Holy Spirit, have mercy on us." In this way he endured his punishment for about a quarter hour. Up to that time, he reacted as if he had not been touched by the flames. Suddenly, he looked up and stretched his arms to Heaven. With the greatest happiness, and tears streaming down, he was heard to say, "Alítheia! Come, my Love! My Life!"

Then the strangest thing happened. A large flame erupted out of all proportion to the wood provided. The body of the prisoner was delivered into the sky or into the ground in an instant and the scaffold was left in flames. Crumpled in front of the platform was a dead Pedro Furia clutching his chest. On the platform, where the prisoner had stood, all that remained beside the charred scaffold was his little book.

The authorities had to break up the crowd and send people home. All remarked that we had witnessed something singular, though whether it was diabolical or the very Mercy of God none could tell.

In testimony of the truth,

Fray Diego Guzman

Doctor Pedro Alameda

In agreement with the original. Forward to Rome!

Archbishop Ximenes de Cisneros

POSTSCRIPTS

We were before the foundation of the world. ^{Clement, Exhortation to the Greeks}

Cornwall, 1632

Thank the Lord for Constantine Comnenus! Before he left Rome to become Despot of the Morea for Bayezid II, he secreted John's confession from the vault of the Inquisition. He may have been helped in this by Pope Leo X (Giovanni de' Medici), godfather to his son.

For what it's worth, I suspect John received his wish for a new life with Alítheia. John IX was executed by burning during the hours of siesta on Saturday the 25th of May, 1504, in the plaza at Toledo. Earlier that year, there had been a regime change in Oran's Ziyanid dynasty. Perhaps his beloved died in that change. Perhaps she was mother of the new Sultan Muhammad VII and found herself the new Valide Sultan.

A year later, Cardinal Cisneros captured Mers el Kébir; and in 1509, as captain-general of Africa, he captured all of Oran, freeing 15,000 slaves. Perhaps he found Alítheia and related to her John's story, or perhaps she was among those freed. Her end is a family mystery. About this time, the Cardinal also reintroduced the Mozarabic Rite, the one most acceptable to Moriscos as reflecting the humanity and adoption of the Christ rather than His inherent divinity.

Three days after John was executed, in a home near the beach at Pesaro, a little boy named Theodore was born to John X and Maria. The boy's grandmother Andrea noted a great resemblance to his grandfather. Family stories say that "From the first day, he would reach out to be held; he could smile; and if we laid him on his belly, he would push himself up to look outside his basket." All his life, he was known for his deep and inexhaustible curiosity. Theodore married his childhood sweetheart, and in his 36th year, he died a very happy man.

In the next generation, I had a cousin, Jacob Palaeologus of Chios, a Dominican clergyman and theologian in Rome. He was burned as a heretic for having Protestant ideas by Pope Gregory XIII in 1585. He was not celibate and had a son named Theodore. I understand Jacob's final words were, *I am with you always* ... but then perhaps this was just coincidence.

Long live the Phoenix!

John Theodore Palaeologus

Christ is all, and in all. Colossians 3:11

London, 1923

The Wisdom of God fated the Ottomans and House Palaeologus to live and die together. The historian Doukas once said the curse of Othman began the day Michael VIII usurped the throne bringing anathemas down on our heads. Doukas said the curse would die with our last descendant in the direct line. If he was right, the Ottomans, their murders and brutalities against the righteous will end with me. Praise be to God.

My ancestor John longed for an Empire of Freedom and a New Age of Tolerance. I pray he found them, and that I might join him there soon.

To you who remain, teach your children kindness, generosity, righteousness and hope ... and to listen always for the voice of Wisdom. If you listen carefully to the children, to the aged, to all who love you and to righteous souls of any religion, you will know. God IS with you.

Johannes Palaeologus Notaras di Pesaro

The Florilegium

Mystic Adam, the Holy Family and the Image of God
Among the Samothracians: *This is ... the ineffable mystery ... that Adam is the primal man. And there stand in the temple of the Samothracians two images of naked men, having both hands stretched aloft towards Heaven, their pudenda erecta ... and the aforesaid images are figures of the primal man, and of that spiritual one that is born again.* Hippolytus, Refutation

Among the Peratae: *The astrologers delineate the center, as it were, a god and monad and lord over universal generation.* Hippolytus, Refutation

Among the Hebrews: *The voice of the Lord is upon the waters. ... With thee is the Fountain of Life; in thy light shall we see light.* Psalms 29:3 and 36:9

Among the Mandaeans: *The name of the Great Mystic First Wellspring be mentioned upon thee.* The Names, a baptismal blessing

Among the Athenians: *The Athenians, while initiating people into the Eleusinian rites display to those being admitted into the highest grade ... an ear of corn in silence reaped. But this ear of corn to them constitutes the enormous Illumination that has descended from the Unportrayable One.* Hippolytus, Refutation

A Phrygian Mystery of the Great Mother: *Whether thou art the race of Saturn, or happy Jupiter, or mighty Rhea, Hail Attis, gloomy mutilation of Rhea. Assyrians style thee thrice-longed-for Adonis, and the whole of Egypt calls thee Osiris, celestial horn of the moon; Greeks denominate thee Wisdom; Samothracians, venerable Adam; Haemonians, Corybas; and the Phrygians name thee at one time Papa, at another time Corpse, or God. ... Thou art Pan, as thou art Bacchus, as thou art the Shepherd of brilliant stars.* Hippolytus, Refutation

In the Vedas: *May I attain to and enjoy that goal of his movements, the Delight, where souls that seek the godhead have the rapture; for there in that highest step of the wide-moving Vishnu is that Friend of men who is the fount of sweetness.*
Rig Veda 1:154

Among the Naaseni: *They divide him as Geryon into three parts. For, they say, of this man one part is rational, another psychical, another earthly. And they suppose that the knowledge of Him is the first principle of the capacity for knowing God.* Hippolytus, Refutation

In the beginning God, before making the world, from the Wellspring of His eternity and from His divine and eternal Spirit, begat for Himself a Son ... He is excellent, he is reason, he is the Word of God, he is Wisdom. Lactantius, Epitome

Son of Man is the sign for the Alpha-Omega, the *image and likeness* man was to resemble, Moses' column of fire, the Tree of Life, the Burning Bush, the Precious Stone, and the Pole of the Word. In a reference presaging the *Vesica Pisces* or the Christ-in-the-Mandorla, the Mandaeans called Him *He who is within the Veil, within his own Shekhinah.*

This Great Adam consists of three elements: Horologium (legs and erection of the Father); Phoenix (torso and Spirit); and Aquarius (head and Son).

When the Phoenix is remembered as the Son, Aquarius is the vulva of the Great Mother. This sign is home of the Cosmic Cross, the Creation and the Flood. The Son of Man incarnates our once-and-future king at the Crossing of the River of Life. He is the Word.

For the Lord thy God is a consuming fire.
Deuteronomy 4:24

God of Truth

For there are three that bear record in Heaven, the Father, the Word, and the Holy Spirit; and these three are One. 1 John 5:7

His Name is called the Word of God. Rev. 19:13

If you speak often with God, you will see the Word itself — that is, God. Georgius Gemistos Plethon

There is the one, absolute Wisdom. ... This is the one God. Nicholas da Cusa, De Pace Fidei

He is the Rock, His work is perfect: for all His ways are judgment: a God of Truth and without iniquity, just and right is He. Deuteronomy 32:4

Wisdom comes from the Holy Spirit, our friend, brother and father Ahura-Mazda. Vendidad, Yasna 44:11

Supremely exalted is therefore Allah, the King, the Truth. Koran 20:114

He has created the heavens and the earth with Truth. Koran 16:3

By Truth is the Earth sustained, by the Sun the heavens ... Rig Veda 10

When he, the Spirit of Truth, is come, he will guide you into all Truth. John 16:13

The Son is Wisdom, and Knowledge, and Truth. Clement, Stromateis

God and the gods

Apollo, mystically understood in terms of the absence of plurality, is the one and only God. Finally, this fire in the likeness of a column and the fire in the tree are symbols of the holy light which crosses from Earth and runs up again to Heaven by means of the Word. Clement, Stromateis

The ancients took those for gods whom they found to move in a certain regular manner, thinking them to be the causers of the changes of the air and the conservation of the universe. Phornutus, De Natura Deorum

Avatars, Saviors and Prophets

For whenever there is a withering of the Law, and an uprising of lawlessness on all sides, then I manifest Myself. For the salvation of the righteous, and the destruction of such as do evil; for the firm establishing of the Law I come to birth in age after age. Bhagavad Gita 4

The victory created by Ahura-Mazda we praise. Saoshyant, the victor, we praise. Vendidad, Yasna 58:3

He shall deliver the needy and the poor. ... He shall redeem their souls from deceit and violence, and precious shall be their blood in his sight. Psalm 72:11-14

I have made thee (Moses) a god to Pharaoh; and Aaron, thy brother, shall be thy prophet. Exodus 7:1

I have exalted one chosen out of the people. I have found David, my servant; with my holy oil have I anointed him. With whom my hand shall be established; mine arm also shall strengthen him. ... I will beat down his foes before his face. ... My faithfulness and my mercy shall be with him. Psalm 89:19-24

Hail, great physician of the world, all-hail; hail mighty infant, who in years to come shalt heal the nations, and defraud the tomb. Swift be thy growth! Thy triumphs unconfin'd! Make kingdoms thicker, and increase mankind. Thy daring art shall animate the dead, and draw the thunder on thy guilty head. Then shalt thou die, but from the dark abode, rise up victorious, and be twice a God. ^{Ovid, Metamorphoses Bk II}

The Lord thy God will raise up unto thee a Prophet from the midst of thee, of thy brethren, like unto me; unto him ye shall hearken. ... I will raise them up a Prophet from among their brethren, like unto thee, and will put my words in his mouth, and he shall speak unto them all that I shall command him. ^{Deut. 18:15-18}

According to al-Biruni, in his *Chronology*, the above passage was a prophecy regarding Muhammad.

We inspire thee (Muhammad) as We inspired Noah and the prophets after him, as We inspired Abraham and Ishmael and Isaac and Jacob and the tribes, and Jesus and Job and Jonah and Aaron and Solomon, and as we imparted unto David the Psalms. ^{Koran 4:163}

Behold, I send My messenger, and he will prepare the way before Me. And the Lord, whom you seek, will suddenly come to His temple, even the Messenger of the covenant, in whom you delight. Behold, He is coming," says the LORD of hosts.
Malachi 3:1

The Word

Now the Word issuing forth was the cause of Creation. ^{Clement, Stromateis}

Harih Aum! AUM, the Word, is all this, the whole universe. A clear explanation of it is as follows: All that is past, present and future is, indeed, AUM. And whatever else there is, beyond the threefold division of time – that also is truly AUM. ^{Mandukya Upanishad}

I AM. ^{Exodus 3:14}

A party from among them indeed used to hear the Word of Allah, then altered it after they had understood it, and they know this. ^{Koran 2:75}

Of this libation of mine thou shalt drink, thou who art a Guardian of the Sacred Fire, who hast asked and learnt the revealed law, who art wise, clever, and the Word incarnate. ^{Khorda Avesta 91}

The world discerned only by the intellect is nothing else than the Word of God engaged in the act of Creation. ... Man ... was molded after the image of God. Now, if the part is an image of an image, it is manifest that the whole is so too; and if the whole creation, this entire world perceived by our senses ... is a copy of the

Divine image, it is manifest that the Archetypal Seal also, which we aver to be the world descried by the mind, would be the very Word of God. [Philo, On the Creation 24-25]

The burden of the Word of the LORD for Israel, saith the LORD, which stretcheth forth the heavens, and layeth the foundation of the earth, and formeth the spirit of man within him. [Zechariah 12:1]

Alpha-Omega, the moment of regeneration

The Word is called the Alpha and the Omega. [Clement, Stromateis]

The foundations of the earth are out of course. [Psalm 82:5]

There was once an eclipse of the Sun that remained a whole month when it extinguished; and a New Sun was created to rise in the East. [Xenophanes]

And afterwards, he (the evil spirit) came to fire, and he mingled smoke and darkness with it. The planets, with many demons, dashed against the celestial sphere, and they mixed the constellations; and the whole Creation was as disfigured as though fire disfigured every place and smoke arose over it. And 90 days and nights the heavenly angels were contending in the world with the confederate demons of the evil spirit, and hurled them confounded to hell; and the rampart of the sky was formed so that the adversary should not be able to mingle with it. [Bundahishn 3:24-26]

Hell is in the middle of the Earth; there where the evil spirit pierced the Earth and rushed in upon it. [Bundahishn 3:27]

When the primeval Bull passed away it fell to the right hand, and the Great Adam afterwards, when he passed away, fell to the left. [Bundahishn 4:1]

The sun shall be darkened, and the moon shall not give her light, and the stars shall fall from Heaven. [Matthew 24:29]

Great earthquakes shall be in diverse places, and famines, and pestilences; and fearful sights and great signs shall there be from Heaven. [Luke 21:11]

The Lord maketh the earth empty, and maketh it waste, and turneth it upside down, and scattereth abroad the inhabitants thereof. [Isaiah 24:1]

The earth shall reel to and fro like a drunkard. [Isaiah 24:20]

This sign shalt thou have of the LORD, that the LORD will do the thing that he hath spoken: shall the shadow go forward ten degrees, or go back ten degrees? Hezekiah answered, It is a light thing for the shadow to go down ten degrees: nay, but let the shadow return backward ten degrees. [2 Kings 20: 9-10]

In that day, the Lord with his hard and great and strong sword shall punish Leviathan, the piercing serpent, even Leviathan, that crooked serpent; and He shall slay the Dragon that is in the sea. Isaiah 27:1

I am Alpha and Omega, the beginning and the ending, saith the Lord, which is, and which was, and which is to come, the Almighty. Revelation 1:8

I AM HE; I AM THE FIRST, I AM THE LAST. My left hand has laid the Foundation of the earth, and my right hand has spanned the heavens. When I call unto them, they will stand up together. Isaiah 48:13

There have been, and will be again, many destructions of mankind arising out of many causes; the greatest have been brought about by the agencies of fire and water.
Plato, Timaeus

When ... the gods purge the Earth with a deluge of water, the survivors ... are herdsmen and shepherds who dwell on the mountains, but those who ... live in cities are carried away by the rivers into the sea. Plato, Timmaeus

There is no old opinion handed down among you by ancient tradition, nor any science which is hoary with age. ... The stream from Heaven, like a pestilence, comes pouring down, and leaves only those of you who are destitute of letters and education; and so you have to begin all over again like children. Plato, Timmaeus

There really did happen, and will happen again, like many other events of which ancient tradition has preserved the record, the portent ... which tells how the Sun and stars once rose in the west, and set in the east, and that God reversed their motion. ... The reversal which takes place from time to time of the motion of the universe ... we may consider to be the greatest and most complete. Plato, Statesman

There is a very ancient tradition in the form of a myth, that the stars are gods and that the divine embraces the whole of nature. ... If we strip the original doctrine of its later accretions and consider it alone ... it teaches that the prime substances are gods, and is a relic of that perfect flowering of the arts and sciences which must have been often achieved and often lost. It is, so to speak, the surviving relic of an ancient treasure, allowing us a fleeting glimpse of what our early ancestors thought. Aristotle, Metaphysics XII:8

Only the Righteous Survive

The Word of the Lord came again to me, saying, son of man, when the land sinneth against me by trespassing grievously, then will I stretch out mine hand upon it, and will break the staff of the bread thereof, and will send famine upon it, and will cut off man and beast from it: Though these three men, Noah, Daniel, and Job, were in it, they should deliver but their own souls by their righteousness, saith the Lord God.

... Or if I send a pestilence into that land, and pour out my fury upon it in blood, to cut off from it man and beast: Though Noah, Daniel, and Job were in it, as I live, saith the Lord God, they shall deliver neither son nor daughter; they shall but deliver their own souls by their righteousness. Ezekiel 14:12-20

Righteousness

The divinity has no place on Earth more allied to his nature than a pure and holy soul. Pythagoric Sentences of Demophilus

Righteousness is this, that one should believe in Allah and the last day and the angels and the Book and the prophets, and give away wealth out of love for Him to the near of kin and the orphans and the needy and the wayfarer and the beggars and for the emancipation of the captives, and keep up prayer and pay the poor-rate; and the performers of their promise when they make a promise, and the patient in distress and affliction and in time of conflicts ... these are they who guard against evil. ... By no means shall you attain to righteousness until you spend benevolently out of what you love. Koran 2:177 & 3:92

The Word of God speaks, having become man, in order that such as you may learn from man how it is even possible for man to become a god. Clement, Exhortation to the Greeks

True sacrifice is fetched not from a box but from the heart, and such sacrifice is made not by the hand but the mind. ... Sacrificed victims, sweet odours, silver and gold, precious jewels – what value have these, if the worshipper's mind is impure? Righteousness alone is what God seeks after. It is there that sacrifice and the true worship of God are to be found. Lactantius, Epitome Chap. 58

One came and said unto him, Good Master, what good thing shall I do, that I may have eternal life? And he said unto him, Why callest thou me good? There is none good but one, that is, God: but if thou wilt enter into life, keep the commandments. Matthew 19:16-17

One Great Family

Philosophers call form "a man" and matter "a woman," since whatever is in act is generated from preexisting matter and an active form as from the union of a male and a female. ... The emission of form into matter by God ... is just like the emission of understanding from its own Essence to the thing understood. Dominicus Gundissalinus, Procession of the World

And all things that exist derive their share of being from Him who truly exists, who said through Moses, "I am that I am"; which participation in God the Father extends to all, both righteous and sinners, rational and irrational creatures and absolutely everything that exists. Origen, First Principles Chap. III

One, self-begotten, lives; all things proceed From One; and in His works He ever moves: No mortal sees Him, yet Himself sees all. Eusebius quoting Orpheus, Exhortation to the Greeks

All animated beings are kin, Pythagoras taught – and should be considered as belonging to one great family. Clement, Stromateis

The Boeotian Pindar, being a Pythagorean, says: "One is the race of gods and men, and of one mother both have breath." That is, of matter, and names the one creator of these things, whom he calls Father, chief artificer, who furnishes the means of advancement on to Divinity, according to merit. Clement, Stromateis

For if we have been created by one God, and sprung from one man, and are linked together by the law of blood-kinship, we ought, in consequence, to love all mankind. Lactantius, Epitome

One righteous man, then, differs not, as righteous, from another righteous man, whether he be of the Law or a Greek. For God is not only Lord of the Jews, but of all men. Clement, Stromateis

Children of God

Only the God-fearing man is … the image, together with the likeness, of God. So the prophet openly reveals this gracious favour when he says, "I said, ye are gods, and ye are all sons of the Most High." Now we, I say, we are they whom God has adopted. Clement, Exhortation to the Greeks

We must accept the traditions of the men of old time who affirm themselves to be the offspring of the gods. Plato, Timaeus

The hierarch, who "desires all men to be saved and to come to the knowledge of truth" by taking on a likeness to God, proclaims the good news to all that God out of his own natural goodness is merciful to the inhabitants of earth, that because of his love for humanity he has deigned to come down to us and that, like a fire, he has made one with himself all those capable of being divinized. Dionysius the Areopagite, Ecclesiastical Hierarchy

For as many as are led by the Spirit of God, these are children of God. For you didn't receive the spirit of bondage again to fear, but you received the Spirit of adoption, by whom we cry, "Abba! Father!" The Spirit himself testifies with our spirit that we are children of God; and if children, then heirs; heirs of God, and joint heirs with Christ; if indeed we suffer with him, that we may also be glorified with him. … For the Creation waits with eager expectation for the children of God to be revealed. Romans 8:14-19

Be Ye Perfect

I am the Almighty God; walk before me, and be thou perfect. ^{Genesis 17:1}

Plato says there are four virtues – prudence, temperance, justice, and fortitude. ... These virtues, when inherent in a man, render him perfect, and afford him happiness. And happiness ... is assimilation to the Deity. ^{Hippolytus, Refutation I Chap. 16}

Be ye therefore perfect, even as your Father which is in Heaven is perfect. ^{Matthew 5:48}

A man's one task is to strive towards making himself perfect. ^{Plotinus, Second Ennead}

Purification

The heavens rain oil, the wadies run with honey. And I know that Aliyn Baal is alive, that the Prince, Lord of Earth, exists. ^{Ugaritic poem}

With thee is the fountain of life. ^{Psalm 36:9}

They have forsaken the Lord, the Mikvah of living water. ^{Jeremiah 17:13}

Impure indeed is man. He is foul within, in that he lies ... and water is pure.
Sata patha Brahmana III

A spring or mikvah in which there is plenty of water, shall be clean. ^{Leviticus 11:36}

Unless one is born of water and the Spirit, he cannot enter the kingdom of God.
John 3:5

(Baptism) shall be a forgiver of sins for them and theirs, and for our fathers and teachers, and for our brothers and sisters who have departed the body and for those living in the body. ^{The Scroll of the Baptism of Hibil Ziwa}

Allah's Messenger ... poured water with his right hand on his left hand and washed himself. He performed wudu as is done for prayer. He then took some water and ran his fingers in the roots of his hair. And when He found that it had been properly moistened, He poured three handfuls on his head and poured water over His body and subsequently washed his feet. ^{Aisha, youngest wife of Muhammad}

Suffering

Excessive desire begets suffering. The suffering of birth and death as well as the leading of a weary life are all caused by greed. ^{Enlightenment Sutra}

Misery ceases on the absence of delusion; delusion ceases on the absence of desire; desire ceases on the absence of greed; greed ceases on the absence of property. ^{Gaina Sutra}

Poverty and the Way

The young man saith unto him, "All these commandments have I kept from my youth up: what lack I yet?" Jesus said unto him, "If thou wilt be perfect, go and sell that thou hast, and give to the poor, and thou shalt have treasure in Heaven: and come and follow me." Matthew 19:20-21

Pray

And above all this pray to the Most High, that he will direct thy way in Truth. Sirach 37:15

When you pray, enter into your inner chamber, and having shut your door, pray to your Father who is in secret, and your Father who sees in secret will reward you openly. Matthew 6:6

Celebrate the praise of your Lord and ask His forgiveness; surely He is oft-returning to mercy. Koran 110:3

Prayer is an ascent of the spirit to God. Evagrius Ponticus, On Prayer

Repent

Surely after that I was turned, I repented; and after that I was instructed, I smote upon my thigh: I was ashamed, yea, even confounded, because I did bear the reproach of my youth. Jeremiah 31:19

The final cure is to betake ourselves to repentance — not the least of the virtues, because it involves self-correction, to the end that, when we happen to slip in word or deed, we may without delay return to our truer selves and confess our fault, praying God for forgiveness, which He will not refuse unless we persist in our transgression. ... Nobody can be so just as never to need repentance. Lactantius, Epitome Chap. 67

One who repents experiences a kind of rebirth through changed behavior and has a renewal of life. Clement, Stromateis

Repent, for the kingdom of Heaven is at hand. Matthew 3:2

Return

That day, which you fear as being the end of all things, is the birthday of your eternity. Seneca, Epistle 102

This philosopher, Pythagoras, said that the soul is immortal, and that it subsists in successive bodies. Wherefore he asserted that before the Trojan era he was Aethalides, and during the Trojan epoch Euphorbus, and subsequent to this Hermotimus of Samos, and after him Pyrrhus of Delos; fifth Pythagoras. Hippolytus, Refutation V Chap. 2

The spirit of Elijah doth rest on Elisha. And they came to meet him, and bowed themselves to the ground before him. 2 Kings 1:15

How do you deny Allah and you were dead and He gave you life? Again He will cause you to die and again bring you to life, then you shall be brought back to Him. Koran 2:28

Allah caused him to die for a hundred years, then raised him to life. Koran 2:259

The Wise is one, knowing the plan by which it steers all things through all. Heraclitus

But concerning the resurrection of the dead, have you not read what was spoken to you by God, saying, 'I am the God of Abraham, the God of Isaac, and the God of Jacob'? God is not the God of the dead, but of the living. Matthew 21:31-32

Pythagoras held that all beings were interrelated, and that there was a system of exchange between souls which transmigrated from one bodily shape into another. If one may believe him, no soul perishes or ceases from its functions at all, except for a tiny interval – when it is being poured from one body into another. Seneca, Epistle 108

For already have I once been a boy and a girl, a fish and a bird and a dumb sea fish. Empedocles 117

The soul has neither beginning nor end ... coming into this world strengthened by the victories or weakened by the defeats of previous lives. Origen, First Principles

Wisdom

Wisdom ... is more beautiful than the Sun, and excels every constellation of the stars. Compared with the light she is found to be superior, for it is succeeded by the night, but against Wisdom evil does not prevail. Wisdom of Solomon 7:21-30

Wisdom was created before all things, and prudent understanding from eternity. ... The Lord himself created Wisdom; He saw Her and apportioned Her, He poured Her out upon all His works. She dwells with all flesh according to His gift, and he supplied Her to those who love Him. Sirach 1:4-10

Accept Wisdom, even if it is found in the languages of the Polytheists. Muhammad

For nothing is secret, that shall not be made manifest; neither any thing hidden, that shall not be known and come to light. Luke 8:17

The Limit of Mankind's Memory

The priests of the Egyptians, reckoning the time from the reign of Helius to the crossing of Alexander into Asia (334 BC), say that it was in round numbers twenty-three thousand years. Diodorus Siculus, First Book of History

The Egyptians and their priests declare that from their first king to this last-mentioned monarch ... was a period of three hundred and forty-one generations ... in

which entire space, they said, no god had ever appeared in human form. ... However, in the times anterior to them it was otherwise; then Egypt had gods for its rulers, who dwelt upon the earth with men, one being always supreme above the rest. The last one of these was Horus, the son of Osiris, called by the Greeks Apollo. ... Osiris is named Dionysius (Bacchus) by the Greeks. ... Apollo and Diana are the children of Bacchus and Isis. ^{Herodotus, The History Bk II}

One God

No race anywhere of tillers of the soil, or nomads, and not even of dwellers in cities, can live, without being imbued with the faith of a superior being. ^{Clement, Stromateis}

The Son sees the goodness of the Father, God the Saviour works, being called the first principle of all things, which was imaged forth from the invisible God first ... as also Empedocles says: "But come now, first will I speak of the Sun, the first principle of all things." ^{Clement, Stromateis}

Both poets and philosophers testify to one God. Orpheus speaks of a principal God, creator of Heaven and Earth, of sun and stars, of land and sea. Moreover our poet Virgil calls the supreme God now spirit, now mind, declaring that mind, as though poured into limbs, sets in movement the body of the whole world; that God passes over seas and lands and through the depths of Heaven, and from Him all creatures derive their life. Even Ovid knew that the world was made by God, whom he calls now the framer, now the architect, of all things. ^{Lactantius, Epitome Chap. 3}

Good and Evil

Just as courage, if you be fighting for your fatherland, is a good thing, if against it, an evil thing; so too the passions, if put to a good purpose, will be virtues; if to bad uses, they will be termed vices. Anger has been given us for the checking of offenses. ... A desire for gain has been granted, that we may seek earnestly for life's necessities. ... Lust itself is inborn that we may beget children; but those that overpass its limitations employ it for mere pleasure alone. ... The passions need to be controlled and directed aright; then, even when men are ardent, they cannot be charged with guilt. ^{Lactantius, Epitome Chap. 61}

What is the Highest Good that all our lives and acts may be directed to that. ... Aristippus placed the Highest Good in bodily pleasure ... Hieronymus ... in the absence of pain. Diodorus in the cessation of it. Zeno ... 'to live in harmony with nature.' Epicurus ... pleasure of the mind. The Peripatetics ... good things of mind, body, and fortune. The Stoics ... virtue. Erillus ... Knowledge. ... In all which doctrines ... they go astray from reason because they know not God. That alone is blessed, which is incorruptible; that alone is incorruptible, which is eternal.

Immortality, therefore, is the highest good. ... Towards this we direct our steps; to win this we are born. As a consequence, God sets before us virtue and justice, that we may secure that eternal prize as the crown of our labors. ^{Lactantius, Epitome Chap. 33}

Immortality

The Milky Way girdles the zodiac, its great circle meeting it obliquely so that it crosses the two tropical signs, Capricorn and Cancer. Natural philosophers named these the "portals of the Sun" ... Cancer, the portal of men, because through it descent is made to the infernal regions; Capricorn, the portal of gods, because through it souls return to their rightful abode of immortality, to be reckoned among the gods ... the soul descending from the place where the zodiac and the Milky Way intersect.
Macrobius, Commentary on the Dream of Scipio

An infant Phoenix from the former springs,
His father's heir, and from his tender wings
Shakes off his parent dust, his method he pursues,
And the same lease of life on the same terms renews.
When grown to manhood he begins his reign,
And with stiff pinions can his flight sustain,
He lightens of its load the tree that bore
His father's royal sepulcher before,
And his own cradle: this (with pious care
Plac'd on his back) he cuts the buxome air,
Seeks the Sun's city, and his sacred church. ^{Ovid}

Zoroaster, Plato says, having been placed on the funeral pyre, rose again to life in twelve days. He alludes perchance to the resurrection, or perchance to the fact that the path for souls to ascension lies through the twelve signs of the zodiac. ... In the same way we are to understand the twelve labours of Hercules, after which the soul obtains release from this entire world. ^{Clement, Stromateis}

The hero justly fix'd among the stars,
Yet is his progeny his greatest fame:
The son immortal makes the father's name. ...
Mean-time, your hero's fleeting spirit bear,
Fresh from his wounds, and change it to a star:
So shall great Julius rites divine assume,
And from the skies eternal smile on Rome.
This spoke, the Goddess to the senate flew;
Where, her fair form conceal'd from mortal view,
Her Caesar's heav'nly part she made her care,

Nor left the recent soul to waste to air;
But bore it upwards to its native skies:
Glowing with new-born fires she saw it rise;
Forth springing from her bosom up it flew,
And kindling, as it soar'd a comet grew. ^{Ovid}

He who has been earnest in the love of knowledge and true wisdom, and has been trained to think that these are the immortal and divine things of a man, if he attain Truth, must of necessity, as far as human nature is capable of attaining immortality, be all immortal, as he is ever serving the divine power; and having the genius residing in him in the most perfect order; he must be preeminently happy. ^{Plato, Timacus}

For mortal to aid mortal – this is God; and this is the road to eternal glory: by this road went our Roman chieftains. ^{Pliny, Natural History Bk II}

Now if souls were to bring with them to their bodies a memory of the divine order of which they were conscious in the sky, there would be no disagreement among men in regard to divinity; but, indeed, all of them in their descent drink of forgetfulness, some more, some less. ... Truth is more accessible to those who drank less of forgetfulness because they more easily recall what they previously knew above. That is why in Greek the word for reading (Anagnosis) *means "knowledge regained."*
Macrobius, Commentary on the Dream of Scipio

With regard to the Druids ... the main object of all education is ... to imbue their scholars with a firm belief in the indestructibility of the soul, which, according to their belief, merely passes at death from one body to another. This doctrine alone robs death of all its terrors, and enables the highest form of human courage to develop.
Julius Cesar, De Bello Gallico

Let virtue alone comfort us, the wages of which is immortality when it has overcome pleasure. Once the passions are quelled, there is no difficulty in mastering other faults, at least for one who is a follower of God and Truth. ^{Lactantius, Epitome Chap. 64}

God created man for immortality ... he who is a Gnostic, and righteous, and holy with prudence, hastes to reach the measure of perfect manhood. ^{Clement, Stromateis}

The soul takes another life as it approaches God ... a self wrought to splendor, brimmed with the Intellectual light, become that very light ... raised to Godhood or, better, knowing its Godhood, all aflame then. ... The man formed by this mingling with the Supreme must – if he only remember – carry its image impressed upon him: he is become the Unity. ... The self thus lifted, we are in the likeness of the Supreme: if ... we pass still higher – Image to Archetype – we have won the Term of all our journeying. ^{Plotinus, Sixth Ennead}

For noble souls, their light unaffected by the vagaries of fortune, have a kingly something that urges them to contend on equal footing with persons of the most massive dignity, pitting the Freedom of Speech against arrogance. ^{Philo, Every Good Man is Free}

Every good man is free. ... He who adjusts himself and his to fit the present occasion and willingly and also patiently endures the blows of fortune ... he indeed needs no more to make him a philosopher and a free man. ... No one can compel him, since he has come to despise both pain and death, and by the law of nature has all fools in subjection. ... There are others born in slavery, who by a happy dispensation of fortune pursue the occupations of the free. They receive the stewardship of houses and landed estates and great properties; sometimes too they become the rulers of their fellow slaves. ^{Philo, Every Good Man is Free}

In Greece there flourished the sages ... in the outside world where are those who spread the message by words and deeds, we find large associations of men of the highest excellence. Among the Persians there is the order of the Magi. ... In India, too, there is the order of the Brahman. ... Among the Jews, the Essenes are known for their holiness. ... Such are the athletes of virtue ... by whom the Liberty which can never be enslaved is firmly established. ^{Philo, Every Good Man is Free}

The one salvation of the soul ... which liberates her from the wheel of life ... is her return to intellectual form and a flight from every thing which naturally adheres to us from generation. ... Of her horses, one is good and the other contrary. One of these leads her to generation, but the other from generation to true Being. ... The soul being winged governs the whole world, becoming assimilated to the Gods themselves. ^{Proclus, Commentary on the Timaeus 330A}

Ancient Christianity

O My Soul, the time I trust will be, when thou shalt be good, simple, single, more open and visible, than that body by which it is enclosed. ... Thou shalt one day be full, and in want of no external thing: not seeking pleasure from anything, either living or insensible, that this world can afford; neither wanting time for the continuation of thy pleasure, nor place and opportunity, nor the favor either of the weather or of men. When thou shalt persuade thyself, that thou hast all things; all for thy good, and all by the providence of the Gods: and of things future also shalt be as confident, that all will do well, as tending to the maintenance and preservation in some sort, of His perfect welfare and happiness, who is perfection of life, of goodness, and Beauty; who begets all things, and containeth all things in Himself, and in Himself doth recollect all things from all places that are dissolved, that of them He may beget others again like unto them. ^{Aurelius, Meditations Bk X}

The last great Age, foretold by sacred Rhymes,
Renews its finish'd Course, Saturnian times
Rowl round again, and mighty Years, begun
From their first Orb, in radiant Circles run.
The base degenerate Iron-off-spring ends;
A golden Progeny from Heav'n descends;
O chast Lucina speed the Mother's pains,
And haste the glorious Birth; thy own Apollo reigns!
... The jarring Nations He in peace shall bind,
And with paternal Virtues rule Mankind.
Virgil, Pastoral IV

Have Heaven for your homeland and live there constantly – not in mere word but in actions that imitate the angels and in a more god-like knowledge. Evagrius Ponticus

Happy is the monk who considers all men as god – after God. Evagrius Ponticus

The lovers of Truth have abandoned the passion for material goods. ... They love peace and holiness. In this life they look forward to the coming life. Free of all passion they live like angels among men. They praise the divine name ceaselessly. They practice goodness and every other virtue. Dionysius the Areopagite, Letters

The Son is Wisdom, and Knowledge, and Truth ... He is the circle of all powers rolled and united into one unity. Wherefore the Word is called the Alpha and the Omega, of whom alone the end becomes beginning, and ends again at the original beginning without any break. Clement, Stromateis

Plato, all but predicting the economy of salvation, says in the second book of the Republic as follows: "Thus he who is constituted just shall be scourged, shall be stretched on the rack, shall be bound, have his eyes put out; and at last, having suffered all evils, shall be crucified." Clement, Stromateis

To restrain one's self from doing good is the work of vice; but to keep from wrong is the beginning of salvation. Clement, Stromateis

He who obeys the mere call, as he is called, neither for fear, nor for enjoyments, is on his way to Knowledge. Clement, Stromateis

Christ becomes present in each individual in such a degree as is warranted by the extent of his merits. Origen, First Principles, Bk IV

It is when a person freely rises to the knowledge of the Truth by a process of self-discipline and learning that God calls him to the position of son, and that is the greatest progress of all. ^{Clement, Stromateis}

"God has taken his place in the council of the gods, in their midst he will hold judgment over the gods." Who are these gods? Those who have mastered pleasure, those who keep themselves aloof from their passions, those who understand all their actions; Christian self-discipline is God's greatest gift. ^{Clement, Stromateis}

It was not by virtue of being God that he did divine things, not by virtue of being man that he did what was human, but rather, by the fact of being God-made-man he accomplished something new in our midst — the activity of the God-man. ^{Dionysius the Areopagite, Letters}

Notices that Atlantis Would Be Found

The sun and moon and the other stars do not rise and set at the same time for every observer on the earth, but always earlier for those living toward the orient and later for those living toward the occident. For we find that the phenomena of eclipses taking place at the same time, especially those of the moon, are not recorded at the same hours for everyone — that is, relatively to equal intervals of time from noon; but we always find later hours recorded for observers towards the orient than for those towards the occident. And since the differences in the hours is found to be proportional to the distances between the places, one would reasonably suppose the surface of the earth spherical, with the result that the general uniformity of curvature would assure every part's covering those following it proportionally. ^{Ptolemy, Almagest}

An Egyptian priest said to Solon: *In those days the Atlantic was navigable; and there was an island situated in front of the straits which are by you called the Pillars of Heracles, an island larger than Libya and Asia put together, and was the way to other islands, and from these you might pass to the whole of the opposite continent which surrounded the true ocean; for this sea within the Straits of Heracles is only a harbor, having a narrow entrance, but that other is a real sea, and the surrounding land may be the most truly called a boundless continent.* ^{Plato, Timaeus}

The world and this ... sky whose vaulted roof encircles the universe, is fitly believed to be a deity, eternal, immeasurable, a Being that never began to exist and never will perish. ... Its shape has the rounded appearance of a perfect sphere. ... The firmament presents the aspect of a concave hemisphere ... which would be impossible in the case of any other figure. The world thus shaped then is not at rest but eternally revolves with indescribable velocity, each revolution occupying the space of 24 hours; the rising and setting of the sun have left this not doubtful. ... To us who live within it the world glides silently alike by day and night. Stamped upon it are countless figures of animals and objects of all kinds ... in one place the figure of a bear, in another of a bull, in another a wagon, in another a letter of the alphabet, the middle of the circle across the Pole being more radiant. ^{Pliny, Natural History, Bk II}

The inhabited world ... forms a complete circle, itself meeting itself; so that, if the immensity of the Atlantic Sea did not prevent it, we could sail from Iberia to India along one and the same parallel. ^{Strabo quoting Eratothenes}

Find the Isle of Purgatory
Now had the sun to that horizon reach'd [It was dawn in Atlantis ...]
That covers, with the most exalted point [when noon the zenith ...]
Of its meridian circle, Salem's walls [resided at Jerusalem.]
And night, that opposite to him her orb [Midnight reigned over the Underworld.]
Rounds, from the stream of the Ganges issued forth, [And if you follow the Tropic of Cancer, the solstitial Sun ...]
Holding the scales, that from her hands are dropt [in the time it takes Libra to fall from the North ...]
When she reigns highest: [starting June 21st,]
so that where I was, Aurora's white and vermeil-tinctured cheek [to Atlantis]
To orange turn'd as she in age increased. [voyage can be made by the equinox.]
Dante, Purgatorio Canto II

I have made the said reckoning of stadia from India to Iberia, is less than two hundred thousand stadia. ^{Strabo quoting Eratothenes}

In a long day (summer to fall) a vessel generally accomplishes about seventy thousand fathoms, in the night sixty thousand. ... [Crossing the Black Sea] ... where the Pontus is wider than at any other place, is a sail of three days and two nights; which makes three hundred and thirty thousand fathoms, or three thousand three hundred stadia. ^{Herodotus, The History, Book IV}

If 100 fathoms = 1 stadia; and 24 hours sailing = 130,000 fathoms or 1,300 stadia ... and if India to Iberia is 200,000 stadia ... then the transit from India to Iberia is less than 154 days sailing and the Isle of Purgatory (Atlantis) can be reached in between 74 and 90 days!

The Great Center
Such things taught Pythagoras, though advising above all things to speak the Truth, for this alone deifies men. For as he had learned from the Magi, who call God Ahura Mazda, God's body is like Light, and His Soul is like Truth. ^{Porphyry}

This divine and wholly beautiful universe, from the highest vault of Heaven to the lowest limit of the Earth ... is guarded by the king of the whole universe, who is the center of all things that exist. ... Helios the most mighty god ... The planets dance about him as their king. ... He is established as king among the intellectual gods, from his middle station among the planets. ^{Julian, Hymn to King Helios}

God granted the ancients a longer time of life on account of their virtue, and the good use they made of it in astronomical and geometrical discoveries, which would not have afforded the time of foretelling the period of the stars unless they had lived 600 years, for the Neros year is completed in that interval. ^{Josephus, Antiquities I:3.9}

He is glorious and preeminent, all-seeing and even all-hearing – this I observe that Homer ... held to be true in the case of the Sun alone. ^{Pliny, Natural History, Bk II}

They have another sacred bird called the Phoenix, which I myself have never seen, except in pictures. Indeed it is a great rarity, even in Egypt, only coming there ... once in five hundred years, when the old Phoenix dies. ^{Herodotus, The History, Bk II}

But you, fair Nymphs, as the daughters verily
Of mighty Jove and of Nature divine,
The Phoenix's years tenfold do multiply. ^{Plutarch quoting Hesiod}

Helios is, as we know, the father of the seasons. ... Now besides those whom I have mentioned, there is in the heavens a great multitude of gods who have been recognized as such by those who survey the heavens. ... And it is Dionysius who is the giver of the Graces ... is said to reign with Helios. Why should I go on to speak to you of Horus and of the other names of gods, which all belong to Helios? ... The ancients also thought that Athene Pronoia shared the throne of Apollo, who, as we believe, differs in no way from Helios. Indeed, did not Homer by divine inspiration – for he was, we may suppose, possessed by a god – reveal this Truth? ^{Julian, Hymn to King Helios}

They say that the seat of the oracle is a cave that is hollowed out deep down in the Earth, with a rather narrow mouth, from which arises breath that inspires a divine frenzy. ... Now although the greatest share of honor was paid to this temple because of its oracle, since of all oracles in the world it had the repute of being the most truthful, yet the position of the place added something. For it is almost in the center of Greece taken as a whole, between the country inside the Isthmus and that outside it; and it was also believed to be in the center of the inhabited world, and people called it the Navel of the Earth. ^{Strabo, Geography Bk IX}

To Make a Knight
Nobility of manners and good upbringing are necessary if nobility of a virtuous heart is to be recognized. Every knight must know the seven virtues. ... Faith will teach you hope; love loyalty and service to the Truth – defend Her unto death. Hope will

give you strength and courage, and will sustain you through danger and hardships. Love unites virtue with virtue, and will lighten the burdens of your great responsibility. Justice is the foundation of a knight – without it, he is a knight no longer. Prudence teaches us to recognize good and evil – to love the one and fight the other. Strength is the virtue in your heart that defeats the seven deadly sins. Temperance takes the middle way between too much and too little – audacity, eating, drinking and spending. Fear God ... and pray for the glory eternal. Maintain your arms, your discipline, your art. Keep always your discretion and use of reason. Promote always the common good. ... Knighthood is not in your horse or your weapons – Discipline is what makes you a man and not an animal. Ramon Llull, La Orden de la Caballeria

Use the occasion of a holy day to induct a knight. ... Let the applicant fast and stand watch the night before. ... Let the knight learn the articles, commandments and sacraments that he may obey, be saved, and know the obligations of a knight. Let him pray to God for grace and the blessing to be able to serve Him all his life. Let the noble who would knight the candidate have all the virtues of a good knight. Let the candidate not be knighted merely to add numbers to the order, but for his merit and virtues. Let the candidate kneel at the altar with his eyes and hands lifted up to God. Put on him a sword. ... Kiss him and strike him, that he may remember his word, his responsibility, and his honor. Show him off a knight that day to as many as possible, that they may hold him to the standard of his order. Let the lord who knighted him show generosity to all that day, that the knight will learn to be generous. Ramon Llull, La Orden de la Caballeria

Know This
Never were so many cities captured and depopulated ... and after their capture repeopled by strangers. ... All these calamities fell upon Hellas simultaneously with the war. ... The real though unavowed cause I believe to have been the growth of Athenian power, which terrified the Lacedaemonians and forced them into war. Thucydides, Peloponnesian War Bk I

It is likely that everyone normally possesses the natural virtues from which, when Wisdom steps in, the perfected virtue develops. After the natural virtues, then, Wisdom and, so the perfecting of the moral nature. Plotinus, First Ennead

With time and hard work, and with adequate help, the Truth will shine out. Clement, Stromateis

There are two paths of reaching the perfection of salvation – works and knowledge. Clement, Stromateis

Men and Beasts the Breath of Life obtain;
And Birds of Air, and Monsters of the Main.
Th' Etherial Vigour is in all the same,
And ev'ry Soul is fill'd with equal Flame: Virgil, Aeneis Bk VI

Whole Droves of Minds are, by the driving God,
Compell'd to drink the deep Lethaean Flood:
In large forgetful draughts to steep the Cares
Of their past Labours, and their Irksome Years.
That, unrememb'ring of its former Pain,
The Soul may suffer mortal Flesh again. Virgil, Aeneis Bk VI

The happy man has good inclinations of the soul, good desires, and good actions.
Aurelius, Meditations Bk V

The ambitious supposes another's act, praise or applause to be his own happiness; the hedonist his own pleasure; but he that is wise, his own action. Aurelius, Meditations Bk VI

To look back upon things of former ages ... we may also foresee things future, for they shall all be of the same kind; neither is it possible that they should leave the tune, or break the concert that is now begun, as it were, by these things that are now done and brought to pass in the world. It comes all to one therefore, whether a man be a spectator of the things of this life but forty years, or whether he see them ten thousand years together: for what shall he see more? Aurelius, Meditations Bk VII

Apparently, Aurelius saw two ages of the gods repeating in 10,000 years.

Infinite are the troubles and miseries you suffered for one sole reason: though you were happy, you wanted more. Aurelius, Meditations Bk IX

Concerning the gods, there are some who say the Divine does not exist, others that it exists but is inactive and indifferent and takes no thought for anything, others again that God does exist and takes thought but only for great things and things in the heavens, but for nothing on earth; and a fourth class say that God takes thought also for earthly and human beings, but only in a general way, and has no care for individuals: and there is a fifth class, to whom belong Odysseus and Socrates, who say where'er I move Thou seest me. Epictetus, Discourses xii

Difficulties are what show men's characters. Therefore when a difficult crisis meets you, remember that you are as the raw youth with whom God the trainer is wrestling. 'To what end?' the hearer asks. That you may win at Olympia: and that cannot be done without sweating for it. Epictetus, Discourses xxiv

The Wise is one alone, unwilling and willing to be spoken of by the name of Zeus.
Heraclitus

There should be something unconquerable, some man against whom Fortune has no power, who works for the good of the commonwealth of mankind. Seneca, On Firmness

A good man differs from God in the element of time only; he is God's pupil, his imitator, and true offspring, whom his all-glorious parent, being no mild taskmaster of virtues, rears, as strict fathers do, with much severity. ... To win without danger is to win without glory. The same is true of Fortune. ... Mucius she tries by fire, Fabricius by poverty, Rutilius by exile, Regulus by torture, Socrates by poison, Cato by death. It is only evil fortune that discovers a great exemplar. Seneca, On Providence

When I speak of philosophy, I do not mean Stoic, Platonic, Epicurean or Aristotelian. I apply the term philosophy to all that is rightly said in each of these schools, all that teaches righteousness combined with a scientific knowledge of religion, the complete eclectic unity. Clement, Stromateis

The woman does not possess one nature, and the man ... another, but the same. Clement, Stromateis

The virtue of a man and woman is one and the same. Plutarch, Moralia

What of the stage? ... There comedy discourses of debaucheries and illicit loves, tragedy of incest and parricide. ... These plays are watched by the young, whose critical years – which should be rigorously controlled – are actually trained by these representations to vice and sin. Lactantius, Epitome Chap. 63

No one chooses evil qua evil. He is led astray by the accompanying pleasure, supposing it good, and he thinks it right to choose. Clement, Stromateis

Every art and every inquiry, every action and pursuit, are thought to aim at some good. For this reason, the Good has rightly been declared to be that at which all things aim. Aristotle, Ethics

Few inquisitors there are who would escape conviction under the very law which they cite for the inquisition; how few accusers are free from blame. ... Even if there is any one who has thoroughly cleansed his mind that nothing can any more confound him and betray him, yet it is by sinning that he has reached the sinless state. Seneca, On Mercy

No doctrinal system, then, is perfect when handed down only by words; it becomes perfect when fulfilled by deeds. Lactantius, Epitome Chap. 50

Do This

Every man should view himself as equally balanced: half good and half evil.

Likewise, he should see the entire world as half good half evil ... so that with a single good deed he will tip the scales for himself, and for the entire world, to the side of Good. Maimonides, Mishneh Torah, Laws of Repentance

Scorn poverty; no one lives as poor as he was born. Scorn pain; it will either be relieved or relieve you. Scorn death, which either ends you or transfers you. Scorn Fortune; I have given her no weapon with which she may strike your soul. Seneca, On Providence

To hold to the Truth and have opinions conformable to Reality is good. Clement, Stromateis

REVERENCE THE DEITY. Xenophon, Memoirs of Socrates

Philosophy, Greek and non-Greek, has made of eternal Truth a kind of dismembering ... in the theological understanding of the eternal Word. If anyone brings together the scattered limbs into a unity, you can be quite sure without risk of error that he will gaze on the Word in his fullness, the Truth. Clement, Stromateis

What is the use that now at this present I make of my soul? From time to time and upon all occasions you must put this question to yourself. Aurelius, Meditations

What then do I care for more than this, that my present action ... may be the proper action of one that is reasonable; whose end is the common good; who in all things is ruled and governed by the same law of right and reason, by which God Himself is. Aurelius, Meditations Bk VIII

When a man speaks evil or does evil to you, remember that he does or says it because he thinks it is fitting for him. ... If you act on this principle you will be gentle to him who reviles you, saying to yourself on each occasion, 'He thought it right.' Epictetus, Discourses

The first purification which takes place in the body, the soul being first, is abstinence from evil things, which some consider perfection, and is, in truth, the perfection of the common believer – Jew and Greek. But in the case of the Gnostic, after that which is reckoned perfection in others, his righteousness advances to activity in well-doing. Clement, Stromateis

First honor the immortal god ... then reverence thy oath ... then honor your parents, and all of your kindred. Among others make the most virtuous your friend. ... What brings you to shame, do not unto others, nor by yourself. ... Let justice be practiced in words as in deeds. ... Bear, whatever may strike you, with patience unmurmuring. ... The speech of the people is various, now good, and now evil, so let them not frighten you, nor keep you from your purpose. ... Think, before you act. ... Do not neglect the health of the body. ... Avoid all things which will arouse envy. ...

Never let slumber approach thy wearied eyelids, ere thrice you review what this day you did: Wherein have I sinned? What did I? What duty is neglected?. ... If you have erred, grieve in your spirit rejoicing for all that was good. ... Never start on your task until you have implored the blessing of the Gods. ... If this you hold fast, soon will you see ... how everything passes and returns. ... Let reason, the gift divine, be thy highest guide. ... Then should you be separated from the body, and soar in the aether, you will be imperishable, a divinity, a mortal no more. Pythagoras, Golden Verses

To model ourselves upon good men is to produce an image of an image: we have to gaze above the image and attain Likeness to the Supreme Exemplar. Plotinus, First Ennead

First say to yourself, what manner of man you want to be. When you have settled this, act upon it in all you do. Epictetus, Discourses

But one refuge remains for the man who is to reach the gates of salvation, and that is divine Wisdom. Clement, Exhortation to the Greeks

First extirpate the vices, then implant the virtues, from which the fruits of immortality sown by the word of God may spring. Lactantius, Epitome Chap. 60

There is every reason to marry – for patriotic reasons, for the succession of children, for the fulfillment of the universe. Clement, Stromateis

The soul is immortal, able to endure every sort of good and evil. Thus we live dear to one another and to the gods, both during our sojourn here and when, like victors in the games, we go round to receive our rewards. And thus both in this life and in the journey of a thousand years we shall fare well. Plato, Republic Bk X

Religion for All the World
What a great fortune it would be if ... every man on earth could be under one religion and belief, so that there would be no more rancor or ill will among men, who hate each other because of diversity and contrariness of beliefs and of sects! And, just as there is only one God, Father, Creator, and Lord of everything that exists, so all peoples could unite and become one people, and that people would be on the path to salvation, under one faith and one religion, giving glory and praise to our Lord God.
Ramon Llull, The Gentile and the Three Wise Men

The Knowledge of things divine and most honorable, is the principle, cause, and rule of human blessedness. Theages, On the Virtues

Become wise and yet harmless; perchance the Lord will grant you wings of simplicity (for it is His purpose to supply earth-born creatures with wings) in order that, forsaking the holes of the earth, you may dwell in the heavens. Only let us repent

with our whole heart, that with our whole heart we may be able to receive God. Clement, Exhortation to the Greeks

The great, shining, ever-lighting Sun is the apparent image of the divine goodness, a distant echo of the Good. Dionysius the Areopagite, Divine Names

Know thyself a man, and be a God. Plutarch, Life of Pompey, inscription on a gate leaving Athens

There is a resurrection of the dead, and there is punishment, but not everlasting. For when the body is punished the soul is gradually purified, and so is restored to its ancient rank. Origen, First Principles

The Noble Eightfold Path:
1. *Right Knowledge*
2. *Right Thinking*
3. *Right Speech*
4. *Right Conduct*
5. *Right Livelihood*
6. *Right Effort*
7. *Right Mindfulness*
8. *Right Concentration* Buddha

Now the high priest's robe is the symbol of the world of sense. The seven planets are represented by the five stones and the two carbuncles, for Saturn and the Moon* ... are rightly represented as placed on the breast and shoulders; and by them was the work of Creation, the first week. ... The broad gold mitre indicates the regal power of the Lord ... the breastplate ... the symbol of work, the oracle indicated the Word Logos ... the symbol of Heaven ... the luminous emerald stones ... in the ephod signify the Sun and Moon ... twelve stones, set in four rows on the breast, describe for us the circle of the zodiac ... Clement, Stromateis

*Watch for their 2º conjunctions 13 times in 2014 and 14 times in 2019.

Gnosis

Jesus said: "Throughout the ages I will pass; all mysteries I will unfold, all forms of Godhead I will unveil, all secrets of thy holy path styled Gnosis I will impart." Hippolytus, Naasseni Hymn (Refutation of all Heresies V:5)

Gnosis is a light infused by God in one's heart. Abu Talib

The extraordinary man is as obvious as a torch in the darkness; the perfect soul does not see itself but that of the Divine Intelligence, whose emanation has become one's own. Seneca, Epistles

Gnosis is fire and faith is a light; a believer sees by the Light of God, and a Gnostic sees through the eyes of Allah. Al-Sarraq

*He whose pride is destroyed and is free from the corruptions,
such a steadfast one even the gods hold dear. ...
Calm is his mind, calm his speech, calm his action ...
who has put an end to good and evil and vanquished his desires,
he indeed is a supreme man.* Dhammapada

*When all the desires that surge in the heart
Are renounced, the mortal becomes immortal.* Brihadaranyaka Upanishad 4

Some consider the highest level of understanding Allah as fusion, others as identification, and others as intimate union; nevertheless, these are all inexact expressions. When one has arrived at this state, it is better to be satisfied and say: "I refuse to manifest what I feel, but consider me happy and do not ask how." Al-Gazzali

Love is the lifting of the veil, the revelation of what was hidden to the eyes of men. One day I looked into the Light and did not stop until I became the Light. Ahmad al-Nuri

Love is the firstborn, loftier than the gods, the Fathers and men. You, O Love, are the eldest of all, altogether mighty. To you we pay homage! Greater than the breadth of Earth and Heaven, or of Waters and Fire ... in many a form of goodness, O Love, you show your face. Grant that these forms may penetrate within our hearts. Atharva Veda 9.2

*As water pure into pure water poured becomes even as that pure water is,
So too becomes the self of him, the silent sage who knows.* Katha Upanishad

In sum, we must withdraw from all the extern, pointed wholly inwards; no leaning to the outer; the total of things ignored, first in their relation to us and later in the very idea; the self put out of mind in the contemplation of the Supreme; all the commerce so closely There that, if report were possible, one might become to others reporter of that communion. Plotinus, Sixth Ennead

There are three effects of Gnostic power: the Knowledge of things; second, the performance of whatever the Word suggests; and the third, the capability of delivering, in a way suitable to God, the Secrets veiled in the Truth. Clement, Stromateis

My notes shall serve as kindling sparks; and in the case of him who is fit for Knowledge. Clement, Stromateis

Wise souls, pure as virgins, understanding themselves to be situated amidst the

ignorance of the world, kindle the Light, rouse the mind, illumine the darkness, dispel ignorance, seek Truth, and await the appearance of the Teacher. Clement, Stromateis

Politics

What then ... is the first origin of political societies? When owing to floods, famines, failure of crops or other such causes there occurs such a destruction of the human race as tradition tells us has more than once happened, and as we must believe will often happen again, all arts and crafts perishing at the same time, then in the course of time, when springing from the survivors as from seeds men have again increased in numbers and just like other animals form herds — it being a matter of course that they too should herd together with those of their kind owing to their natural weakness. Polybius, Histories VI 5

This race, the men of the present time, was not the first. As for the previous race, all in it perished. These current men are of the second race, which multiplied again from Deucalion. Concerning those earlier men they say the following. They were extremely violent and committed lawless deeds, for they neither kept oaths nor welcomed strangers nor spared suppliants. As punishment for these offenses the great disaster came upon them. Suddenly the earth poured forth a flood of water. Heavy rains fell, rivers rushed down in torrents, and the sea rose on high, until everything became water, and all the people perished. Lucian of Samosota, De Dea Syria

Nothing ... on Earth is more gratifying to that supreme God who rules the whole universe than the establishment of associations and federations of men bound together by principles of justice, which are called commonwealths. Cicero, Scipio's Dream

That old passion for power ... in man increased and broke out as the Empire grew in greatness. In a state of moderate dimensions equality was easily preserved; but when the world had been subdued, when all rival kings and cities had been destroyed, and men had leisure to covet wealth which they might enjoy in security, the early conflicts between the patricians and the people were kindled into flame. ... They were driven into civil war by the same wrath from Heaven, the same madness among men, the same incentives to crime. Tacitus, Annals Bk II

Before the destruction of Carthage the people and senate of Rome together governed the Republic peacefully and with moderation. There was no strife among the citizens either for glory or for power; fear of the enemy preserved the good morals of the state. But when the minds of the people were relieved of that dread, wantonness and arrogance naturally arose, vices which are fostered by prosperity. Thus the peace for which they had longed in time of adversity, after they had gained it proved to be more cruel and bitter than adversity itself. For the nobles began to abuse their position and the people their liberty, and every man for himself robbed, pillaged, and plundered. Thus the community was split into two parties, and between these the state was torn to pieces. ^{Sallust, The War With Jugurtha}

Aristides having drawn up his answer in the form of a decree, and called upon all the ambassadors ... bade those of Sparta tell the Lacedaemonians, "That the people of Athens would not take all the gold either above or under ground for the liberties of Greece." As for those of Mardonius, he pointed to the sun, and told them, "As long as this luminary shines, so long will the Athenians carry on war with the Persians for their country, which has been laid waste, and for their temples, which have been profaned and burned." ^{Plutarch, Lives, Aristides}

Monarchy first changes into its vicious allied form, tyranny; and next, the abolishment of both gives birth to aristocracy. Aristocracy ... degenerates into oligarchy; and when the commons inflamed by anger take vengeance on this government for its unjust rule, democracy comes into being; and in due course the license and lawlessness of this form of government produces mob-rule to complete the series. ... Lycurgus, then, foreseeing this, did not make his constitution simple and uniform, but united in it all the good and distinctive features of the best governments, so that none of the principles should grow unduly and be perverted into its allied evil.
Polybius, The Histories Bk VI

He kept the public good in his eye, and pursued the straight path of honor. For the most part gently leading them by argument to a sense of what was right, and sometimes forcing them to comply with what was for their own advantage. ... The two engines he worked with were hope and fear; with these, repressing their violence when they were too impetuous, and supporting their spirits when inclined to languor, he made it appear that rhetoric is (as Plato defined it) the art of ruling the minds of men, and that its principal province consists in moving the passions and affections of the soul, which like so many strings in a musical instrument, require the touch of a masterly and delicate hand. ^{Plutarch, Lives, Pericles}

It appears to me that Justice ... may be called the mother and nurse of the other virtues. For without this a man can neither be temperate, nor brave, nor prudent. For it is the harmony and peace, in conjunction with elegance, of the whole soul. ^{Polus, On Justice}

For the Romans themselves not only belong to the Greek race, but also the sacred ordinances and the pious belief in the gods which they have established and maintain are, from the beginning to end, Greek. And beside this they have established a constitution not inferior to that of any one of the best governed states, if indeed it be not superior to all others that have ever been put into practice. For which reason I myself recognize that our city is Greek, both in descent and as to its constitution. Julian, Hymn to King Helios

The three kinds of government ... all shared in the control of the Roman state ... and in its subsequent administration it was impossible even for a native to pronounce with certainty whether the whole system was aristocratic, democratic, or monarchical. ... For if one fixed one's eyes on the power of the consuls, the constitution seemed completely monarchical and royal; if on that of the senate it seemed again to be aristocratic; and when one looked at the power of the masses, it seemed clearly to be a democracy. ... For when one part having grown out of proportion to the others aims at supremacy and tends to become too predominant, it is evident that ... none of the three is absolute, but the purpose of the one can be counterworked and thwarted by the others, none of them will excessively outgrow the others or treat them with contempt. Polybius, The Histories Bk VI

Things born increase until they arrive at their consummation, whereafter they age and perish. ... Every human empire has shown three distinct stages of growth, fruition and destruction. In the beginning, being destitute of goods, empires are engrossed in acquisition, but after they become wealthy they perish. ... The end of self-satisfaction and insolence is destruction, but poverty and narrow circumstances often result in a strenuous and worthy life. Hippodamus

The Serpent

It was the 'Spirit of God' who 'moved upon the waters,' as it is written, in the beginning of the creation of the world. ... The expression in the song of Habakkuk, 'In the midst of the two animals' (or the two living creatures) 'thou shalt be known', should be understood to refer to Christ and the Holy Spirit. Origen, First Principles Bk I

According to the Peratae: *To those ... of the children of Israel were bitten in the wilderness, Moses exhibited the real and perfect serpent; and they who believed on this serpent were not bitten in the wilderness. ... This serpent is the power that attended Moses. ... No one, then ... can be saved or return into Heaven without the Son, and the Son is the Serpent.* Hippolytus, Refutation V Chap. 12

According to Clement: *Why, then, is the serpent called wise? ... Wisdom being manifold, pervading the whole world, and all human affairs, varies its appellation in each case. When it applies itself to first causes, it is called Understanding. When ... it confirms this by demonstrative reasoning, it is termed Knowledge, and Wisdom, and Science. When it is occupied in what pertains to piety ... it is called Faith. In the sphere of things of sense ... Right Opinion. In operations ... it is Art. But when, ... by the observation of similarities ... it is called Experiment. But belonging to it, and supreme and essential, is the Holy Spirit.* Stromateis

On the Cataclysm

For a small moment have I forsaken thee; but with great mercies will I gather thee. In a little wrath I hid my face ... for a moment; but with everlasting kindness will I have mercy on thee, saith the LORD thy Redeemer. ... For the mountains shall depart, and the hills be removed; but my kindness shall not depart from thee, neither shall the covenant of my peace be removed ... and all thy children shall be taught of the LORD; and great shall be the peace of thy children. [Isaiah 54:7-13]

Thou hidest thy face, they are troubled; thou takest away their breath, they die, and return to their dust. Thou sendest forth thy Spirit, they are created; and thou renewest the face of the Earth. [Psalm 104: 29-30]

Then the earth shook and trembled; the foundations of the hills moved and were shaken because He was angry. Smoke went up out of his nostrils and fire out of his mouth. ... At the brightness before Him thick clouds passed and hailstones and coals of fire. ... Then the channels of waters were seen, and the foundations of the world were laid bare. [Psalm 18]

When a world-cycle is destroyed by wind ... there arises a ... great cloud ... to destroy the world-cycle. And first it raises a fine dust, and then coarse dust, and then fine sand, and then coarse sand, and then grit, stones, up to boulders as large as ... mighty trees on the hill-tops. These mount from the earth to the zenith, and do not fall again, but are there blown to powder and annihilated. [Visuddhi-Magga]

In the day of the great slaughter ... the light of the Moon shall be like the light of the Sun and the light of the Sun shall be sevenfold. ... Behold, the Name of the Lord cometh from afar, burning with His anger. ... His lips are full of indignation and his tongue like a devouring fire. And His breath, like an overflowing stream, shall reach to the midst of the neck. ... And in every place where the grounded staff shall pass ... like a stream of brimstone doth kindle it. [Isaiah 30:25-33]

Embracing Our Humanity and Our Divinity

If a man could only take to heart this judgment, as he ought, that we are all, before anything else, children of God and that God is the Father of gods and men, I think that he will never harbor a mean or ignoble thought about himself. ... We ought to be proud, but we are not; as there are these two elements mingled in our birth, the body which we share with the animals, and the reason and mind which we share with the gods, men in general decline upon that wretched and dead kinship with the beasts, and but few claim that which is divine and blessed. [Epictetus, Discourses]

I have been all things unholy. If God can work through me, he can work through anyone. [St. Francis of Assisi]

When I call unto them, they will stand up together. Isaiah 48:13

Blessed are all they that wait for Him. Isaiah 30:18

On the 27th of February, 2013, if the reversal has taken place, it will be time for a new calendar. The Milky Way will be back parallel to the horizon, looking more as one might expect of our home in the stars. If humanity survives Ekpyrosis with its season of deadly challenges, it will certainly be by the grace of God. If the New Creation has been postponed, we should then be thankful and watchful for the other signs. For example, when the number of the fallen on Earth approaches the more than 10 billion angels in Heaven, Revelation 5:11 *the East raises an army of 200 million,* Revelation 9:16 *Israel is reestablished,* Ezekiel 37:21 *and all the world seems content to talk peace while waging war,* Jeremiah 6:14 & 8:11 *know that the time is near.* When the Cross returns to northern skies, let us remember the religion that once united all mankind in the mysteries. Our religions were never meant to be cults of the dead; ours is and was a God for the living. We were never supposed to be cults of the End Times; we are celebrants of all Creation. We were not born here to suffer or to punish each other with our greed. We came here to seek the Truth and to assist the Sun of Righteousness Malachi 4:2 *in building a better world!*

Acknowledgments

When I asked Dr. Haris Kalligas, then-director of the Gennadius Library in Athens, where I might find the ship manifests of Captain Doria, who reportedly had taken Byzantine refugees to Venice, she sent me a translated copy of the log entries. The name I had hoped to find, John Palaeologus, was there, as was a former surname that, in my estimation, could have kept John alive. That log is the only evidence I encountered showing such a King Arthur figure could have existed. Palaeologus family histories show a John the son of Thomas or of Manuel *el Ghazi* – and no sons for the last emperor, Constantine XI.

Captain Doria's log in Actes du XIIe Congres International D'etudes Byzantines, pp. 172-173

I have to thank Dr. Fannie R. Linder, my parents Ken and Barbara, my son Ken and my daughter Sonya for their support and encouragement reading the manuscript as it proceeded, providing me questions and comments.

I owe another debt to my sister Kathryn for proofreading the original manuscript. Of course, any subsequent errors in fact, spelling or grammar are due to my own oversight, obstinacy and misinterpretation.

Thanks as well to my niece, Rocio Alba Crespo, for working with Biblioteca Nacional de España for permission to publish the quote by Saint Bernard.

Finally, I must thank my wife Maria. Her patience, kindness, courage and generosity still amaze me after 35 years. I lack the words to express the wonder I felt when she told me to stop commuting to D.C. and to do whatever it might take to write this book. Without Dulcinea's great Faith, this Quixote would never have attempted to tell a great Truth.